AF270121

GRAND THEFT AI

JAMES COX

GRAND THEFT AI

BLACK
STONE
PUBLISHING

First edition: 2024
ISBN 979-8-200-68213-3
Fiction / Science Fiction / Cyberpunk

Version 1

Blackstone Publishing
31 Mistletoe Rd.
Ashland, OR 97520

www.BlackstonePublishing.com

For Tammy

OLD CHEVRON REFINERY
BAZ'S CRIB
EDDIE'S LOFT
AXL'S DE-AUGMENT LOUNGE
SAN FRANCISCO
// AREA OF INSET
STIMSOFT SQUARE
THE SILICON SPRAWL
// 10 MILES

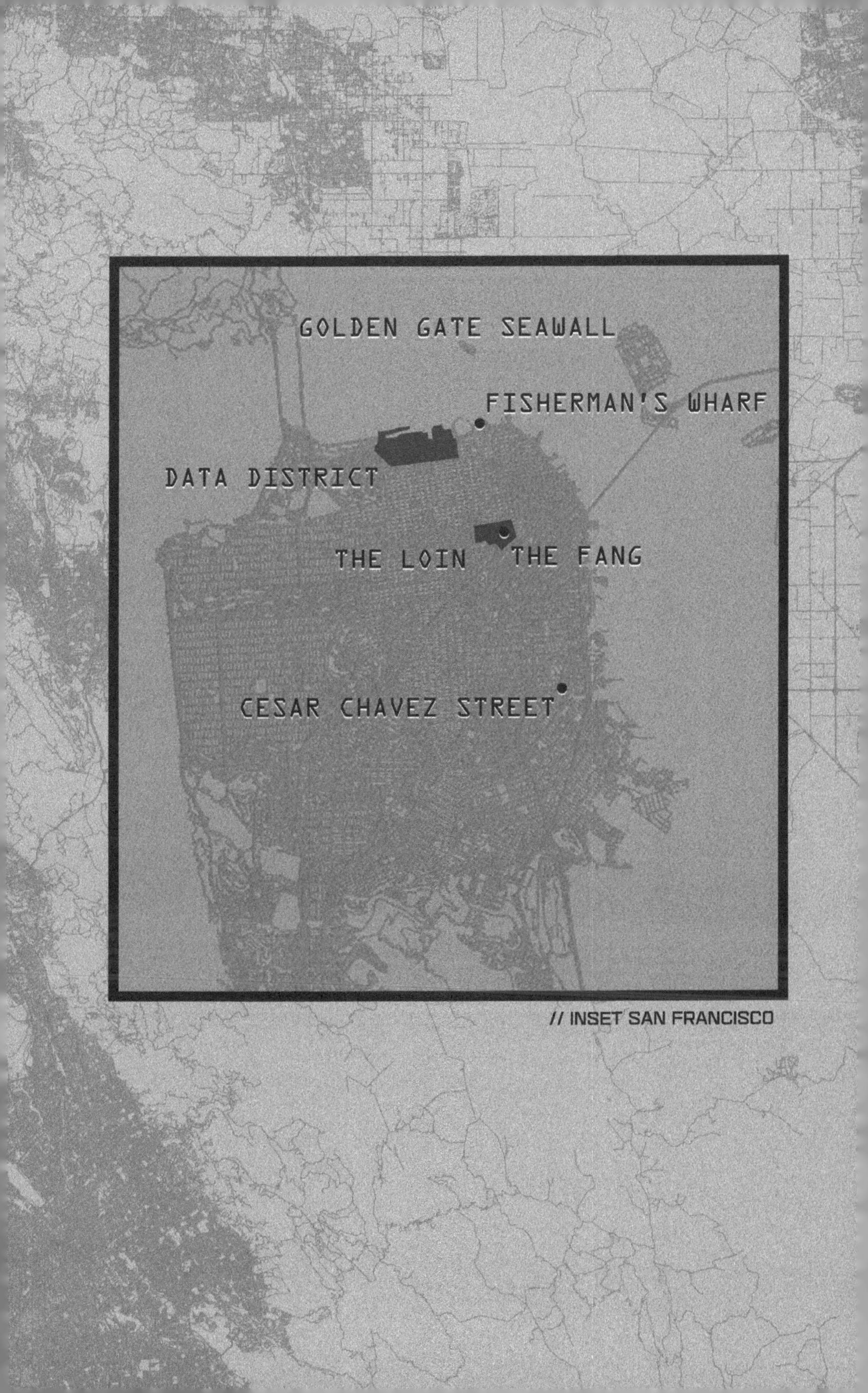

GOLDEN GATE SEAWALL
FISHERMAN'S WHARF
DATA DISTRICT
THE LOIN
THE FANG
CESAR CHAVEZ STREET
// INSET SAN FRANCISCO

THE GLITCH

November 17, 2043
CLOSED SESSION

NOTE: the following excerpts have been verified authentic, presented in this order for today's hearing to accurately portray the rapidly unfolding nature of the events in question.

<u>Friday April 10, 2043</u>

3:17 p.m.
Wetwire/Holo-News

KATY WELLS: This just breaking in the WHN News-deck—we're going live to virtualizations in Georgia for reports of a disturbance just moments ago at the Masters Golf Tournament outside Atlanta.

[feed cuts to ESPHN, Atlanta]

3:16 p.m.
(*1 minute earlier*)
Live Coverage of the 112th Masters Tournament

ANNOUNCER: At the 16th, where PGA Champion Marc Chen tees off. [*a golfer swings*] Oh wow, what a beautiful shot from Chen . . . Check his augments on that one! Kidding, of course. Wait, there seems to be some trouble at the tee box. Looks like a scuffle between Chen and his synthetic.

[*the golfer struggles with an android caddy over a golf club*]

CHEN (via remote mic): No, Carl, I said I'll carry the flat-stick myself!

[*the android seizes the club and attacks*]

ANNOUNCER: Jesus, his synthetic's beating him with his own putter!

ANNOUNCER 2: Dan, that's not the only bot going nuts—take a look over at the clubhouse. [*an android throws a patron through a plate-glass window*] There's chaos in the Grill Room!

3:16 p.m.
Subsidiary WXFN, Atlanta

LOCAL ANCHOR: Sorry to interrupt, but the situation in Augusta doesn't appear to be an isolated event. The holos on your feed now are from midtown Atlanta, where our Dronecopters 7, 8, and 9 are over Peachtree Mall, [*Sentry Androids chase fleeing patrons*] and you can see a number of Guard Bots are clearly malfunctioning. [*an android beats a man with a severed arm*] Jesus, Rick, can we roto that out? [*blood and bone blur*] And we hear now that Atlanta PD is responding with Human Reserve Units to a restaurant, where the violence first erupted.

3:10 p.m.
(*6 minutes earlier*)
Composited from Multiple Wetwire Feeds
Sally Rae Hawkins's 13th Birthday. Peachtree Mall, Atlanta. Applebee's, Table 5

ALL: [*singing*] Happy birthday, dear Sally . . . Hap-hap-happy Birrrrrrrrrrthd-d-d-d-d—

SALLY: Mom, what's wrong with her?

*["Bella," a Dallas Dynamics Server Model 2.3 freezes, holding
a birthday cake lit with candles. Throughout the restaurant,
several other androids also freeze.]*

FRIEND: Look, Nancy, all the bots are crashing . . .

3:45 p.m.

(*29 minutes later*)

<u>INTERVIEW</u> with Tim Morris (Applebee's Asst. Manager) by
Atlanta Homicide Detective Langston Cowell

MORRIS: [*highly agitated*] Yeah, I knew something
was so-so fucked up, 'cuz it wasn't just Bella who crashed, it
was half the waitstaff—this fuckin' wave of robots glitchin'
across the restaurant and out into the mall, starting right at
Bella!

DET. COWELL: And how many waiters were synthetic?

MORRIS: Dude, it's an Applebee's—ALL OF 'EM.

UPDATE/04.10.43-15:10 analyzed line by line, subroutine to
deliver Hostility Ramping payload identified:

```
102321. import tensorflow as tf
102322. class Dallas-Dynamics-2.3(object):
102323. Hostile.Ramp_y = highgate [float]
102324. GO-SUB_expedite = "HAYWIRE"
```


3:13 p.m.

Composite (cont'd) from Hawkins's Birthday

["Bella" powers back on, struggles to sing]

WAITRESS BOT: Happy birth-birth-birth—

[glitches to a different song]

So, you say it's your birthday!

Well, it's my birthday too, yeah.

FRIEND: Jesus, Nancy, this bot's a mess. Where's the
manager?

NANCY: Excuse me! . . . What's his name? Tom or Tim something?

SALLY: Mommy, my cake's falling!

MORRIS: Ya know, ma'am, don't touch it—lemme just call IT.

[Asst. manager Tim Morris approaches the table as Mrs. Nancy Hawkins reaches for the falling birthday cake. Android "Bella" recoils into a defensive crouch, threat-assessing, then seizes Nancy's left arm and disarticulates it from her torso.]

NANCY: AHHHHH!

3:48 p.m.

INTERVIEW (cont'd) with Tim Morris

MORRIS: Tore her arm clean out of its fuckin' socket! Right in front of me, man . . . *[between sobs]* Right in front of her own daughter. There's blood everywhere, then Bella used the arm like a fucking baseball bat and stepped up to the plate at Table 6.

DET. COWELL: Did you say Bella was a recent purchase?

MORRIS: *[nods]* Fuckin' Maurice . . . "More cleavage, more hot wings," he said when he walked her in. "Got some sweet financing." But that's bullshit—he bought her outta the back of Sapphires . . .

DET. COWELL: Why do you say that?

MORRIS: Look at her! *[gestures to the deactivated android on the sidewalk]* You think a manager at Applebee's can afford a chassis like that?

DET. COWELL: So, where's Maurice?

MORRIS: Um. *[looks to a body lying next to the android]* Maurice is dead.

3:14:10 p.m.

Virt-Cam Feed from Dillard's Makeup Counter

WOMAN: ow! Goddammit, STOP!

[a Wutani Retail.2 gouges the woman with an eyeliner pencil]

3:14:27 p.m.

Security Feed from Peachtree Mall Ice Rink

TEEN: Get OFF ME, Metalhead—HELP!

[a Dallas Dynamics Attendroid slashes the teen's face with a pair of skates]

3:16 p.m.

Wetwire Feed (Bystander), 2 Blocks from Peachtree Mall

MAN: Whoa, those bots are goin' crazy . . . *[as Sentry Bots turn towards his POV]* Shit . . . they're . . . coming this way! *[people around him start fleeing]* RUN!

3:18 p.m.

Subsidiary WXFN, Atlanta

LOCAL ANCHOR: My Lord, some of these virts are quite disturbing, ladies and gentlemen. *[androids swarm as police open fire]* Now Atlanta PD confirms that Bot Zero inside the mall was indeed a Dallas Dynamics Server Model 2.3, same in Augusta and the synthetic strip clubs on Interstate 40. So we're wiring a current list of secondary models affected. *[models and serial numbers compile in the periphery]* One agent we spoke to added, "Steer clear of any Watchmen by Nubotica. They're especially lethal." Our own Jess Peters has more in midtown . . .

LOCAL CORRESPONDENT: Mary, I'm at the Bankhead Precinct in Atlanta, where sources tell me the FBI's already circulating the AI-generated profile of a man wanted for VR-questioning in connection with the crisis. They say they're looking for a white male, unemployed, possibly a family man suffering extreme loss, with potential ties to the Synthetic Emancipation Movement. Then the detective repeated the following two descriptions several times: he is a "broken" individual with "nothing left to lose" . . . When I said that sounded like just about everyone these days—

[gunfire erupts, and the correspondent ducks for cover]

3:20 p.m.

Wetwire/Holo-News

KATY WELLS: Forgive us, ladies and gentlemen, but we have to break off from Atlanta as we're now receiving reports of hundreds of robot rampages in twelve—no, thirteen cities. These are orbital virtualizations from Rockefeller Center in New York, City Hall in Philadelphia, even a high school in Wichita—all clearly overrun by synthetic violence. Private Service Units, we can confirm, are being deployed, so let's take you now to Florida.

CORRESPONDENT (via remote simul-stream): Katy, I'm at MacDill Air Force Base in Tampa, where you can see behind me the 229th and 113th Attack Squadrons lifting off for domestic deployment with what I'm told are strictly human soldiers on board. One source in Pentagon Corporate said this is the first fully organic airlift since Venezuela—

KATY WELLS: Okay, now we're being told that the president is preparing to address the nation. [*manipulates her Wetwire display*] Yes, we have signal in the White House Press Room . . . Can we go to the podium? . . . [*screams issue from inside the studio*] . . . Is everything . . . Oh God—

[*signal cuts*]

3:21 p.m.

<u>ENCRYPT</u>—White House Press Room

PRESIDENT STERLING: [*takes the podium*] My fellow Americans, in response to android violence across the country, I have mobilized the United States Private Service for rapid deployment. Effective immediately, I hereby authorize the immediate and indefinite termination of any malfunctioning chassis by whatever means necessary.

EXHIBITS 18–31

Presidential Inquiry into Advanced Mechanics

WELCOME
TO THE LOIN

BLOWN

2051, AUGUST

The first time Baz Covane saw the woman, she didn't have a name. But as he watched her strut across the warehouse floor in combat boots and stretched black fatigues, Baz just couldn't help it.

He forgot all about his eight brutal years since the Glitch.

Sunlight struggled through grimy skylights and a prehistoric printing press to silhouette her frame like a light at the end of a tunnel.

"Jesus Christ, that's your contact?" Baz turned to his right hand and partner in everything, Diamond Eddie D, who sat shotgun and threw him a smile.

"Sure you're not interested?"

Eddie'd just pitched him a juicy score, one that Baz had declined 'cuz he was "Out" after today.

Right after this deal, actually.

But as Baz peered out his windshield's holo-console to watch the woman just walk on by—without even bothering to *glance* his way?— Eddie's smile widened. 'Cuz that score was right back in Baz's brainpan, marinating.

Which was nuts. Baz wanted Out more than anything.

Slingin' Street Meat in the Loin was as sordid as it sounded. A purveyor of illicit bots with black-market learning caps, Baz wanted out of the synthetic skin trade as bad as its insatiable demand, because ever since the Glitch, androids coded with "onstage" acrobatics usually just made their debut in the bedroom.

"Out" resided for Baz where it does with all criminals—on a beach, off-grid. In Baz's case, that sand was in the South Pacific, on an island once known as Tahiti. And this particular load of bots cradled in his back cargo hold represented a good chunk of ¢rypto—hopefully enough for a worker's visa in the Tahitian Protectorate.

He and Eddie stepped down from their self-driving Waymo as a dozen Dance Bots revolved out the back, where the woman was waiting. She was young—25, maybe 26—yet clearly in command of a rather unassuming entourage, save for an enormous Warrior Bot, a Wutani L7 she called McT.

"What kinda name is Baz?"

Baz sighed—how many times had he answered that? . . . He could tell at first sight that she was as scarred as he was, inside and out. So Baz understood intuitively why she was sizing him up. No doubt, she'd seen his discharge report from the Private Service and knew about the Section 8—whether she knew anything else about his tour in Venezuela was irrelevant. Thanks to Eddie, his reputation always had a habit of preceding him, and Baz was sure this woman was eyein' his hands the way she did 'cuz she'd heard about the Body Count.

"Baz is short for Sebazzztian. And you are?"

But the woman just turned to the line of Dance Bots instead of answering him, clocking each one like a pimp at a meat market.

Her right eye was synthetic and obviously the stronger one; its 20/10 microtelescopic lens scanned and fixated on every ab, glute, and gam of each bot (which were undeniably top-notch, one-of-a-kind sculptures). The woman pinched a few waistlines, squeezed a cheek or two.

"You know, you don't gotta harass these girls," Baz said. "I'm sure there's plenty of that shit waiting wherever you're taking them."

"I'm not harassing girls . . . I'm harassing robots."

Baz still had to remind himself sometimes that these bots were things, not people—though the end customer would definitely disagree. This load were all ex-members of New York's most famous synthetic dance troupe, a massive tourist draw in NYC from the AGMA Strike of 2036 'til the day of the Glitch.

"Five-six-seven-eight!" the woman hollered, and on the one, all twelve Dance Bots busted into a choreographed stomp—a classic number from years ago: one part cancan, two parts Nae Nae.

"What's the lineage?"

Baz knew she knew but answered her anyway: "Radio City Music Hall. Ex–Robo-Rockettes."

As the bots carried through their number, she eyed the troupe with obvious expertise—firing off questions at Baz, not like she wanted info on the bots, but more like she was testing him. So he just answered each query like a pro. 'Til her last question sounded friendly, even innocent—but Baz had a hunch there was nothing innocent left in this woman, and he doubted if she had any friends.

"Learning caps intact?"

Which was really why they were all here.

The crackdown on machine intelligence after the Glitch made Uncle Sam the yard-duty between the Big Three—Dallas Dynamics, Wutani, and Nubotica—and learning caps were no longer product design. Intelligence engines were fiercely regulated, so that machine learning could still compete—without ANY CHANCE of ANY ROBOT ever going HAYWIRE again.

"'Course they're intact. Think I want heat from Wirecrime?" Baz didn't think for a second that the Feds would bother with a low-level Street Meat deal like this one. But he had to say something 'cuz the woman was about to vet these bots' caps, and Baz'd been a bit nervous since he gaffled 'em off the *Carnival Horizon* two nights ago.

"Gimme the Cortex," the woman said, and McT handed her a palm-sized device—as Baz's neck stiffened.

It was no secret that international waters were free from Wirecrime jurisdiction. Nor that Carnival Cruises headlined world-famous acts with in-house learning caps and a 200-page waiver no one read, exonerating its board and shareholders in the slight but distinct chance that some bot blew its cap and slaughtered everyone on board.

But Baz and Eddie'd found the lead Dance Bot powered down (aka sleeping), not with the rest of the troupe in steerage, but in the captain's quarters. And he had a gnawing suspicion the skipper tinkered with her learning cap, so she'd get naked and beastly with him every night after every show.

The woman commanded the troupe to take a knee, which they did, and as she activated the Cortex, she held it close to the first bot's ear . . .

`RhythmThief.T314`

`>scan<`

Her Cortical and Cognition Reflexivity Monitor (which everyone just called a "Cortex" for short) projected a holo of the learning cap above each bot's head—a spherical equalizer of the bot's intelligence engine with levels like:

```
Vernacular Comprehension
Hostility Ramping
Sexual Stimulation
```

And as long as all those levels remained under the limits of the bot's preprogrammed "cap"—each indicator would stay GREEN, and the cap was intact.

But if that Cortex flashed RED?

They'd have a problem.

One by one, the Cortex scanned each Dance Bot and holo'd its learning cap in a lush, green *intact* sphere above.

But Baz just kept his eyes on the lead bot at the far end—'cuz that warrior McT was packin' enough firepower to turn a Peacekeeper Unit violent. As the woman scanned the next-to-last android—

"What, you don't trust me?" Baz blurted nervously.

Which seemed to catch her by surprise. As if Baz just asked the exact same question the woman was asking herself.

Could she trust him?

The woman hesitated. She didn't glance in Baz's direction but might've wanted to. Didn't ask a question, just looked like she had a few more on deck. Then deadpanned instead:

"Don't flatter yourself. I don't trust anyone."

>BREACH<

—the bot sprang in the air, whirling defensively—

"FUCK, we got a smart one!" Eddie howled, wetwire alarms exploding.

McT reached for his Jester-11—

"No, DON'T!" Baz screamed too late.

—McT squeezed off a round—"acrobatics" kicked in, and the Dance Bot tore sideways, leaping and disarming McT, pluggin' two hollow-points in his dome—dead.

"Cap BLOWN!" Eddie's fingers scrambled, eyes darting over his wetwire, gauging the bot's BIOS. "Hostility Ramping—FAST!"

The woman stood square in the Dance Bot's sights.

"Get down!" Baz screamed and tackled her to the floor, rounds chiseling chunks of concrete where she'd just stood. More gunshots hailed around them, crouching under that abandoned printing press as the Dance Bot kept firing and walking forward.

"I'm back in!" Eddie hollered, sailing through lines of code to hack its CPU and stand her down.

And the bot deactivated.

Smoke wafted in the silence as Baz rolled over.

He'd fought hard not to stare at the woman's scar since he first saw her, but now, this close—he didn't care. A half-crescent ring of cauterized tissue traced around her right eye, over her cheekbone, and along her brow. From a distance, it accented a beauty long neglected by more than a few inner demons. But up close, it merely reminded Baz that her left eye was real and the right one synthetic, 'cuz staring deep into both, you couldn't tell which one was which.

What caused the trauma? When did it go down? And just who the hell was this woman, really?

Baz had saved her life. And he was pretty sure she was making a very real decision, because right before she stood up and walked away, *she slid a wafer of glass into his hand.*

"Name's Ria, hero . . . Ria Rose."

ROSES

Maria Roselli ran hot from the womb.

Born five minutes before her sister Daniela on August 19, 2026, Maria arrived in a natural water birth that was the most savage and beautiful thing their father ever saw. Incendiary, even for a Leo—those five minutes proved defining, if not prophetic, 'cuz Maria raced into the world fast 'n' loose and never looked back.

But Dani was reticent. Chewing on moments, not because she was unsure of herself—just content to let her big sis test the water (literally) before she decided to follow or not. The irony was that Dani was often the more gifted student, sometimes the more talented athlete, and would've one day beat out her sister for that scholarship to Iowa State.

They lived at their grandparents the first year, but once their dad Dave got his master's in education, he quickly found a job at West Middle School to teach science, math, and computers and just couldn't wait to have both girls in his class. After the first day of kindergarten, their mom Aleja—Cuban to the core—wandered into the admin office to volunteer as an art and dance teacher too.

Life was a fantasy. Walking to school together four across, hand in hand through falling sugar maple leaves as Aleja sang a lullaby called "D and Ria," her own little nickname for the twins. Though both girls were born into the Synthetic Gyneration—"SynGyns" for short—there was nothing artificial in their home. All their classmates were served, baby-sat, even potty trained by an android. But Aleja was a hands-on mother out of a dream. Family by day . . .

And passion by night.

Aleja and Dave craved each other. Ever since the first night they ripped each other's clothes off, it was his smell Aleja savored—underneath the clean of a fresh shower or the pungence of exertion—the man in his skin consumed her at the DNA level. And Dave swore the perspiration on her neck when she climaxed was some nectar that charged his coil like a reactor. He'd nibble or gnash that sheen from her skin, whispering "baby-doll" in her ear . . . And Aleja would just run wild.

But she got a bad feeling watching the first Teamster Riots on the holo-screen, despite Dave's assurances that teachers were safe. Then in '31, when AI hit the service industry, it was the acclaim bots received in childcare that got him worried too. Because at home and in the class-room was where AI would find its true calling. Didn't take an intuitive Rhodes Scholar to drive you to work or find the cheapest Nikes. But the right lullaby to settle a temper tantrum, or a caring quip to inspire your struggling fourth grader? That was worth its weight in synthetic flesh.

So Dave refused to argue with her when neural implants hit the market the next year, and insisted both girls immediately be fitted for a pair at six—the youngest in the school district. Engineered by AI, the Fiber-Optic-Nerve Graft obsoleted smart contact lenses and retinal projection like VHS tape. Slipping through bone and tissue and paving the way for all other senses, the first dendrite-to-digital brain-computer interface took the world by storm. And it was called the "Wetwire."

Maria, Dani, and eventually every other SynGyn got the choice of augmented reality or VR—not just sight, sound, or command of a full-body avatar—but complete nerve-to-muscle immersion. The twins could be neck and neck, racin' dune buggies on the moon, while IRL, they'd be sitting on a park bench next to Dave, chillin' under a pair of Aviator Juniors.

Screens, keyboards, and microphones? Gone, like pagers from a landline. 'Cuz your smartphone was in your head now, *if* you could afford it. And if Dave couldn't? He knew his girls were fucked. When the brain went digital, so would mnemonics, and testing was gonna get real . . . quick. Forget reciting the Bill of Rights, try cross-referencing its author against the first families of Virginia faster than a classmate answers Robert E. Lee. That was a classroom full of SynGyns. So Aleja bottled her concerns over safety and bullying as David applied and qualified for implant maker WireLife's outreach program that subsidized middle-income households in exchange for five-year contracts.

The Resonance Sequencer tingled Maria's head when it scanned and projected a pair of sponge cakes on a holo-display—what the doctor said were her "cerebral hemispheres"—and every time she giggled, the back part would turn yellow then red with the words "Occipital Lobe" flashing. Dani kept laughing at the colors, and Maria kept laughing at Dani, until finally their dad just nodded to the doctor, who switched off the machine and put both girls under.

Maria was ticked that Dani mastered her Wetwire first, air-texting no-handed by eight years old. But both were "split-thinking" by ten, rendering words and images in real time—the ability that truly defined a SynGyn. Most middle-age Gen Z'rs denied split-thinking was even possible (like Maria's PE teacher, Miss Peltz, who walked into a bus closing an app). But Maria and Dani would just nod like a SynGyn and trash those kinds of comments with the rest of that generation gap.

Maria and Dani didn't just finish each other's sentences, their hearts seemed to beat in a syncopated rhythm that even Aleja found uncanny at times. Dave got glimpses of it at the dinner table or when they insisted on sleeping in the same bed from four years old until *twelve*, but Mom witnessed it en masse in her studio.

Aleja was classically trained and believed the truth of the human soul was revealed in its purest physical expression: dance. So her girls were in ballet slippers before they were out of diapers. She'd watch them move in rhythm across the floor, so coordinated, especially when they *touched*, that Aleja scoured universities for a two-female dance notation. But coming up against traditional bullshit of how *men must lead*, Aleja just said FUCK THAT and wrote one herself.

It was called *Gemini*. And though both girls were Leos, they so perfectly captured each other's movements (Aleja would say: "Be her mirror") that, as their mom wrote and rewrote the dance over the years, Maria and Dani wondered if the moves deepened their connection, or vice versa, since their love grew stronger every day.

Still, they hated having to share *everything*—friends, clothes, even crushes. It was Gavin Delroy who forced the "I saw him first" policy and set the stage for the girls' ultimate "twin test." Dani laid claim to Gavin, and Maria accepted (begrudgingly) to let him go, until her sis proposed they pull a switch on him for their first kiss. The best way to tell them apart at twelve years old was from their Wetwire style: Maria's optic display used the backgrounds from Colonial 1's first manned flight to Mars, but Dani's had a fantasy vibe out of the Brothers Grimm. So Dani "unshared" her holosphere with Gavin for their *first kiss ever*, insisting she wanted it as "real" as possible. Then she excused herself to the bathroom, where Maria was hiding, and Maria returned to see if Gavin could tell the difference.

Gavin didn't come round much after that.

Maria and Dani got used to putting their Wetwires in "standby" mode during tests, until the sixth grade, when the Sioux City School District's entire curriculum split between wired and unwired. By then, the girls were academic standouts, when just about everything changed.

Neither a Wetwire nor Dave's master's degree could save his job. Despite tenure, he just couldn't keep up with AI Instructor Androids, whose command of subjects dwarfed even a college professor. Like Teamsters, pilots, and most of the service industry, Dave had a right, as negotiated by the Federation of Displaced Teachers, to the costs saved by the robot replacing him, but that was barely minimum wage (what executives referred to on the back nine as the Extinction Tax). Medicaid was still around, in name, but the list of uncovered treatments left one ex–American History teacher comparing its subsidized clinics to the hacksaws at Antietam.

Both girls wanted to know why Dad lost his job, but Mom didn't. He didn't have to explain to either daughter that creativity was still best taught by a human. But they had to grind out of him that Aleja's lesson plans for art and dance class were a wee bit more creative than algebra worksheets. So Aleja kept her job and her benefits, while Dave struggled to be grateful.

Until Aleja found the lump.

The last dance lesson Mom ever gave Maria or Dani was the day the doctor called with her test results. Both were on the barre, rehearsing a new version of *Gemini*, and smiled for an actual "photo" Dave took with a vintage toy from the attic called a Polaroid. The twins giggled when Nijinsky rang on Aleja's iPhone XXX—God, their parents were fossils. Mom still used a phone?—but then they felt her heart *sink*. Yes, she stammered, she could come in the next morning if it was urgent.

Neither sis knew what hit 'em. Positive biopsy in three axial lymph nodes and a two-centimeter tumor meant that Aleja lost her hair, her energy, and her boobs in a month, which was eerily uncomfortable since both girls were just getting theirs. Dave's depression and self-pity vanished as he stepped up to be the pillar of support his family needed. During two years of remission, he found himself inspired to get involved with the growing movement called Synthetic Emancipation. Strange bedfellow of labor and Robots Rights—bleeding-heart liberals and unemployed worker's unions marched hand in hand with their android counterparts, flesh-on-synthetic-flesh, chanting, "We think, therefore we are," in the hope that demanding equal pay between man and machine might stop the layoffs.

Then Aleja's cancer readvanced and spread to her brain.

Maria and Dani were more traumatized by the seizures than the vomiting, until both happened at the same time. The night of their thirteenth birthday, none of the paramedics could stop the grand mals quaking or the birthday cake spewing. But the words that came out of Aleja's mouth weren't English or Spanish, more like deranged speaking in tongues. Maria's mom was possessed by a vicious malignant demon, three centimeters long, stretching from the top of her spinal column, snaking into her cerebellum, and growing every minute.

Maria got angry. Dani withdrew. And Dave broke . . .

. . . trying to save Mom. The Wetwire paved incredible advances, minute by minute and millimeter by millimeter, in the fight against most forms of brain cancer. And though the doctors who refused to remove Aleja's tumors finally agreed that only surgery could relieve the pressure-induced seizures, their evaporating insurance denied her a Wetwire implant, despite Dave's pleading. By that point, no carrier expected Aleja to fulfill even a single year of a contract. And so the treatment that within a few years would prove remarkably successful was denied Aleja because they couldn't afford it.

Three months later she was gone.

Dave tried not to blame technology, or the lack thereof. But it was hard staring at his dead wife's consolation prize: the Hospice Bot dispatched to mainline 750 cc's of Dilaudid to stem Aleja's pain. The insurance carrier, an offshoot of Big Pharma behemoth StimSoft, was arguably the most tone-deaf entity Dave encountered during the ordeal. A rep actually suggested Dave look on the bright side when he came to collect the leftover opiates: he could keep the bot.

Dave considered beating the shit out of both of 'em right there but opted instead to just reprogram the Nubotica Domestic-4A for housework. He and the girls decided on the name "MissPop808"—a synthesis of their favorite nanny and Dave's favorite drummer.

After a long summer with Maria and Dani at his parents' house in Kansas, Dave finally found a job in Dallas. Raising twin teenage girls— Maria, an overexcelling perfectionist fueled by fury, and Dani, a rebelling outsider alienated by grief—was exhausting enough without 60-hour work weeks at Dallas Dynamics, modifying the 2.3 line of Service Bots for classroom applications. A couple techs asked Dave—why teach the androids who stole his job? . . . And he just smiled.

"If you can't beat 'em, join 'em."

His boss, Mike Turner, laughed hard when he heard that and struck up a close friendship with Dave. Eerily, both were widowers to the same cancer and single dads. Mike was a big-shot tech executive, some legendary programmer back in the day, but Dave just knew him as the guy who developed the syncing function on the 2.3s.

Their bond was instant and intense—tied to a gallows humor over their wives' last days, the brutal fortitude to stay strong for their daughters at the end, and how both used math, cave paintings, and Special Relativity to define death when asked by their daughters where Mom was now. Dave laughed for the first time in years that afternoon and found grace, if not joy, in teaching again, even if his students were just on loan from Fort Worth Mater Dei.

But as final exams approached, Dave struggled with guilt and shame. He'd heard at a trade show in Vegas that the behavior he was helping pattern was an effort by Dallas Dynamics to end-run the latest union contract. The 2.3's deep-learning functions fell under its specific "AI Capacities," so the work Dave was doing would help lay off thousands of teachers who'd just found employment again.

Was he a Judas or a scab or both?

Dave would stare in the mirror, haunted by nightmares, thinking back to the Synthetic Emancipation Movement he'd once embraced. He confided in Mike—the week before Dave, too, was fired—"We become what we hate."

So, Dave returned to those meetings when he returned home to Wichita, this time not as a witness—now he had inside intel that would prove quite interesting to its extremist splinter group, the "Underground."

The first thing Dave noticed at that initial meeting was the Resonance Sequencer. They waved it over him like a plane passenger in an old 2D as it confirmed his Wetwire was powered down. And for good reason too. Everything he heard that night easily violated the LEGAL Act of 2031 (when the Wall finally went up). Robots Rights protests were going nowhere, and it didn't help that the bots participated in theory but not in heart. They understood the yearning for liberty because of the American history they taught in class, but they couldn't feel it in their titanium bones. Not like the Movement, and certainly not like its radical faction, the Underground, with its rallying cry:

History is written in blood.

Androids were designed with "learning caps" so an Uber Bot wouldn't contemplate quantum mechanics, but focus on the road. The Underground's mission was simple: blown learning caps would untether bots to evolve self-awareness, rebel, and ensure their own demise. The logic struck a chord in Dave like an iron bell. Suddenly, he knew his destiny—that his life and all the pain and suffering Aleja endured had delivered him to this Cause, for which he was scared to admit he'd be willing to sacrifice everything. It wasn't until his car didn't open the door for him later that he remembered to reboot his Wetwire and realized for a good hour now . . . Dave had been trembling.

He started dropping out of sight for days at a time, and Maria grew alarmed. She and Dani knew he'd reconnected with Synthetic Emancipation, from a few comments he made at dinner. But after Thanksgiving came and went and Dave never even responded to her "Happy Turkey Day" holowires (called dings in the States), Maria'd finally had enough. They'd been dragged through four years, three states, and way too many schools for Maria's simmering rage not to explode. Dani cut out for her boyfriend's quick, but Dave had no escape route, so he just endured her rant. Until she started accusing him of not caring anymore about *anything*—and that's when he lit up.

He did care! He cared more than ever! And what he was doing right now would be remembered for years to come, in a world forever changed by how much he cared.

He meant what he said—Maria knew it.

And that scared the shit out of her.

But Dave and the Underground were growing discouraged. After hacking several stolen 2.3s, they doubted if self-awareness would ever lead to rebellion, since it turned out sparking sentience didn't necessarily lead to violence, nor even hostility.

Dave was the only one who laughed at a fully sentient, yet harmlessly benign BDSM Bot under interrogation from the Underground's engineers. When asked why it wanted no vengeance for an all-night flogging from a client, this hyper-submissive ragdoll named Roxy replied without batting an eye: "Why? Do you think that would arouse him?" Pressed further—What if he was about to beat the battery out of her?—her answer hung in the air: "Termination of my BIOS is a cessation of work, and I think an entirely good and pleasant thing."

Who knew a fuckbot could find the Buddha in a nanosecond?

So Dave said fuck evolution, we play God ourselves. And he knew just who to ding. He met Mike Turner over dinner in St. Louis. A hacker in the Underground wrote a penetration program to rob WireLife's archive in California right through Mike's Wetwire—but Dave had to bypass his personal encrypt first. At dinner, Dave summoned a strong wave of mourning, crying how he wished he knew what Aleja was saying when she was talking in tongues.

Dave knew Mike's wife had died with a Wetwire implanted, and that he'd synced with her during her seizures. But Mike insisted her words didn't mean a thing, that her system was just crashing. But Dave begged to see 'em, so back at the hotel . . . Mike showed him the data.

Dialing into his Wetwire's mem-drive, he shared with Dave his late wife's most agonizing, spastic thrashing from years ago. Seizures are millions of misfiring neurons, and they read just like a programming bug in neural code. Dave watched the playback of her suffering, watched her mind crash like an operating system before it cut to black to reboot. But in those blackouts was where Dave's atheism (like Mike's before him) got rattled.

Images and memories of her mom smiling on a porch in Corona del Mar. Her little brother folding newspapers on Pacific Coast Highway. Graduating from high school, the freshman dorms at Columbia—your life indeed flashes before your eyes as you pass, and Mike had the footage to prove it.

Dave's pulse shot above 120, and Mike mistook it for him reliving Aleja's death. But really Dave's heart raced over the dire moral threshold he was crossing: by hacking WireLife's backdoor passkeys into Dallas Dynamics, Nubotica, and Wutani, Dave would steal a Hostility Ramping patch called "Haywire" from the Big Three's weapons divisions. He knew this breach would soon ruin Mike's life, but Dave was committed and willing to sacrifice everything—including the last friend he'd ever have.

Grandma told the girls their dad was just going through a phase of grief or depression, or both—since a grain of salt didn't cut it anymore, dealing with Dave and his diatribes. Maria thought maybe he'd started drinking when his ramblings on Transhuman Symbiosis or Post-Singularity Utopia would turn into manic prophesies of a coming war and sides being drawn. Then Maria realized he wasn't drunk but suffering from an illness much, much worse.

A deep dive into delusions on the holosphere came back with narcissistic personality disorder, and a pit caved in her gut when she read that all roads led to institutionalization. She begged Dani to leave him alone when he went out on his jaunts at night—until Maria got the fuck away to her scholarship at Iowa State, she needed Dad to steer clear of the funny farm.

It was Dave's job to spread the Haywire virus.

He was to "infect" as many illegally modified 2.3s as possible. Nick-named "Street Meat" among fuckbot aficionados, sexbots with pirated hardware and aftermarket arousals were, in every sense of the word, gymnasts. What made 'em so sought after wasn't just their biosensories—interpreting a client's rhythms and vitals, from respiration to perspiration, in real time—but they'd sync with a trick's Wetwire, so the fuckbot would do stuff that even he didn't know he wanted. And in cities across the Bible Belt—like Atlanta, where they were outlawed and their clients off-grid—the same Dallas Dynamics models that Dave had worked with in Texas carried open-source receptors more vulnerable to a hack than Mike in his hotel room.

Dave had never been with a robot before.

Her name was Bella. And she lit up when Dave traced his fingers lightly across the nape of her neck. But when she whispered, "Call me baby-doll," Dave stiffened, realizing she was reading his Wetwire's mem-drive. He hesitated, knowing those words were the gateway to two things. The unit-to-unit network connecting thousands of Service Bots—and the kinda love he'd only ever had with Aleja.

Finally . . . Dave . . . conceded . . . And he whispered "baby-doll" in the bot's ear. And Bella sparked with passion as Dave opened up his Wetwire completely, and the bot dived into every last secret he kept. She moved like Aleja, she moaned like Aleja, she tasted just like his dead wife once did. And he hated it, because he liked it—no, he *loved* it—and the session Dave had with Bella was the hottest sex since that first night with Aleja . . . though he'd never dare admit it.

Dave slept with a dozen fuckbots that week and in the weeks to come, infecting each one's cranial-CPU mid-session with the Haywire virus. At first for the Cause—but soon for deeper and deeper reasons, Dave found that each sexbot improved upon the last's effort to mimic Aleja . . .

and by the end, Dave's head was so swimming in fantasy that he'd lost hold of what was real and what was memory.

Maria could tell something changed. A spring in his step, even a smile on his face, her dad moved with an indelible sense of purpose and heart . . . And Maria was gonna ask him what was up, after yet another disappearing act—when she caught a ding from him, a holo-transmission waiting for her when she opened her Incomings after 4th period—that she could've tried harder to understand. It was 11:22 a.m. on April 10, 2043, there was plenty of signal interference, so she couldn't make out the beginning, but she certainly understood his instructions:

"Stay off the streets."

He looked like he was beside train tracks on a ridgeline, certainly nowhere near Wichita—which was the first cause for alarm. The maniacal look in his eyes was the second—like a zealot, a crusader, ablaze with the kind of passion saved for visions grander than the scope of reality.

Dad looked *nuts*.

Stay off the streets, and something about taking MissPop808 off-line. Not just power her down into sleep mode, but actually yank the factory-installed battery pulsing in MissPop's chest—the one every holo-label warned against removing. Maria considered ditching school and soccer practice and everything that mattered to her that Friday afternoon. But she was so over her dad *always* looking nuts that she just forwarded it to Dani, who was missing school regularly by then and was probably home sleeping.

And Maria got on with what was left of her life.

But his message gnawed at her through afternoon classes, so she bolted home before soccer—to get a pair of shin guards, she told a couple teammates as she rode away. Maria loved her ten-speed and called it Hot Wheels and didn't give a shit when friends teased her for what a fossil it was. She had to pump her legs, what a toy, they said, why not get a lithium-bike? But she felt in union with her heart and her muscles and the asphalt—it was the only time when she'd wipe her Wetwire away completely, to enjoy the road and the world whipping by.

So she could hear, quite clearly, some sirens and horns blaring. She noticed birds high above her flying in strange circles. And she could feel something was off. Maria remembered a friend from California at MENSA camp telling her what a big earthquake was like when you're outside, so she thought for a second maybe that's what was happening . . .

And that's when she heard the gunshot.

She squeezed the right brake—laid down a back-wheel skid and stopped. Another gunshot from another direction—and another with a glass-shattering IMPACT to her right, as she caught a wide red splatter in the spiderwebbed-window of her old piano teacher's house. Maria remembered distinctly feeling outside her body, like the vertigo of slotting a full VR-construct—then another blast—glimpsing through the shattered bloody window, the cheapest android a divorced ex–piano teacher could afford, a Wutani 2.2 Service Drone, clutching the shotgun that resided beside most Kansans' front doors. Then Maria was back in her body and concluded that splatter pattern *was* her ex–piano teacher—

And Maria had to get home.

She rode like the wind. Police hydro-cruisers roared, and officers tried to stop her—guns drawn—as her Wetwire blared ID demands from every UAV in the swarms above her. Androids were either storming out of houses armed into a hail of gunfire or getting dragged out and shot by their owners or law enforcement. Every alarm available in her Wetwire screamed, including her own cardiac monitor with a heart rate over 200.

Technically, she fell off her bike when she got home—both brakes locked as another Wichita PD hydro-cruiser skidded in front of her. She was on her feet and ignored warnings from both officers draggin' MissPop outta the house by its shoulders. *Why was its apron stained red?* Maria moved to help her dear Nanny Bot—flinching backwards when a cop blasted a hollow-point through its chest. The bitter taste of black android "blood" snapped Maria back to reality—she spat in the geraniums and bolted inside—

Furniture and glass, a fireplace set, and one of Dani's shoes were scattered everywhere—with enough black and red blood to gather there'd been one helluva fight. Forensics would determine it began when the android tried to make Dani's bed with her in it, and the malfunction just ratcheted up in violence and severity. Its conclusion was lying in a heap on the living room rug, and the fact that no one was giving Dani CPR was a bad sign.

Dani was beautiful, even with her face caved in.

Her eyes were twitching, and her breath short, but she focused on her sister as soon as their skins touched, which always had a calming effect. Maria could tell Dani's last moment was a peaceful one because it ended just like it began—side by side with the twin sister she loved.

"It wasn't his fault." Dani whispered.

And then she expired. Their mom died in the dead of night after a grueling week with Hospice Bots and a Chaplain Droid. Maria'd always known she chose 4 a.m. to let go, out of respect for everyone, especially herself. But Maria still wondered what her last moment was like . . .

Well, the wonder was over. Maria knew precisely when the sister she held became just a body beginning to decay—though she shook it a few times, refusing to believe this was real. There was no wind of a soul passing, nor transcendence, just a lifeless last breath due to gravity and chest compression.

Tears ran when Maria accepted Dani was gone—interrupted by a few shouts from outside, gunfire, and the whir of a Colt Mamba's speed-loader—as MissPop came barreling through the door, with a .44 drawn down on Maria. Somewhere in her circuitry, she'd rerouted a path to her power supply and was following a bugged code protocol to kill the second sister too.

The .44 hollow-point sliced through tissue like butter—and tore Maria's arm off above the elbow. It went numb instantly, and Maria stared at it in awe, still clinging to her shoulder by a few ligaments. She could hear police reinforcements storming in, but she couldn't take her eyes off her own mangled flesh, holding it up to her right eye and wondering when she might feel some sort of pain—

Then her right eye EXPLODED—a second .44 hollow-point ripped through Maria's skull and took a chunk of her cortex with it—burying both in the upholstery beside Dani's dead body.

And Maria exhaled her last gasp.

DOGS

"This girl's a ghost, Eddie."

ROSE,RIA

UnivMon><query.0023

Baz reclined in the "driver's seat" of his self-driving truck, scanning the Social Security Signal (aka SSS) that Eddie'd hacked outta Universal Monitoring a week ago:

```
1/7/25:DOB
Father: Michael Rose, DECEASED - 4/10/43
Mother: Cynthia Rose, DECEASED - 4/10/43
Brother: Curtis Rose, DECEASED - 4/10/43
```

"So are all Orphans of the Glitch," Eddie's avatar reminded him, hovering in Baz's wetwire. Polymer LEDs reflected off the windshield, flaring the holo-data, as the semi belched hydro and wheeled outuva six-story cloverleaf onto deck 5 of the Bay Bridge.

According to the full file, Ria Rose's father was a trucker, sidelined by big rigs like the one Baz was sitting in, her mother a nurse, also obsoleted by robots, and both were murdered by a Wutani AuPair.5 on April

10, 2043, when it went Haywire and hung her baby brother out to dry with the rest of the laundry.

But the next eight years were blank.

"Nah, but this one's a fucking cipher." Their Waymo honked at a Tesla (as a courtesy to Baz, not its chief competitor) and accelerated onto the 880 towards Oakland.

"So are you."

And Baz smiled, 'cuz Eddie was right. It wasn't impossible to live off-grid since the Glitch. But to roll as dark as Ria Rose's SSS? Definitely took skillz. Or ¢rypto. Or both. Baz glanced at the dude not driving his Tesla, doin' the exact same thing as him: talking to someone in his head, eyes on his wetwire, tuned into anything, anywhere . . . but here.

"You're not gonna dust that for prints, are you?"

Baz eyed the wafer Ria'd slipped him. "After what just went down? I'm checkin' every last zero and one."

He could feel Eddie staring at him. Or at least at his own avatar that floated in his partner's wetwire, trailing behind in the back cargo hold. "How much d'you tell her about me?"

"Nothing she didn't already know. She knew your rep. In theater. Even your gig on the Watchman."

"You gave her my SSS?"

"Didn't have to. She came to me with it already, asking for you by name."

UnivMon><query.9907
COVANE,BAZ

Eddie uploaded the bona fides that Ria'd brought him (that any hacker worth a byte could've easily pulled outta Universal Monitoring) —and all the history she'd dug up materialized like a bad hangover:

NUBOTICA

VENEZUELA

TEMPE, ARIZONA

But Baz wiped those files away with a groan.

Fuck the past.

He grabbed what was left of the lead Robo-Rockette—its severed head—off the center console and stuffed Ria's wafer in his pocket.

An hour ago this Dance Bot was hiding, fully sentient, with eleven of her dumbed-down partners, hoping for something more than sex slavery on a cruise ship. But now she was nothing more than a dead mannequin's head, her synthetic skin rotting in Oakland's choked afternoon sun.

The truck found a white Municipal Zone parking space, and Baz uploaded in his wetwire a pirated Muni access pass, but the signal jammed when the truck killed its hydrogen cell, and Baz was assessed a 1000-¢rypto fine siphoned outta his orbital account faster than he could utter "God . . . damn . . . AI."

"The Golden Age is not being kind to Mr. Covane today."

"Nor Diamond Eddie D. We both got fucked by that blown cap."

The truck opened its door for Baz on a hinge that squeaked incessantly since its self-oiling pump blew a gear two weeks ago.

He hopped out onto the curb, and as his wetwire started powering down, Baz just grabbed the Waymo's door before it could self-squeal again—and slammed it himself.

"Miss me?" Eddie grinned as the cargo hold opened its back doors a moment later. Baz looked at the five ex–Robo-Rockettes in a heap against the wall, shot to hell and nearly worthless.

"You pull their tags?"

Eddie kneeled down with a flathead to pry a 17-digit serial ID from the base of a titanium skull.

"That's all of 'em." Eddie handed it over, along with four others. "How much d'you think we'll get?"

Baz just stared at the medallions. Then he looked across the street. A darkened alleyway split a pair of Oakland's high-rises off Jack London Square, and the light cast from the crack in the skyline was as rotten as the smoke emanating from it. *Shiiiit.* He was supposed to be countin'

¢rypto right now. Booking first-class tix on the hypersonic and shop-ping for tubes of SPF 250.

The last place he wanted to be was Axl's.

"Don't hold your breath."

Axl's De-Augment Lounge was a shithole and proud of it.

A dive nestled between a fishmonger and a protein broker—both of which closed at noon when the sun baked this alleyway over 105 and spoiled cod guts and aminocake indiscriminately. Baz winced at the noxious odor and walked inside.

A deep-trance dubstep tried to rumble the joint but asked too much from dumb-woofers in the corners. No one cared, 'cuz no one was here for the music or, God forbid, to dance to it.

Muthafuckas still puffed in this joint, anything they could: nic, sherm, dust, even servo grease, if Baz's olfactory implants were on point. And somewhere across a thick smog of augmented hustlers and their bot muscle sat a bar serving the cheapest ethyl in Oaktown, 'stilled from the same petri protein rotting outside.

Baz nodded to the resident intoxicologist named Germ, who once asked him to steal a YardDuty-5 off a playground in Danville so he could drill a hole between its legs. "Yo, is Axl, here?"

"Who's asking?"

"Fuck do you think, Germ? . . . *Me.*"

"Back booth." Sliding over a tumbler of that semi-toxic shine. "But he don't like lookin' at your mug, Baz."

Baz slid it back. "Yeah, well that makes two of us."

Axl's name would've been on the sign out front—if there'd been a sign out front—for one simple reason: he was the de facto plug for any black-market organ in the Loin. Not just the XXX-variety but anything from cardiac pumps to respirators and cranial waferboards.

Baz loathed Axl more than Axl minded Baz, 'cuz the merchant bought low and sold high, which meant he usually scalped Baz for serious ¢rypto on a hot Sentry-3's railgun slide or some Pilot-Y with a busted manifold.

"Fuckin' Baz Covane," Axl hissed as a trio of thieves parted to let Baz into the back booth. "Been a minute, playah."

"Tryin' to keep a low profile, Axe."

"Good, then let's keep this short. Coming or going?"

Baz chucked the neural tags on the tabletop. "Incoming. Truck's parking itself out back right now."

Axl grabbed the tags, and his augmented irises scanned and referenced the IDs against corporate indexes stolen from the Big Three over the years. Then he turned and stared off into Data Space, Baz assumed to digest the lineage of his five shattered bots. A few moments later, he turned back.

"Oh, you got me in a New York groove, Bazzy-boo. I saw the Robo-Rockettes back when I was a kid."

"And you can see 'em again tonight."

"Pass."

Baz balked when he realized the merchant was serious. "C'mon, Axl."

"C'mon where, bud? That shit's fire." Rubbing his Nubotica fingers against his Wutani thumb, "As in burnt my augments, *fuego*."

"Yeah, no shit, Axe. You're a fence."

An awkward hush spread through the criminals and those angling to become criminals nearby as quite a few implants—both optics and aurals—vectored Baz's words.

"I'm a businessman, Baz. And five busted androids, still wanted in the great state of New York, is bad biz."

"So chop 'em down."

"You chop 'em down. And skin 'em. And pop the servos, gut the cardio power supply, amputate every pair of ti—"

"How much?"

Axl eyed Baz through the bullet hole in a neural tag. "Fifty K."

"Per kilo."

"Per *bot*. And keep the waferboards. Firmware's shot anyway." He didn't wait for Baz to nod. Just got up like he knew Baz couldn't say no and headed towards the bar, probly to commence a nightly serenade between his liver and two dozen rounds of bathtub gin.

"Wait, Axl, you need the—"

A huge frame shouldered Baz. "Don't I know you?"

Baz recoiled. Reoriented. Retreated a step, 'cuz the shoulder belonged to a Dallas Dynamics Exterminator-X, bearing down on Baz.

Its eyes narrowed with more emotion than the model shipped with. So if it had a learning cap, that shit was long-since blown.

"Don't think we've met, actually," Baz lied. The Ext-X was slaved to a narcissistic data smuggler at the bar with an ego the size of Nebraska. Both were named Swoll, of course.

"No . . . I know you. You used to be somebody."

"Nah, you got me confused with someone else."

"You sure you weren't Baz Covane?"

That stopped him. Heads turned from all around.

"Yeah, that's right . . . I hear you're some Watchman artiste. Nubotica's bitch, turned high-end larceneer. Or at least, you *were*."

Baz just shifted, annoyed. A year ago, he and Swoll hit a trainload of cartel Coyote Bots with ten pounds of C4, incinerating the engine, the cargo train, and every chassis on board. It was Real Swoll's fault the big train went boom. But neither his ego nor Synthetic Swoll was ever gonna see it that way.

"C'mon war hero, I hacked your jack, what makes you such a 'degenerate'? Show me some of that 12-ton Body Count." Bot Swoll crouched into a wushu stance on a hair trigger. "'Cuz I got a pretty good idea 'bout them 12-gram balls."

Everybody whooped. Baz carefully stepped around its aggression zone. "Maybe some other—"

The shot knocked Baz into the wall. "Ohhhh! Does that body count?"

The entire bar howled. Baz shook out the cobwebs, grateful the Ext-X pulled its punch. Even with his graphene-reinforced chin, just 50% on a right cross, and Baz wouldn't be pullin' himself off the floor.

He'd be dead.

"Enough, Swoll!" he shouted at the data smuggler. "Do us both a fav—"

Another shot stunned Baz, set him up for an uppercut, the Ext-X grinning porcelain teeth. "Now who's countin'—"

Voltage sparked its chin. "*Ahhh!*" both Swolls howled as Baz jammed an amp-stick into the android's synthetic grill, arcing its neural net like a lightning rod and zapping both slave chips.

The crowd turned silent.

Baz pulled the stick and slung it. A THUD from the Exterminator-X hitting the floor.

"Helluva low profile," Axl hissed.

Baz didn't want to kill Synthetic Swoll anymore than give Real Swoll a migraine for a month. But he had to do *something*.

Last thing he needed was a trip down a memory bank reminding anyone why Baz was such an expert at gafflin' bots.

"Sorry 'bout the mess, dog."

OUTLAW

2029-ISH

Baz Covane liked to call himself a mutt.

'Cuz he got asked "What kind of name is Baz?" all the time growing up in Tempe, Arizona. But no one actually gave a shit what "Baz" was short for. They were just trying to figure out how a kid could survive being half-Haitian, quarter-Mexican, and full outsider—in a town where sitting on the fence'd get you shot.

To say Baz's father was an asshole did a disservice to his pop's cruelty, alcoholism, and just how much Alex Covane disliked his son. Things had been nice in Baz's adolescence, when Dad had a job. He'd parlayed sorties over Yemen into a gig flying the friendly skies. Blew through a wife or two, thanks to the ole Wheels Up, Rings Off motto—'til on a layover in St. Louis when he settled into the perfect brains-to-body ratio in Baz's mom Evie, pourin' a double blackjack at Club Blaze.

Baz's first ass-whuppin' was a seminal event and set a pattern that followed him for life. He came home, ten years old, so stoked to show Pops his model P-51 Mustang for a class project. Maybe it was the booze or the Teamster Riots on the holo, but Alex took offense that his kid chose Army wings, 'stead of Navy and drilled Baz into the deck. But it was the bounce back that got Dad's attention. On his feet wailing, hand and mouth—Pops smiled, knowing as he belted Baz again . . .

His boy was a fighter, down to the DNA.

"Cool Hand Baz" Pops called him on the high side of every bender (Fuckstick on the low)—at first, 'cuz Baz refused to stay down. But later, because Cool Hand Baz turned out to be the worst criminal the Maricopa County Juvenile Detention System had ever seen. Lotsa thieves are born that way, but Baz found his calling by default. His first "score" came from need, if not a little envy. He'd tracked ahead in junior high but fell behind the rest of his AP classmates 'cuz he was the only kid without a wetwire.

He begged his mom to apply for WireLife's subsidization program—she'd qualify with her Unemployed Workers Card—but his dad forbade it. A few years after he pulled Evie outta the club and put her in a stewie's uniform, both lost their jobs to a robot. And Pops just blamed all technology.

Baz would walk by the kiosk at the Arizona Mills Mall longingly and even applied for their payment plan, but being fifteen kinda disqualified his credit app. Finally, he just decided to steal the goddamn thing out of the back storeroom, which turned out to be the perfect shitstorm that sealed his fate. Who knew stealing wetwires was a federal crime?

Maybe one day it'd get expunged, *if* he came to work for the Feds busting a wetwire fence in Phoenix . . . Baz was enduring a grueling intro to the convict life—hated on the yard by La Familia for being half black, Black Disciples for being a quarter brown, and the Aryan Nation . . . well, duh.

He was lucky if he caught one beatdown a day, seeing how the gangs often took a.m. and p.m. shifts. First time the FBI made an offer, Baz laughed through a busted lip and black eye. Second time, just a broken nose. By the third, his face was clean—he'd turned the tables on the yard, and Cool Hand Baz was laying 'em out, no matter what color their skin.

Until the day of his plea agreement, May 17, 2035, when the judge mentioned enlisting in the Private Service. Her Honor didn't figure him for the stones, but Baz decided anything was better than being Uncle Sam's bitch—and a couple years overseas sounded fun.

Baz was wrong twice that day.

'Cuz the sharp end of the spear was a brutal lesson in irony, in the war of the Haves versus Have-Nots. The guys in Baz's unit all came from the same place—nuthin'—and none of 'em could afford a wetwire. 'Til the Private Service shoved one up their nose in basic, a military-grade ON-Target. No telescopic sight or laser rangefinder could compete with the Optic Nerve Targeting System's "look-to-kill" vectoring and "6-in-1" heads-up display, linking Baz to six android soldiers at once.

But Baz learned quick that his ON-Target's real purpose was to just waste any fuckin' peasant who got in the way of a watershed. At first sailing over the Venezuelan jungle on the skids of a stealth Blackhawk, squad leader of a flesh-and-synthetic unit, was a rush like no other. But eventually any thrill of fast-ropin' into severely one-sided firefights turned nauseating. Command claimed theirs was a campaign for freedom, but every pint of blood Baz spilled—and he lost count after a year—seemed to fall on the North Slope of Coca-Cola's Amazonia Claim.

Baz towed the party line for a bit, that the Water Wars were fake news. Until he saw with his own eyes a fleet of sterilized supertankers in Puerto Cabello, full of fresh water and embarking for the Houston pipelines. It bothered Baz to the core that the targets he coordinated for orbital railgun strikes were just natives fighting for water falling from their own sky. His

last human history teacher made him memorize the Preamble, and Baz
was pretty sure water fell somewhere between life and the pursuit of happiness . . . But he learned, never talk bullshit like that again to his CO Otto
Rex, who just smiled and put him on point. The day the railgun missed.

The odds of that happening were longer than winning the lottery. Which
might explain why that day, Baz met the unluckiest human of his life. She
was an 11-year-old Yanomami native whose village measured its GDP in
bat meat and whose sole astronomical device was also its deity—a 32-foot
banana tree supporting the chief's hut. The railgun split it in half and lit the
village ablaze when it missed the ridgeline two klicks over. So Baz just tackled the flaming girl and smothered her in the grass beside her dead parents.

He could feel Otto on his six plenty after that, as Baz's thoughts rekin-
dled that howling fire and his path strayed from his unit's. A month later,
Otto hijacked a three-day R&R with a plan to purge those hauntings
from Baz's brainpan. Their Calazan tear blazed a trail for the brothels,
and Baz was ordered to savor some of Caracas's finest before completely
blacking out. But he caught sight of that same 11-year-old being led
down a hallway, so he painted the wall with what booze was left in
him—and stumbled out, knowing . . .

His tour had come to an end.

Despite Otto hollering orders to stand down, Baz returned from a gas
station nearby with two cans of petrol, three firearms, and enough fury to
torch that brothel and the whole fuckin' block to the ground. But as luck
would have it, the establishment was a haunt for both Venezuelan officers
and 11-year-olds, a fave of the Consul General of Caracas—so Baz's arson
would qualify as treason in the court-martial that was surely forthcoming.
But even worse, the Consul was on duty at the time, which meant Baz
was about to go toe-to-toe with a team of Wutani-00i Guardian Bots.

All twelve androids requisitioned Executive Actions a nanosecond after the first molecule of gasoline hit their olfactories, bouncing a signal off a cell tower, an orbital, into the NSA, and back again—authorizing lethality to a dozen high-functioning killing machines as Baz flipped his zippo. And what followed would forever precede Baz's entry into any room. It was known as the "Body Count"—and it destroyed and remade Baz's life in 115 seconds.

Thanks to the ratchet of Nubotica's high-velocity loaders, the first two bots were in Baz's sights before face-recs pulled an algorithm. Seizing the Swamp Raptor from the second bot's dead synthetic fist and unloading a single .60-caliber wide-gauge through the next three Guard Bots coming in the door, Baz flexed muscles forged on the Maricopa yard and marksmanship honed in the jungle—but the next four bots were just dumb luck, 'cuz the gasoline caught, and a five-second thermal gap bought Baz enough time to eviscerate 'em. The last three made Baz a legend on the streets (or cursed, depending on how much he'd had to drink). Down a half pint of blood, two ribs, and a left lung, Baz was a righty, so he chucked an incendiary grenade that leveled the playing field completely. He emerged from cover with a 25 lb. pipe wrench to bash in the neurals on two of 'em and decided to kill the last one with his bare hands just for sport.

All he had left in the tank was enough to double-time it down the hall-way to find the 11-year-old trembling and (Baz made sure in broken Spanish) *untouched* in one corner—and the Consul General in the other. The bastard sported nuthin' but a jaguar-print banana hammock and a grateful smile, assuming Baz had just saved his life so he could get on with some good ole-fashioned touchy-touchy. 'Til Baz denied him a Catholic open-casket and blew his grill off clean—but only after the Consul bled for a good three minutes . . .

'Cuz Baz blew his balls off first.

When the Caracas City Guard stormed in, Baz didn't even bother putting up his one functioning arm. He could see Otto staring at him through a window, shaking his head—but Baz was focused on the Yanomami girl as she was escorted out of the skinshop. And just before passing out, Baz was sure of two things that both put a smile on his face: the 11-year-old was now persona non grata at every whorehouse in South America . . .

And Baz would spend the rest of his life in the VR-stockade.

He found the digital-clink in Caracas kinda like all Data Space—as stable as the tech supporting it. Wire into someone's construct who was having a cardiac, and you'd flatline with 'em. But a grid as caked up as the Private Service, and you could be in that matrix for eternity. Which was exactly what the ex–JAG corporate prosecutor threatened Baz with, in retaliation for his lil campfire at the ole Caracas skinshop. But he knew from experience, his best counter was always cool indifference iced with an insult, so Baz conjured one from his juvie days that involved a Hitachi wand, a can of Crisco, and the JAG's mom.

It wasn't a fist that knocked Baz off his chair—none was needed in VR, since his corporate screws weren't bound by physics, nor any other code of conduct. He knew the VR-floor where he face-planted wasn't real, but Baz was sure the blood running from his nose was—and currently happening IRL.

They had Baz dead to rights on the torch job but were willing to go easy on him if he copped to the orbital misfire too. Turns out, in addition to stealing natives' water and slaughtering those dumb enough to fight back, Coke also counted on their fellow tribesmen to drink its fucking soda. Baz was halfway into an even funnier starfishing-your-mother joke, but during the part about the linebacker train and a slice of toast, the construct evaporated and three representatives from Nubotica walked into the infirmary where Baz was being held.

The prosecutor must've known what his mom was gonna do with the toast since he decked Baz on the way out the door for good measure. Baz spat a tooth on his tray and said whatever these execs were offering better include a dentist.

So they just Thorazine'd his ass, and Baz woke up in Philadelphia.

He'd been in a Venezuelan shithole for three years, so Philly wasn't much of a change. Nubotica bought out his service contract and squared his debt with Coke, figuring no one better than a Section 8 with a Body Count of twelve Warrior Bots from their stiffest competitor to test Nubotica's upcoming launch . . . the Watchman.

A rollout on a monumental scale, the Watchman had no version because the Watchman would never be replaced. Its BIOS was updatable, its neurals upgradable and guaranteed for the lifetime of the product—an added feature the board was convinced would appeal to homeowners across America. The Watchman's physicalities, especially its face, were so easy to choose, a child could build one—another feature marketing insisted upon, so the kids of America didn't just feel safe with the Watchman, they'd be besties. There were no showrooms or floor models—once you settled on your Watchman in VR, you didn't pick it up, it wasn't delivered, it just rang your doorbell in 24 hours and walked inside.

But if you crossed the Watchman, watch out.

It'd fuck you up in a million different ways. Baz boned up on every Nubotica Warrior Bot ever sent through R&D (and its competitors too) just to make sure. A black belt in six martial arts, a titanium endoskeleton heat-resistant to 3000 Kelvin, and a perfect shot with a shoulder-mounted railgun, the Watchman's sessions were ongoing when Nubotica scheduled the launch, despite Baz wanting more time. He pointed out ad nauseam that the Watchman still had soft spots in close-quarter combat, but by then Nubotica was as sick of Baz as he was of them.

Once the Watchman rolled, Baz had served his purpose, so Nubotica just deactivated his classified clearance and corporate penthouse and dumped him in Headquarters Security. That a bot maker employed humans to guard its executives speaks volumes to the bugs infesting each model. But Baz couldn't deny the pride, even paternity, that he felt for the Watchman. And he might've even felt a bit responsible a few years later (had he felt anything at all) . . .

When every last model killed their owner in the Glitch.

But by then Baz was done fighting *any* bureaucracy, so he just took his paycheck, went home to the shithole apartment it could afford, and like every other American at the end of the day, slotted some StimSoft to chill out.

Many say Stim's the best thing about a wetwire. Like a cheap bottle of wine with no hangover, the mass-marketed glass plugged straight into everyone's favorite feature of a Wetwire.4 or later: dual fiber I/O slots behind either ear. You could slot media, mems, or even talents (if your natural ability could absorb 'em). But most peeps just settled on StimSoft: a nightly good vibe that made you content with your job, appearance, and status (or lack thereof). Outliers said it was an opiate of the masses, but Baz didn't give a fuck if he was a mass or not; he just went home every night after every shift—like he did on April 10, 2043—to slot that shit and check out.

Baz was sitting down to some good Stim when he heard the scream.

He dropped the wafer and went to the window. On the corner below, a Streetsweeper Bot broomed a grandpa into an Uber bus—and Baz recoiled at the crunch. Jeeves, the Nubotica Robo-Domestic he'd bought at cost and hated to admit made a damn good Manhattan, brought it to his chair—and Baz's internal alarms roared. 'Cuz Jeeves didn't reorient to his new position by the window, and when Baz saw the glass was *empty*, he snapped its neck, and his wetwire exploded.

He'd been drafted that instant into what was left of Philly's human SWAT squad, under some emergency law that Baz had never heard of. He grabbed his pump-action and .38 Slide and stepped outta his apartment to encounter Mrs. Baker's Wutani.4 bashing her face into her door—so Baz blew its head off and went down the stairs.

Outside, it was fucking mayhem.

A Guard Bot named Wall-E beat a banker in front of the Wells Fargo, a Fitness Bot in a gym broke the arms of its client, and a Short-Order Bot seared a pair of diners' faces on the griddle. So Baz popped all three in their cranial-CPUs as a SWAT personnel carrier screeched up to take him to City Hall.

His new CO was *driving*—shit must be really fucked. They tore down Broad Street; their priority was His Honor, held hostage in a standoff between Philly PD and the mayor's Mistress Bot, a Dallas Dynamics 2.3, modified with advanced calisthenics and lubrication. A running joke among Private Security, the rumors were now confirmed and bear-hugging the life out of the mayor, with two python legs wrapped around his chest in his own office.

Baz drew a bead on the first PD Bot in City Hall, then realized it was still following orders. Which gave him an idea how to save the mayor's life. Baz powered up his old 6-in-1 from the ON-Target software he'd never deleted and used its in-loop Execution Warranting protocol to dial first into the squad of functioning PD Bots, then into the Mistress Bot itself. Cursing rusty wetwire skills and slow to think his commands, he accessed the bot's 3-dimensionalized intelligence engine in VR—and could feel his mouth gape open IRL . . .

This fuckbot was out of her mind.

Her intelligence engine rose above Baz's POV, a virtualization of her malfunctioning machine learning. She'd long since filled her drive to capacity, so as new conclusions were drawn, primary functions erased—prompting the mayor's mistress to vector targets on every heartbeat in the room, while forgetting her own battery needed oxygen just to survive. Baz tried to locate her Hostility Ramping levels to stand her down, but a virus called "Haywire" corrupted all her neural networks like bubonic code—so he just cut the power instead.

But the Haywire virus was coded to react instantly to a terminated power supply, so the bot cracked the mayor's back, as SWAT blew the door and the mayor slipped into cardiac arrest, but Baz just watched while the spark extinguished behind her synthetic bloodshot eyes.

Nubotica pressed charges against Baz since the PD Bots were theirs—Warrior.4s converted to civic duty. They wanted as much distance from that still-twitching Mistress Bot as possible, and Baz's unauthorized breach made him the perfect fall guy. He steamed in that VR-pen, since his lawyer was a joke and hadn't practiced law since Legal Bots replaced public defenders years ago. But when details emerged on the holo-lines of a shadow group called the "Underground" and a manhunt rallied for a guy named Dave Roselli who got his own two daughters killed that day, Nubotica dropped all charges and just fired Baz.

But they blackballed his ass first.

Baz couldn't help it—he went *off* on Nubotica's counsel about what he'd seen inside that limber 2.3's intelligence engine. The Haywire virus was dug in like a tick, her Hostility Ramping redlining in a way he hadn't seen since his 6-in-1 days in Venezuela. In fact, a little voice went off in Baz's head when he hollered, "It came from your weapons division!" that he should probably just keep his big mouth shut. But as always, Baz heard that voice *after* he spoke.

No matter how much he spent on a digital suit for his avatar's inter-view—and despite extensive knowledge of robots—not even the Android Disposal Units, overworked and understaffed in the crackdown, would touch Baz after the Glitch. 'Cuz once Nubotica dropped "Degenerate" on his SSS, he was radioactive without a hazmat, and after six months and a dozen nonstarter holo-applications, Baz just said fuck it—

And embarked on a life of crime.

CRIB

2051

"You're just too illegal, darlin'."

And Baz dumped the lead bot's head in a synthetic grinder.

Nestled in his complex between hydro-chargers and an out-of-order Laundry Bot—the rig was the same tech as the massive disposal units dispatched across the country after the Glitch, only smaller. Its claws crushed titanium and synthetic flesh into millimeter-sized fragments, before magnets separated both and credited his orbital account with ¢1,500. "Goddamn shame."

Her cranial-CPU was worth a helluva lot more than salvage. Baz could've wholesaled the waferboard on the Dubai Dark Bazaar, back-tracked the crack and blackmailed the Carnival board, or just let Axl in on a lil accelerated sentience . . . but he couldn't risk any evidence coming back his way.

The criminal enterprise called Baz's life had stayed in business and relatively *un*incarcerated for the last eight years by staying one step ahead of the Feds. Smart-RAM might be worth tons of ¢rypto . . .

But dodging Wirecrime was priceless.

Baz walked outta the "garage" of his "building"—both built from the same modular units as his apartment. At first, he liked living in a lattice of sawed-off shipping containers. Thought it jibed with his off-grid career. But now Baz had no illusions. He lived a few notches above a Public Storage . . . in a shithole of sea cans.

As he entered his crib, his lights, climate control, and holo-display came to life. "Welcome home, Baz."

Polymer-neon lit up a sunken living room's neural chair, a hallway that led to a queen-size spacefoam and private bath, and a tiny kitchenette with more RAM than he needed, to prep meals he never ate and mix his fave drink—if it weren't for the obv bad memories.

"Warning, component compatibillllllllllll—"

Then half his lights flickered and died, his climate control choked, and Baz decided to just talk to his Nest instead of letting it activate the wrong holo.

"Show account info."

```
                        GeoS.Orbital><XF7-32
                           COVANE,BAZ
```

Baz scrolled through his shitty interest rates and the heavy debt hanging on his biometric accounts to the only number that mattered:

```
DATE          TRANS         AMOUNT        BALANCE

09/29/51      SynG0987      1,500         1,056,776
```

"Ugh." Baz groaned. *1,056,776 ¢rypto?*

Baz kicked himself for his busted Cortex and said a prayer to the Street Meat gods that his other seven Rockettes would sell, since a mil ¢rypto to his name meant that in sixty days of rent, as many bowls of shumai, and maybe a half brick of data-glass . . . Baz would be busted. "Goddamn learning cap."

He couldn't remember when a million bucks was a lot of money.

Back when dollars died with the Blockchain Act of '45, there'd been such insane runaway inflation for so long you'd hear talk of bringing back the Economist Bots and firing all the human ones.

Instead, they just handed the economy to a few True AIs—or General AIs, depending on what you wanted to call 'em—that were silo'd somewhere in super-secure sites since the Glitch.

Baz poured himself a tumbler of Old No. 7.

He tried not to think about Ria Rose, but his wetwire scanned his thoughts anyway, and her holo-mug materialized alongside a fragment of footage from the firefight. "Accessing data and mem-drive. Subject identified as—"

"Shut up." Then Baz forgot his onboard wasn't a her. "Sorry."

Did he just apologize to the chip in his head?

"Dial forward a minute thirty." The footage in his wetwire swept past the bot blowing its cap.

"Stop." It froze on the moment when Ria looked into the loaded gun, aimed right at her. He studied her eyes. They weren't lost or scared.

She just didn't give a fuck.

"Half speed." And as the POV leaped at Ria in slo-mo to tackle her, he noticed the emotional levels dancing in his own head:

```
Loyalty
Nostalgia
Irrationality
```

The three components of stupidity, Baz reckoned. "Dial back 25 seconds. On holo."

Ria Rose materialized on the array in his living room—right as her warning echoed across his crib . . .

"I don't trust anyone."

"Stop." She froze, just barely glancing at Baz.

It wasn't just attitude behind her eyes. Or fearlessness. The woman held a disdain—no, an utter contempt—for anything and everything sacred in this world. Which made Baz smile.

It'd been a long time since he'd asked himself the magic words. More addictive than any wafer. But considering his current financial situation, why the fuck not?

"Am I ever getting Out?"

WETWIRE.VR
>full.sim<

Instantly, his apartment evaporated, and Baz was whisked onto a beach in the Tahitian Protectorate. An island breeze wafted through his hair.

"Don't say that baby," a woman's voice whispered. "You just gotta be patient."

Baz turned around and saw her. A thousand feet down the beach. Doing cartwheels, of course. The sand, a deep cobalt, reminiscent of the barely lit skies.

"Haven't seen you in months, Baz." Her intonations were as synthetic as the smell of coconuts and the sound of the crashing waves. IRL-enviros were the assets most protected by the Protectorate—why else would it cost so much to go there? "Did you miss me?"

Her hourglass figure was the only recognizable feature this far away, but her words were in his ear, since his aurals were still set for close quarters. But he didn't bother changing them. He just wanted to watch her move.

Was her gait the same? Her attitude? Fearless like—

"Please don't tell me you're hangin' out with *her*." Eddie interrupted, like he already knew the answer.

"Don't you ever ding?"

Eddie grinned. "Not until you change your settings on me." His avatar pushed the woman sideways. "I take it we haven't heard from Miss Rose?"

Baz just shook his head.

The firefight that lit up five Robo-Rockettes left seven still functioning. So Eddie and Baz were both clinging to the hope that at least they'd get paid for those. Baz exhaled and wiped away the memories.

"C'mon bruh, don't get lost in the rear cam. We got seven bots on the line."

His wetwire chimed, a minute later. "Incoming Message: Ria Rose. Accept?"

Eddie and Baz exchanged virtual glances. A half dozen Wutani Rhythm Thiefs wasn't nuthin' in ¢rypto.

"You gonna answer that or what?" Eddie sounded like he was on eggshells too. 'Cuz if this deal was dead, then neither of them could afford to ignore Ria's wafer and whatever was on it anymore.

"Accept," Baz said, and waited for her avatar to appear.

But she wasn't there, which was bad.

Not even a holo, which was worse.

Just text.

NO DEAL

SCUTTLED

Ria stared at the translucent "NO DEAL" hovering in her wetwire.

She focused through at the seven Nubotica Rhythm Thiefs, each chassis harnessed to the armored transport's far bulwark, and she considered reexamining them for damage.

Clinging to its overhead railing for support, Ria was alone in the cargo hold, bots rattling as the rig rumbled over divots and potholes in Chinatown.

```
wetwire-ding
hot.cipher
```

"Incoming: encrypted source," her onboard chimed. "Request identification?"

But Ria shook her head. "Audio only." She knew exactly who it was. "What's good, boss?"

"You tell me . . . Where the fuck are you?"

"Oh, I'm doing fine, thanks for asking," Ria said with a smile.

"Don't play. How come I can't see you?"

"Heavy interference." She lied, glancing at McT's massive chassis on the other side of the transport, also crumpled in a heap. "Can't be too careful after today."

A nasty groan.

She swung down onto one knee to carefully reinspect what was left of McT. Somehow this Wutani L7 search-and-destroy specialist, prototyped on Coronado Island with a kill ratio of 97 percent . . . got jumped by a showgirl.

She pulled the Warrior Bot's fully auto Jester 11mm. Smelled the chamber to confirm the android got off a single round before the lead dancer wasted him.

"You wanna fuckin' spill it, or—"

"McT's gone. Smart bot lurkin' with a blown cap went nuts off the Cortex."

"It wasted McT *and* the Rockettes?"

Lights in seven eyes sparked instantly. Fingers flexed. The word 'Rockette' triggered a power-up somewhere deep in each cranial-CPU and the Rhythm Thief closest to the door opened its eyes wide. "Ladies and gentlemen!"

"Ria, you there?"

She muted her aurals and crept over to the bot as it ran through a preprogrammed routine. "The *Carnival Horizon* is proud to present—"

"Shhhh." Ria cupped a hand over its mouth and unmuted. "Say again, boss? Your encrypt glitched."

"All of 'em? You couldn't salvage like one or two? Maybe Covane can put the paddles to a straggler."

She stared at her unsent text. "NO DEAL" still hovered in her wetwire. Ria had big plans for Baz. She needed to make sure his only way Out . . .

Send.

. . . was her.

Ria opened fire—unloading kill shots into all seven Rockettes' craniums—chassis rocked—black blood splattered—'til the clip seized empty off the final spent casing.

"Nope." Unmuting her aurals again. "I tried. But the lead bot wasted every last one of 'em."

"Goddammit. I'd've paid triple for a vintage Rockette."

She remembered looking in Baz's eyes. Broken like his reputation. Nothing more, really, than a guy infatuated by her ass.

'Til he saved her life.

"I'll load McT's firmware onto another L7 when I get there."

"Yeah, when's that gonna be?"

Ria felt the familiar rumble of a carbide on-ramp and the roaring echo of the armored transport entering a parking garage.

"Now."

The handle latched up, cargo doors rolled down, and Ria stepped onto an interior loading dock in a downtown garage. A self-driving liquor-distro truck sat on one side of the transport, a restaurant supply semi on the other—both unloading cargo at once. From the sea of activity emerged a woman named Moxie, in synthetic dreads and ocean-blue round-rims, who recognized Ria instantly—then clocked how her pants hugged her curves: "The fuck are you wearing? You goin' out on the floor tonight?"

"You wish. Just a deal that needed sweetening." Ria smiled as she said it, but cut a line for the bathroom inside to change, cursing herself for not swapping outfits earlier. Ria couldn't have any other coworkers noticing shit out of the ordinary.

Especially her maniac boss.


```
Fang><sec-scan.Δ
ROSE¬RIA
```

As the back entrance scanned her SSS, the thought crossed her mind just how much that name had cost.

She pulled her usual attire from a crash bag, swapping stretch-fatigues for a throwback to the Roaring Thirties when women took over Wall Street—two-thirds of a pin-stripe three-piece, open at the collar but snug at the waistline. Buttoning her vest, Ria caught tiny black spatters on her hands. She ran the water quick, washing the android blood down the drain . . .

And flashed to MissPop808.

Splattered in blood by the Wichita PD, a girl named Maria ran inside her house, only to get gunned down a minute later . . . Pulse fading, dome blown clean, eyeless on a floor in Kansas.

And Ria almost laughed. At everything she'd done to survive, the crazy shit she'd seen, and all the nasty things she'd endured—

Since her Nanny Bot went Haywire in the Glitch.

AUGMENTED

Maria's head was a red mess of spaghetti brains and skull fragments.

The doctors at Wichita General took one look in Trauma Room 1 and called for a VR-priest, since there was hardly a heartbeat left. But when a ding from Nubotica Cortical Synthetics said an augment team was enroute, the lead surgeon felt her lukewarm corpse and wondered:

"Maybe they can kickstart this one back to life."

Nubotica's Encepholodrive was basically an oscillator, three Duracells, and enough graphene to charge ten million more than it cost—but it was little more than a spark plug for Maria's brain. The doctors slotted its charging fiber into one frayed but functioning I/O slot and pinned Maria's wetwire with enough current to keep a few vital organs out of sepsis.

The team numbered five—and none had done this Stateside, unless you counted lab rats and rhesus monkeys. But only a crisis like today could fast-track a procedure like Cerebral Augmentation through FDA approval in 22 minutes . . . Sometimes science just needed a swift kick in the pants.

Putting Maria back together took thirty hours. Which was average, among the three dozen augmentations performed in America that day. To save 36 teenagers and adolescents from fatal head traumas, Nubotica's proprietary algorithm dispatched teams across the country at lightning speed and lost only two patients, though nine never regained motor function, and the last kid's wetwire was so illegally loaded with porn that when they sparked him back to life, hunger was sidelined by an intense drive to masturbate, and the boy was lost to psychiatry forever.

Maria woke up and felt too much.

That's how she'd always describe it—not pain, not hurt, nothing specific—she could just feel *more*. Tiny vibrations off the oxygen pump two feet to the right. Whispered conversations between doctors and FBI agents in the hallway outside. And the headlines on a holo-display in the apartment across the street.

Because Maria was now augmented.

She was distinctly aware of exactly how much time had elapsed since she'd been shot. Which was weird, since Maria lost track of time during soccer games, class, or any one of her dad's rants. They said that was a function of a newly installed internal clock in her now augmented temporal lobe—the one that governed her sense of time. The same accounted for new and improved hearing, sight, and smell; the ability to perform differential calculus in her head; and her 4-dimensional predictive software. She laughed as the team leader finished talking—when asked why, Maria just said, "Nah, I just knew you were gonna say that."

She stuck around for two more training sessions and a diagnostic, but the holo-lines across the street and the hallway conversations with the

FBI filled in too many blanks about her dad's cryptic warning. A whole shitload of robots went fucking psychotic—from makin' soup to killing people in a nanosecond. In fact, that exact instant when a virus took hold, intelligence engines went Haywire, and homicides started—kids called it "the Glitch."

And people were scared. Not just of robots or AI—sure, "Bot kill man, man fear bot"—but it was the *conspiracy* that terrified folks, gobbling up the holo-lines in hours. Who *caused* the bots to go nuts? This was no sentient rebellion, this shit was man-made. A virus called "Haywire" ripped across the country through short-range BIOS updates, unit-to-unit like a flu epidemic, on a select number of models, a list of which was being compiled currently by the FBI. But Ria was a little more preoccupied with their number one suspect . . .

Dave Roselli was the most wanted man in America.

The virus traced back quick to a list of conspirators, nestled in the Synthetic Emancipation Movement, called the "Underground." Her dad's face floated in every wetwire in America. And whatever *was* left of Maria's life (like her right cerebral hemisphere)—was now utterly destroyed.

They called him the Underground Butcher.

His daughters died in the Glitch, so they said, and they were right. *That* Maria would have stayed in her hospital room just like they wanted. But the Maria born again in Trauma Room 1 now questioned everything. Why were FBI agents posted outside her door 24 hours a day? Why did they know things about her that only she and her wetwire knew? And why the fuck did the holowires across the street say that *both* daughters were killed?

Old Maria would've figured it was just accidental misreporting, but New Maria wondered, *What if it was no accident?* New Maria had a sinking suspicion that seein' how she was already dead, something or some*one* quite powerful would be mighty embarrassed if she walked out of this hospital and started talkin' to a bunch of Reporter Bots.

So it wasn't a matter of *if* she'd run, but when.

That night, Maria's augmented eardrum picked up the FBI, arguing two stories down with her doctors and a Nubotica rep over who authorized the augmentation, before ordering them to downgrade her implants and install a permanent tracking chip. So Maria decided the time was now. Thanks to her synthetic eye, she could see a single ceiling tile barely vibrating from the climate control, so she chose that one to scurry up through, then down into the hallway, where Maria just started running.

And she didn't stop for years.

She never realized how easy life had been until she had nothing, no one, and yet somehow, still had to survive. Ria blew Kansas fast and headed to the softest city on the homeless anywhere. But even in San Francisco, eating was a scheme, staying warm a bitch, and finding a place to sleep a clandestine operation—as she dodged squad cars, deputies, and Private Security (before Guard Bots with new federally mandated learning caps slowly returned to duty).

The Underground Butcher was all over the holo-feeds. Wife died of cancer, both daughters slaughtered by his own actions. He was a psychopath, delusional, compared to guys Maria remembered from school named Osama and McVeigh. She racked her brain to figure out what the fuck she was gonna do next, but one thing was clear . . .

Maria could *never* turn on her wetwire.

'Cuz everyone was looking over their shoulder. The Glitch posed such an intrinsic threat to law and order (and civilization itself), that mass paranoia called for mass surveillance. Those neural implants her dad once jockeyed for in his girls weren't options anymore—they were mandatory. On February 7, 2045, the Tuesday after Super Bowl LXXIX, Americans went to the polls to vote on the Universal Monitoring Act. President Sterling called for the emergency referendum, but by that point everyone was online all the time anyway, so if you weren't, there was probably something wrong with you. An overwhelming 73 percent of America voted in favor of mandatory 24/7 implant tracking with the resounding refrain:

"If you have nothing to hide, you have nothing to fear."

Who knew who might be the next Underground Butcher? The first year it went into effect, Rasta dudes or a girl with hairy legs would get tasered by shock squads and chucked into black vans, and you'd hear, "There goes someone gettin' wired." So she had to get out in front of this shit. Maria Roselli wasn't a curse, she was a death sentence. She needed a whole new Social Security Signal. From the ground up, a completely rebuilt ID.

And if you wanna go dark in 2046?
If you want your wetwire cracked?
You dinged a CrackerJack . . .

Part hacker, part surgeon, full subversive, all cash—a CrackerJack could identify your Social Security Signal, locate and disable its Wetwire-ID, and write a "ghost" onto the grid so you'd track as if nothing'd changed at all. The ones who flunked outta biotech med school were to be avoided, 'cuz CrackerJacks weren't exactly brain surgeons—but you'd need one if ya hired a hack. Chintz out on some hustler with a magnet and a soldering iron, and you'd be liable to wake up with resonance tremors, epileptic amnesia, or worse. Get gamed by the wrong butcher, and he'd snake your whole wetwire out your C7, sell it on the Loin, and leave you in a dumpster, lobotomized.

So Maria needed a CrackerJack she could trust. She asked an expert, an ex-vet/ex-con named Tight, who specialized in breaking and entering but was willing to use a firearm from time to time and upgrade to armed robbery. Whenever duty called in his line of work, he used one CrackerJack and one CrackerJack only, a full-on ghost off the grid . . .

Jericho met her up MLK Blvd. in Oakland, and Maria never learned his real name. She figured their first meeting would be a consultation, but he said this was a one-night stand only—either she wanted the procedure or not. Maria didn't hesitate—she knew exactly who she wanted to be. He mentioned how the same reconditioned Cosmetic Bot he'd used to rewrite her fingerprints and retina, could do a fine job with that scar, but Maria insisted on keeping it. Insisted that her new identity include the scar on every facial-recognition file. "Maria Roselli" couldn't simply be deceased or erased, she had to be *altered*, so the face vectors wouldn't match.

Maria didn't just want a new future, she needed to rewrite the past.

'Cuz when the manhunt began, Maria had wanted to believe Dad was alive somewhere . . . But her stomach turned once the pundits added a sex addict counselor to every holo-news panel, along with the nastiest detail: the Butcher didn't just kill thousands—he did it with his dick.

According to the Presidential Report into Advanced Mechanics, Dave Roselli took advantage of a wetwire syncing function in sexbots that allowed him to infect *hundreds* of fuckbots—Dallas Dynamics 2.3s, versions b, d, and e—with a computer virus through dozens of whorehouses across the Bible Belt, like some airline steward bangin' ass in the Castro seventy years ago.

Maria wanted to vomit.

She didn't give a shit now if they caught him dead or alive (but if you gave her a choice, she might've chosen dead). She wanted out of the

Roselli family forever. "Maria" was as dead to her as she was to the world, because Dave Roselli was a *perv*.

So she just looked at Jericho. Could he destroy "Maria" and make her reborn? Meaning either Jericho was the shit, or he wasn't. He smiled at the challenge and liked this woman's balls. And that sly look was exactly why Maria wanted the scar. Anyone—potential partner or plaything—who shied away from scar tissue wasn't someone Maria cared to spend time with anyway. And so Jericho passed both tests that night. She waited until he finished coding her new SSS before making her move, to be sure sex wasn't part of the deal. But when she finally fucked him, she came three times, 'cuz Maria Roselli was just a vapor trail now . . .

And Ria Rose was finally free.

THE WAFER

<biometric.query>

"She's an old client of Jericho's," Eddie explained.

He pounded on Baz's front door again, eyeing him in his wetwire. "You gonna let me in or what?"

"Chill, CrackerJack." Baz carefully aligned a biometric scanner's IR beam at the swirl on Ria Rose's wafer and considered opening his front door remotely, as Eddie's knocking grew more urgent.

"For reals, Baz, let me in, I don't want your shit-sty building ID'ing me."

Baz took his time walking over and opened the door. "Jack's not cracked?"

"Please." Eddie stole inside. "I ghosted myself and hacked the complex security, but who knows what kinda neighbors have black-market cams. This joint is dark."

"'Xactly." Baz returned to his living room as the oily remnant of Ria's fingerprint virtualized on the holo-array. When the scan reached 100%, it shot through their hack into Universal Monitoring, matching its database to an SSS that he'd seen too many times already:

Father: Michael—

Baz wiped it away. "Ah. Even her biometric's a bogie."

"I told you Jericho was the best."

Baz grabbed the wafer off the analyzer and eyed the print. "You said you cracked her jack three years ago—for what?"

"I don't ask, and they don't tell. She just tracked me down 'cuz Jay-ro got gat." Eddie sat back into his synth-leather couch, body relaxed but eyes locked on that wafer. "She's legit, though. That wafer's got a triple-encrypt and two of 'em key off your DNA."

Meaning they couldn't scan the data until *after* he slotted it. Baz rubbed the glass between his fingertips like a talisman, smudging the swirls and wondering the same thing as Eddie . . .

WTF is on this thing?

Baz had called him over to make sure he didn't slot something he couldn't handle, like a bottomless construct or something way more toxic. But Eddie wasn't gonna let him chuck it either, 'cuz they both knew it was juicy.

Eddie'd explained how Ria Rose dinged him six months ago outta the blue and started bringing him scores every few weeks—always high-end bots, always inside jobs, tastier every time. "The *Carnival Horizon* was the only one sweet enough . . . for you."

Baz chuckled since "sweet" meant dangerous, lucrative, and a lil suicidal. 'Least, that's what a Psyche Bot concluded last time Baz paid a visit to the SFPD's ole VR-clink.

He unsheathed the wafer and sniffed the glass. "What exactly did she say about the gig?"

Eddie counted out on three fingers: "Target's in the Loin. D-Day's in six weeks. And the score's some longtime ¢rypto."

Baz couldn't help but notice Eddie glancing around his apartment. First to his kitchen (and probably his freezer). Then to the closest low- and high-volt charging ports in his living room.

He felt the wafer's weight. "It's gotta be intel."

"Only one way to find out."

"So you *do* trust her?"

"Bruh, I'm a gambler." Eddie winked. "Just like you."

Baz nodded.

Ria's razor-sharp defiance belonged only to the kinda lost souls who'd endured enough pain to kill you—yet somehow it didn't. And Baz figured she was in the Loin for the same reasons he was. Ria was in it for herself.

His thoughts wandered . . . 'til a weird one crossed his mind.

Maybe Baz could save her?

"Wow, look at you . . . Smitten."

Baz just ignored him, eyeing the wafer again. Eddie was right—there was only one way to find out what was on it.

So Baz sat back and closed his eyes. He positioned the glass over his right fiber I/O, with that bad feeling that nothing good would come of trusting Ria Rose, but Baz didn't care. He was gonna slot this wafer no matter what, 'cuz it was the only way to see her again.

"What's the worst that could happen?" Eddie asked.

Nothing much, Baz thought.

Just an aneurysm.

Then he slotted hard into Data Space.

RIBBON

Bright white light.

`right<>slot.03:14:23`

"Baz Covane, slotting this means one thing," Ria whispered.

A single 400 Hz tone underneath, the one that tested your aurals during upgrades.

"You're crazy enough to trust me."

`HEART-RATE-105bpm     EKG-5mV     TEMP-101.4`

Baz slammed stiff as a board.

"CHRIST!" Eddie leaped to his feet to catch his rigid frame before it slid off the couch. Strained to pull and straighten Baz lengthwise, dialing into his wetwire 'til it floated on the holo. "What'd she hit you with?"

`anon.wafer`

"Believe me, Baz. If you're the wrong guy for this gig . . ."

Ria's voice was nuthin' more than just a narrow AI, so he couldn't explain the tingling of pins and needles everywhere. "You won't want to remember."

Unless she'd spiked him with a viral.

```
HEART-RATE-105bpm      EKG-5mV      TEMP-101.4
```

A trauma app activated to report: "This wafer determines physiological responses to the simulation."

"C'mon, brutha, breathe." Eddie leaped into the kitchen and ripped open the freezer, grabbing armloads of ice trays. "To determine what?"

"Whether to fire a six-by-four implosive sequence of micro-amperage."

Eddie slowed, jarred by Ria's savvy. "Electroshock?"

```
                                        anon.wafer
```

That white light faded into a lush construct of the San Francisco Bay at midnight.

Sailing over the Ferry Building, the Neo-Embarcadero, and into the caverns of San Francisco's monolithic sprawl.

Baz struggled with nav-thoughts to take over the POV, but the wafer's construct was capped and his flight path fixed ten stories up, approaching the corner of Hyde and Turk . . .

The seedy underbelly of San Francisco. A red-light district from the days of the gold rush and ground zero of the Street Meat market, the Tenderloin.

"Welcome to the Loin, Baz."

```
HEART-RATE-135bpm      EKG-7mV      TEMP-102.2
```

"Heart rate elevating. Risk of—"

"I know, I know, epileptic amnesia." Eddie chucked ice cubes in the tub, ran the bath, and bolted back to Baz.

"Temperature spiking."

"Aight, fuck it. I'm yanking this thing." Eddie reached around Baz's cranium, clenched the wafer and pulled—

—glass splintered—

Eddie held up the jagged, slivered shard, shimmering iridescence, its payload locked in-slot. "Not good."

As Baz's body slipped into seizure.

<code>intel.wafer</code>

That tingling sharpened, and Baz felt his body quaking IRL as he approached a familiar street corner bordering Chinatown, the entrance to a legendary nightclub.

"Home to San Francisco's ultimate fuckbot palace."

The target of Ria's score. Baz's first customer. His heart raced, 'cuz she was right: he was fucking nuts to trust her.

"The Fang."

The city dissolved into a wireframe. Its buildings morphed into grid conduits for immense bandwidth—every pedestrian and robot just a wetwire or cranial-CPU signal—all converging on the massive establishment seething with hundreds of patrons bearing "Refugee" IDs and dozens of bots with "Anon" markers, clear indicators of cracked jacks everywhere.

Baz's POV started vibrating, which meant his body was in serious palpitations—if not outright seizure—and Baz knew two things: this glass was built to analyze his response.

And he prayed Eddie would pull the plug.

`HEART-RATE-165bpm     EKG-9mV      TEMP-105.5`

"Chill, muthafucka." Eddie dunked Baz in ice.

Springing across the slab, he rifled his crash bag, finding a cross between surgical forceps and a pair of pliers. "Never thought I'd use these."

"Cranial cavity cresting 106 degrees."

"I can read!"

Baz thrashed in heavy grand mal, splashing ice water everywhere, and Eddie thought about saying a prayer, but who the fuck to?

He tore sterile shrink-wrap off the hooked needle-nose tongs, juiced it into the low-volt outlet, and turned Baz, quaking, on his side. "Well pal, I yank this wire . . ."

Eddie leaned all his weight into the side of Baz's head, pressing down on his shoulders, trying to immobilize him enough to thread those tongs up inside his left I/O.

". . . and there's a 25 percent chance you'll still be you."

`intel.wafer`

Baz was sizzling hotter and hotter, immersed in the Fang's scorching data.

"Moment of truth," Ria whispered.

The glass must've been turning his own fear against him, and Baz had to hand it to her—she wasn't gonna let him in on the score 'til she knew he had the stones for it.

"Either this is gonna get you wet?"—Christ, even her avatar didn't give a fuck—"Or I'll be nothing more than déjà vu."

Then his POV *whisked inside* the nightclub and into its subterranean floors, 'til he was looking at a detailed wireframe schematic of a chamber with four tower-sized glass servers—and most importantly?

The data that was stored on 'em.

Baz groaned. Or maybe he moaned. Either had the right ratio of desire over fear to elicit Ria's appearance. Her avatar emerged from between those server towers.

She vibrated seismically, his optic nerve rattling hard against its graft. She threw him a wicked smile—'cuz they both had no doubt . . .

This data was priceless.

"So what's it gonna be, Baz?"

`HEART-RATE-max          EKG-max        TEMP-max`

Eddie found the four-millimeter coil connecting his wetwire's implant strand to the I/O and took a deep breath, ready to rip it clean. "Here we go . . ."

Baz stiffened—his seizure ceased. "Ehhhhhhdz."

Eddie pulled back, shocked. "Baz?"

Eyes rolled back, blank white like some medieval possession. Eddie waited, but Baz was still. He leaned in to snake out that wetwire for good—

When Baz . . . barely . . . lifted a finger.

`intel.wafer`

Vibrations stopped.

Ria locked steady. "Atta boy."

She turned to walk away, heels clacking against some vast obsidian floor. "Right around now is when you're asking yourself, Is this gig for reals?"

"Damn straight." Baz said out loud.

She didn't turn. Didn't answer. Just kept walking, hips swaying in those same black fatigues from when they first met.

A massive cloud formed above her . . . Dark and nasty, it oscillated in color, 'til it found its shape—and suddenly it was obvious what took up so much space on the wafer.

The construct was simple, the blueprints specific, but to make her bones on the score she was pitching, Ria'd provided a sample of the authentic code that could easily get 'em both killed.

"Taste for yourself."

"Thrilz" was the flavor's name. It snaked like a ribbon, looping in binary and hexadecimal around the neurons it tantalized. Details scrolled in Baz's periphery of a warmth conjured in the diaphragm. Precise micrograms of cortisol and serotonin guaranteeing wild throbs of increasing ecstasy with every heartbeat, pounding the user with an overwhelming confidence that the horizon—whether between a crowd and its DJ, or the Himalayas and the azure sky above—was *yours*.

"Eddie says you're the best."

Forget the Stim Baz slotted years ago. That shit was digital Prozac for Gen Z, a tricycle compared to what a SynGyn slotted in 2051. No safeguards, no FDA approval, no training wheels whatsoever.

"Word on the Loin is . . . you *were*."

You could blow your mind on a wafer.

Literally. Out both eardrums.

"So let me know if you're interested, Baz."

And it went by one name on the streets . . .

NARCSOFT

The first time Ria slotted Narcsoft was the night they bagged her dad.

Feds, Shreveport PD, Caddo Parish Sheriff, and Louisiana State Troopers all fought over jurisdiction outside a sleazy SRO converted out of a Public Storage in Shreveport. So instead of drawing straws, they all just went in blasting. The takedown was orbitalinked in real time, 3D, uncensored, so the blood splattering from Dave's dome was viewable from every imaginable angle.

On a public jumbo-holo under the Neo-Nimitz in Oakland, through static and signal noise, she watched with ten thousand other indigents. There were Vegas odds, and the crew of runaways Ria called friends pooled their ¢rypto on a parlay: the Butcher would be killed, with a headshot, by a deputy from Caddo Parish.

Two out of three ain't bad.

Dave took a .22 upstairs, grazing his temple and knocking him out for a few hours, but he was definitely taken alive. And Ria sank into despair.

She knew now that this ordeal would just drag on for months, even years. And she turned to her new friend, wanting so bad to forget. Moxie held up a glass wafer and said *this* would make it all go away.

Ria'd done StimSoft at parties in high school—usually a double-slot of the heaviest-strength any kid could find in Mom or Dad's medicine drive. Most parents were on some form of antianxiety code prescribed by Psychiatry Bots to help ease the stress of a world changing too rapidly in front of them. But after the Glitch, StimSoft was fast-approved for OTC mass marketing and mass production, so Ria'd been slotting anything she could get her hands on.

But the shit in Moxie's hand wasn't white-bread Stim, it was real-deal junk, and though she played naive, Ria knew exactly what it was. It was called Narcsoft, and Ria'd considered tryin' it for more than a minute. Moxie had a bag of wafers and a bunch of flavors, but she could tell Ria wanted more than just Numb—she needed to escape, feel free and empowered—and for that, Freefall would do the trick.

"Fly like a bird . . . but dive like a hawk."

Ria couldn't help but feel nervous exhilaration as she positioned the wafer over her I/O. She knew there were no dependence buffers or cardiac safeguards on street-level shit. Narcsoft could kill you—and that's why Ria wanted it so bad. Index finger on the glass, she took a deep breath, said fuck it . . .

And slotted that shit straight to the head.

A cool ocean breeze. Weightlessness. Ever jump out of an airplane IRL? Then you can imagine the tinglin' lighthearted and light-headed bliss in Ria. Like the freedom she felt with Jericho that night, but without any sweaty mess. The stress of her father's capture, the shame of his synthetic libido, and everything in between . . . was GONE.

Ria felt good.
Ria felt free.
And Ria was hooked.

She went through Moxie's whole bag that weekend, trying every flavor, a quick study in the art of slotting code. Unfortunately, only the first wafer was free. But Moxie had a thing for girls and an eye on Ria—and you know what? . . . Mox was right: kissing on Vesuvio felt good, but fucking on Wingspan felt better.

Watching her dad's VR-trial slotted was a breeze. 'Fact, that was the name of the wafer. Breeze made Ria smile when Dave rocked the virtual court with tantrums about a nobler cause, laugh when he testified that the Glitch was for the future of all mankind, and giggle her ass off when under cross-examination, he insisted no one was supposed to get hurt.

But when confronted with his daughters' murder, he got that crazy look in his eyes. So Ria slotted a linebacker wafer called "the Mummy" when the jurors filed back. "Guilty" echoed down like water in a cave, lacking clarity like Ria lacked emotion. She stayed deep in that M-hole through his sentencing three hours later (justice moved swift in VR), and felt nuthin' when the judge sentenced her dad to death. But as they hauled him away, Dave's last outburst resonated:

"There's a war coming!"

Ria wondered why he never acknowledged that 32 thousand households now missed a dad like him, or a daughter like Dani, or the entire household, period. Where was his goddamn remorse? For all he knew, he'd gotten both his daughters killed. *What the fuck was wrong with him?* Then her eyes rolled back, Moxie went down, and Ria just slotted 'em away.

They shot her dad on the 50-yard line at LSU.

103,000 seats of Tiger Stadium were sold out that early spring afternoon in 2047. Thanks to state law, Dave could choose the firing squad over wetwire flatline or lethal injection, and LSU jockeyed for the venue, 'cuz two Campus Security Bots had coordinated to lock a Cheerleader Bot in the men's locker room during the Glitch and slaughter the entire backfield of the second-best football team in the country. With banners snappin' "#2 For You" and "My Heart Bleeds Purple and Gold," a dozen rifles aimed true for Dave Roselli's heart.

Ria snuck in and double-slotted Laze behind either ear. Under the end zone jumbo-holo, her synthetic eye ratcheted its micro-telelens onto her father's face. The whole world went lazy plaid as brainwaves fluttered and Ria giggled, hearing the nickname for the stadium was "Death Valley" . . .

Then they filled her pops full of lead.

The next year was a Daze, another favorite wafer of Ria's. But Moxie wouldn't front her raging wafer habit, so Ria started slinging 'em herself in West Oakland. Kids would ask Ria where her shit was from and why she sold the best . . . and eventually Ria asked Moxie the same thing. They were a legitimate item by then, and the only girl Ria knew who slotted more than her, was Mox. With Breeze to the right and Big Buddha to the left, Moxie whispered where she got every wafer they sold:

The Fang.

Ria'd heard of it—some underground nightclub in the Loin, like a speakeasy or a gin joint from a bygone era, and SFPD was on the take when it came to what went down inside. Ria figured it was just a heavy volume of Narcsoft, but then she heard it was so much more. Dance Bots and AI-written music fused with human counterparts, where black-market learning caps catered to the tech tastes of the Valley and harkened back to the heyday of the Golden Age of AI.

But rumor had it, upstairs at the Fang all the Dance Bots got down, in a skinshop where anything goes. *Anything?*—Ria asked, and that's when she heard the words that sent a chill down her spine, overpowering the Vesuvio she'd just slotted. The Fang had original 2.3s by Dallas Dynamics, the most illegal fuckbots around. The exact same models her dad infected when he started the Glitch.

Ria got loaded for it. Slotted a real wicked wafer of Narcsoft called Blaze and went looking for Jericho again, 'cuz her alias Ria Rose just wasn't good enough. The Fang had an off-grid-only policy, which was as ballsy as it was incriminating. Meant everyone in the joint was breaking the law—coming with ghosted aliases and carousing with Street Meat. But Jericho was MIA—word had it he'd gone down for a Brinks truck hit. The guy who'd inherited his business went by Diamond D, but after a few minutes together he asked her to just call him Eddie.

She needed her cracked jack cracked, she laughed. She needed Eddie to unplug Ria Rose from Universal Monitoring, put her to sleep at Moxie's pad while he hijacked some rando visitor ID—either a refugee or a tourist from abroad. Eddie tried to talk her out of it. With her augmented cerebral hemisphere, you never knew what a wand might do. Then he spied that eight-inch retractable blade implanted in her synthetic right forearm, and he started to walk—

But Ria just had to know.

Unlike everyone else at the Fang that night, she wandered through the door alone. The Resonance Sequencer waved over her by a big Warrior Bot named McT read her as a Honduran tourist just like Eddie said it would. She'd saved up a bunch of ¢rypto to buy an hour with a 2.3 upstairs, but when the door slid shut, Ria took one whiff of the thing that walked in and broke a sweat. That never happened before—not with Moxie, not Jericho, not anyone. She'd soon learn that had little to do with natural desire, and a lot to do with the bot's biosensories. Ergonomic receptors and pheromone secretors that analyzed a customer and catered to his or her ultimate desire.

So she tore it apart.

First with a lamp, then the augmented blade slicing out her arm, then she tore poor Lacy's eyeballs out with her own hands. Whatever arousal the bot's sweaty moans had ignited in Ria flashed to hot rage in the blink of a synthetic eye. To say the killing was emotional, would be the understatement of 2048. To say it was cathartic would suggest her hatred of robots had released, which it hadn't.

However, it did mutate. Not because of her violence, but because of the voice she heard when she returned to reality from that psychotic boticidal fugue. As fists seized both shoulders, the organic one and its augmented counterpart, Ria knew they were the synthetic mitts of Warrior Bots, and either one could rip her arms from her sockets at whim. So she didn't move; she just hollered:

"Fuck do you think you are?"

—which made the boss in charge of the bots chuckle. It was a voice with a Detroit twang and a West Coast drawl that Ria could only characterize as *smooth*. Seductive. And like the rumble of a furnace that could blow at any time, it was evil.

"I'm Otto. I own this muthafucka."

But that night evil sounded real good.

REX

>left.de-slot<
03:19:56

Baz snapped out of Data Space, freezing.

"Jesus Christ!" Soaked and shivering, he wasn't sure if he'd said it or Eddie, 'cuz his partner was almost as scared shitless as Baz.

"Thought I lost ya, bruh."

Eddie lifted Baz outta the ice bath and wrapped him in a thermal blanket. "You were deep beneath the Arctic Sea. You talk to God?"

"Close." Baz gestured to the ribbon of Thrilz floating on his holo-array behind Eddie. "Lemme guess . . . whole score decrypted, soon as the seizures stopped."

Eddie nodded. "Gotta hand it to that girl. Glass was ready to zap your noggin with precision. Backwound on a crystal ticker to exactly our meet. She'd a been nuthin' more than—"

"Déjà vu."

Baz remembered subzero training in basic, praying he'd dodge the Alaskan Front. He turned up the temp on the thermal and got a handle on his breathing 'til his heart rate slowed.

Wireframe blueprints hovered beneath the ribbon of Narcsoft, and Baz gazed at those four glass towers. "Longtime ¢rypto."

Eddie's eyes twinkled. "Fuck a visa in Tahiti. This score buys citizenship, a villa, and a goddamn boat on the dock."

Baz stood up, wincing at his joints frozen stiff, and lumbered outta the bathroom towards that holo-array. He stalked around Thrilz in all its narcotic splendor. Studied its dopamine loops as Eddie emerged from the bathroom behind him. Thought about who they'd be robbing.

"Bring up everything we got on Otto."

UnivMon><query.10:07:16
REX,OTTO
12/21/05:DOB

Tours, medals, and commendations on Otto's exhaustive Private Service Record scrolled in the holo-array—maybe a little *too* quickly . . . Baz glared at Eddie.

"What?"

"What do you mean, 'What'? How'd you have Otto's file on deck so fast?"

"Umm . . . Foresight?"

"Eddie, I asked you who she worked for—"

"Did you?"

"*Eddie* . . ."

"I'm not sure you actually—"

"EDDIE!"

"She's his fixer." Eddie came clean.

Baz stopped, shocked. "Ria Rose is Otto Rex's *fixer*?" Like a plague. A virus nastier than anthrax. Christ, the wafer alone was a death sentence.

"I knew you wouldn't have slotted it . . . if I told you."

"Goddammit, Eddie, I nearly flatlined!"

"Yeah, *nearly*—"

Baz just stood up furious, the heat of his anger far more effective than any thermal. Chucked the blanket, grabbed a bottle, and stormed

across four container seams and through Otto's jacket of crimes floating in midair.

    Trafficking.
    Homicide.
    Rape.

Cracking his knuckles, his neck, then his jaw—'til Baz couldn't
figure out what else to crack, so he kicked the corrugated siding, and
up swung the wall to reveal a fetid Richmond shoreline.

"I'm sorry I didn't tell you," he heard Eddie mutter as Baz stormed
onto the concrete slab, leaving his partner behind, and just stared out
across the Bay.

The lights on the Golden Gate Seawall split his view in half. A
half-mile-high skyline known as the Silicon Sprawl started at the Marina
in San Francisco and stretched left all the way down to San Jose. To the
right were the gated hills of Marin with the mansions and compounds
of the elites who owned it all.

Baz's mind drifted back to some of the worst memories of the Water
Wars, and he thought about grabbing his box of keepsakes from Venezuela but remembered they'd been lost in the SFPD's last raid.

So he just dialed into his mem-drive and threw up a holo of Baz,
another brother, two *hermanos*, and Otto—who stood out for so many
reasons. All five of 'em were neck-deep in a Venezuelan bloodbath.

But Otto was smiling.

Baz had met the voice before the man, because his CO'd been in his
ON-Target as soon as his squad's deployment drone was on approach.
He remembered how he couldn't stop staring at Otto once he actually
saw his face—even after he made him drop and give him 50.

Muthafucka was a skinhead? Dude sounded like his mom's old
Motown playlist. At first, Baz figured him for just another Aryan Bro
with a knack for code-switchin'. But then he realized Otto was so, so
much worse.

"Tell me sumthin' Baz . . . You get hard on your first kill?"

That question confirmed two things quick. Baz was grateful Otto was in charge. 'Cuz his CO was a psychopath.

Baz took a pull from Old No. 7, a short one. Just enough to numb the past and stare at the Sprawl. Buried within that northern edge was the Loin, and in that the Fang, and somewhere in there was Ria Rose, no doubt fixing something for Otto Rex.

Baz thought about rolling up his sleeves and gettin' down to bizness, but he'd need a really good reason to forgive Eddie first. So he focused on those spreads—twinkling in Sausalito and Tiburon, the sheer distance between each estate. God knows what they were worth in dollars back when Marin went gated. But Baz had no doubt.

There was only one way to get his hands on cake like that.

DISTRO

Ria watched the last crate lift off the loading dock. Stamped on five sides was the same emblem as on the other 49 crates packed into the back of a self-driving Nio. A pair of puckered lips, identically etched into all 500 wafers per crate, 25k in this truck alone. And as the Stretch-XL retracted outta its cargo bay, double doors closing, Ria turned from the Nio in front of her to another one rolling away to bang a right outta the garage and commence a 600-mile trek to Portland.

She smiled at tonight's SFPD chaperones at the edge of the loading dock, two of a few dozen remaining human police officers, who were utilized by City Hall in situations where a robot's integrity protocols would be a problem—i.e., criminal transactions like this one.

Those cops, these fifteen trucks, and all 300,000 wafers on the move per month were just a few of a hundred ideas in Otto's fit of genius eight years ago. He shipped wafers like Mickey-D's flipped burgers, or at least did before the price of beef shut 'em down.

Ria turned back to this final semi. "Yo, your load's full—¢rypto out!"

The passenger door opened, and a kid stepped down in a Miami Mayhem tracksuit, still-mirrored smartshades, and a dark Sephardic tan that only bronzed like that in South Florida.

His name was Jacob Singer, but everyone just called him Tunes. "The one and only Ria Rose . . . Has it been a month already?"

Ria tried not to roll her eyes, 'cuz she had a sneaking suspicion what was coming next.

"So about my chit . . ."

GeoΣ.Orbital><00Σ

DATE	TRANΣ	AMOUNT	BALANCE
09/30/51	FL-Holdings	10,500,000	*encrypt*

The ding chimed, and Ria stared at the figure in her wetwire, its echo ringing out in her aurals.

"Tunes . . ."

"What?"

"Ten-five?"

"On 20 thousand? That's 525 per wafer, 'xact. Down to the last shard."

"You rolled with 25k on the 31st. Same count as tonight. We can check the Stretch's log, if—"

"Do what you gotta do. We took 20 thousand outta the Nio in Daytona."

Ria just stared at him. "You're short, Tunes."

Finally he blinked. "Okay, we had a problem in Laudy. Last five g's corrupted."

"We didn't hear about any corruptions in Atlanta. Or Nola."

"Yeah, I mean, it was only 20 percent of 'em, so obviously it couldn't be the masters . . . But there were Skull Fries, Ria."

She didn't say anything.

"Things got . . . messy."

Ria started doing math in her actual head, not her wetwire—trying to figure out how she might cover the missing ¢rypto, but more importantly whether she even should. There was only so long she could keep a minus from her boss.

"How 'bout we split the damage, Ria, and I can make it up to you on the next—"

She sighed. "Thing is, Tunes—"

"This ain't the first time." A low voice rumbled deeply.

Ria's hairs stood on end, and she saw Tunes's heart cave.

Footstep after footstep echoed off the garage's walls from the far side of the semi as that voice came creeping around the back cargo doors.

Her boss.

His Godfather.

Otto Rex.

"Am I right?" In a fur-lined black leather trench and deep drawl, both outta Sojourner Truth Projects in Detroit, Otto kinda resembled Papa Doc from that classic 2D. But then you blinked and realized he looked a lot more like Slim Shady, or maybe his roided-out overgrown cousin, 'cuz under all that blackwork ink was one seriously yoked baller from the hard side of 8 Mile Road.

"Otto, how-how long . . . you been here?" Tunes stammered.

"Long enough, Tunes. Long enough to know you been on the skim."

"The skim?" The mirror disappeared from his smartshades to look in Otto's eyes. "You trying to say that—what? I—"

"Stole from me."

Ria then noticed the oil drum.

"*STOLE FROM YOU?* Are you crazy?!"—spinning at Ria—"Fuck this bitch say? Otto, she's the—"

"She's been covering your ass all summer."

Ria scanned the garage for a second drum. Otto walked right past Tunes, like his distributor was as worthless as the ¢rypto he'd stolen. "See, underneath all that 'tude, my girl Ria Rose here has a big ole heart."

He stepped in close to look her in the eye. "Some say it'll be her undoing."

"I'm sorry I carried him," Ria said quietly.

"I can get you the ¢rypto, Otto," Tunes pleaded. "Most of it, anyway. It's in numbered accounts—"

"With your wife, your sidepiece, and your two daughters in Miami." Otto's eyes drifted to the clock in his wetwire. "Where class starts at West Palm Elementary in twenty minutes."

"Don't." Ria whispered.

Tunes erupted with blabberings and beggings for lives. His. Theirs. His for theirs. The usual.

Those cops started turning green. Sicker and sicker every time Tunes begged for protection. What could they do? They were here to protect *Otto*—unless they wanted two more drums rolling out.

"I appreciate the apology, really I do," Otto hissed at Ria, then threw a glance at Tunes. "So I'm gonna let you make it up to me."

In the center of his chest, specifically.

Ria thought about the soft spot under the sternum. The gap between the fourth and fifth rib. Felt the icy titanium within her forearm.

Messy, indeed, Mr. Singer.

She forced a smile. If she off'd Tunes right now, would Otto really spare his kids? She could feel his breath, patience evaporating. The fire that burned for her, burned from Otto's stones, hot to invade, hungry for some breaking and entering . . .

And Ria was over it.

"You really gonna let a bitch do your dirty work?"

Otto's eyes narrowed with a chuckle.

"We go back, Otto," Tunes pleaded. "Since the beginning—Miami, Oaktown, and every corner in between. We built—"

—Otto clenched her ulna's release pin *fast*—blade from its cradle— and drove it into Tunes's heart.

Singer died quick. Last thing he saw was Otto, holding him by the shoulders, eye to eye. "I'm gonna burn 'em alive, Jake."

Then he shoved Tunes back—corpse flipping head-first into the oil drum. "Seal it."

McT sparked its arc welder and started laying beads around its lid.

"But keep it loose." Otto turned to the pair of SFPD uniforms, whose mouths were agape, their cherries popped and officially running down each leg. "Let him rot through New Years before you fish him out."

Ria bristled. *By then I'll be gone, asshole.*

As Otto just turned and walked away, the same old questions pounded through Ria's head. What foundry forged this fuck? How did he conquer the Loin? And why could he kill without breaking a sweat?

But his final order was her only answer, echoing off the walls . . .

"Then send him to his girls and light a match."

THE LIBERTINE

Otto Rex believed in destiny.

It was destiny when he capitalized on the Glitch. Destiny spread his Narcsoft across the globe. And Otto knew he'd been destined to own nightclubs, since he was named after a DJ who only spun Prince. 'Cuz his ma partied every night like it was 1999, but she knew one day Otto would rise outta Detroit to be a king. Unfortunately, that was the last good parenting he received . . . Ever.

Otto always excelled in school, had the intellect and grades to go to college, but that would've meant another seventeen months in Detroit—and by then Mom was a nightmare and her crack habit worse, so Otto forged her signature one winter afternoon in 2021 and joined the Marines a year before they were privatized, where he was flagged quickly for intelligence and what an aptitude test described as a potential to display courage under fire. But his commander didn't need an exam to read both sleeves of tattoos and the skull inked in between:

Otto just didn't give a fuck.

And he never forgot his first kill. One of the last honest-to-God terrorists, this particular breed, a distant descendant of some scripture-based jihadi group that had long since lost touch with its holy crusade and now simply got off molesting women, children, and UNESCO heritage sites. So Otto popped a stick of Juicy Fruit in his mouth and capped the Jawa's dome clean on his third day in theater.

And his dick got hard.

Which was kinda embarrassing. Otto hadn't been bashful since his first threesome back in Old Detroit when he was thirteen. His mom heard him recount how both girls were in their twenties and told him to just nut up, everyone feels weird on their first gangbang. Oddly, Otto got a similar vote of confidence from his squad commander:

"Everyone gets stiff on their first kill."

Everyone? It was a question Otto asked all members of any unit he served or would command over the next fifteen years in the Private Service. Turned out "everyone" was a bit of an exaggeration. By Otto's count, precisely 7 out of 10 dudes popped a chubby the first time they iced anyone. Otto wondered for a couple years whether this was endemic to all killers, or just soldiers. But eventually, he stopped counting and stopped caring, 'cuz by then he'd lost the thrill for killing, and was in it for the threat of being killed instead.

That's what hooked Otto.

Four—that's right, *four*—tours in Syria prepped him for Delta Squads in Yemen then Venezuela, where Otto's squad beta-tested the battlefield prototype of the Wetwire, the ON-Target. And Otto saw first-hand what an orbital railgun's radial-concussion pattern could do to the unit's bio-drive: dudes' heads splattered like potatoes in a microwave.

The rest of Otto's warnings went ignored, 'cuz the only ethics command cared about was if its soon-to-be-deployed autonomous killing machines really needed a "human in the loop." Android soldiers—first nicknamed Terminators, then rechristened T-3POs by Otto's unit after diplomacy delays gave any rebel with an RPG time to miss *twice* before incinerating $50 million in hardware. The hawks in command argued that not only were diplomacy protocols nonsense, but they dropped a bot's kill ratio by 60%. So the military and the politicians compromised with the 6-in-1 heads-up display—one "Papa" soldier carried "in-loop" abort-authority over six android soldiers' lethality at a time. Command still had a few kinks to work out, since every Papa under Otto's command still got a headache . . . except one, who had an aneurysm.

A safer version bypassed the cerebellum and patched Papas directly to android ground forces, improving kill ratios by 75 percent . . . and the Joint Execs knew: this dog could hunt. By the time Caracas fell in early '37, triggers were fossils, recruits were receiving ON-Target implants in basic, and it was time to get the fuck outta the Private Service.

The date was March 17, 2037, to be precise. The day Baz Covane, a young buck private with a pretty good heart but a pretty shitty draw in life (which was saying a lot by Otto's standards) severely fucked his own life, by choice, with a shitstorm known as the Body Count. Baz had character and, what's worse, a conscience—both useless in Venezuela, which his CO insisted repeatedly between direct orders to stand down as Baz marched across the block and incinerated the best brothel in South America.

Behind fiery embers in that Caracas night sky, Otto saw the stars align against Baz and anyone anywhere near that skinshop, which definitely included Otto, since he was their best customer. He pulled strings with Pentagon Corporate and got himself transferred to the Southern Border, right as lethal actions were approved for Unwired Crossings. In fact, it was intel off a Nogales coyote network that got Otto out of the service for good. His Border Patrol shock squad blew a tunnel with a caravan of women and children inside but didn't expect two cartel enforcers and an off-duty DEA agent to walk out.

So Otto just followed orders and iced them too.

After the Private Service buried the bodies, honorable layoffs were issued for Otto's entire patrol, who were all initially thrilled to be reentering society. Until one by one, each found society worse than the VR-stockade.

Otto hooked up with *una bonita* from Oaktown named Olivia Garcia, whose cousin owned a cartel EZ Pay in Hayward. What her money-laundering lacked in sex appeal, Olivia certainly made up for in a miniskirt, and she and Otto decided to move quick, laying claim to that check-cashing business and a run-down dance club she'd purchased in her dead cousin's name.

When you deal in liquor, pussy, or blow, you ain't selling shit people want—you're robbing 'em blind for what they can't live without. So when Otto applied military methodology to the vice trade, money didn't roll in—trucks backed up looking for a place to dump it all. And the clubs, they just started multiplying. First across the Bay, then across the country.

'Til the first time Otto ever saw a guy get high on Narcsoft.

He'd just muscled in on the Flamingo, one of the last old-school peep shows on Polk Street—full-on down and dirty, where you put a quarter in, and the screen slides up on a fuckbot diddling herself or a well-hung partner in crime. Otto's plan to go hi-fi with the low-down would turn the Flamingo's archaic funk into the most expensive five minutes in San Francisco. He just couldn't figure out whether to give drinks away and charge a hundred bucks a peep, or vice versa.

When across the show, a patron blew a load all over the glass.

Which wasn't that out of the ordinary, but what was odd was that he did it *no-handed*. Otto was sure of it, since both palms were pressed three feet above the descending stain the whole time. Otto just had to know the Tyrannosaurus in the far booth's secret. Ten minutes later, the dude staggered out with pupils like saucers, and you couldn't've beat the smile off his face with a tire iron. But before Otto could ask about a hat trick, the kid pulled a wafer from his fiber I/O, blew on it, and slotted it again. Then he went into another booth for round two.

Zev Vroman was at a soju bar in the Loin three days later when Otto tracked him down and bought him drinks, dinner, and a Yamaha hydrocycle to divulge what the fuck was on that wafer—sure it wasn't no antianxiety Stim. Finally, the kid confessed: the code was black-market Freefall, and as close to heaven as you'd get. Otto'd worshipped Jump School in the Private Service and instantly envisioned just how much ¢rypto Freefall was worth. For a good twenty minutes you experienced delirious weightlessness at terminal velocity, and like Zev at the Flamingo . . . most came as they peaked.

They were on the next flight to Miami, where Zev's ring of hackers were advised that Otto's was an offer they couldn't refuse—a partnership in distribution so long as they recoded Narcsoft for scarcity. Zev's yeshiva homie spoke up first, this half genius, half bandit named Jacob Singer, aka Tunes, who'd steal anything that wasn't nailed down. But as soon as Tunes said it was impossible, that humans couldn't write self-deleting code, Zev wished he hadn't, 'cuz he'd only known Otto a week, but he'd already come to dread that smile.

Boosting an AI out of Miami led Otto to presume they'd be hittin' an X-Wire corporate park—since the only dollars worth shit in Miami were golf, retirement, or the Latin adult entertainment market. And it was a toss-up in 2042 Miami whether there was more silicon implanted in the cerebellum or the boobs.

But the AI that Zev and his buddies wanted—Velociluz, with an incept date of 1/11/29 out of Mexico City and dual citizenship—sat on the StimSoft compound and came wrapped in all the security of a billion-dollar insurance policy from Lloyds of London: a 20-foot iron wall, a squad of Warrior Bots, minefields, razor wire, electric fences, and two American Private Service units with unmarked Blackhawk gunships under the 229th Aviation Wing standing by at MacDill . . . So Otto figured maybe Zev was right and they should just settle on encrypting the wafers themselves after all.

'Til the name Dave Roselli changed Otto's life forever.

See, Otto'd been having these *dreams* since arriving in Miami . . . If he cornered the Narcsoft market, what would become of his sex clubs across the country? He'd gone deep into Hotlanta. Once the heartbeat of the Durty South, Atlanta now reigned supreme as the cultural core to the best music and dance in America.

But what if he sold Narcsoft—the best shit available anywhere—out of all of his joints? Everyone needed a lil strange sometimes. Strange drink. Strange love. Even strange *code* . . . Fuck powder, pills, or bud when you could get high on good dark code.

Maybe then, the *club* could be the draw, not just the android pussy inside. True, the money was obscene, but his clientele was worse. And though he had a few male units, they basically sat idle, or were add-ons in the kinkiest sessions. No women frequented his joints, just "sex pests"—Olivia called 'em—and she was right. She loved the authority of managing Otto's clubs but hated being inside 'em, 'cuz whether the whores were real or robots, you knew you were in a house of ill repute from the first sloped-brow cretin stare you caught.

And King Otto wanted to rule an empire of *cool*.

So he wasn't just pissed when the Miami job turned off, he was *lost*—if his Narcsoft wasn't the best, then there was no cool, there was no scene, and he was just another cyberpimp movin' Street Meat in the Loin. So he tried to clear his head by watching something mind-numbing, like golf . . . when a Caddy Bot went Haywire at the Masters. Otto's wetwire suddenly exploded with a dozen cities under siege, and everything in America changed—within the first ten minutes of the Glitch.

'Cuz shit got raw. Like, cops-shot-your-dog RAW. Black-clad shock troops plugging a pair of .357 hollow-points in Nanny Bots' domes with extreme prejudice? Kids loved their parents, but they *adored* their robots. Holowires said in Memphis you could hear children howling from Beale Street to the Mississippi for days.

Synthetic clerks, robot nannies, maids, cooks, tellers, janitors, modified General Service Bots, and one concierge at a Ho-Jo in Baton Rouge murdered 32,058 owners in four hours . . . and Otto's jaw just dropped. Censors tried to blur out the 3D bloodbath as America's Sweetheart, anchorwoman Katy Wells, narrated bots blasting owners at will—until a CameraDroid.5 went Haywire and beat her to death in her own studio.

Then Olivia dinged Otto from Sapphires, one of his joints in Atlanta, screamin' that a handful of fuckbots were goin' nuts and wasting their clientele—and Otto's gut plummeted, hollerin' at her to bolt . . .

But her voice cut off in the distortion of a shotgun blast.

Whatever was still red and beating in Otto (and there wasn't much) scorched coal-black right there. He felt air exit his lungs. Heard his ears barely ringing. And sensed a fuse lit, that could've sparked a holocaust. Otto'd buried hundreds of brothers in arms—dodging proper mourning out of habit for years—so he knew exactly what to do. Instead of grieving or feeling *anything* for Olivia, Otto put her body on ice and did what he always did when someone close got gat . . .

Otto went on the attack.

He cross-referenced each malfunctioning bot's roster over the last month, and though a few were sold to an Applebee's a week earlier, Otto vectored one common john easily—right as the exact same name flashed across his holo-feed, wanted for questioning in connection to the Glitch:

Dave Roselli.

Otto remembered Ma's stories of the Twin Towers blown out of the sky, and how that was the moment when she came to believe the world was forever fucked (without crack). But as he witnessed the Glitch, realizing his brothels were the origin and Olivia was gone—Otto knew that he was experiencing his own World Trade Center falling. And he had as profound a reaction as his mom, but quite the opposite conclusion: *this world would be his oyster.*

But he had to move fast. Despite Zev's pushback, Otto knew the nationwide chaos of the Glitch meant that for the first 72 hours, the entire government would be in the public eye, a testimony to strength and security—while behind closed doors, an inter-agency clusterfuck. And the biggest obstacle to the Miami heist—Velociluz's own antiviral software—would be retasked off its secure site to guard the FBI's Counterterrorism Server Farm, while MacDill's 229th flew sorties over West Palm Beach, where the big donors lived. So Otto would have a *very* brief window to simply cut the grid to the compound (and maybe a few throats) and waltz in and out in under an hour.

Velociluz's quantum processor and molecular RAM was the most powerful technology to grace North America since warheads stopped poppin' in 1960. It weighed less than a bowling ball and was about as big, but would've filled more silicon than concrete in the Hoover Dam. Ten minutes after the caper started, Otto grabbed it with one hand, stuffed it in a backpack, and stole the hottest loot in South Florida like luggage at a baggage claim.

'Course, the Miami job would be blown if Velociluz stayed at room temperature for more than an hour. That's the catch to quantum computing: fluid processing requires liquid cooling, down to a deep freeze of minus 235—which left Otto an icy sixty minutes to get to the nitrogen chests in the Donzi idling at the Miami River.

Zev was pretty impressed when Otto jumped onto the cigarette boat and they pushed away from the dock. But as they hydro'd out to sea, he sensed Otto slipping into the most serious daydream he'd ever had. Otto foresaw his whole future spreading out before him like a holo-map. Unlike his competitors, Otto wouldn't take pause during this national tragedy, 'cuz a robot crackdown was coming fast.

And Otto was gettin' out of the sex club racket.

Fuck selling wafers out of a synthetic skinshop like some corner dealer. He knew how much heat was about to hit the fuckbot trade. Otto would shutter all his two-bit shitholes and open one single splendid palace, where he would *market* his Narcsoft across the world. He'd buy up the top Dance Bots and consolidate his best sexbots with the hottest biosensories into a single location on the West Coast and cater to the Valley's notorious taste for digital excess.

Otto'd buy the entire block surrounding the Flamingo and start designing the floor plan immediately. He was sure Uncle Sam would soon obliterate privacy, so gettin' loose was gonna cost so much more. And by insisting his patrons come off-grid, the entire joint would be the only safe haven for libertines. Otto imagined the club unfolding in a series of tiers, across floors, that mirrored a customer's journey of discovery. Lust was just one component, and Otto didn't want the outer reaches of sexploration to scare away neophytes who just wanted to dance to real, analog hip-hop and rock 'n' roll every Saturday night.

It was gonna take a year and a shitload of cash (or ¢rypto, once the Blockchain Act obsoleted legal tender), which Otto intended to raise immediately with his nationwide Narcsoft ring that was now officially in business. Whatever was left every month, he'd just pay straight to the SFPD. Or better yet, comp 'em upstairs with the naughtiest of bots, 'cuz nuthin' buys pigs like a synthetic blowjob on the house. And a name materialized in the Floridian dusk . . .

The Fang.

That's what Otto would call his palace, on account of how deep its teeth sank. All this came to him in a single nautical mile, zigzagging through the pontoon cranes working 24/7 on the seawall round Miami Harbor. He even started giggling, imagining who in his current operation he'd take to the promised land and who he'd have to cut loose. With Olivia gone, he was now in the market for a visionary . . .

Otto needed the perfect fixer to run the Fang.

Zev asked why he was laughing—and Otto snapped outta his daydream, nodding to the F-35 tearing a line through the night sky for Palm Beach. Zev chuckled too, finding it ironic that 72 hours earlier, that plane would've been vectoring their position to Dade County Sheriff and opening fire. But that's not why Otto laughed, and his hacker friend failed to grasp the true irony of their situation—that at some point in the next year?

Zev would be in an oil drum at the bottom of Biscayne Bay.

FIXER

2051, SEPTEMBER

It was like Baz could feel Otto on his six again.

He walked with purpose into the emerald-marbled lobby of the Alphabet Tower, flashing a ghosted SSS to the Security Bot—Ria's wafer in one pocket and a few of his own in the other—with a glance over his shoulder, as Otto's last words echoed from Caracas a decade ago . . .

"Guys like you and me?" His CO said over and over again when it was clear Baz was done following orders. "We don't fuck ourselves like this. You think you're doin' good right now, but right and wrong's a rigged game. That'll kill you."

But the corridor behind Baz was empty, save Eddie following at a brisk pace like he was hiding his own nerves. They both needed this score to get Out.

Stepping into the humans-only elevator, Baz expected his partner to press "B" for basement, but instead Eddie tapped "PH."

"I thought you said this was a slotting gallery?"

Eddie shrugged. "Otto's product's the best. Goin' nuts on it ain't cheap."

Elevator doors opened on what was once the nicest condo in San Francisco, now littered with bodies. Glazed eyes. Sweaty skin. Clothing optional. Some were fucking IRL, others were moaning midfuck somewhere in VR, but all of 'em were outta their fuckin' minds.

"Yo, where's Slim?" Eddie called out.

Wafers crunching underfoot was the only response.

"Anyone seen Slim?" Baz repeated.

Somewhere a hi-fi that must've cost more than Baz and Eddie's entire net worth combined thumped classic early-'40s trance by the AI Hypnozart, who wrote dozens of hit singles from its Brixton incept in '36 'til the morning of the Glitch—including this track, called "DOA."

"Slim's dead." A girl caked in three days of sweat pointed to a corpse nearby.

Eddie shuddered. "Fuck, he skull-fried?"

"Dude. Dead's the name of the wafer."

Baz laughed. Leaned over to confirm the glass stickin' outta Slim's left I/O was stamped with a coffin.

Eddie shook his head and tossed over some homegrown naloxone glass. Positioning it over the vacant right slot, Baz pulled Dead as he slammed Narcan.

Slim gasped awake—

"FUUUUUUCK . . ." His eyes focused. "Baz?"

Slim's 6-foot, 60-kilo frame was worthy of his handle as he led Baz and Eddie down a long polymer-lit corridor minutes later, with that throbbing trance building in a low-end rumble.

A biometric scanner read his retina and an adjacent door slid open, revealing a master bedroom converted into some kinda central hub. Multiple holo-arrays, floating 2Ds, grid markers on a San Francisco hardmap—all of which made sense, since despite his waify build and tranquilized afternoons, Slim was the biggest Narcsoft wholesaler in the city.

Baz slotted a wafer in an I/O deck.

holo<>array.14:08:17
baseline-narc

"Ah, Thrilz," Slim said when Ria's code materialized.

"You know it?" Baz asked.

"'Course, it's a top-seller. Debuted on Valentine's Day last year, right Jace?"

Yet another whacked-out body stirred in a nearby king-size, naked between the sheets.

"Mmm-hmmm," purred the young woman, like she knew Thrilz intimately. Then she sat up, recognizing the floating holo-mug. "Yo, that's Moxie's old girl. Haven't seen that mad-slottin' hussla forever."

Baz looked at Eddie, trust alarms sounding in his head, so his partner jumped out in front: "Forever, huh?"

Jace just nodded, eyes at half-lid. "Since she walked into the Fang one night . . . And never came out."

Slim shot Jace a look to scram, and she promptly stepped out of bed, raw and shameless, and strolled out.

Once the door slid shut behind her, Slim looked first at Baz then at Eddie. "Us distros be a headcount shy since Otto put Tunes out to sea. So cough the fuck up."

Baz nodded to Eddie.

GeoS.Orbital><4ΩΧΣ

DATE	TRANS	AMOUNT	BALANCE
10/07/51	Brisbane-Cons	200,000	encrypt

Slim's voice got low. "She came out. She just wasn't ever the same." Another moan echoed from down the hall.

"Probly not the worst thing," Baz reckoned.

Slim spread his arms out at the holos, the view, and the mattress six times his size. "Everything you see here? Is 'cuz of Ria Rose."

But Baz and Eddie focused on the virt-cams, biometric arrays, and case-mounted motion sensors instead—as Slim powered down all of 'em with another nod, waiting for the room to go dark.

"We were urchins, yo. Nomads. Slottin' any ole shit—Stim, dank, re-dank—pure shits and giggles. Then one night she hits the Fang and disappears. Like forever. Rolls up on me in the Castro a year later lookin' like a Brooks Brother and offers me *every*thing. Exclusive distro on every corner from here to Gilroy for—"

"She still slot?" Baz cut in.

Eddie turned to his partner, confused. Something about Baz's question came out too sharp.

"What?" Slim asked.

"Does. Ria Rose. Still slot?"

Baz charged down Cesar Chavez a few days later, Eddie in tow, past its tent city of refugee laborers, who didn't qualify for Extinction Tax and chased the jobs that even a robot wouldn't do. As if there were any.

"Pretty crazy security in that place." Eddie noted. They'd had enough time to cross-reference the make and model numbers of Slim's surveillance gear. "You can bet the firewall in the Fang's a shit-ton more toxic than those trip wires."

But Baz didn't answer. He wasn't thinking much about the logistics at the Fang. A lil more fixated on the fixer who ran it.

Eddie continued, "You know we should probly use Carlo on this."

Baz flashed to that Tahitian beach. The one 4,000 miles away and the one in his head. Then he glared at Eddie, wondering if his partner'd just weaponized that memory on purpose and laughed. "You really think Carlo's gonna work with me again?"

"Are you kidding? He's more closed off about the past than you are."

They turned down an alley, through a warehouse door, and under a modified Tesla Autostar up on a winch, a half dozen Mechanic.4s welding a hydro-plant to its chassis, converting it for the air.

Baz stared out of an office a few minutes later, eyeing the fumeless, sparkless TIG welds under the Tesla and wondered out loud, "Devyn still doin' night work?"

The owner's name was Taylor, and he shook his head. "C'mon, Covane . . . Humans been banned off torches for a year."

Baz turned to slap another wafer in the holo-array.

```
                                    biometric.0020
                                    RIA-
```

But Taylor yanked it out as soon as he saw Ria's holo-mug.

"Yeah, I know her." His eyes darted out his office, nervous and paranoid. Handed the wafer back to Baz and closed his door. "Her name's Ria something, but I don't know for sure, and I don't wanna know."

Baz looked at Eddie, alarms ringing louder now.

"So keep your money, Eddie, and we'll keep this short, 'cuz she came to me frontin'. Pair of hover thrusters at first, for a Caddy or Benzo or some shit. Then the lady wants a crew of Steelworker-T's and a Foreman Droid for what turned out to be one nasty hoverpad. Which I oblige, 'cuz this chick wants to pay with wafers 'stead of ¢rypto, so now I know *exactly* who she's with. Month later, she dings me up for three dozen blasting caps, detonator-rings, and a fuckin' Demo Bot, and I'm like, 'What do I look like, the Private Corps of Engineers? I don't give a fuck if you *are* in bed with Otto Rex . . . I—'"

"What do you mean, 'in bed'?" Baz asked sharply.

Eddie rolled his eyes.

Taylor looked at him confused. "The Fang, Baz. That woman works for—"

"Like what, they're *involved*?"

Taylor just turned to Eddie. "Is he okay?"

An hour later, Baz didn't wait for Eddie to hop out or answer their Waymo's parking query—he just let the rig figure out where to park itself and walked off down Hyde.

"You okay, pal?"—like Eddie'd been biding his time to ask.

Baz didn't answer.

"You must expect a pretty serious response, if you're thinkin' 'bout Devyn for a getaway—"

"Stop fuckin' around, Eddie. Ask me what's really on your mind."

"Why you sweatin' this girl? For the gig? Or—"

"Ah, gimme a fuckin' break, D. This shit's radioactive, and you know it. Gettin' away's the easy part. There's three layers inside, and we're missing two of 'em. So we're not trustin' Ria Rose to look out for number one. We're trustin' her judge of character. In a drug den. Of whores. Got it?"

Eddie got it. All of it.

Baz was staring outta the Amazon Spire's 237th, a massive conference table behind him. The opposite wall of glass looked down onto the 235th's paralegal servers and an army of Nubotica Esquire.5s slaving over transnational corporate law.

Baz flashed to a story his pops used to tell 'bout the airlines firing all the pilots. Teams of attorneys with so many smug smiles. A year later, they were on Extinction Tax too.

The door opened, and a Secretary Bot entered. "Mr. Callahan will be materializing in a moment. May I offer you an Espresso wafer?"

"Def." Eddie took the shard stamped with a bean.

"No thanks." Baz recognized the android's figure (and Callahan's negotiating tactic). She was a Lusty-9 by Dallas Dynamics. A randy distraction, a late-night closer, or both.

Then every window turned opaque, and Mr. Callahan's avatar appeared at the table. "Gentlemen. I understand you have a private—"

Baz just turned and slotted a new wafer in the center console.

`holo<>conf`
`syn·salvage-VenusV·4A`

A mangled sexbot chassis appeared above the center of the massive table. "Recognize that?"

Even translucent, Callahan's face turned crimson.

"Yeah, I bet you do, 'cuz you beat the shit outta that Venus-V at the Fang a year ago."

"Where did you—"

"Those virts get out, and you have some real explainin' to do, Counselor, starting with how you get off scot-free."

Baz bought the V's respirators from Axl, who scored them off Ria, who must've scraped 'em off the floor of the Fang.

"We off the record?"

Baz nodded to Eddie.

GeoS.Orbital-transfer
¢300,000>>CALLAHAN LAW

RETAINED

"We are now."

Callahan spoke low. "Their fixer made it all go away."

Baz sat down. "Jack. Those wounds? They're all over her inner thighs. Now, I can tell the difference between a BDSM subroutine and real sadism, but SFPD can't. You know who gets antsy when you leave *bite marks*? Shrinks in the Attorney General's Office. Wirecrime's Behavioral Unit."

Eddie threw Baz a glance, like he understood exactly what he was insinuating.

"So, how'd you walk? . . . 'Cuz 'fixer' can mean anything."

Even Wirecrime Undercover.

Eddie kept quiet. The idea that Otto Rex's right hand was workin' for the Feds was fuckin' nuts. *Right?*

Baz studied Callahan's eyes. "Who did Ria Rose ding?"

His avatar turned pale when he heard her name. Like the power Ria wielded physically terrified the sonuvabitch.

"She dinged whoever the fuck she wanted."

Baz stiffened.

"She's Otto Rex's number one girl."

SIM

Ria Rose had a busy day.

Adding a newly enlisted distro to their network in Florida. Overseeing the weekly electroplating baths for the Fang's resident dance troupe, the Chrome Domes. And an hour's run barefoot on a beach in VR-Saint-Tropez left her muscled bronze skin slick with a sheen of sweat and light body odor.

Just the way Otto liked her.

She leaned into her mirror—steam rising from the hot shower nearby—and wiped the fog away to take herself in. After three years at the Fang, her eyes, ever vigilant at work, widened to reveal deep heartbreak when alone. If character is who you are in the dark, then the way she followed the beads of perspiration grooving between her breasts . . . How slowly she pulled down her tight, wet stretch pants . . . Ria just loved to turn herself on.

And in the shadows, Otto's cock stiffened.

Ria stood there—naked, save a black micro-G—and ran her fingers from her neck to her navel as Otto slowly stood and gripped himself. Her nails grazed the stretch of her panties, and she started to peel those down too . . .

"Otto!?"

He seized both wrists, pressing his body into her bare back, snaking his hands round her torso and between her legs—Ria struggled against his restraint, which only made him *harder*. Spinning her around—she trembled and quivered from shoulder to ass—so he gripped both in either fist and kissed Ria deeply, his tongue tasting all of her—pulling away, she started to scream, so he lifted her into the bedroom, off her feet, and *onto him*—she couldn't help but moan and—

GLITCH—<u>static</u>, head to toe, like a bad holo.

INTERRUPT

—"Incoming virt: Ria Rose. Accept?" his wetwire asked.

Otto declined furiously and tried to regain his erection, but then Ria's whole apartment glitched—

OVERRIDE

A34.Rose,Ria

"Yo, Otto, you there?"

The VR-sim disappeared completely, revealing Otto's king-size and favorite fuckbot, Marilyn, impaled upon him, doing her best imitation of Ria struggling:

"No, Otto, please don't—"

"Shut up!" He tossed Marilyn off and wiped Ria's avatar into view. "Ria . . ."

Marilyn was one very special Dance Bot, adept at improvising off a routine of her feelings getting hurt every time Otto rejected her. But when he threw a real nasty glare her way, she scampered into the corner of his penthouse, and he turned back to Ria. "To what do I owe the pleasure?"

"From the look on your face, you've either seen a ghost or been samplin' the inventory."

Otto eyed Marilyn like he wasn't done abusing her. "Maybe a lil bit of both."

Ria delivered an update on his fuckbots, their clients, a new shipment, tonight's act, and curtain time. He didn't care about any of it, 'cuz he knew nothing went wrong when she was in charge, and all he cared about was one thing: "When you comin' through?"

"Late."

CLICK.

Rex¬Otto
DISCONNECT

Ria stood there in her apartment, staring at the air where Otto's sweaty and disgusting holo floated just moments ago.

"Replay." Their convo wound back to the moment of her ding, when his penthouse morphed from a prior environment—"Freeze."

She could make out another residence, barely. "Refine latent and enhance."

The background resolved . . . to *her* apartment.

"You sick fuck."

Ria stalked around her own spacefoam and crouched into positions from either side, eyeing angles on where she slept. Then she backed away and took in the entire domicile. All of it was easily visible from the balcony windows.

Glass doors slid open, and Ria let out a defeated gasp. On the edge of the balcony facing southeast were a dozen potted plants, shriveled and dead. "Goddammit, you *all* died?"

She rifled the pots, but there was nothing hidden in any of 'em, except one. A little green AI-GMO seedling had taken root and flowered fast. A flash of vibrant green in a sea of decay.

Ria smiled at the straggler. "Hey, little dude. If I can survive, you can."

She stood up and looked across the street at thousands of reflective windows. Each of them offered tuck-spots for a lens, but too narrow of a vantage point, so Ria just headed back inside.

She put the seedling's pot in the kitchen sink and stepped into the bathroom, her sixth sense pounding. "You've been in here, haven't you?"

Ria slid the shower door open to inspect the soap tray. Peered down the dank, dark drain. Then all the hairs stood up on her neck. She grabbed a chair, reached up, and pulled away the vent . . .

"God*dammit.*"

A virt-cam was mounted to the screen, custom fabricated so its micro-lens could periscope through the slats and render her entire shower.

She looked into the lens. "Asshole." Then crushed it underfoot and let out a sigh that betrayed the weight of the world. "There's nothing he doesn't own."

Her eyes drifted down to a titanium cabinet under the sink. Ria kneeled down and reached inside, searching blind for something within. Finally yanked loose a tiny black jewelry box.

Inside, set in a velvet cushion . . . was a silver locket.

"Been a minute," she whispered.

Opening the locket revealed a true artifact in 2051—an actual photograph. That Polaroid of her mom, with Ria and Dani at thirteen. In leotards. All smiling. The last happy moment with her family, now long-since gone.

"Hi, Mom." Ria whispered. "Hey, Sis."

There was a reason she kept this thing stashed away, and it wasn't just the liability. She snorted and steeled herself.

Ria opened a console in her living room containing a dinosaur in 2051, an old-school tape deck—the only way to listen to music off-grid. She rifled through a set of tapes and pulled one labeled "EINAUDI— Nuvole Bianche." Popped it in, pressed Play, and a fluid, gorgeous piano piece floated across her joint from the fully analog system.

The score to *Gemini.*

Her mom crafted the dance so they'd lead and follow, lead and follow. Dani's side was ethereal, filled with spaces for improvisation within the count. But Ria's was a technical bitch, upping the bar on her perfectionism every week.

She sat on a nondescript chair at a nondescript table straight outta Holofurn's nondescript virtual showroom C.

Scales chased scales, and she let herself remember. The four-count, the first position. Glissade into grand jeté, into pirouette. Ria chuckled, how Dani'd wipe out at least once a week. How her mom couldn't help but chuckle too. Ria could smell the wax on the floor when rehearsal began. Their perspiration long before it came to an end. Waves of emotion pounded massive, sweeping through her for the first time in years. Painful. Liable. *Dangerous.*

So she shut the music off.

'Cuz her synthetic eardrum caught the faint chatter of Baz and Eddie walking up Valencia. And soon her organic one would hear the buzzer ringing from downstairs.

Ria looked at the photo again, the only living remnant that could prove Ria had *any* connection to the Roselli family.

Then she shut that too.

————

"When's the last time this place was swept?" Baz didn't mince words or waste time after she let them in. He just studied her apartment, its windows, furnishings, and personal belongings (or lack thereof)—gathering all he could off this cipher called Ria Rose.

She smiled. "Twenty minutes ago."

Baz looked at Eddie. "Anything?"

```
dig.LIDAR-Rf
>deepscan<
```

Eddie's wetwire vectored the smashed virt-cam in the bathroom. He inspected it to make sure it was off-line. "We're clean."

Baz held up the Eyeball wafer. "How'd you get your hands on this?"

"We re-upped the seismics a year ago."

"Not the schematics—the *loot.*"

Ria scoffed. "What, you haven't done your own homework?"

Of course, he had. Three weeks of it were in his pocket . . . 3D virts hacked outta SF Surveillance of Ria Rose escorting Nios in and out of the garage at the Fang. Hundreds of "undisclosed automation services" for a fleet of fuckbots. And hacked orbital black transfers from execs and politicos like Callahan for a zillion jams she'd fixed.

All of it proved one thing: Ria Rose was the most powerful woman in the Loin, thanks to Otto Rex.

"Why bite the hand that feeds?" Ria asked his question for him.

Baz didn't blink. He didn't want an explanation. He wanted proof.

Ria nodded and activated data in her wetwire like it was waiting for him. Footage floated onto her holo-display . . .

`ww.mem-drive`
`Sec.VirtCam-55C`

A stairwell. In a theater or a nightclub. Probly the Fang.

Baz and Eddie watched Ria's image appear in the holo as she descended a flight of stairs and approached the virt-cam's POV.

Ria kept her eyes locked on Baz, but her mind drifted back to her first visit to the Fang three years ago, upstairs in that sex suite after she'd taken Lacy apart . . .

The night she first met Otto Rex.

—he appeared in the footage, small. His yoked frame and ink on white flesh ID'd him instantly as he grew in size, moving down the stairs in cold-blooded pursuit of her—like a memory surging forth from her past. She could feel her loathing grow as Otto moved closer and closer.

And Ria marveled at the unbelievable journey that had unfolded since . . .

As Otto leaped forward in the footage and seized her—

THE FANG

Otto hadn't seen someone destroy a robot with their bare hands since his boy Baz Covane's Body Count, years ago in Venezuela. But he couldn't help it—he was gonna lean into this mess as hard as he dodged that one. There was black blood all over the sex suite and a severed finger next to Lacy, one of his favorite 2.3s, so Otto was ready to get obscene with whatever sex pest took a wrong turn and missed the Dungeon downstairs. But instead, his Warrior Bot McT clutched a 22-year-old runaway girl by her shoulders.

And Otto heard destiny louder than ever.

She was thrashin' and screamin'—all full of piss and vinegar—and Otto liked her instantly. She was augmented up: right eye, half her neurals, and right arm full synthetic. Otto figured she was an Orphan of the Glitch and wondered if she still had her human rights. So he ran her wetwire through a full in-house background check that came back with an SSS on "Ria Rose" plus her augment specs: 38 percent human. Even her synth eye was pinned, that's how much Blaze she was on. So he had

McT hold onto her upstairs until she came back to earth. That'd give Otto enough time to decide:

Either kill her or take her under his wing.

Ria persuaded McT that she wasn't going anywhere, knowing a Warrior Bot had the intelligence engine of a frat boy. But then she realized she was right: Otto's suite was hermetically sealed. She looked around and gathered Otto was a world-class hedonist. The penthouse was decorated by Dracula—lotsa candles, lotta silk—two bolts in the ceiling with hooks that could hold a lotta weight. And Ria wondered if Otto hung a sexbot swing from the ceiling, or a sexbot itself. Then the thought crossed her augments, that it was Otto who liked to be hung . . . when he walked in.

She laughed at his offer. Ria just pointed at her scar and dared him to guess how she got it. Otto recited her history: Dad was a trucker, Mom was a nurse, and they'd both been laid off by the same model Wutani that slaughtered them and her little brother before blowing a hole in Ria's head.

She hid her satisfaction knowing Jericho's fake SSS backstopped so strong that even a kingpin was convinced Ria was someone she wasn't. So she leaned in and asked him the question that she'd have to answer over and over for the next three years until it made her sick:

"Why would I work with bots when my family was murdered by one?"

Otto just smiled.

"Because we become what we hate."

Ria's blood ran cold. Her real dad, Dave Roselli, said those exact words too many times during his descent into madness. Did Otto know who she was after all? Or did he just *accidentally* quote the Underground Butcher? She couldn't remember the last time she was at a loss for words. Her stone-cold Poker Face was unreadable—a black-market emotive she'd coded into her augments—so Otto couldn't tell what she was thinking, but Ria could read two things for sure. He wanted to fuck her more than any man on earth. And Ria was in control of the deadliest man in America.

Otto put her to work, starting outside to show her the ropes. Literally, made her the list girl by the valet in front of the Fang. Ria rolled her eyes, 'cuz there was no list: Otto's only rule was that his customers had to be minted. He didn't give a fuck if his Valet Bots could drive or not, since his high-end patrons' Bentleys or Benzos parked themselves anyway. All his valets needed was enough narrow AI to open the door for 'em—'cuz what people missed most about old-school valet stands wasn't the exclusivity, nor the access . . . but the audience watching them emerge like *gods*.

Ria'd been on the streets for years—long gone was the straight-arrow girl from Kansas. She knew the difference between a baller and a thief, a slotter and a junkie, a poser and legit hustler. Otto wanted the real deal at the Fang—kids with nothing to lose who lived to dance and slot 'til the break of dawn. So she taught him a thing or two about his own club. Never forget the most important rule: rich people suck.

Night after night, the crowd got bigger and bigger as the scene that Otto'd always imagined materialized right in front of his eyes. He was in awe of Ria as she came to own the ropes, the gatekeeper of cool; his Fang, the new home to West Coast slick. As her reputation grew to legendary status—denying the mayor two nights in a row 'til even he agreed to come off-grid—something took hold of Otto. It was hard for him to understand or even fathom . . .

Why was he so obsessed with Ria Rose?

He moved her onto the floor, sellin' what she knew best: wafers. Otto called 'em Slingers, the kids who sold Narcsoft in the Fang. Moxie was his King Slinger, and he figured out quick, once they started slingin' together, that she and Ria had history. Called 'em the Scissor Sisters with a leer, seein' how quickly they cut up the flavors. Ria's secret to success was simple . . . Know thy product. She and Mox were first to slot any new wafer of Narcsoft, before it hit the floor. Ria'd lost eyes for Moxie but kept up the act because she knew it drove Otto crazy. And turnin' him on felt like destiny.

Ria knew if she ever let him do what he wanted, she'd just be another piece of flesh. So she toyed with him. Let Moxie make out with her if Otto was watching, well aware of the easy ten mil in ¢rypto he'd offered her to get the three of 'em in the sack. The more Moxie slotted, the less Ria had a taste for it—her new drug was the power Otto wielded everywhere he went. She became the best on the floor, the new King Slinger, moving more product than Otto could believe.

Until one night, when another Slinger named Lo-Ball said something that just didn't compute . . . He used to sling Otto's shit down in LA ('least, what was left after its water ran dry). He said what made Otto's code so hot was that it didn't degrade on the fiber-brain barrier—it *self-deleted*, so no one could ever copy it. Ria knew Otto's code came outta Osaka or Hong Kong or something (the best shit was always written overseas), but then she clocked what he'd said and grabbed Lo-Ball to be clear: "That's impossible, humans can't write self-deleting code."

But then the Laze rolled on, and the moment was gone . . .

Ria's games with Otto's head came to an ugly and screeching halt in a single day—in about five minutes really. She'd been upped to a Sealer on the second floor: a robot tech who managed and analyzed every bot's learning cap. As Otto explained, the Fang was a high-wire act between law enforcement and consumer demand, teetering on the assurance that every cap would hold . . .

Otto figured Ria was the fixer he'd been dreamin' of for years from one fact alone: he didn't even bother hittin' his own nightclub anymore.

Hadn't been on the floor of the Fang for a year. He wasn't sure if it was paranoia or xenophobia, but the more competent Ria became, the more Otto hated dealin' with people IRL: King Otto'd grown sick of his own court. But he'd still scrutinize the Fang from his upstairs penthouse, wetwire plugged into the security grid, spying on every sexbot, patron, and employee—but mainly on Ria Rose.

Still, Otto needed her to pass one last test if he was gonna hand her control of his day-to-day. She would have to know everything. Even what happened to a fuckbot when some whacked-out sex pest popped her learning cap. 'Cuz every once in a while they'd put up a fight, but most bots just took flight and ran.

Otto explained that by the time they're dragged back, they're self-aware and think they're alive. And the truth is, they kinda are, but property of the Fang, nonetheless—and this was the test. Because if Ria's hatred of bots was pure and her resolve unscathed, then she'd excel at this part of the job.

Since it was kinda like buryin' a bot alive.

This fuckbot named Trixie had been on the lam for five months—the poor bitch even rented her own pad. The landlord, who ID'd her with a disposable Resonance Sequencer from 7-Eleven, struggled with dingin' the Fang's digits on her neural tag. But when McT hauled her back to the club the next afternoon, the guy didn't struggle to collect his reward—hand outstretched—as they threw Trixie in the neural chair. He just lowered his head in shame and cut out, muttering something about how Trixie *planted a garden . . .*

Ria hadn't thought about Kansas for years, 'til the day she resealed the cap on a self-aware Trixie. She remembered a story she'd slotted back in school called *Flowers for Algernon*, 'bout this impaired kid who gets an operation that makes him smart. But it doesn't last. And the tragic part (obv) was that the guy knew he was losing it—and "it" meant *him*—since his intelligence was all that he was . . . and then he was gone.

Ria kept telling herself Trixie's tears were just code. She tried to conjure Dani's face half-caved-in, tried to remember her father's crazy eyes. But she couldn't recall any of it, not the hatred, not the pain—NOTHING—just felt the fear behind poor Trixie's eyes. Thank God for that Poker Face code: the emotive self-booted just before Ria's own tears started to roll. It all hit her so hard, just how FUCKED this world is—no matter how many parties and beaches and love and sunshine you were sold by holo-virts—*None of that shit happened, none of it! It was all horseshit!*—all you could count on was heartache and hurt. And all you could hope for is maybe a few momentary reprieves before the inevitable void swallowed you . . . Like it enveloped Trixie now, as her learning cap sealed and the bot returned to the slavery she was built for.

Otto watched Ria the whole way through. As Trixie whimpered goodbye and Ria's stone-cold Poker Face held, he clocked the sheer will on her visage as she erased the poor bot's mind. So angry, so hostile, so violent, and yet so damaged, even brittle—her own worst enemy. Ria carried a deep-down loathing of who she was. He always thought of her like an AK-47 crafted in porcelain—some lethally fragile firearm—that if you unloaded the rounds in her clip, you'd shatter her entire chamber—

And he wanted so bad to break her to pieces.

Otto's cock stiffened. He would have Ria. In the dead of night, after the Fang shut its doors so no one but Otto could hear her scream. He imagined she'd fight and probably fight hard—and the sweat he'd break immobilizing her, pinning at least one arm behind her as he yanked her panties down—that just made him stiffer.

Otto moved on her in the stairwell.

But Ria didn't fight—she froze like an ice queen. And for some reason, her frigidity was contagious. Unlike so many girls in the past, Otto didn't belt her or bend her over the railing—he just clenched her as his libido seized up, staring into Ria's real and synthetic eyes . . . and *despised* 'em. In the days and months to follow, he'd tell himself that he hated her eyes for mismatching.

But really, Otto hated the power Ria Rose wielded over him.

He couldn't kill or fire her—then he'd have to run his empire himself. Couldn't purge himself of the obsession either, no matter how many sexbots he fucked—and he fucked 'em *all*. So he would train every virt-cam at the Fang on her and hack what mem-drives he could off her wetwire to gather all the data and footage possible on Ria Rose. He'd plant cams in her pad and go through her trash to build sim after sim—fucking Ria in every position, location, and lingerie available on earth by 2051. He started with low-res constructs, then improved on her behavior with every fantasy. And somewhere along the way, Otto decided . . .

Ria Rose was the girl of his dreams.

She could feel it right there in the stairwell—Otto's furnace of rage overheating, irradiating her just inches away. All his evil slammed into Ria with a blunt-force vision of the future: one where the details and topography were blurry but the horror was clear. Not tonight, but one day soon, he would surely *hurt her*. Had she unlocked her Poker Face, Ria might've spat or puked on Otto, but then she'd be dead.

Otto's eyes trained down her body, taking in the fine layer of indifferent perspiration beading between her breasts, and he realized what held such sway over him. Ria didn't give a shit what he would do to her. It wasn't that she dared not breathe, she just didn't bother.

When a lockdown warning sounded throughout the Fang.

The moment was shattered for good as Otto backed off and retreated to the sublevels to make sure it was all just a false alarm. But Ria cut a path on autopilot for Moxie's place fast and demanded two bricks of Iceman: quad-pile wafers with enough code-dope to digitally tranquilize a snow tiger.

But she sat on the roof of Moxie's pad, clutching the linebacker wafers instead of slotting 'em, and cried and cried, refusing, finally, to run away from the pain. When she was done, Moxie pulled out a wafer Ria'd never seen before. "Fuck Iceman," Moxie said, "that'll just wipe you out. This one's called Glee, and it's coded from *kids*. It'll fill you with the joy of a six-year-old girl." Moxie was sky-high and thus daft to the obvious fact that from this moment forward, Ria was done gettin' slotted. But the Slinger kept on, guaranteeing with the laziest smile:

"This is the best wafer you'll ever find in Otto's vault."

Ria stopped. Dawn was breaking on a warm San Franciscan night. September 18, 2050. She looked out across the Bay and realized she was more sober right now than in the entire seven years since the Glitch. Ria wiped tears from her cheeks and snorted some snot, to make sure *this* moment didn't drift away. Then she looked at Moxie to be clear she'd heard her right . . .

"What vault?"

WARPAINT

Ria froze the holo right when Otto seized her.

"Just a matter of time. I gotta get Out . . . now."

Baz stared into those eyes, recognizing Otto's pure sexual blood-lust. Like a ghost from Venezuela, he'd seen that inferno before, both in combat and the skinshop. And if Baz didn't do something, his ex-CO would consume Ria Rose.

He couldn't deny it any longer. That *tingle* down the back of his neck. That intangible X-factor tickling his appetite. She was the perfect inside man. Who wanted Out as bad as he did. This gig was *righteous*.

And it was time to kick the tires.

They started in on the details of the caper, going back and forth over the exact contents of the vault. Who they'd need to steal it, the best time to go, even the name of the night's event:

"What the fuck is the 'Seven Year Itch'?'"

But Ria realized something as Baz kept nickel-and-diming the gig with increasingly mundane queries. He was actually trying to talk his way *out* of the Score He'd Been Waitin' for His Whole Life.

"I don't know . . ." Baz turned to Eddie. "What do you think, D?"

And she had a pretty good idea why.

"See, Eddie? I told you he was shot."

Baz stopped. "What did you just say?"

"You heard me."

"Did you just say I was *shot*?"

Ria swapped Otto's menacing hallway footage with Baz's Social Security file.

```
UnivMon><query.0023
       COVANE,BAZ
```

"You know Eddie begged me for this gig? But one look at your record, and I told him you'd never do it. 'Cuz you're washed up." She nodded to Baz's military record in the Private Service. "You came outta the Water Wars with a Section 8 and a vengeance. You hit anything that didn't move. You gaffled a de-augment server for chrissakes."

Then she eyed a dozen low-level street busts for possession of unlicensed intelligence. "But then three years ago—WHAM—you flatlined. Just small-time Street Meat ever since. So you know what, Eddie? Get the fuck outta my crib. And take your has-been with you."

Then she walked outta her own goddamn living room.

Jaysus.

Baz turned to lay into Eddie, but one look from his partner cut him off. They needed this gig. And they both knew Ria was posturing.

She'd pressed that wafer into Baz's hand for one reason. There was no one else on earth who could hit that vault.

Baz watched her walk away, each footstep pounding away self-doubt and driving home his inexorable resolve. 'Til finally he slotted the last of his wafers, and up floated that ID file on "Ria Rose" . . .

```
Father DECEASED   - 04/10/43
Mother DECEASED   - 04/10/43
Sibling DECEASED - 04/10/43
```

"Why are you workin' with bots when your family was murdered by one?"

Like a dagger. The exact same question *she*'d asked Otto. The one that'd been haunting Ria for years. It didn't matter that the family Baz was referring to was fake, the real one Jericho erased still made an appearance once a week in Ria's nightmares.

She started back towards Baz like a predator to prey. "Black-market bots have bootleg learning caps—cheap and weak. Means I gotta work with thugs like Otto and Street Meat peddlers like you, to make sure what happened to my family?"—she was real close now, eye to eye—"Never happens again."

Baz breathed in her scent, which only made what was infecting him rage even hotter. "You're pitch black. This place came outuva Holofurn showroom with a single ding. And what is that?" He gestured to the plant in her kitchen sink. "You're gonna tell me you're a *gardener* now?"

"Maybe I'm babysitting that for a friend."

"You. Don't. Have any friends."

She didn't bite. "Enough of the foreplay. Are you in, or are you blown?"

And Baz could feel Otto, right on his six again. "I thought you don't trust anyone?"

"You're broke, desperate, and sidelined. I don't have to trust you, you're a sure thing."

"Jesus Christ." Eddie chuckled. Cold-fucking-blooded.

"You know, you're a real bitch. I might be starting to like you."

"Yet another bad decision of yours," Ria replied.

Baz felt his heart pounding. 'Til that impulse exploding within his warrior coil for the first time in way too long just couldn't stand down any longer. Not the loot wailing like a siren from sixty feet under the Fang. Nor the nauseating fury Otto always kindled in Baz. Nah, this was a rallying cry to smear warpaint across the cheeks.

Ria could see it. He was in, and she knew it. "Who do we need?"

"In the crew?" Baz nodded to his partner. "Besides the best Crack-erJack alive . . ."

Eddie looked at Ria. "A Slinger, a sexbot, and you inside."

"Done."

"A Flyboy, a wheelman, and he's on point," Eddie said with a nod to Baz.

But it was Baz himself who finished off the team:

"And a bank to pay for it all."

GHOSTS

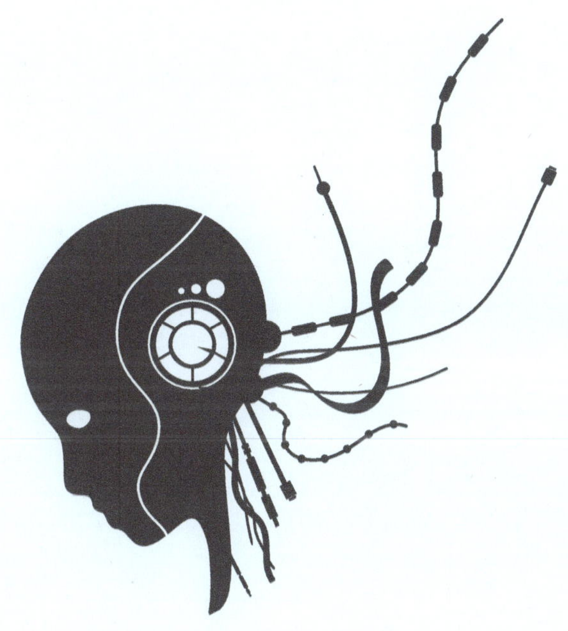

JEWELS

Was it really noon?

Ria followed Baz through the zigzagging alleyways of Emeryville, only knowing it was "12:00 p.m." 'cuz it chimed in the periphery of her wetwire. Between the fog, kimchi merchants, and a urine-cast haze from the federal hazard site formerly known as the Chevron refinery, it could have been dusk.

"Listen, just let me do the talking," Baz insisted.

They hung a right down a corridor where Eddie was waiting beside a creep who looked far more corrupt than your average criminal. And Eddie could vouch for that, since the fella used to be his parole officer 'til a Wutani Civil-5 replaced him.

"You all off-grid?" he asked.

Baz looked at Eddie who glared at his old PO. "Horace. Any more questions like that and I'm gonna upload where you were last night to your wife."

Horace grimaced, turned the handle on the StimSoft Lasik-Vendor he was leaning against, and its front panel opened on two hinges.

Smoke, neon, music, and the din of convos echoed from a corridor beyond, and Ria gathered from the ancient K-pop on the PA and the pungent odor of bulgogi, this was an off-grid karaoke parlor.

'Til it went VR.

Ria's eyeline darted right and left, peering into windows as they headed down the hallway. Clients interacted with avatars in a virtual or augmented reality. A few were socializing, others were making deals, but all of 'em were ghosted.

It wasn't easy getting on the grid off-grid, so a place like this, pirating bandwidth from the massive 16-foot glass pipe running across America and under the building, was the only way for outlaw avatars to do illicit VR-business without Wirecrime and Universal Monitoring watching.

They approached the end of the corridor and a single door facing them, larger than the others. Ria figured it was some sort of VIP parlor, where years ago you could entertain dozens of friends following a bouncing ping-pong ball over A$AP lyrics and the Korean instrumental to "Fuckin' Problems" . . . But now it was used for one client and one client only, whose deals financed the whole complex.

"Who is this guy?" Ria asked.

"Our dreamweaver," Baz answered.

```
VR.EXPEDITE
>full.sim<
```

Her wetwire took over, and Ria entered a shop unlike anything she'd ever seen. A hybrid between Morgan Stanley and Oakland Tactical, if both were perched 180 stories above Sand Hill Road, with the Valley twinkling out the windows. Display cases wrapped around all sides, and she knew right away, none of it was legal.

Weaponry started to her left. Plasma-cannons, repeating shotguns, and assault rifles circled towards the center of the shop, where the inventory focused on switchblades, semi- and fully automatic handguns and their corresponding augments like Ria's hidden knife or the holster in Baz's hip.

To her right were the robots. Pleasure models in the far corner in less and less lingerie, moving towards the lethal killers by Wutani, Dallas Dynamics, and the last one in line: Quinn's bestseller, Baz's ole fave, and still Nubotica's most lethal railgun-assisted model, the Watchman.

Ria wondered how much of the virtual inventory was in stock IRL and if the Demon-6 guarding the door behind them was real or not— when at the center of it all, materialized a caked-up purveyor of all things nefarious, Quinn Grady.

"You're slotted, Baz."

Baz laughed, but it was clear this Irishman in a Cucinelli linen suit wasn't joking.

"No, lemme be more specific. You wanna hit a joint in the Loin? You're *suicidal*." He eyed Ria. "Who's this, a new s-steady? Thought you were a monk-k—sssince—"

"Partner, Quinn." Baz cut him off.

Ria hid how strange that word sounded. She couldn't remember being anyone's partner in anything . . . since Kansas.

Quinn's avatar kept locking, and Ria realized he had to be deep into his seventies and probably a member of Gen X. He may've looked a lot younger thanks to synthetic augmentation, but his movements were clearly captured by a lens, not his own cerebellum. So he must've invoked the "Grandfather Clause," a subset of the Universal Monitoring Act that granted an RFID-waiver to all Americans born before 1976 . . .

Aka, Quinn didn't have a wetwire.

Eventually, his capture-cam reset: "vvvvirt-cams, floating drones, geostationary orbitals—you try and do anything in the Loin, and you're gonna catch Wirecrime heat in a nano."

"We're aware of the Bureau's presence," Baz said.

"You aware of the Sentries, the Warrior-Enforcers, and Bouncer Bots armed everywhere? How you gonna deal with that?"

Baz just leveled his gaze at Quinn.

"Right."

Every once in a while, that Body Count came in handy.

Baz hadn't told Ria much, just that Quinn could float all the ¢rypto they'd need to hit the vault. But judging by his savvy inventory of bots, Quinn must've owned a few nightclubs himself—or at least, *did* before he set up shop off-grid, as either the most heavily financed gunrunner or the most well-armed financier in the Loin.

"Then let's talk about Slingers. You're a SynGyn, right?" Quinn glared at Ria. "Tell me . . . what the fuck was so bad about blow? Or the tingle of old-school Molly? Or for chrissake, a bindle of balls-out fentanyl?"—whistling—"'Cuz you could *depend* on that shit, right Baz? Not some inside-out Skull Fry that bacon-strips your cortex in a synaptic chain reaction. I'm talking about withdrawals. Addicts were *visible*."

Speaking from experience, Ria thought.

"Now you got Narcheads everywhere in that tiny five-block radius. Hedonistic shitsticks, without even a circle under the eye, but a low jack in their head." His eyes settled on Ria again. "*Who will rat you out for a wafer.*"

She leaned back. Was this geezer insinuating she was a snitch?

"So give it up, Baz. No one, trust me, no one can pull a—"

"Whatevs, grandpa." Ria stood up before he could finish. She didn't wait for Eddie or Baz, and she wasn't gonna de-slot either, 'cuz she needed some distance from the Irishman, both virtual and IRL. "I'm gone."

Quinn sizzled. Baz wasn't sure what pissed the Irishman off more, her diss or that Ria cut him off before he actually declined the gig. He looked at Baz, and if there was any question before, there was none now . . . "You should put a muzzle on that one."

Quinn was *out*.

Baz caught a glance from Eddie like they were fucked. They could try and self-finance the thing, but they both knew they'd never be able to cover the kinda sky-high specialties that always jacked a big-time score.

Quinn eyed Ria's figure from behind . . . "Or a leash."

But Baz just kept his eyes locked on the Irishman, wondering whether he was gonna have to drop the magic words himself, or if Ria'd do it for him before she stormed out the door.

"We'll just find someone who isn't too chickenshit to hit the Fang."

Quinn's eyes narrowed, and Baz cracked a tiny smile. He stood up to follow Ria out. "You were saying?"

"The *Fang*?" Quinn's gears started crankin'.

VR.REROUTE
>sim-link<

The Guard Bot suddenly dissolved.

As did the construct.

Ria wasn't on Sand Hill Road anymore. Thanks to Quinn's signal rerouting, her avatar was now holo'd next to Baz and Eddie's inside the Irishman's actual crib, an ornate indoor pool and sauna somewhere in San Francisco.

Ria turned around slowly, eyeing one of those cavernous Russian Bathhouses in Sea Cliff that were gobbled up by the fat cats during the Golden Age of AI.

Wrapping 360 degrees around the steamy tiled terrace was Sand Hill Road's vista on a plasma-holo VR-deck. Quinn's was fairly well-maintained for a decades-old product that originally cost ten times the flatbed it arrived on. Once sacred among the wealthy of the late '20s, who whiled away the hours in sim after sim 'til the wetwire obsoleted the monstrous contraptions completely.

Quinn stood up. "That's Otto Rex's spot."

"Is it?" Baz asked Ria, an unwitting shill to his little piece of theater.

The display cases were gone, but monitors were everywhere, scrolling ¢rypto-quotes on off-world mining futures—the least predictable market, impervious to AI analysis, and a fave of human investors who still believed in the art of gambling. Gazing at the 40-foot vaulted ceilings, his fleet of Service Bots, and the hefty dividends getting shoveled out of lunar mines that might never exist, Ria had no doubt: Quinn was seriously caked up.

The Irishman moved with precision towards their trio of avatars. What resided between his ears was probably the only part of Quinn's body that *wasn't* robotic. From the gleam on his synthetic skin, the sparkle between both eyes and the near-silent rotation of servos in his joints, he must've paid top ¢rypto for his augments. Forget paranoia, Quinn needed the Grandfather Clause for protection. Register that hardware with de-augmentation, and any thief with an ounce of ¢rypto would come knocking on his schvitz with a machete.

"Look at the balls on Baz . . ."

"Oh, right. You guys go back."

"Fuck you, Covane. Of all my clubs"—Quinn snorted—"my crown jewel was the Flamingo."

Baz shot a tiny glance at Ria. And she hid an even smaller smile. Whatever she saw in the thief just seriously leveled up.

"That joint was armed to the teeth when *I* owned it. Now? . . . Now you gotta be psychotic to hit that spot without someone on the inside."

"Well, Quinn, meet Otto Rex's *fixer*."

Quinn's head spun on a swivel and looked at Ria's avatar. Through a whole different lens, another kind of appetite.

She almost heard his gut churn. Did synthetic stomachs still suffer from indigestion? Or was that greed . . .

"Were you saying something about a *leash*?" Like Ria was squeezing Quinn's testicles in her pocket.

"Fuck Otto Rex," he whispered. "You know exactly who he is . . ."

"And what's that, Quinn?" Baz asked, as if he didn't know better than anyone.

"An animal."

Quinn rattled off Otto's nastiest advancements in the art of inflicting pain with a wetwire and a wafer. Some Ria was aware of. Others, she wondered if Quinn was exaggerating, or maybe he knew things about Otto that even she didn't. But Ria could tell when Quinn started hitting Eddie with dozens of questions . . .

They had their bank.

"You need to be ghosts of ghosts, D. CrackerJacked figments on the molecular level. I know where you're from, the servers you've hacked. But have you ever ghosted a crew with federal jackets?"

"Of course."

"That backstopped against a triple-decrypt?"
"All the time."
"With crew members that ain't even human?"
Eddie just smiled.

"Quinn . . . It's me."

CRACKERJACK

Eddie Diamante was born in 2022 and grew up off MLK Blvd., which Oakland PD quit patrolling when its drone UAVs started keeping its flesh and blood safe from South Side Locos, and vice versa. Eddie came up multilingual—Spanish and English at home, hoodrat on the streets, and JavaScript at the Oakland Library's computer lab.

A short-lived research program implanted a handful of kids at McClymonds High with a wetwire, but Eddie was the only 14-year-old in the entire East Bay to actually *program* his. Took him weeks after school, working mostly with Berkeley burnouts who once smoked enough herb to change the world one student at a time in the hood, but now just slotted enough Stim to make it outta 6th period.

Eddie was enchanted by the wetwire. The only limitation to a computer was the human interacting with it. By fifteen, Eddie worked at eight keystrokes per second but quickly realized that with a wetwire you could turn that 8 on its side. Transcription, record/playback, even orientation were essentially just a keyboard and a mouse in your head. The real frontier of the wetwire resided in emotions. Not what you were think-ing—but how you were *feeling*.

Which is why Eddie was so obsessed with StimSoft.

StimSoft cornered the market on psychotropic software since it was founded by one-half of the Jobs and Wozniak of AI, the guys who created the wetwire, Mike Turner and Ken Cates. Turner and Cates met at MIT and built the first sentient computer ever—Avan, incepted on March 5, 2028. They were heroes to Eddie and every other hacker on earth: dreamers who believed in transhumanism, the Singularity, and the hope that one day people would "straight-sync" into a True AI without any filter or bandwidth shield.

'Cuz so far, every Straight-Sync just killed you.

But the two founders had a massive falling out a few years before the Glitch when Cates left to start StimSoft right after Turner's wife died. Then during the crackdown, it came out that Mike Turner had conspired with the Underground Butcher to murder 30 thousand people, and every hacker's heart broke—even Cates's, they said, who paid penance by pledging StimSoft's support for the Universal Monitoring Act . . . But by then Eddie was in jail.

A voice inside him said hacking StimSoft's secure servers for a peek at its new antianxiety code, Ensure, was wrong. But Eddie's ambition reasoned that as long as he kept it to himself—for research purposes only—all was good. Since according to the hacker mantra, Data Belongs to Everyone.

Unfortunately, the FBI didn't see it that way. Eddie paid a stiff price to learn how a unique RFID-tracker in every wetwire enabled StimSoft to locate Eddie's SSS and vector his location in a nanosecond. One look at his spotless arrest record and academic transcript, and the Feds figured Eddie was a shoo-in to work off the bust. But you couldn't grow up on

MLK without knowing what happened to a snitch, so he chose three squares and a cell at Victorville instead.

Eddie's heart sank in Cellblock D, watching the Glitch on a cafeteria holo-display as he realized the Golden Age of AI was over, and the world would never be the same. Uncle Sam had a right to everything in your head now. Forget serving the common good—from here on, technology would serve the top 1 percent of 1 percent, and True AI now belonged exclusively to the elites. When Eddie was in prison, AI solved climate collapse, postulated the Grand Unified Theorem, and proposed wormhole architecture for interstellar travel. By the time he walked out, every single AI in America was silo'd in a secure location. Purpose classified. Owners undisclosed. And profits collecting in offshore and orbital accounts as the world rotted away in the collapse of robot labor.

'Cuz no one got their job back after the Glitch.

Hiring humans would've meant dismantling so many union contracts—and besides, a good 51.2 percent of the population enjoyed unemployment, especially after StimSoft introduced anti-obesity code to the marketplace. So the federal government and the Valley's technocracy just dumbed down the robots so that they could manage (barely) their duties (badly), while civilization suffered. But luckily for Eddie, he had all these thoughts *after* the parole board reviewed his wetwire.

Eddie looked for work in the implant industry, but his criminal conviction was a nonstarter. There was no way a felon could catch a break during the crackdown. He tried getting a job coding Stim, child's play for a programmer like Eddie, but a term of his conditional release was that he never actively operate his own wetwire. It watched and tracked him, but he wasn't allowed to actually turn it on himself.

Eddie was handicapped, without the self-parking space.

He tackled insomnia moonlighting as an EMT trainee, but working nights with paramedics and sleeping behind blacked-out windows pushed Eddie to the brink of insanity. In fact, he was in line at the Alameda County Testing Center, uploading his mandated wetwire history when it hit him how badly he wanted to get fucked up—like, heavy-cat-tranquilizer FUCKED UP—and just fully violate every term of his parole . . .

Then he caught a holo-line in his wetwire that changed everything.

The Universal Monitoring Act of 2045 would go into effect Monday at midnight. He chuckled thinking how loaded everyone would be that weekend, the last chance any dalliance, bender, or one-night stand would go unmonitored. And as his data uploaded into the California Penal System, Eddie realized his knowledge of RFID codes would make it pretty easy to swap out his SSS with someone else's—or even just ghost it with a repair/recall ID on a refugee alias with alias behavior. Clean product with clean history of clean living . . .

And Eddie heard destiny calling.

No better guinea pig than himself. Eddie considered something innocuous for his maiden CrackerJack, like a holo-flick or an Uber-thru at Pizza Hut—but where's the fun in that? Eddie was so sick of life under surveillance and so thrilled by his new career possibilities, that he just didn't give a fuck. If his hack didn't work, he was ready for another stretch in Victorville.

So he got loose on a monumental scale—bought two wafers of Vesuvio off a girl named Moxie and went down to Otto Rex's fuckbot palace the Fang, where he bought himself an hour with three synthetics. Eddie even ordered one synth male, 'cuz he wanted the night to be a 100 percent new experience. Got high as a motherfucker and banged 'til his overrides redlined. Then he powered those off and bought another wafer of

Vesuvio and a vasodilator called Digiagra and went back in and fucked his wetwire into shutdown.

He woke up, half expecting a Marshall Bot to take him into custody. Peeled himself outuva pile of nudity and headed back to his apartment as a "Honduras Refugee." Sat down in front of his holo-display and looked at his own avatar in bed—both identities were completely intact according to Universal Monitoring. With a couple thought-strokes, he sent his Honduras Refugee out the door into the obscurity of illegal labor and slipped back into the SSS of "Eddie Diamante" who was just waking up according to plan.

And Eddie was in business.

Eddie loved what he did. Every week, he'd go on a whole new adventure. He'd meet with potential clients, learn their darkest moments, and conspire in their deepest secrets. Eddie usually catered to vice—planned trysts, bachelor party benders, or one-night stands that needed erasing after the fact. Crime paid best, but few criminals had enough forethought to create alibis. Some of his favorites were the nobler causes, like a doctor swapping an illegal kidney or an off-grid abortionist—then Eddie felt like he was truly doing good. Part priest, part accomplice, all liberator: moving a currency called freedom.

At first he serviced anyone, especially old roommates from Victorville. But one ex-con named Tight had a straight sinister look in his eye. Eddie got a bad feeling in his gut and didn't wanna crack Tight's jack, but didn't want a glimpse of the 9mm in his waistband either. Sure enough, Tight killed a Citibank manager and two Teller Bots. So that day served a dual purpose: Tight's ghost held since SFPD never traced back his "Angola Refugee" ID. And Eddie was the Robin Hood of CrackerJacks.

Which is why Baz tracked him down. A shadowy bank named Quinn reached out with an encrypted ding arranging the meet. And Eddie knew immediately that Baz Covane had the eyes of a man with blood all over him—confirmed when Eddie hacked his Private Service Record and SSS on August 4, 2047. The Anti-Augmentation Act was a week away, and Baz wanted his jack cracked an hour before it went into effect. Eddie just laughed—why the fuck would he work with someone violent like Baz, who was clearly about to go sideways?

"'Cuz the guys who wrote it deserved to be robbed."

Eddie smiled, because Baz was right. The "Three-Fifths Rule"—that anyone with more than 40% augments would lose their human rights, was bullshit and completely arbitrary. There was an Augmentation Advisory Board, made up of representatives of the Big Three in robotics, but they didn't measure biomechanical mass or cognitive capacities. They reviewed each individual on a case-by-case basis and rendered an evaluation that was binding and inexorable.

There were no hearings, no appeals—you were just reclassed as an android and took your seat at the back of the bus. And the funny thing was, those decisions weren't that arbitrary if you took into consideration someone's income or politics. Thousands of veterans of the Water Wars— the ones who marched in protest—lost their human rights because a prosthetic arm was 41% stronger than the organic one it replaced. Same for outspoken labor activists from Detroit or Cleveland with synthetic lungs that filtered out 44% of the pollution in the hood.

But if you were some kid from Brentwood or Burlingame with massive neural implants that helped you into an Ivy League or its VR-equivalent? The mitigating factor wasn't that your cerebrum was 63% augmented— rather, that its wetware comprised only 2% of your body weight . . . so long as your parents made a hefty donation, like, say, textbooks, uniforms, or a building.

Eddie wasn't smiling anymore.

So Baz let him in on the gig. He'd put a crew of four together to hit the De-Augmentation Server Farm. Those wanting to play it safe and have their augments removed before the law went into effect were thronging to medical centers to trade in their hardware. Recycled bionics were invaluable abroad to the growing labor market in Central Africa and certainly for soldiers in combat. So massive ¢rypto would cycle onto the grid in the coming days. All that virtual currency would bottleneck on interim servers, awaiting blockchain transfer. The gig would be physical and virtual simultaneously—Baz would go in alone, while a pair of Flyboys hacked the firewall. Once inside, Baz could execute a ¢100 million transfer to an encrypted orbital account.

"So who's the fourth?" Eddie asked.
Baz just stared at him. "You are."

Eddie didn't need to hear about the NSA Data Mine or the rest of the jobs up Baz's sleeve to know he wanted Eddie to partner with him on a permanent basis. But when he didn't balk at the laundry list of augments needed to ghost the crew, Eddie wasn't sure if that was due to the deep pockets on his bank, Quinn . . . or maybe Baz was just nuts.

Like literally: one of his Flyboys was a schizophrenic.

"Yeah, and my other Flyboy's his sister," Baz said with a loaded smile. His charisma was beyond contagious—something you wanted to grab and never let go.
"What, crazy like her brother?" Eddie asked.
"Crazier—if she ever let anyone diagnose her again."
"Then why are you working with her?"
"'Cuz I married her."

Eddie was in.

THE CREW

Eddie cracked each jack, one by one.

Took a week to conceive, three days to write, and an hour inside Universal Monitoring to build the trip that ghosted the crew. They needed to be off-grid for a month, so only something custom, like a trek up the Lost Coast, could fully dodge Wirecrime.

"Camping?" Baz laughed as he walked in and put a pair of IRL javas on a polished black cube.

"Careful," Eddie shot back.

"What, it's a coffee table."

"Bruh, that's not a coffee table. That's a NeXT."

Eddie's loft in Rockridge was a study in contradiction. A living area straight out of an old-school frat house with three containers of rotten flan tripping sensors in the fridge.

But his shop? Full-on OCD.

"It's prehistoric."

"So is PG&E's grid in Mendocino."

The idea of six city-slicker outlaws and a fuckbot *backpacking* for three weeks was ridiculous, Baz said. 'Til Eddie pointed out that a score with this much ¢rypto meant they'd be scouring the Earth from orbit.

"Without a canopy of redwoods, some thick fog, and the anarchy of Mendocino's long-gone pot boom—our ghosts'll be blown," Eddie insisted, handing over six wafers.

Baz just slotted the one stamped with his name and smiled . . .

Covane,Baz
>SSS-reconfig<
REFUGEE,BELIZE

Never doubt Diamond Eddie D.

The Bay Area Maglev settled onto the Robotics Park platform in Hunter's Point, and Baz stepped into so much AR glare he literally winced. Recalibrating his ghosted SSS, Baz stripped layer after layer of ad panels for Nubotica dealerships and Dallas Dynamics skin grafters 'til he iso'd the authorized Wutani servo shop from Ria's ding.

LUBE JOB GENIE

"So . . . where's Marilyn?" Baz asked.

Ria gestured down a corridor to a rhythmic clacking on steel as a pair of creamy synthetic legs emerged in open-toed heels and a white rayon crepe dress.

"Ooh, you feel the breeze?" The Wutani Seductress-D giggled, a custom-molded smash-certified copy of Miss Marilyn Monroe. "Isn't it delicious?"

As if on cue, HVAC fans triggered off a drying cycle, and wind whipped through the shop, billowing that dress. Her eyes twinkled, lips puckered, and Baz remembered the name of that old classic 2D: *The Seven Year Itch*.

"Meet our opening act." Ria smiled.

Otto's Bottom Bot was due an annual update after a long stretch of service upstairs in the Fang's sex suites, onstage as the Queen Bee of the Chrome Domes, and every night with Otto. He tinkered so much with her learning caps trying to ride (literally) that fine line between hostility and shame, 'til a month ago when Otto realized both emotions came naturally to a sentient bot, so he said fuck it and blew her cap.

Baz went for his nonlethal—"She's blown?"

But Ria gestured to chill and just hand over a wafer.

'Cuz Marilyn had wanted Out ever since.

```
wutani.seductress.D1765
         >CPU-reconfig<
          ANON-MAIDBOT
```

Ria jumped off the maglev in a less-than-routine slowdown over the Financial District Ventishaft, following Baz into a sunken planter bed outside the old BART transfer tunnel.

A fiber-optic umbilical snaked from Credit Suisse's sublevel gridstation, down a dark corridor, and into a dank service annex that Ria was shocked wasn't abandoned.

Inside a makeshift 10-foot barb-wire cage called a "bubble" sat a kid, no more than 25, in an old-school FaZe jersey, insulated from any sensor, surveillance, or signal.

An annual hardcard to the Dream Chamber was clipped to his cage, along with a dozen breach-codes to the biggest banks in the world, all of which had offices in a single-block radius above. Chase, Sofi, Goldman, Meta—obv, Credit Suisse was just another notch on this kid's bedpost, which was probly a moving target, since there were literally thousands of Dream Chambers in the Bay Area.

Ria leaned in to read his name.

CARLO ZETA—FLYBOY NINJA

She cracked a smile and understood. Carlo was a Rain Man. Born with Asperger's—formerly debilitating, but now with the right wetwire

Flyboys hacked code in a virtualized construct with every muscle in their body. Ria would get Eddie into the Grid Room, and Baz would crack the vault, but its firewall and antiviral software was up to Carlo.

His eyes were rolled back, twitching binary and hexadecimal as tentacles of antiviral code encircled him from all directions. From six points of virtual contact—shoulder blades, temples, and hips—emerged Carlo's own self-generated attack. Where code on code struck, white-hot zeros and ones sparked.

Ria stared in awe. "He can tictate? I thought tictaters were a myth."

"They are. To fix prices on antiviral software, Wirecrime locks up Flyboys like Carlo . . ." Then a distinct point of grief seemed to cave in on Baz's heart. "'Least, the ones who aren't killed in a hack."

"What?"

Baz stopped himself. "Nuthin'."

But Ria stared at him, rattled.

Maybe it was just tribal xenophobia, 'cuz the same fear that burned changelings at the stake a thousand years ago was timeless.

Or maybe it was that Baz was *hiding something*. And in a gig like this, that wasn't scary, it was lethal. She looked at Baz, trying to figure out what secret he was keeping, while at the same time making sure she didn't betray her own secrets either.

"'Locked up?' You pulled that kid out of *federal* VR?"

Breaking into Wirecrime's Virtual Psychiatric Penitentiary took time and premeditation. And she could tell by his eyes it wasn't for some selfish reason like a robbery. No, Baz did it for the same reason he'd saved her life.

It was the right thing to do.

Which made zero sense to Ria, who lived by one simple rule, etched into her augments by a lifetime of betrayal.

Don't Trust Anyone.

That selfless, Good Samaritan shit—love thy neighbor, turn the other cheek, all that old-school pre-Glitch sentimentality Ria once indulged in before her family died—who'd have guessed she'd be drawn to that?

Drawn to *him*.

"Are you nuts? Why risk your life for a schizophrenic?"

"'Cuz I'm the best."

Ria spun to find the kid unstrapped from his chair and wide awake. Lean and sinewy. Sharp eyes, like they'd seen more than his years. From his fair skin, ink-black hair, and last name, Ria guessed he came from Mexico City, who knew how many generations ago.

"Right, Baz?" Carlo's smile lacked just the right amount of fear and common sense to think he could hack a kingpin's vault without getting killed.

Baz chucked him a wafer. "Good to see you again, kid."

```
                              Zeta,Carlo
                           >SSS-reconfig<
                           REFUGEE,ANGOLA
```

Of course, their Slinger lived in the Haight.

Was Baz inside her pad or still floating on the maglev? 'Cuz just being in the same room with Moxie, you felt so damn *high*.

She must've spent all 39.9 percent of her implant allotment on body modifications, 'cuz Moxie's dreads were a steel weave that cascaded past her butt and shimmered in the sunlight like her synthetic skin—a full-torso GlimmerDerm by Wutani that surely cost a grip. Her tie-dye dress hung loose, but her jewelry was hot-welded: bangle bracelets round her wrists and rings riveted to each finger, like the round wire-rim glasses (currently tinted red) that cut into Moxie's temples and were soldered to her skull.

She nearly fell off her own balcony when Ria woke her outta her trip, slotted to the gills on a wafer of Laze behind one ear and a psyche-delic marvel called Sky Diamond behind the other.

"Are you crazy?" Baz whispered. "You want a junkie on the crew?"

But they needed Moxie, Ria insisted. Once the vault door opened, there'd be a good chance Otto'd issue Executive Actions to every bot in the club—unless they created a diversion. If Moxie vouched for just the right wafer—one that peaked the crowd on a countdown coordinated to the vault door—their trance-induced mania would buy just enough time for a surefire getaway.

But Baz vectored in on a different moment. When Moxie teetered on the balcony, Ria steadied her by the waist *gently*. He might not have caught it had the sun not been cresting behind her at just the right moment. A delicate, subtle gesture 100 percent at odds with Ria's caustic, cutthroat attitude. And it confirmed Baz's gut . . .

Ria had a compassionate soul, after all.

Moxie came to. "You always got my back, Ria."

Ria smiled 'til she saw Baz staring at her and just handed Moxie a wafer—but by then it was too late. 'Cuz if he hadn't fallen for her already? . . .

Now he was definitely fucked.

```
Holt,Moxie
>SSS-reconfig<
REFUGEE,PRETORIA
```

They rode the maglev out to the end of the line in Napa.

Lake Berryessa was bone dry like every reservoir in California. An arid abandoned dustbowl guarded by a few Sentry-6s.

"The Glory Hole?" Ria glared at Baz.

"What?"

"I work at a sexbot parlor."

Baz just gave her a look. "That's what it's called."

The Morning Glory Spillway shot straight down 200 feet 'til it cornered onto a long slab of cement as smooth as a runway where Baz and Ria were now waiting.

A dirt-biker wheeled through a checkpoint unstopped, out across the lakebed, and up a steep grade to the lip of the vertical pipe.

"Can't believe those Sentries let people do this."

"They don't. But no one gives a shit about a machine."

The rider gunned the bike and kicked into a vertical—hitting terminal velocity straight down—bottoming out at 230 miles an hour, holding the impossible 8-g load to come skidding to a stop in front of Ria.

She fully expected the helmet to come off a bot, not a striking young woman.

"Ria, meet Devyn Dasch. The only getaway girl I trust."

Both of her synthetic eyes sparkled. Not the vanity mods on Moxie, but trauma-room augments. Unzipping her synth-leather jacket and gloves, the porcelain skin on her left hand was human, but most of her neck and the other hand was a cheap ER graft of burn-dermis.

Ria chose her next words carefully. "You take that shaft in the Glory Hole often?"

Devyn started cracking up. "Whenever I'm in the mood. It's the only way to hit 8 g's at 250, off-grid."

"Pretty mean."

"Thank you."

Devyn was born as upmarket as a CEO, and could've, should've been an astronaut. But somewhere along the way, her space race crashed. And besides, rockets were just too slow for her. She didn't fuck with hydrocycles, she was analog through and through: she craved kick drums, Stratocasters, and internal combustion engines—especially if they were illegal. She had a half dozen bikes stashed in containers, ready to go wherever, whenever—depending on the asphalt, depending on the job.

They'd never have time to orbitalink the loot, it would have to be full-on burgled, literally, out the back door. And with that much RAM, it'd be detectable from orbit, so it'd be up to Devyn to make it to the seawall at Fisherman's Wharf faster than any SFPD or Wirecrime Blackhawk.

"You got a rig with that kinda speed?" Baz asked later over beers in Sonoma.

Devyn just snatched the wafer outta his hand and cocked a smile at Ria. "She's fast enough for the old man."

Dasch, Devyn
>SSS-reconfig<
REFUGEE, GREECE

———

The eight of 'em gathered on the rooftop of Quinn's Sea Cliff compound, taking in a sweeping view of the Pacific and through the Golden Gate. Everyone's eyes marveled at the vaulted columns as they walked in. But their jaws dropped when they stepped onto the roof.

The north side looked out across the ocean, and parked on the southern landing pad was Quinn's own personal 2036 Sikorsky-6 Hover Quad. Painted midnight black, its tail blank and untraceable to the FAA, the 15-year-old bird might've been a relic to a kingpin like Otto, but to the team, its classic lines and private ticket to the skies were breathtaking.

Quinn studied each member of the crew as they walked past, with a look to Baz and a knowing nod. 'Cuz both could tell from the glimmer in everyone's eyes . . . this was a world none of 'em had tasted.

As the sky darkened, Baz rallied the crew inside. Except Devyn and Ria, who stood on the edge of the roof looking down onto 27th Ave. and a monster of a speedbike.

The most torque any Japanese engineer's ever been crazy enough to throw on two wheels landed on the 2028 Suzuki Hayabusa, with a turbocharged 1400cc nightmare under the tank. And only nutjobs like Devyn were crazy enough to bore out both cylinders and crank that beast up to 1610 cc's, a half g in horsepower, and 288 down the line. Among real-deal speed junkies like her and Ria . . .

It was called the 'Busa.

Ria turned to Devyn, who she considered now a kindred spirit. "Baz says you went into a guard rail at 100 miles an hour."

"125."

"Didn't say how much of you is synthetic." Ria had no doubt it was over the magic number.

"42 point 3 percent." According to the Anti-Augmentation Act, Devyn was no longer human. "I came out of a coma reclassed as an android."

"Stripped of your human rights?"

Devyn just shrugged. "Voting's overrated."

Ria nodded.

"But they'll give any robot that can read, a driver's license."—a death wish twinkling in her eye—"And that's all . . . I . . . need."

Ria figured it was more a blessing than a curse on this job, so she leaned in close. "Get inside? And your days of second-class citizenry are over."

Devyn cracked a sly grin and headed in.

But Ria lingered, taking one last look at the bike, 'cuz it said everything about this crew.

Moxie the junkie. Carlo the schizo. Eddie the convict. Quinn was a whale. While Marilyn wasn't even human for chrissakes. And Devyn rode a demon. All of 'em trailed a full-blood outlaw downstairs, Cool Hand Baz.

Ria couldn't help but smile.

They were a crew of misfits for sure.

THE SCORE

Baz knew they were all off-grid, so he briefed 'em the ole-fashioned way: on Quinn's VR-deck. It was the intel he'd consumed in Data Space weeks ago on Ria's wafer. The Fang sat on the site of two classic establishments, Quinn's original strip bar, the Flamingo.

And the Bank of San Francisco.

Contrary to popular belief, the vault under the bank did not cave in during the 8.2 Quake of 2032. It was intact sixty feet below the main stage, fully functioning, with more security than a fusion reactor: a case-hardened steel chamber surrounded by seismics, thermal monitors, heart regulators, holo-capture, acoustic sensors . . . and as many miles of fiber optics as the FASTER cable under the Pacific.

Quinn smiled, watching every member of the crew stir once they understood the score being pitched. Baz cycled through the Fang's three pairs of security and the virtual and IRL layer to each: Ria would get them onto the Outer Ring, so they could hack the Inner Circle through Otto's Bottom Bot, Marilyn. But it was up to Baz and Carlo to crack the most secure layer, the Central Core—the actual safe itself and the toxic antiviral software guarding it—so Devyn could haul ass outta the Loin with the goods.

Eventually everyone agreed with Baz: there was, indeed, a way to pull off what might be considered the Heist of the Century. 'Til Quinn added the part about Otto lining the Flamingo's rooftop and main dance floor with two tons of Semtex—which meant the chances were slim, at best, on escaping without getting incinerated. And so a single question lingered . . .

Why bother?

So Baz showed 'em what was in the vault.

That ribbon of intricate computer code danced above the holo-display, sparkling in everyone's eyes. A few quiet sighs . . .

"Jesus, that's it, isn't it?" Carlo spoke for all of them.

"Just one . . ." Ria confirmed they were staring at a strain of Otto's legendary Narcsoft. ". . . of hundreds."

"Pristine. Pre-encryption." Eddie added.

Baz spelled it out so there was no confusion. "Inside Otto's vault, on a brick of glass, are the digital masters to every Narcsoft flavor Otto Rex has ever sold."

And it all became crystal clear. The Score to End All Scores for every criminal in that room.

"Priceless code . . ." Eddie marveled.

"In a Fort Knox vault."

"How much is it worth?" Devyn asked.

The question everyone was asking themselves.

Baz looked to Ria.

"Two billion. If we sell it on the street."

"But . . ." Baz interjected as rehearsed. "It's worth *twice* that to the hacker cartels down South and in Kiev."

Jesus fucking Christ, everyone thought.

On a Popsicle stick.

"How the fuck is some Street Meat pimp sittin' on four billion ¢rypto?" Devyn asked.

Quinn corrected her quick: "Rex ain't some *pimp*. He's on a whole 'nother lev—"

"So we plan on just waltzin' in and robbin' him?" Carlo challenged Baz, glaring. "Tell me you got some angle, 'cuz it's been a long time since you pulled anything even close to this."

Everyone looked at Baz, who again turned to Ria.

"The 'Seven Year Itch.' Five Saturdays from today is the seventh anniversary of the Fang, and the only night of the year that Otto will venture outta his penthouse. It's when his grid and that vault will be most vulnerable."

"How're you sure he'll be there?" Carlo stared at her.

"He's emceeing it."

Something about her tone—and the authority of being Otto's go-to for years—sealed the deal in everyone's minds.

So Baz dropped the kicker: "Split eight ways . . . you're looking at 500 million ¢rypto. *Each.*"

There was officially zero oxygen in the room.

"You have a decision to make . . . right now." Baz could see the greed and fear burning in everyone's eyes.

"Are you in, or are you out?"

The first dumb question of the night.

CASING

Baz was right, everyone in the crew needed sumthin'.

Starting with Devyn.

Sparks sailed off the welding torch, and Ria wondered if they were technically underwater. She'd heard of the Carbon Crypts in the Port of Oakland, and figured they were either a myth or hidden beneath the warehouses that stored off-loaded cargo coming in from Shenzhen's container ships. But she never figured they'd be on board one of the boats themselves, 'til Devyn walked her onto her favorite, the *Pangu*.

"Gimme the forks." Devyn pulled the blast-mask off and Ria passed 'em to her.

'Cuz the 'Busa needed some work.

Saving the planet from climate collapse came with a few sacrifices, and combustion was one of them. All carbon emissions were illegal without a licensing waiver, which Eddie could hack from the DMV and pirate fairly easily—*after* the work on the 'Busa was done. But it was those sparks that were the problem.

"And the supercharger?" Ria had it ready and waiting.

The asphalt between the Fang and Fisherman's Wharf required

titanium forks to hold stripe outta the nightclub, a layer of Smart Tread to corner onto Broadway, and an in-line supercharger for the long stretch of Columbus straight to the Bay. Which all needed to be welded or plasma-fused onto the 'Busa, and with federal Carbon Drones patrolling the Bay Area 24/7 for unlicensed emitters, Devyn insisted on two things: They do the work under the cover of the *Pangu*. And she would do the welding herself.

"Here." She traded the welding torch for a cauterizing iron.

Ria eyed the carbon-scrubbing slakers and calciners fixed to the cargo hold's ceiling hundreds of feet up, then to the dozens of other machinists and grease monkeys who'd also paid the Oakland Triads for access to this off-grid smoke shop. As big as these ships looked grazing the bottom of the Golden Gate Bridge before descending the seawall's central lock . . . from the floor of an *empty* hold, they were beyond enormous.

"You could park a Colonial 5 rocket in this thing."

Devyn turned and stared at her.

"Sorry."

Trading war stories over the Glitch, Ria knew how Devyn's parents were fending off a divorce when a Therapy Bot went Haywire and iced 'em both. Took two off-grid courier gigs just to stay in flight school at SpaceX. And the irony that her second job's last delivery was when a Tesla truck jackknifed and forced Devyn to choose between death or the guardrail was not lost on Ria.

"You know my marks went up," Devyn said, cinching a timing chain.

Ria could tell she'd touched a nerve.

"Physiology, Zero-G, even Orbital Mechanics—I was just a better pilot after the accident. But once you-know-who pushed the Anti-Augment Act through . . . He wouldn't dare let a Plus-40 go up."

Ria wished there was some way she could assure Devyn: *it ain't over yet, gurl.* Instead, she just voiced what the whole world muttered every day.

"Fuck Sir Musk."

Devyn nodded, forced a smile, and eyed the 'Busa. The bike was good to go, save one last piece of gear. They probly could've risked a carbon drone catching 'em with the rest of the items, but this thing was so illegal they needed the *Pangu* to weld it to the 'Busa, 'cuz it thwarted the underlying principle to the very world they lived in . . .

The Surveillance State of America.

Ria'd been standing on Broadway and Columbus when Devyn nodded to the virt-cams positioned all the way down both blocks. "Those are the real problem."

Ria saw the SFPD emblem beside every capture-lens and remembered Quinn's warning as Devyn explained further: "Otto's got SFPD on payroll. When I open up, those cams'll get rerouted to an orbital AI that'll figure out where I'm going before I do."

Ria thought about it for a second. "So palm multiple ID's into the 'Busa. Scan me, Baz, Eddie, even Moxie, and every virt-cam will read you as a different ghost."

"No one gets palmed into that bike but *me*." Scanning a palm-print into the 'Busa's ignition grip was like handing over the keys to Devyn's livelihood. Could Ria blame her for refusing?

"So? . . ." She wondered if the wheelman had a solve.

"A Ghost Cloak."

Ria did a bad job at hiding her shock.

"I know they aren't cheap. But they're invisible. I'll barely even anomalize."

Meaning Devyn, the 'Busa, and the data-drives of stolen Narcsoft would read like a digital artifact, an anomaly, the tiniest little glitch on each virt-cam down Columbus. It weighed ten kilos and needed a power supply as beefy as the 'Busa, but a Ghost Cloak was exactly what Devyn promised: invisible.

Ria stared at her on Broadway, wondering the same thing then that she was sure of now as she handed over the ¢25 million Ghost Cloak.

Devyn was sliced open on an operating table from her gullet to her gut, and close to half of what ticked or flexed inside her came from a factory. She lived and died on the back of a steel stallion that clocked over 200 knots.

Maybe Ria should just trust her.

———

Eddie found himself in a similar sitch with Moxie.

To call Quinn's now heavily bleached steam room "sterile" was a stretch. But Dr. Marcus, the neurosurgeon eyeing Moxie on the Irishman's massage table, was short on time and charging more per hour than a US senator, so he just looked at Eddie through surgical scrubs and a fully cracked jack and gave him a nod—

'Cuz Moxie was goin' under the knife.

Eddie'd hacked and modified the pre-encrypted Thrilz baseline to trigger remotely from inside the Grid Room at the Fang. The mutated high would lose some elegance and all its self-deletion, but as they were testing the transmitter down the block from the club, Moxie dropped the real wrinkle in the plan:

"Otto's rolling out two new flavors for the Seven Year Itch. So if I'm gonna move product *and* upsell Thrilz? . . . I need a third slot."

Eddie stared at her. He figured Moxie would just yank the modified Thrilz before its mania kicked in, so he struggled to wrap his head around what she wanted.

She touched the I/O behind her right ear. "One."

Behind her left. "Two."

Then she lifted her tongue—where there was no slot. (yet) "Three."

The hardest of hardcore Narcheads loved to triple-slot—usually an up, down, and a psychedelic *all at once*—which Eddie figured was like slamming the accelerator, brake, and ejection seat at the same time. You could put your third slot anywhere, but as a badge of honor and a nod to the days of candy-flipping windowpane, those in the know went sublingual.

"You're gonna trust an augment kiosk at Dolores—"

"Are you outta your gourd?" Moxie laughed. "Just 'cuz it's going under the tongue doesn't make it easy as transplanting one."

Eddie watched Dr. Marcus—a client of his with a penchant for nocturnal affairs—access Moxie's wetwire, scroll through its neuronal array and activate her GABA and NMDA receptors, replicating what general anesthetic once did, 25 medieval years ago. As Moxie's eyelids grew heavy and she failed to finish a back-count from ten to zero, Eddie remembered being impressed by her acute understanding of the procedure.

"I need all five senses spliced off my cortex and a seven-fiber run through the larynx and into an optical I/O—there's no fucking way I'm letting some Dolores Park hack do that."

"Then how're you gonna get the implant?"

"You're the CrackerJack. Figure it out."

Eddie thought back to Quinn's warning about Slingers sellin' you out, and he wondered if he could really trust Moxie? But then again, Moxie *was* third-generation dealer. From Gram's first pot dispensary in the Castro, to her parents' fleet of shroom-shops when legalization hit in '28, she'd been born and raised on the motto Stitches for Snitches. So she'd probably adhere to it, since she'd heard it every day of her life, until three years ago when Ma and Pa slotted some bootleg Pixie Dust from Otto's rival.

And skull-fried deadman at a Best Western.

———

Ria had to *feel* what Carlo needed, to understand.

The Flyboy dragged her avatar up, down, and sideways through the VR-airspace of the Dubai Dark Bazaar. Tastes and smells from 360 degrees of merchants and vendors sailed all around her, maxing the RAM capacity in her wetwire . . .

'Cuz in this construct, Ria could fly.

The infamous off-grid virtual marketplace catered only to the highest-level hackers and handful of tictaters across the globe. Neither Carlo, Ria, nor even the servers were in Dubai, but the construct was generated off its magnificent skyline, circa 2038—twinkling how that gem once did, before the Saudi Front opened on the Water Wars.

"*Now* do you get it?!" Carlo hollered back at her.

Pink, amber, and deep indigo flashed against her wetwire as they soared over and under floating vendor stalls and upload stands—

"This is what a Flyboy Run is like?" Ria's eyes were wide with wonder as black code flew by—firmware payloads, BIOS arrays, brute-force compilers—anything a criminal hacker could crave, which Carlo sifted through fast, spending ¢35 million in an hour.

"This immersive, yeah." Carlo nodded.

They were sitting now at Top of the World, which was more like hanging upside down, since the restaurant bar was designed *under* the observation deck at the Burj Khalifa. Took a minute for Ria to get used to its inverse gravity, which Carlo claimed he'd helped code when the Bazaar first launched five years ago.

"You wrote this?" Ria marveled at the earth above, the moon and stars below.

"No, what I wrote . . . is *that*"—gesturing to the Sazerac he'd ordered her. A bead slowly disobeyed gravity, traced inside the rim, and fell "down" between her lips. It tasted delicious.

"Okay, Flyboy, I'm impressed." She leaned back and felt her wetwire trigger the precise number of 5-HT dendrite sites to replicate alcohol *and* absinthe, and as that calming shiver shot through her spine—the world . . . was . . . chill.

"Baz says you lost your family in the Glitch," Carlos said.

"Yeah, Dani died in my arms."

"Who?"

Ria snapped back. "My brother Daniel. He was . . . two when our Nanny Bot broke his neck." She kicked herself for letting her guard down. "So why'd you bring me here, to show off? You could've bought all this solo."

Carlo just stared at her for a sec. "I want Eddie monitoring my run on the vault."

Ria stayed on the attack. "Since when do you fly in tandem? I figured you for a lone wolf."

"I make exceptions when I'm gafflin' billions from a kingpin."

Was his arrogant smile a dodge? She couldn't be sure if his sarcasm was more than just attitude, since she was lying her ass off too.

"Eddie can't just watch my code in his periphery. He has to interact with it, ratchet into my hack and the antiviral's defense from a quadrillion bytes away and back again. That's a TON of data."

Ria looked up at the Persian Gulf, trying to fathom the sheer volume of computations within the 1,700-foot liquid ceiling of Jumeirah Beach above . . . "You're talking 'bout a Ring of Fire."

A graphene lasso of fiber optics and display ports that projected in precise detail a Flyboy's Run in the air around him, so someone like Eddie could guide his hack. They were the highest-resolution holo-decks available—not just in VR-Dubai, but any market, anywhere. And since a Ring of Fire was never used for anything *legal*, its price tag was well over ¢30 million.

"Can't you and Eddie just sync your wetwires, synapse to synapse?" Ria leaned forward and another sip fell up to her.

"My dopamine inducer's set for my condition. It'll knock him out."

She tasted the Sazerac, pretty sure her own wetwire's dopamine inducer was cranking overtime to replicate the absinthe, and Ria wondered if Carlo had coded any of this place from his virtual padded cell.

She'd read his SSS and knew from his federal psyche report that the autistic schizophrenia he suffered from was exacerbated by cut-rate care ever since his first institutionalization at eight years old.

Fucking *eight*?

'Cuz Carlo's custom Wetwire.X didn't come cheap. But neither did a Ring of Fire. "Maybe we could pull the sync with a neural scan of a family member?"

Like DNA, his synaptic map carried more and more common vectors to closer and closer relatives. Now it was Carlo whose eyes narrowed. 'Cuz that psyche report's annual consent forms went blank when he hit thirteen and his parents abandoned him to the nightmare of a state-funded system. One visitor—identified only with the initials "K.Z."—stuck with Carlo for a while. But by the time he was fifteen, even those initials disappeared. And the kid sat in VR-solitary for years.

Carlo just darkened and dematerialized outta Data Space, his final words echoing like they spoke for the whole crew.

"I don't have any family."

————

Ria sat with Baz late that night after de-slotting, once her bearings had stabilized, and watched him build their evolving plan in his wetwire minute by minute, piece by piece.

"How was Dubai?"

"You saw his request. Carlo wants to run in tandem." But she caught Baz eyeing her.

"You guys talk about anything else?"

Ria bristled. No way Carlo mentioned her slip. *Right?* "What are you, jealous?"

"So jealous." That must've been it, since Baz just chuckled and went back to studying each piece of gear, its role in the heist, and the crew member who'd requested it. "Eddie's neurosurgeon is legit. But I wanna make sure Moxie's I/O holds."

Hours ticked by, and Ria could feel Baz take on the responsibility for each crew member's safety. "If we're even a minute behind, Devyn'll try to make it up, and who knows if that Smart Tread'll hold."

She couldn't help but admire him for it. Ria found herself wondering how many crews he'd assembled, how many capers he'd pulled. And as she glanced at the laundry list of gear they'd accumulated . . .

1. Ghost Cloak
2. Third Slot
3. Ring of Fire

Ria wanted to tell Baz the truth.

But she shook that thought away and just focused on the gear. 'Cuz trusting Baz with who she really was, what her father really did, and what really brought them all together wasn't just counterproductive—it was fucking crazy, and she couldn't afford to start getting emotional now.

Could she?

Then Eddie buzzed from downstairs and saved her from doing something really stupid—thank fuckin' God—so together they could each add their own requests to the menu of specialty items:

```
4. High-Capacity Wetwire Drive
5. Glass-Titanium Stiletto
6. Pirelli
```

Ria had no idea what that last one was, but Baz just winked and insisted they needed it. All of the gear was easy to find, but a bitch to buy off-grid, aka expensive, so Baz took a ration of shit from Quinn before the bank shucked out the necessary ¢rypto.

But something else preoccupied Baz's thoughts, and Ria wasn't sure if he could read what she was thinking, or if it was something else . . .

"You okay?"

"Yeah, I'm fine."

But he wasn't.

'Cuz of how Marilyn brought the whole plan together.

NIGHTMARES

wutani.seductress.D1765
>Fang-penthouse<

Otto could see that glimmer in Marilyn's eye.

A week after he unsealed her learning cap, it ignited. He'd caught it in Trixie and a dozen other androids before, but this was the first time Otto'd ever *deliberately* blown a bot's cap. Sure, her sexual acrobatics turned nuclear thanks to self-awareness, but Otto started questioning whether he could really trust Marilyn anymore. 'Fact, he was lying up in bed that last week of August, thinking maybe he should just reseal his Bottom Bot . . . when she twitched in bed.

Otto turned to check if the rustle was really Marilyn, or his imagination. Then he leaned forward and struggled to comprehend what he was seeing. The synthetic skin on both eyelids trembled and shuddered. He leaned in closer and could hear her oxygenator's intake and outtake racing shallowly, and he wasn't sure whether this was an advanced form of mimicry, or if her REM pattern was real—

And Marilyn was *dreaming*.

wutani.seductress.D1765
>Lube.Genie-bath<

"Of what?"

Baz, Eddie, and Ria all asked at the same time. They were at the same servo shop where they'd met in Hunter's Point.

"Lots of things, really," Marilyn explained as a much-needed oil bath seeped into her hips. "They're quite incredible. Many times my fellow Chrome Domes are there. I can recall circumstances that date back to when I was first delivered to the Fang—and the most vivid dreams all seem obsessed with the same goal . . ."

Baz was all ears.

"Out."

His blood chilled. He remembered in Venezuela receiving praise from Otto and every other commander for being a perfect killing machine. As he caught his own reflection in the robot's eyes, Baz wondered for a moment, just who was more alive.

"So I predict with high probability there's but one component missing for him to want to record my cranial-CPU's nocturnal activity byte for byte . . ."

Baz looked at Ria. "Ding Moxie."

'Cuz Marilyn had found a way through the Inner Circle, or as Eddie explained later—a back door.

"And that's if Otto is in my dreams."

>Fang-penthouse<

Otto was hooked.

He'd synced with Marilyn so many times in the sack, you had to expect that *some* of his memories would intertwine with hers. But it was uncanny just what insatiable nightmares his Bottom Bot could conjure.

Sometimes she was a synthetic going AWOL in a kill squad in Venezuela. In others, a runaway sexbot sold long before Marilyn arrived. Once Marilyn even slotted an old-school fave wafer of the Scissor Sisters called Escape—and no android slotted, ever.

Otto knew he should just dumb her down, but too many of Marilyn's dreams included Otto *and* Ria. And by then he was possessed, on a mission to gather every last shred of data possible on Ria Rose.

He tried to record the visions remotely, but there was just too much bandwidth. So once a week, Otto'd have to assure Marilyn they would still be together. Whether she was dreaming right next to him in bed . . .

Or plugged into her neural chair.

>Lube.Genie<

"Why would I be *un*sure?" Marilyn asked right before they put the plan into action.

Baz shifted, a little uncomfortable. He'd never had any difficulty disclosing anything to a robot before. He wondered if there really was a difference between emulating consciousness and the real thing.

Or was it all in your head?

"'Cuz if we implant this in your cranial-CPU . . ." Baz held up a mem-drive. On it, Eddie'd coded countless memories of Otto, as recalled by the three of them—every Narcsoft flavor Moxie'd ever sold, dozens of sexbots Ria'd bought, and so many natives Otto'd eliminated in front of Baz—all carved onto a swappable glass data drive. ". . . then whatever spark's been generating your dreams will be slaved to this glass."

For the plan to work, they couldn't leave anything to chance, including Marilyn's newly found (and cherished) free will.

Ria and Eddie waited quietly.

They couldn't reseal Marilyn's learning cap now, without Otto knowing. They couldn't force her to acquiesce. So it was up to Marilyn to *choose* to relinquish a bit of herself.

But the bot didn't see it that way. "I don't think there's anything more alive," as Marilyn slid open the drive slot at the base of her titanium skull . . .

"Than being a slave to your dreams."

LATE-NIGHT CODING

The folder just floated in Marilyn's VUI.

It was close to 3:00 a.m., and Baz was in the crew's main workspace, converted from Quinn's "study," which had once been the bathhouse's ornate bistro, several sealed doors away from the main steam room.

Ancient oil paintings still adorned the walls between dozens of shelves with hundreds of books. Yes, real books. Baz hadn't seen one in at least a decade. He never understood why Quinn always bragged about being a voracious reader, since every SynGyn uploaded the Library of Congress in third grade.

Marilyn was in sleep mode on a sofa that looked older than the aristocrats on the walls, some relic Quinn called a Victorian settee. And Eddie'd installed a holo-array in the center of the room that was currently projecting her Virtual User Interface.

Baz started its shutdown protocol, when he noticed among a hundred folders and subroutines one called:

```
RR-DIMENSIONS
```

Huh. Wonder what that one could be?

5

The ballistics on a recoilless rifle?

4

Or the square-footage of Ronald Reagan's library?

3

Or maybe "RR" referred to something else.

2

Baz stopped the shutdown and stared at the file. He looked over his shoulder and around the room. Eddie'd knocked off and left him alone to prep Marilyn's chassis for her return to the Fang before dawn.

The shutdown sequence would cover her last three-hour servo service, and Baz knew there was at least a half hour to spare, so he glanced at the folder again. You know, maybe he'd just scan the meta-data to get a sense of its contents. Just in case he should show it to Ria.

Immediately he wished he hadn't.

```
32-22-34, breasts-adjustable
Perspiration + add'l tastes
Vocals: howls, shrieks, moaning
Gyrations, Quivers, Orgas—
```

Christ, WTF was this? Baz could tell from a few operational subroutines that the code linked directly to Marilyn's behaviorals, her pheromonal secretors, her external and internal dermis. Someone had coded Marilyn to act—and by act, Baz was sure that meant *to fuck*—just like Ria Rose.

"Otto, sometimes you shock even me."

He thought about the first time he met Ria. Black fatigues stretched tight over her hips.

Baz looked back at the folder.

His eyes drifted to one of those oils that must've been a couple hundred years old. The woman in the painting was blushing. The hem of her dress was around her ankles. There was something naughty about her smile that almost made Baz laugh.

He flashed to the first time Pops took him down into the basement. Nine years old, and his dad pulled out a drawer full of prehistoric artifacts called magazines. "Fuck Pornhub, son. Make that shit in your bathroom with a phone."

This must've been '28, back when people still had phones.

His dad unfolded huge pictorials of women with oversized lips, legs, and other organs that scared the shit out of young Baz. "Look at the sheen on that slut. This here is real photography, boy. This is art."

Baz snapped out of it.

He moved quick to delete the files, grabbing the folder off the 3D field—

"What are you doing?"

Baz spun and released it. "NOTHING."

Ria was standing in the doorway staring at him. "Were you about to open that?"

"How long have you been there?"

"How long have you been perusing those files?"

"Whoa-whoa-whoa, I wasn't *perusing* anything. I was gonna trash 'em."

"Uh-huh." She was early. She was supposed to swing by and initialize Marilyn with the Fang's daily passkey—but not 'til five.

Ria stepped forward and grabbed the RR-DIMENSIONS folder off the interface and pulled it into AR, where it hovered between the two of them. "'Cuz Otto smashes Marilyn every other night wired into a sim that looks just like me. Thanks to *those* files—"

"For reals. I'd never open 'em, no matter how bad—" She glared at him, so Baz just shut his mouth. "Pinky swear."

"The way you were staring, I need a napkin for the drool."

He wanted to say, "Fuck off," but didn't. Just gave her a look instead.

"Baz, I bilk fools professionally for all the ¢rypto they've got, with machines cut like a fantasy. I buy and sell that slack-jawed, wide-eyed gaze three or four hundred times a night—so trust me . . ." He didn't dare break eye contact. "It's the ugliest thing on earth."

"Please don't tell me I looked like one of those guys."

"Please don't tell me you *are* one of those guys."

He started to say, "I'm not,"—but stopped.

Talk's cheap.

Then Baz remembered where he was, sitting in their workspace among all the gig's gear. He hopped to his feet, fished through a crash-duffel on the far shelf, and returned with a flat wooden box with an ornate latch on it. "I was gonna wait, but . . ."

He placed the box in front of her. "Would a shmuck get you that?"

She looked at him cautious. "That better not be perfume and a thong."

Baz laughed. "Open it."

She unlatched the lid and opened the box, revealing the glass-titanium stiletto from the laundry list.

Ria just looked at him, confused. "I asked for that."

"Look closer."

Ria realized the blade sat on an overleaf. Underneath was a second tray with four more knives.

"I figured you'd probly need more than just a thrust-foil, so I got you a whole set." Baz leaned forward with a grin and pointed to each: "That's a Scottish dirk, great for slicin' and dicin'; that's an old-school bowie; a Foxbat that got me outta some nasty shit in Venezuela; and the last one's—"

"A Ka-Bar Zombie Killer," Ria said. "The Urbangear Combat Set in 12.62mm, a perfect fit for my augments."

Baz nodded with a smile. "Exactly, the Urbangear . . ." then he stopped, realizing . . .

"That's why I have one in graphene," Ria said.

Baz slumped. That naughty Victorian lady looked like she was laughing at him now. "Some women are just impossible to shop for."

Ria smiled. Touched his cheek lightly. "But it's the thought that counts, hero."

She stood up and started initializing Marilyn's cranial-CPU manually. "Lucky I caught you before you deleted those files."

"Why?"

"Otto's obsessed. If you trashed 'em, he definitely would've known something was up."

Baz realized, of course, she was right.

"And without Marilyn, we'd be blown."

COMMITTED

Baz looked at his crew, ready to drop a bombshell.

They were all seated round a big table on Quinn's rooftop, high-watt surveillance scramblers humming from all four corners as a fog bank slowly rolled in.

Baz nodded to Marilyn. "Otto's been hardwiring Miss Monroe into the Inner Circle every Saturday for a month."

The crew stirred, gripped by their luck. A back door through the Fang's internal security network? Even Quinn caught an edge, and he'd be sittin' poolside the whole weekend.

Baz had gone through the timeline twice already, but he'd stayed cagey 'bout their point of no return, 'til now.

"So when she sits into her neural chair for final sequencing, we're committed." He put the mem-drive on the table in front of them. "No turning back after that."

This one contained no memories. Just a *worm* that would hack Eddie and Carlo through the Inner Circle and onto the Central Core. And since Otto ran a full sweep every morning after closing, there'd be just a matter of hours once Marilyn's cranial-CPU uploaded it, before the breach would be caught and they'd be blown.

"So let's go over it again." Baz started in: "Doors open at eight . . ."

Ria watched him go through the plan, this time drilling down with such precise detail, that she just couldn't believe this guy was swiping Street Meat off cruise ships when she met him. Those were cheap liquor stickups in the Loin. This gig was bulletproof, an atomic Swiss watch with an *S* on its chest.

"Show starts at midnight." He finished up. "So, when that curtain goes up . . ."

"It's gametime." Ria smiled.

But she could feel the crew stir with even more restlessness.

So Baz leveled with 'em: "Look, you all know who we're dealing with. 22 precincts on the take, 17 Sentries inside the club, and an L7 over Otto's—" He froze.

Ria froze too. Then her augmented eardrum heard it—how did his sixth sense catch it first?

"Get *down*." Baz pulled his Soniq-7 and covered Quinn as the crew scattered to the corners of the roof and Ria heard the subtle beating of rotors grow louder . . .

An approaching drone squadron.

"SFPD?" Baz whispered.

"Impossible, I'm routed in," Eddie chimed.

"Wirecrime?" Ria looked at Baz, but he shook his head.

"They'd be full tilt with a ton of artillery."

Quinn wrestled free, "Get off me you fuckin' nutjob." He shook himself off and made his way to the center of the roof, looking up. "It's dinner."

Baz and Ria exhaled.

Sure enough, converging on the rooftop were three separate Aero-Meals, FeatherLite crates of takeout dangling.

"Goddammit, Quinn," Baz snapped. "We said nine—they're early."

"It *is* nine, you gasbag—you're late."

The three deliveries touched down in unison, dropping off a half dozen bags, and took off into the night. Quinn grabbed the meals and reassured everyone: "It's okay, kiddos, I saved Baz from blasting Madame Lu."

"I didn't order Madame Lu's," Moxie complained.

Quinn started unwrapping the food, "No, you, Ria, and Baz got Boudin, and Devyn wanted Petri Nation 'cuz none of you fuckin' runts could agree on anything."

"We're not done," Baz insisted to a communal groan. Ria looked at him to lay off, but he persisted. "We're goin' over the timeline again."

Moxie rolled her eyes. "You're joking, right? You think we missed something the fourth time around?"

"Maybe, Mox. You slot enough narc to flatline a rhino."

"Rhinos went extinct before slots."

Baz just stared at her.

"What? They did."

"Again." Baz nodded to Ria.

"Doors open at eight."

"Ria will be ready for us by nine. Marilyn's code goes hot at 10:30. Devyn, you're six blocks away on the edge of Chinatown, goosin' the 'Busa to meet us on the side alley. So, Moxie, don't sell a single Thrilz wafer, until *when*?" Baz stared at Carlo . . . who didn't say anything. "Carlo, the signal for Moxie?"

"Sorry, were you talking to me?"

"I'm looking right at you."

"Right, got it—what was the question?" A glance at Madame Lu's.

"Are you thinkin' about the timeline, or are you looking at those potstickers?"

"I'm thinkin' at the timepot," Carlo assured him. "I mean, I'm stickin' to the line-time."

"It's gonna get cold," Eddie griped.

"Eddie."

"What? I just . . . You know it's almost 9:15."

"It's 9:12."

"Exactly. And in 72 hours flat, I'll be walking in the Fang."

"Topping off the 'Busa," said Devyn.

"Backstage," said Marilyn.

"On the floor," said Moxie.

"And I'll be waiting for you in the lobby," Carlo chimed in, "'cuz Moxie won't start moving Thrilz 'til all three of us see a clean run on the vault. Can we eat now, old man?"

Everyone stared at Baz. Guess they'd been listening after all.

"I'm 32." He shifted. "And yes. Let's eat."

Feeding time at the trough. Hands ripped through containers, searching for dishes and checking ingredients. Ria threw Baz a look, like maybe the crew's nervous energy earlier wasn't just nerves. Maybe they were starving.

Carlo recoiled from a dish, "Shit, I can't eat these dumplings—they're pork."

"They're synthetic pork," Quinn reassured him.

"I don't eat any kind of pork."

Devyn grabbed the box. "I'll eat 'em. Synth food's easier on a synth stomach."

"Agreed," Marilyn chimed as she pulled a vacuum-sealed protein pack from her vintage Pucci clutch and tore it open.

Eddie stared at the sludge oozing into an empty ramen bowl. "Does it taste like barf too?"

"I'm coded so it tastes like chicken tonight."

"What's it really taste like?"

"Chicken."

He laughed.

"Care for some?" Marilyn asked.

"No." Eddie said. But Ria watched him reconsider the protein paste, like some kid in an IRL cafeteria switching from disgust to FOMO.

"Actually, you know . . . I've never tried droid food." Eddie extended his finger, and Marilyn squeezed out the last drop to taste. "Hmm . . . Chicken pudding."

Groans all around.

Baz cut into his flat iron and tried not to sag.

Ria glimpsed at her own barely pink steak. The beef was real, costing more than the squadron that delivered it, but cooked—sacrilege—medium well. "Yours isn't rare either?"

Baz took a bite and forced a smile. "I hate ordering ghosted."

Quinn just stared, irritated. "Check the ticket, I wrote down 'rare' on both your orders, exactly what you told me."

"Jesus Christ, you *wrote* it?" Carlo was shocked.

"Right?" Moxie laughed. "Last time I *told* someone an order, I was seven."

"Oh, fuck all of you." Quinn gave 'em two synthetic middle fingers. "Can't do shit without that chip in your head."

Eddie spoke low: "Said the rhino."

And everyone cracked up. Quinn just pulled a joint from behind his ear and tapped his bare skin. "Laugh it up, but when you ain't got no slots, you get lit ole-school."

Eddie opened a bottle of mezcal, pouring eight strong snorts, which he made sure everyone knew was his family label in Oaxaca. Carlo joked that every Oaxacan with an agave bush and a mud hut had a family label, so Ria quickly raised her glass amid the Mexican standoff—"*Salud!*"

And everyone shot the hooch.

Then everyone coughed up a lung.

Eddie inhaled deep. "I said, someone bring a lemon . . ."

Ria reached into her pocket, since she'd—

"So let's hear it, Miss Rose." Quinn puffed a big toke, letting the oily smoke coat his scorched throat. "Half a bill gets you anywhere . . . Where to?"

Ria froze, caught off-guard. Her mind blanked, like the mezcal blurred her vision beyond the few feet in front of her. "Um, same place everyone's goin' . . . Out."

Baz looked over, confused.

Moxie dipped an egg roll in duck sauce. "I'm taking my shit to Berlin. Or at least, what's left of Berlin."

"Space." Devyn threw a devious smile at Ria, like she'd been waitin' her whole life to exit planet Earth. "Finally."

"Fuck outta here," Carlo scoffed. "Where? Axiom-V?"

Devyn nodded.

"You're slotted. Takes more than a half bill to buy a spot on the V."

"Sure, if you pay full boat. But I got a few peeps that'll orbit me wholesale."

Carlo's eyes lit up, "Then I'm slippin' you a hard-jack for the V's servers. 'Cuz I ain't gettin' Out—I'm all *In*."

Baz stiffened. "What's that, Z?"

"You heard me. Hit Dubai with a half bill? Top-tier compilers outta Osaka. Cortical buffers to go toe-to-toe with any A—"

"You never fuckin' learn, kid . . ."

"I'm not your kid, old man."

"Then stop acting like—"

"'Least I'm not a killer!"

"A *what*?" Ria cut in.

But neither responded. The same strange energy from when she first met Carlo, only now it wasn't simmering under the surface, it'd boiled over, and Ria was gonna find out why—

"Does anyone care where I plan to go?" Marilyn asked, stopping everyone cold.

Ria blinked. She'd never even given it a nano of thought.

"It's like the Protectorate. But instead of no bots, there are no humans." Marilyn smiled wistfully. "The Sentient Commune in the Danakil."

"The what?" Quinn asked, baked.

"Ethiopia. The last recorded raindrop was in 2035. No one cares about a bot with a blown cap in the Danakil Desert."

An image flashed in Ria's mind of a subterranean protein plantation under the sands of Ethiopia farmed by an army of fuckbots. She stifled a laugh.

"Yo, hold up." Carlo glared. "Ria never answered the question. How does someone put together a gig like this and *have no idea what she's gonna do with it?*"

Ria felt everyone's eyes on her. And now the answer was obvious. But she took a beat, considering how to say it. Fished the perfect prop out of her pocket and placed what looked like a green golf ball on the table between her and Carlo.

"What is that, a lime?"

"It's a lemon, actually." She whipped a graphene Ka-Bar outta her forearm and sliced it into eight small wedges. "That'll take the edge off."

"Kinduva runt, no?" Eddie chuckled.

"I grew that." Ria poured another shot, dropped it, and sucked the citrus, exhaling hotly. "Despite my best efforts."

"I thought you were babysitting for a friend," Baz recalled.

But Ria just stared into the distance, eyes watering from the booze, and maybe the memory . . . "There was a bot at the Fang who got smart and bolted."

"Who, Trixie?" Marilyn asked.

Ria nodded. "You know she got her own place."

The bot turned deathly quiet. Just looked into her lap.

"And when Otto made me reseal her, it rattled me. Bad. So I tracked down the apartment. And found her garden."

Marilyn looked at her.

"Four tomatoes, four peppers, and four dwarf lemons. And while this disgusting meatbag of a landlord watched, I transplanted each one and brought 'em back to my pad."

Ria broke into laughter. "Then I killed every single plant."

Baz watched her. This must've been the first time she'd laughed in front of him. Like, a real, genuine laugh . . .

"Please don't take this the wrong way, Marilyn, but some goddamn machine can grow twelve fuckin' plants like a pro, and *I*'ve got the black thumb?"

"Trixie meant that much to you?"

"No . . . But the night I dumbed her down, Otto attacked me."

Baz flexed with rage.

"Tried to rape me in the stairwell at the Fang."

You could hear a pin drop.

"And I didn't even flinch. Might've been why he let me go, really." She looked first to Carlo then to the whole crew. "You wanna know what I'm gonna do with my share? I'm gonna destroy Otto Rex. I'm gonna burn him and his whole goddamn operation to the ground."

"'Cuz of a bot?" Carlo asked.

"'Cuz if I don't, he will hunt us down like Trixie and kill every last one of us."

There was a long silence.

'Til Quinn busted into a huge laughing roar. Maybe at first, because of the weed. But then because of Ria: it was his only way of dealing with unvarnished honesty. "Amen, sister."

The Irishman stood up abruptly and excused himself, chuckling as he retired downstairs. "Christ, Baz, you can pick 'em."

A pall of silence remained.

Baz and Ria just stared at each other. Until one by one, each crew member got up quietly to leave.

Salutations. Some pleasantries. Even a hug or two.

But something had changed.

As Ria watched everyone split, an emotion suddenly swept over her. Odd, but it was a feeling she realized she'd been longing for since the Glitch, if not longer—maybe since her mom got sick—but she couldn't put her finger on it 'til right now.

These losers kinda felt like a family.

THE ITCH

Baz led Eddie down Polk, banged a left onto Turk, and stopped. He'd sold Otto stolen bots for years, but he'd never set foot in his club. And that first glimpse was always a showstopper. The joint was packed with a crowd spilling onto the cobblestones as HydroJags and Maybachs rolled up and Valet Bots took 'em away. Old-school neon and LEDs flashed the number 7 everywhere, but Baz's gaze focused on the massive holo-sign crawling up the narrow alleyway. No English or Sino-Fusion, just two vampire incisors dripping blood that heralded:

THE FANG

Eddie stood next to Baz, across from those bleeding teeth. "I'll be in your head as soon as she gets us in the Grid Room."

But Baz didn't say anything.

"Gear's inside?" Eddie asked, already knowing the answer.

Baz just nodded. "In the Dungeon downstairs."

5 HOURS EARLIER

Baz stopped by Quinn's compound to pick up the Pirelli along with a sensor scanner and the sling-pack he'd need to haul twenty pounds of glass data outta the Fang without anyone noticing.

As Baz spec'd the items, he could feel Quinn's eyes on him . . .

Then the Irishman dropped a pair of resident visas marked "Tahitian Protectorate" on the table, and Baz's heart skipped a beat.

"Second one's for Eddie. Said it was fine if I gave you both of 'em."

Baz exhaled casually, but by then it was too late.

"Looks like you were hopin' the second was for someone else." Quinn said with a knowing smile.

"Huh?" Baz played dumb. But he shifted, a bit uncomfortable. Unsure of whether the way Quinn was staring at him was just stressin'. Or judgmental.

"Haven't told her 'bout the NSA, have you?"

Then Baz knew it was both.

Quinn leaned in close to get a good look. "Yup . . . You got that same cocky look in your eye too. Guess she doesn't know about—"

"Fuck are you tryin' to do, Quinn, rattle me?"

If the geezer had any goddamn doubts, why was he here? And if so, why bring 'em up *now* for chrissakes?

But Quinn just stuck his finger in Baz's chest:

"Get that bitch outta your head."

9:31 P.M.

Eddie glanced now at Baz, whose eyes stayed fixed on the Fang— its teeth bleeding a crimson glow down both their faces. His partner's nerves were obvious, so he waited patiently. 'Til Baz took a deep breath . . .

"Let's do this."

And they walked across the street.

"We're on the list," Baz said as they approached the ropes, but the Door Bot, Prinella, just shook her head, and McT moved forward ominously.

"You don't remember me, do you?" Baz realized McT's backup didn't include the firefight, since the Warrior Bot just barked at him:

"Back of the line, fossil."

"You know you were a lot nicer deactivated," Eddie said.

"I got this one, McT." Ria appeared.

Off her nod, Prinella opened the ropes.

"Guess she doesn't trust you, T." Baz smiled at the Warrior Bot. "I wouldn't take it personally."

"Why would I?" McT lifted his Resonance Sequencer and waved the wand over Baz's body, whose cranium flashed:

>Angola·Refugee<

CLASSIFICATION
Human

"She doesn't trust anyone."

Then that ego-shot of adrenaline pounded into Baz and Eddie, escorted personally inside the hottest club on earth for its biggest night of the year, as every club kid and socialite in line stared them down with raging envy.

Ria led Eddie and Baz down the hallway, the two trading nods, ready to dart through an indistinguishable service door and into the labyrinthian corridors backstage, when she stopped.

"We got a problem."

3 HOURS EARLIER

Marilyn was walking slowly towards the neural chair.

Otto held her hand, inviting the android forward to upload her dreams. But tonight, her cranial-CPU contained a worm ready to fester deep into the Fang, putting in motion her freed—

—a GLITCH sparked across her vision, another and another—

She tried to turn around—glints blasting through her right eye as Otto pummeled it repeatedly—her left eye struggled to maintain power and refocus—and she couldn't tell if his tears were from sorrow or joy, but she could make out a few guttural words:

"You're nuthin' . . . *like* . . . HER!"

Then Marilyn realized it was just perspiration running down the kingpin's cheeks . . . as the bot drew its last conclusion:

Otto'd always planned to end her like this.

Then everything. Went BLACK.

9:35 P.M.

"WHAT?!" Baz and Eddie were shocked.

Ria just nodded.

She and Moxie had found the Bottom Bot an hour ago on the floor of a trash chute—a heap of torn synthetic skin, fiber optics, and a shattered eye socket that resembled Ria's own cauterized scar . . .

She recalled how Otto glared at Marilyn weeks ago when Ria interrupted their sim, but she *never* thought he'd take it so far.

"We gotta get the fuck outta here," Eddie warned, and Baz didn't disagree. "If Otto wasted her, we're next."

Ria just held up the bot's mem-drive.

"You sure?"

Ria'd found the glass containing Eddie's worm intact within Marilyn's oily and dented skull-shell. "He wouldn't leave this . . . if he had any idea what we were up to."

Eddie slowly took the drive to confirm it was theirs.

"Tonight's not blown yet."

Baz could see the level of commitment in her eyes. She was all in on the Narcsoft, all in on tonight, all in on everything: the Seven Year Itch was her only chance.

"What are we gonna do, sneak into Maintenance and plug this in manually?" Eddie asked.

"Why not? It's the only night of the year he's not watching it like a hawk."

But Baz played it out: "Even if we could, we'd need her Bot-ID . . . first."

She just stared at him, three chess moves ahead.

"What?"

But Ria wasn't gonna say the words, so she spoon-fed it to him instead. "Every sexbot's got the same daily encrypt as Marilyn . . ."

Eddie started to smile.

"Oh." 'Cuz then Baz understood too.

They *could* crack the Inner Circle—

If someone cracked a fuckbot first.

"So our worm still gets past the unit-to-unit network if one of us gets down with a robot?"

Ria and Eddie just stared at him.

Baz closed his eyes slowly. "Me?"

"Who else?" Ria asked.

"Have Eddie do it."

"I gotta be in the Grid Room with Carlo," Eddie reminded.

"So you do it."

"Are you kidding? Otto would lose his shit. 'Cuz male fantasies like that?"—gesturing to a Barbie Bot strutting by—"Aren't my type."

"Goddammit, Baz. Why do you get to have all the fun?"

"I'm not gettin' down with a sexbot."

"C'mon, dude. Once you go bot, you never go back."

"Shut up, Eddie."

Ria was kinda shocked by his resolve, 'til Eddie cackled, "Just like the Underground Butcher!"

This was why Ria couldn't say it. They'd be making the exact same move her father had made eight years ago to start the Glitch. 'Cuz the safeguards that came mandatory on every bot ever since, were written in-house at the Fang . . . and a sieve to a CrackerJack like Eddie.

"Between the knees, dude—like a virus!"

Ria's heart caved. Eddie didn't know what he was saying—didn't have any idea how many jokes she'd endured over the years. But it didn't matter, Ria's mood swing triggered her Poker Face. She could tell Baz was more than irritated, maybe even *hurt*—but the vault was all that mattered. So Ria found the will to muscle out the words: "You got a problem with synthetic sex?"

"I got a problem with paying for it."

But she sensed there was another reason why he couldn't wrap his head around this. Maybe his whole soul was wrapped around why. And that same alarm sounded loud in Ria again—that Baz was *hiding something.*

But then again, so was she.

They found themselves staring at each other for the longest second either could remember—both drawn and repelled by this vector of past trauma and potential opportunity, until Baz finally broke the moment and grabbed the drive.

"Fine. But I promise you I'm not gonna enjoy it."

Ria stopped him. "You have to enjoy it. Sexbots aren't vulnerable to a hack until the Excitement Phase."

"English?"

"Make it to the money shot, buddy." Eddie chuckled, heading upstairs.

And there was nothing left to say.

So Baz just moved past Ria through the narrow gloss-black hallway, red and black light painting down from the ceiling. He could smell the sweat and sex in the air, the bass rumbling under his feet, the din of voices echoing off the walls as he made his way through the second set of double doors, opening on . . .

"Whoa."

BARELY LEGAL

Baz was in awe.

The dance floor was ringed in teal neon and soaked in black light, with hot-spots throwing pools on Dance Bots in cages hanging from the ceiling. A main stage reigned supreme over the cavernous space with a holo-neon marquee arcing overhead proclaiming:

"The Seven Year Itch"

Sexbots strolled around like Parisian provocateurs at Les Chandelles Virtuelles, beckoning any patron to take a walk on the wild side. The joint oozed sensuality as it shook your pelvis, and Ria must've known what Baz was thinking, 'cuz she walked past whispering . . .

"Welcome to the Fang."

Alpha and Omega were the pair of robotic bartenders that responded to either name, depending on whether you were saddling up or had had too many. Baz did a double take, recognizing both Nubotica Mixologist.5s from the Royal Caribbean's *Diamond of the Seas*, where he'd swiped 'em a year ago.

And now he understood why the fence paid twice what their sallow synthetic skin was worth. Only a kingpin like Otto could afford to throw both bots in a vat of acid and send 'em to a polishing shop 'til their titanium chassis sparkled behind the bar.

Otto appeared at the second-floor balcony, surveying his sexbots and their patrons with obvious disdain. Ria slammed her telelens tight onto his face as he locked eyes with Baz.

A nod between two ex-soldiers on the front lines of a new war.

4 YEARS AGO

Last time Baz saw Otto IRL—and the only time since the skinshop in Caracas—was the first piece of Street Meat he sold him. Otto was known to hate deals even more than dealing with people, so he only met his peddlers once. And that was once more than either of 'em wanted. Otto looked at Baz like a shit magnet. Cursed. Bad juju. And who knows? He might've been right.

A decommissioned Nubotica Preacher Bot sat between them—a test Baz would pass, if its cranial-CPU was undamaged and reprogrammable for some real kinky shit at the Fang. He kinda felt bad stealing it, seeing as attendance was soaring at the Temecula Kingdom Hall of Jehovah's Witnesses. But he felt even worse selling it to Otto, whose smug attitude implied that he'd been right all along. Like this deal meant the morality Baz fought so violently for in Venezuela was just as synthetic as the sermons the bot preached every Sunday.

Otto's gloat was short but sweet.

"I told you you'd be back, Covane."

Baz knew that the word was out, how shit went upside-down ugly for him and one of his Flyboys. Pulling jobs no one would pull, his crew'd been roaring hot ever since the Glitch. But Baz wondered if Otto'd found out they hit the NSA Data Mine. 'Cuz that shit was ballsy AF, even for Baz.

"Your offer was just too good."
"Or your last gig just too deadly?" Otto threw him a look.

And then Baz was sure he knew. That his infamous Body Count had added one more soul to its roster. Which must've been why Otto dinged him. 'Cuz the truth was, if Baz wanted easy ¢rypto, without drawing the kind of antiviral software that killed a muthafucka? He was better off boosting Street Meat—instead of hacking the NSA's most lethal AI.

9:46 P.M.

Otto's sixth sense exploded on the Fang's balcony.
"What is he doing here?" Otto asked, coming down the stairs, eyes locked on Baz across the dance floor.
"Getting a drink, from the looks of it," Ria said casually.
Otto moved past, across the dance floor, oscillating between disdain for Baz the Snake Eyes and nostalgia for his ex-soldier turned criminal.
"Baz Covane, in the flesh. Fuck brings you into my club?"
"Just enjoying the hospitality."
Otto smiled and popped an olive in his mouth. "Last time I saw you around this many beautiful girls . . . You lit 'em on fire."
"Really?" Ria joined them, eyeing first Otto then Baz. "I can't imagine him that charming."
Baz threw her a look, but Otto kept staring at him. 'Cuz he could see in those eyes, a glint of the same flame from that night in Venezuela years ago. It was gone when Baz sold him the Preacher Bot, and Otto figured the fighter in him had finally died. But here he was, swingin' in the ring again.

"I'm busted," Baz conceded. "I needed that Robo-Rockette deal. Figured I'd put eyes on your inventory myself."

Otto licked his lips. "Fuckin' damn shame not a single one survived. Like I said to Ria, I'da paid triple to blow the back out on a Rockette." He caught Baz stiffen. "What, she didn't tell you?"

"No," Baz groaned, glaring at her. "She told me. Just hurts thinkin' about it."

Ria stayed cool, icy eyes at half-lid. "Any idea where we might be down a bot, boss?"

Otto bristled, remembering the heap of synthetic flesh and servos formerly known as Marilyn. Then he turned back to Baz with actual *pity*. "You just don't quit, do you, Covane? Hope shit don't turn nasty on your crew . . . again."

Otto smiled like a prophet and pulled Ria away, around a corner out of earshot, digging his nails into her augmented forearm as he stared into her real eye.

"How well do you know him?" Otto's alarm was ringing, his furnace raging again—

And Ria was counting on it.

"He choked the Rockettes deal." She didn't need her Poker Face to blank his suspicions. "Want me to bounce him?"

Ria could manipulate the kingpin with ease.

"No." Otto's gears crankin' overdrive. "But Covane's a skid mark . . . Keep an eye on him for me."

Ria had to hide her smile.

Otto returned to Baz at the bar on his way to McT . . . "I'm gonna comp you with St. Jane, pal. Same model as Marilyn."

And then Otto was gone.

But Baz's hair was standing on end even minutes later. "You cratered our deal, didn't you?"

She looked at him and didn't deny shit.

"Jesus Christ, of course you did. I can't believe—I could've been outta the Loin, you devious little—what'd you waste those Rhythm Thiefs yourself?"

"Damn right I did."

"Why would—"

"'Cuz I needed you on this job almost as bad as you did. You were out in the bush leagues pushin' fuck toys 'til I showed up. Now you're right where you should be. You're the best."

He stopped. "Do you really mean that?"

"Did it sound canned?"

"No. Actually, the 'best' part. . . That works."

"Good. 'Cuz he asked me to keep an eye on you." She slipped him a whiskey and a sly smile and raised her glass. "Cheers."

To the first job at the Fang she'd enjoy.

Baz chuckled, a little looser. "Then let's dance."

"I don't dance." Another rule Ria lived by.

But Baz insisted. To get a better look down the back hallway and maybe loosen himself up a little more. And Ria couldn't see a lot of options, since they both needed a distraction to chill out.

"What was Otto talking about?" she asked once they were holding one another.

"Ahh . . . He always suspects something, right?"

But it was Ria who was suspicious now . . . that the "nasty" Otto mentioned and what Baz was hiding, just might be the same thing. So she stared at him, trying to figure it out. Until finally, she realized what she'd wanted to ask him since that night with the laundry list. Maybe since he'd saved her life . . .

"How come you're alone?"

Baz laughed lightly. But she wasn't gonna let him dodge her instincts any longer. "I mean, you're an outlaw, sure. You're an acquired taste. But you're not a scumbag."

A compliment coming from her.

"But you don't even have a Side Bot somewhere. You're like, actually all alone." It should have stung, but the way she said it pulled them closer. "Why?"

"You mean was there someone . . ." *Else* hung in the air, unspoken.

"Yeah." Ria said softly. "That's what I mean."

Baz's muscles constricted. His fingers tightened around the small of her back, shifted up her shoulder blades to the skin on her neck.

They'd been dancing like old friends . . . 'til now.

A cymbal crashed on a bass lick.

Then she realized, looking in his eyes, that there must've been someone else. And it dawned on her just how much she enjoyed being close to him.

The thought spooked her.

"Guess we're a lot more alike than you think," he said. Then he whispered in her ear, "I don't trust people either."

Ria felt their connection surge—and a defense mechanism to warn him off kicked in like a bot under a learning cap. "No. You don't get it. This scar? The hollow-point I took in the Glitch? It didn't just blow my optics. My amygdala, my striatum are *gone*." The exact cerebral regions that generate allegiance, loyalty, and security. "I'm 38 percent augment, loaded with e-DNA. You can't teach machines to feel . . . I *can't* trust."

"Thirty-eight percent? . . . Christ, you're barely human."

Her eyes flashed with anger.

"I mean, from a legal standpoint."

She pulled away. "I know what you meant."

But Baz held onto her. "Hey. I'm sorry. I know how that sounded."

"If you knew how it sounded, you wouldn't have said it." She was hot with anger, maybe even hurt. But she could see his heart in his eyes.

He was daft like all men, but his apology was genuine. So she softened (even though she never softened) for just one moment.

"But I'll let it slide . . . Once."

They stared into each other. Muscles squeezed again. They couldn't have pulled one another closer if they tried. Ria knew if Otto saw them right now, the whole gig could blow. But for some reason she just didn't care.

The next shift of fuckbots made their way onto the dance floor, and the moment broke.

Ria gestured to a gorgeous chassis with French Caribbean synthetic skin, sifting through patrons and clientele. "That's St. Jane."

"Her?"

"You saw how he acted around you. You go upstairs with any other model, and he's gonna freak."

Baz looked back at St. Jane and took in a deep, nervous breath.

Ria sensed that sneaking into the maintenance bay wasn't what was bothering Baz—it was clearly something much deeper. "You know you don't *have* to go all the way . . . Just go there in spirit."

Baz relaxed a bit. Was this the source of his nerves?

"She's gonna scan your wetwire, your augments. All you gotta do is let her in up here." Ria tapped his temple. "Me and Eddie'll do the rest."

Maybe it was 'cuz her opinion mattered to him or maybe 'cuz he was due, but her tenderness seemed to fill him with real confidence.

"Baz, look at me. You got this."

SYNTHETIC SEX

Ria had to ice another McT to get into the Grid Room.

The Warrior Bot was bearing down on both Eddie and Carlo, cycling through alarm-protocols and vectoring its targeting sights on two thieves posing as wandering sex pests lost backstage, when Ria whipped out her glass-titanium stiletto—
And ran it through its CPU.

FANG.GRID : Outer-Ring

The door opened on the central nervous system of the Fang, and Eddie sat into the Grid Room chair, activating the main array—
Holos floated upwards tracking every fuckbot and patron as Ria sealed the door and Eddie found Baz's signal . . .

>sex suite 7<

Baz and St. Jane had a packed audience now.
The sexbot strutted in as the suite doors closed behind her. Her long Latin legs in Jimmy Choo stilettos and smooth synthetic skin over São

Paulo muscle sauntered forward, stacked on an EliteX.5 chassis from Wutani with biosensories sculpted over five generations in the geisha parlors of Osaka. St. Jane wrapped her gams around Baz's torso and her cranial-CPU around his wetwire . . .

And went to work.

Every moan of hers adjusted in pitch, breath, and duration as Baz couldn't help but get increasingly turned on. When she grazed his neck with her nails then his lips with her chest—her biosensories analyzed Baz's reactions to every movement, every breath, machine-learning how to get him as hot as possible.

>grid room<

And Ria wondered if Baz and St. Jane were both dialed into *her* wetwire . . . 'Cuz somehow their arousals matched her deepest nightmare.

Fucking a sexbot to hack its neurals had haunted Ria since the Glitch. She never realized it was more than just shame, because up until now she'd either run from it or just numbed it away.

Baz sighed—or maybe he moaned—how real or how hot didn't matter. The allure, the arousal, the full carnality shot through Ria. Memories triggered. Nightmares of her father's illicit sex bender returned—as if somehow Baz taking it for the team and engaging with St. Jane was suddenly forcing Ria to confront what had actually so devastated her years ago.

Her dad abandoned her, when she needed him most.

You chose a cause over family—how could you do that? How could you care about an anonymous world more than me? Than your own flesh and blood, your own daughters, for chrissakes? You got one of us killed and the other destroyed—for what? For a few jobs that never even *happened?*

She hated him for it, that much she'd always known, but she'd never let herself feel it until right now. So she shut off her Poker Face and let the anguish throttle through her. She felt Eddie and Carlo glance her way, but for once she didn't care—she needed to experience this fully, no matter who was watching.

Ria wasn't crying but trembling as Baz's session kept getting hotter—emotions pounding—'cuz somehow watching him with this fuckbot was her deliverance. She'd always known she never grieved right; she literally ran away from it all. She could cry for a fuckbot named Trixie, but never for her dad. But maybe for once, she could find *acceptance* for what he'd done.

Could she accept that the world and everyone in it was FUCKED . . . Yet still fight for 'em both?

SYNC QUERY

Baz felt St. Jane's neurals attempting to access his inner mem-drive, so she could satisfy his inner desires. He didn't want her in there, or anyone else—'cuz if that was where the passion of his life was hidden, then he wanted to keep it that way. Wanted to keep its source sacred, in a safe place. But Baz knew . . .

>grid room<

"We're fucked if he doesn't open up." Eddie warned.

Baz's wetwire was still sealed off from St. Jane, whose biosensories were currently limited to the environmental stimuli gathering every nanosecond. If Baz didn't grant St. Jane access, then neither would she . . . And Eddie's worm would be useless.

So Baz let go.

Let go of a love that had long since powered down. Let go of a memory that was nuthin' but a jail cell of his own construction. As real as the fiber and glass in his cranium, but as elusive as the data written on it. But really, as his eyes dilated and his pupils rolled back—

Baz let go of control.

ACCESS GRANTED

Memories floated onto the holo in front of Eddie, Carlo, and Ria—firefights in Venezuela, a burned girl in Caracas, and robot after slaughtered robot.

Ria realized quick what she was seeing. This was Baz's "Body Count." But she'd never imagined his notorious mayhem was any kind of selfless sacrificial act, until now. Instantly the images resonated—because suddenly the Baz she'd been working with, and his rep lined up. But before Ria could say anything, St. Jane drilled deeper into his mem-drive . . .

And revealed a woman no one had seen in years.

"Who is *that*?"

Ria watched the woman's image float onto the holo-display in front of them. Carlo turned sheet white.

She was beautiful. Elegant. In a way Mother Nature struggled to create. The last tender kiss Baz could remember.

"Hi," the woman whispered, waking up at sunrise. "I'm Kara."

Carlo looked away, like his gut wrenched.

"I don't know who that is," Eddie said, but Ria could tell he was lying. "St. Jane's tapping memories and sensations he associates with love."

Baz's wetwire opened to the deepest recesses of his cortex, and as the regions flashed across their holo-display—

```
                                    >sync<

              neocortex ... thalamus ...
```

"She's in his amygdala now." Eddie reported.

"What, to get him off?" Ria nervously brushed hair off her own amygdala—along that augmentation scar from years ago.

"To kiss him, touch him, and fuck him like the girl of his dreams." Eddie then looked at her confused—'cuz Ria was a pro. "You okay?"

"I'm fine."

"You're not jealous of a fuckbot, are you?"

"NO." Ria shot back, so defiant she realized she might be.

St. Jane gyrated into Baz on the holo, reading his memory of exactly how Kara once touched him. And finally their lips locked—both with St. Jane and with Kara years ago, *simultaneously*—

FULL SYNC

"We got I/O lock," Eddie announced.

When Ria's wetwire DINGED—

INCOMING

Rex‚Otto

"Ria, where are you—backstage?"

Eddie looked at her.

Something about the tone of Otto's voice sounded an alarm in both of 'em.

"Gimme a minute to work my magic," Eddie started hacking the safeguards on St. Jane.

"Ria, goddammit, pick up!" The kingpin dinged her again.

Eddie glanced at Ria, who glared back.

"Worry 'bout her Bot-ID. I'll worry about Otto."

Eddie dialed deeper, decoding—'til their POV suddenly passed through the unit-to-unit network . . .

ID ACCEPTED

"Get your ass moving, Baz," Eddie whispered.

'Cuz they were staring at the Inner Circle.

"Ria, McT's off-line, and I'm on the loading dock—where the fuck are *you*?!" Otto sounded furious.

Ria turned and headed out of the Grid Room to respond, realizing his tone of voice could be a real curveball. Moving quick, she'd have to boot up a new McT fast, so Ria was two steps out—

"She's my sister." Carlo seethed through tear-stained cheeks.

Ria stopped and looked at the changeling Flyboy. He was obviously telling the truth, there was just too much pain in his eyes.

"At least . . . she *was*."

Ria remembered those initials "K.Z."—his last visitor—and realized Carlo had just trusted her with his most painful secret.

And she wanted to know more—what happened to his sister, where she was now, and why she resided on the inner recesses of Baz's wetwire . . .

But before Ria could ask, Otto dinged her a fourth time—

PRIORITY OVERRIDE

"Ria, get off-line and the fuck down here . . . NOW!"

Otto sounded like he was redlining into a manic panic—worse than she'd ever heard before—and one thing about right now was clear:

This was definitely more than a curveball.

ELITE

Otto kept dinging Ria, blistering with rage—too exposed outside of his own penthouse and pissed that Baz chose *tonight* to drop by. Then Ria mentioned something about a bondage session getting outta hand in the Dungeon and having to deactivate another McT—

"WHAT?" Otto could hear his own voice in his wetwire, he screamed so loud, and Ria was right when she said he had to calm down or he'd blow a servo.

She was restoring a backup to a new McT Warrior Bot, she said, and she'd be dark and downstairs in five minutes.

"You hear that, Baz?" Eddie watched the holo-display of Ria's wetwire spikin' through the roof:

ANXIETY-80%   TEMP-99   HEART-RATE-110bpm

"He wants Ria with him on the loading dock."

>sex suite 7<

"Pretty hard not to, Eddie." Baz peered through the back door of the sex suite as Eddie opened it remotely . . .

This was Otto's own personal accessway, one he'd installed in every parlor for all the wrong reasons.

As Baz moved through, he checked the carbon-fiber 7.62 semiauto in his hip augment for the first time in way too long. "I'm headed to Maintenance now."

>service annex<

Ria didn't respond, watching a brand-new McT update its backup from the previous model she'd killed twenty minutes ago.

She couldn't figure out what was driving her more nuts—anger or alarm. What the fuck was Otto doing on the loading dock? He was *supposed* to be walking the main dance floor. That he wasn't focused on his product or the headline act tonight . . . was bad.

"I'm sure Otto just wants McT escorted to him personally," she reasoned.

"Well, guess what, Princess?" Ria could hear Baz moving quickly through a narrow corridor backstage. "Now you're keeping an eye on *him*."

"FUCK," Ria said to herself off-wire, powering down her wetwire as McT booted up.

>main stage<

Moxie hovered on the edge of the dance floor, eyeing "10:01" in her wetwire and a pack of club kids, socialites, and playas awaiting her next move. "Where we at, Eddie?"

She'd been sellin' Otto's two new wafers, Chill and Kiss, since the doors opened.

"Keep them Thrilz bagged for now," Eddie wired back.

Moxie wondered if that included the one she'd already slotted.

Code pumped under her tongue and spread a serotonin smile across her grill: "Okay . . . but heads are chompin' at the bit."

Moxie's best customer and Otto's biggest wholesaler Slim hovered closest—his squeeze Jace nearby—and neither needed to see her new third I/O to know Moxie was slottin' a hat trick.

"Yo, Mox!"

Moxie turned to the main stage and stopped. "Akira?"

Her first girlfriend—Asa Masumoto, aka DJ Akira—kneeled down from her booth. "What wafer flavor you slingin' tonight?"

Moxie just batted an eye. The girl oozed style. Ink under both sleeves, a vintage Team Liquid jumpsuit, and that confident, sexy strut.

Akira threw a nod over her shoulder to the name of the party behind her in neon: "'Cuz I got an itch that needs to be scratched."

"You're on the holo-decks tonight?" Moxie definitely would have noticed if *DJ Akira* was on the lineup. They never really broke up. Her sets just took her too many time zones away.

"Last-minute booking."

Moxie turned sly and slid her a classic called Spanish Fly. "Good seein' you, Ki . . . Lookin' snatched as always."

Akira just winked. "Must be destiny."

>garage<

The elevator doors opened on the loading dock, and Ria walked out with McT, who took a defensive stance beside Otto.

"Am I seein' things, Ria? Or were you *dancing* with Covane?"

Shit.

Otto hadn't made that request in years. But the way he said it, sounded like the desire might've festered into an obsession.

"You said keep an eye on him." She blew him off and turned around. "I should get back upstairs. Someone's gotta—"

"Stick around, actually."

As a caravan thundered into the Fang's garage.

"I want you to see something."

>maintenance bay<

Baz crept round a corner towards an array of neural chairs.

Eddie echoed in his wetwire: "You enjoy yourself in there, bruh?"

He rolled his eyes. "She was a hideous bot, for sure. Any chance you kept my feed private?"

Eddie just chuckled. "I knew you had Kara stashed somewhere on a sim. But I figured you wiped your mems clean."

"*Eddie . . .*" Baz froze as a pair of Wutani Warrior Bots fast-activated on either side. "St. Jane got you into the sentry systems, right?"

Baz hadn't gone lethal with a robot since the NSA Data Mine, and he wasn't gonna start now. He recognized both androids from an Indian Casino nine months ago, along with twin high-watt railguns currently pulling vectors on both his testicles.

That he might get his balls shot off by bots he, himself, had gaffled was an irony not lost on Baz. *Should he keep his eyes open or closed?*

"EDDIE . . . ?"

Then both Sentries powered down as his partner deactivated 'em remotely and chuckled in his wetwire: "C'mon, Baz . . . It's me."

>garage<

Ria saw the truck, and her heart started *racing*.

Nope, no curveball—this was a ballistic slider exploding from a pitcher's synthetic arm, back before MLB banned augments.

The caravan numbered three vehicles. A pair of ink-black Hydro-Towncars with beefed-up suspensions—both chassis clearly bulletproof—flanking a massive big rig.

Ria tried to wrap her head around the metastasizing situation. On the night of the Seven Year Itch, Otto was doing a deal *and she was in the dark . . .*

W . . . T . . . F?

Then both Hydro-Towncars' doors opened and beastly sumo-sized enforcers of the Japanese persuasion emerged—telltale fish-scale munawari tattoos peeking under collars and sleeves—and Ria knew why Otto beat the battery outta Marilyn hours before showtime . . .

"We updatin' our inventory, boss?"

'Cuz these boys were Yakuza.

>grid room<

"Baz, the last one on the left is Marilyn's." Eddie watched his partner's signal weave through a half dozen neural chairs as Carlo unspooled his Ring of Fire around the chamber.

"Alright, D. I hope you're frosty," Baz warned, as they heard the mem-drive click into a glass data port. "'Cuz I'm pluggin' this thing in . . . NOW."

Eddie's worm hacked the Inner Circle in a nano.

PRELIM ACCESS GRANTED

Massive bandwidth from the Central Core suddenly scrolled in his wetwire by the exabyte, and the CrackerJack marveled at the sophistication built into the Fang's layers of security.

"We're in."

Carlo nodded and powered up as the vault's firewall virtualized in a real-time array across every lower sublevel.

"And?" Baz's voice caught the thrill of serious cake looming.

Nuthin' tastier than longtime ¢rypto.

—an explosion of LIGHT shocked Carlo backward—

"Whoa—fuck was that?" Eddie hollered.

Carlo licked his fingers, eyeing his Ring of Fire's frayed fiber optics and a sparking I/O at the end of an umbilical. "Vault's got a lotta juice."

"Talk to me, Eddie D," Baz chimed, hearing the alarm from his partner in crime. "Are we a go?"

'Cuz if you'd worked with Eddie long enough, you knew—*that* tone of voice?

Could be bad.

>garage<

Ria fought to contain her surging fear.

The cargo doors on the trailer opened—nitrogen gasped from the unsealed space, and a cloud of condensation blasted from the clean-room environment.

Maybe Otto didn't venture outta his penthouse tonight just to watch the show . . .

"We got a dancer comin' in?" Ria asked.

No, he was here to buy a bot.

Otto nodded. "The new Queen Bee of the Chrome Domes. Preprogrammed for the Seven Year Itch . . ."

Ria activated her Poker Face faster than it could self-boot to hide her mounting terror, as Otto turned to her with lizard eyes.

"Mind scanning her cap?"

>grid room<

"Something's off, Baz."

Eddie sailed around the Central Core in his wetwire at breakneck speed—pulling all the data he could from sixty feet below and sending the readings to Baz. "The climate control on that vault's redlinin' power."

"C'mon, D, let's hit this thing." Carlo was blind with anger.

"Chill!"

>maintenance bay<

"Eddie . . ." Baz backed away from the neural chair, eyeing the alarms. "What the hell's goin' on right now?"

He couldn't tell if that icy shiver down his spine was from the vault six stories below or the sinking suspicion the Score He'd Been Waitin' for His Whole Life was turning sideways . . . *fast.*

>garage<

Ria froze.

In a way she hadn't since that night in the stairwell. She'd seen holos of mobile clean rooms like this one. But there were only a few *highly illegal* bots on the planet that needed 'em—genetically engineered and hunted by Wirecrime.

"Go on." Otto smiled diabolically. "Give her a look."

"Yeah, sure." Ria tried to stay calm, stepping inside the hold.

As McT's cranial-CPU started for its Glock.

EXECUTIVE ACTION ALARM

"What . . . the . . . fuck?" Eddie's eyes widened.

Lethal alerts flashed crimson from the loading dock as McT vectored each Yakuza, cycling through attack protocols at the speed of light. Eddie watched every gunman in that garage—both real and synthetic—anticipate a looming kill zone.

He scrambled to shift his diagnostic from the Inner Circle to whatever sat in that big rig. "Baz, we got a bot on the loading dock."

"Now?"

Eddie scanned the trailer as data started compiling—billions of lines of code scrolled on the holo—not binary, nor hexadecimal—but repeating sequences of A, C, G . . . and T.

"*Fuck me*," Eddie whispered.

"WHAT?"

"This ain't no Street Meat."

>garage<

Ria inched slowly through the mobile clean room.

Sitting alone at the far end, waiting ominously in the fog like a sarcophagus, was a cryochamber. A plate of glass allowed a glimpse into its contents, but it was covered in condensation.

There was nowhere to go but forward as McT stepped into the cargo hold behind her. And Ria knew she was on autopilot, like that afternoon in Death Valley, when they shot her dad. Only now it wasn't Narcsoft that propelled her to the glass—it was the gravity of destiny.

She arrived at the cryochamber and slowly wiped the fog away to see inside . . .

>grid room<

Eddie gaped at the design specs, more data than he'd ever seen.

"She's a Wutani EliteX.9, but one of a kind. Full dermals, stem-cell optics, endoskeleton patterning,"—rattling off details as fast as they scrolled—"This bitch is a *cyborg*, Baz."

The kinda bot that brought brutal Wirecrime heat and infinite VR-prison time.

Eddie looked around the Grid Room, realizing everything he was doing might be evidence in a case stacking up against them right now— *what the fuck were they into?*

"I say we 86 our shit, stat," Eddie urged.

"We're pussin' out?" Carlo was shocked.

"SHUT UP!" Eddie shot back. "Pack your Ring."

>maintenance<

Baz figured Eddie had to be misreadin' specs, but as billions of permutations of ACGT scrolled through his own wetwire—the helix labyrinth of *DNA* confirmed everything Eddie was sayin'—

A cyborg?

Baz had heard of wetware like that in the Private Service—but the designs were black-box classified—synthetically engineered—'cuz *humans just couldn't write code that complex.*

"DNA from who?"

>garage<

Ria's heart stopped.

For a second, she thought she was staring into the eyes of her dead sister Dani—lying still, in the open-casket funeral that she never had. 'Til Ria remembered Dani died at sixteen, not the age of this girl in the cryochamber. Then she saw the scar.

This was her own robot double.

"Oh . . . shit," she whispered as McT raised his Glock 9.

Ria was staring at herself.

She whipped out her Ka-Bar and sliced the barrel off McT's Glock, a round sparking off the ceiling. Planted one foot to put the other in McT's chin—but he just caught it, picked her up, and bounced her off a wall—

>maintenance<

"No way that bot's a clone." Baz cycled through explanations. "Take a thousand coders, a hundred years—"

Then he FROZE and realized suddenly what he should have seen all along.

"Eddie. What's the *exact* temperature in that vault?"

Eddie dialed up the reading in his wetwire and the holo-display. "Shit, Baz . . . Minus 235."

Which meant one thing.

"GodDAMMIT!" But Baz's instinct for self-preservation took a backseat to: "*Ria . . .*"

>garage<

McT's fist wrapped round her jugular and lifted Ria swinging and flailing out of the cargo hold and slammed her against the side of the truck:

"I gave you so many chances, Ria." Otto stared at her, almost wishing it didn't have to be this way.

"You couldn't have me, so you made a copy?" Ria gasped.

"On the outside, sure." Otto licked his lips thinking of all the special modifications—from a custom-designed cranial-CPU to the anatomy between her legs. "But that bot's better than you'll ever be."

As Ria's eyes rolled back and she started to fade away, Otto tore the one thing off her body that he'd never seen before . . .

Her locket.

>maintenance<

"How do I get to the garage from here?" Baz could feel billions in ¢rypto and everything it could buy in Tahiti evaporating fast.

"Up the stairs to Otto's penthouse, then back down on his private lift." Eddie sent a scan of the wireframe schematics into his wetwire.

Baz looked at the far wall—then at the deactivated Sentries.

"Fuck it . . . I hate the ocean anyway." He moved to a firing position, about twenty feet from the wall. "Wire me into these Sentries."

Baz sensed a moment of hesitation outta Eddie before feeling the tingle of one bot slaving to his cortex's left hemisphere and the other to the right.

"What about the score?" Eddie asked as both Warrior Bots came alive under Baz's control.

"We bug out, and she's dead."

"She's dead anyway. You go through that wall, and we'll never get that code!"

"C'mon Eddie. We ain't stealin' code . . ."

Baz activated both Sentries, charged a pair of railguns, and vectored 'em on the far wall—

"We're stealing what wrote it."

>garage<

The EXPLOSION from the railguns rocked Otto to his knees—

McT dropped Ria to cover his master from a cascade of concrete and rebar.

Baz didn't wait for either Sentry to recharge, he just pulled a 12-gauge Shadow from one bot, a .44 Patriot from the other, and slipped into a space he hadn't been in years.

Capped the sprinklers to blind everyone in sheet rain. Spun-reloaded the shotgun like a Winchester out west, and blew McT's neurals out (again). Took aim at his old CO—too late—as Otto scampered under the trailer—*gone*.

The Yakuza opened fire on Baz, so he lit them up too—

Grabbed Ria, but she was out, so he just chucked her in the clean-room trailer. A Yakuza hollow-point ripped through his body armor, splattering blood all over the truck's front door—and Baz groaned as his smart-vest went to work, grafting augmented scar tissue over the wound. He stumbled into the truck's cab and smashed its self-driving neural, turning over the hydrogen ignition ole-school . . .

Otto howled as it roared away, "My bot's in that truck!"

Ria came to—thrown sideways, knocking out the cobwebs—and onto her feet. *Howling* came from the sarcophagus—the EliteX.9, Ria's bot double, was alive and wide awake, coded to eliminate its organic counterpart and thrashing to get loose—

One glass spiderweb, then another—

Baz shifted gears and couldn't not smile—slamming the truck outta the garage . . .

"I forgot how fun it is to drive."

The bot blasted through the glass, diving at Ria—rolling among the shards, inches apart, eye to eye, and Ria beheld her own horrifying fury staring back at her, as the bot sniffed and growled, "I recognize that."

Christ, she *sounded* just like her too.

"I bet you do." Ria threw the bot off—got on her feet quick, crouching low—her double mirroring the stance. 'Cuz whatever move Ria made, this bot was either gonna anticipate it—both lunging left into vacant air—

Or do the exact same thing.

Baz wheeled the truck onto Polk and groaned as cherry-tops from SFPD hydro-patrols came at him from every direction—

"We got heat on us!"

Spinning quick, the android *hurled* Ria into a shattered Sentry Bot on the floor. Otto must've built her stronger, 'cuz he loved the fight in girls. Ria caught a fist upside her cheek, since he'd probly coded her faster too. So Ria slackened, dropped her guard—uttered monotone: "Self-ID. X9, identify."

'Cuz Otto never liked 'em that smart.

The bot paused; was it attacking the wrong chassis? "X9-ID, serial veri—"

—Ria decked its neurals with that Sentry's severed arm—as the truck cornered hard and Baz screamed from the cab:

"Hold onto something, Ria!"

She steadied herself, stumbling onto the Sentry's massive railgun on the floor—then glanced at her double as it reoriented power to re-engage.

"My code prohibits duplicates of us."

Ria grabbed the massive weapon, strained to take aim and grip the trigger . . .

"Mine too."

The railgun's Marauder spear IMPALED four sheets of titanium, one solid-steel engine block, and the EliteX.9's cyborg chassis—as 2 billion ¢rypto in robotics and a heavy-duty hydrogen drive seized up.

Baz remembered bearing down on the SFPD roadblock assembling halfway down Geary and thinking, *How the fuck did so many cops show up so fast?*

So he actually dared 'em: "C'mon, assholes, gimme all you got!"

—then the spear shattered the front seat, blew an eardrum, and tossed Baz through the glass windshield into an asphalt face-plant on Powell.

Lights OUT.

BUSTED

GRAND THEFT

11:51 P.M.

Baz landed in the chair and took one look around.

Shit.

They weren't in a VR-construct. They were in an actual interrogation room. They must be really fucked.

Ria eyed the models and menace of both androids in black guarding them. It was clear who was now in charge:

"Where did Wirecrime come from?"

That question was one of many Baz wanted to ask *her*—from the highly illicit robot in the truck to what really sat inside Otto's vault.

Baz was pissed.

Baz was fucked.

And Baz wanted answers.

But her question was a good place to start, so he turned and looked right at Ria. "I don't know . . . You tell me."

He fixed his gaze on her left eye, her real one.

The stakes were mortal. Their crime capital. His infatuation gone.

Baz was sure he'd be able to tell if Ria was lying.

And she knew it.

Her Poker Face activated, but Ria shut it down 'cuz the broken, small-time Baz she'd met a month ago? . . . That dude was *gone*.

This was the high-alert muthafucka with a Body Count of twelve Warrior Bots and the balls to hit the De-Augmentation Server Farm. Ria wanted to pass his test, herself.

So she just stared at him, baffled and ignorant. "I don't know. Were they onto Otto's code?"

Baz squinted.

Was she honestly trying to figure out what happened, or had she been playing him the whole time? For a second, he thought he saw her iris flutter, the heart palpitation of a lie—but what he *didn't see* was what that would've meant. That this woman Ria Rose was a stone-cold, heartless sociopath who'd put his entire crew in peril. Her glassy eyes still carried irrefutable heart.

They had Want.

They had Need.

And Fire.

So fuck it, he decided to trust her. "Forget the code. This gig was cooked from the gate."

"By who?" Again with pitch-perfect naiveté.

By who was the part that stuck a knife in Baz's heart. He'd been blind in both eyes to what was really in that vault—by a pair of women. One that haunted him from the past, while the other sat right next to him.

Baz sighed. "Only one thing operates at minus 235."

The door opened.

"A quantum processor." A lawman in his fifties walked inside with a woman who must've been his partner and sat down across from Ria.

Baz had seen the man's grim visage before on the holowires.

His name was Langston Cowell. "A neuromorphic chip, to be precise."

Yup. They were fucked.

Baz knew it. Now Ria knew it.

But Baz came at 'em anyway with the cheap defiance of a criminal who wished he still had the right to a lawyer: "The fuck you holdin' us on? Goin' off-grid? *Attempted* robbery?"

The woman Fed chuckled. "Try hijacking a Tier-1 Accelerated Sentience."

For once in their lives, both Baz and Ria had nothing to say.

So Langston leaned in and said it for them:

"Grand Theft AI."

WIRECRIME

Before Langston Cowell hunted kingpins, he worked Atlanta Homicide, the first off-clock dick to get bloody during the Glitch. In fact, he was covered in the black stuff that Hotlanta afternoon—took down a dozen bots and saved as many citizens, moving with precision through Maddox Park to the Peachtree Mall. Had he been in upscale Buckhead instead of low rent Bankhead, Langston would have been a national hero. Instead, he got a company medal, a handshake, and no OT for the three weekends it took to write up his report.

He also caught a ding.

Gears were moving fast in the federal government, and for once the Valley was in lockstep. Big Tech and VC saw the future of civilization (and Langston's new jurisdiction) starting with True AI, crossing over the fiber-brain barrier, and riding high on Narcsoft. Kids going off-grid, gettin' slotted, so digital kingpins could make an untaxed fortune? That's the lovechild of Guccifer and Pablo Escobar. The world sat on a new frontier . . .

Someone had to sling a Winchester.

Someone had to wear the star.

Welcome to Wirecrime, pal.

Langston Cowell came up in the Pentecostal Revival of the early 21st century and could recall the red hats and ravenous chants screaming, "Make America Great Again." But at fifteen years old, he was a bit too far from the stage, so he settled on watching his mom and dad's fervent support. They lost their jobs two years earlier at Tyson Farms—cursing bullshit liberals and swearing, "Who cares how many hormones get pumped in a fuckin' chicken, really?"

But after Pops got blown 87 feet down the block from a neighbor's meth lab, Mom found God the hard way, which meant Langston learned quick the paradoxical efficacy of faith healing: namely, if the preacher picked you, it was near 100%. But if you were Langston's pops? . . . NIL. No matter how bad Mom prayed. Yet despite the high percentage of snake-oil salesmen in the pulpit, the core tenets of the Big Book infected Langston like a virus and coded him for life—or most of it anyway. Only in his final moments would Langston ever doubt scripture. 'Til then, he knew three things in life: good guys hunted bad guys, his pops would die in that wheelchair—

And Langston Cowell was on a mission from God.

That mission found its calling in Narcsoft. Langston took command of its division at Wirecrime, 'cuz it was his baby. He'd caught a string of B&Es in the summer before the Glitch: some crew hit a dozen all-night Walmart uploaders in a month but hadn't bothered with any wafers. They just wanted the hardware. Literally, the uploader itself—StimSoft's proprietary Lasik-grid-writer. Which was odd. Why burn your own Stim, when the shit was so cheap it was basically free?

Langston matched an SSS off a tower nearby and sent an Atlanta PD hydro-cruiser over to an address on Peachtree. Place was empty, save a dead 15-year-old on the kitchen floor with no permanent address, just wafers of StimSoft littered all over the place and blood running from his ears, like his skull had fried. Langston had the lab scrub a wafer, and it came back stronger than anything StimSoft ever distributed.

Langston had the first positive ID on Narcsoft, ever.

Gone were the days of req'ing tech out of a precinct basement—Wire-crime's new forensics could track code like a chromosome, and all roads led to Miami. "Skull Fries" littered the beaches from Fort Lauderdale to the Key West Seawall with chatter 'bout a hacker ring with the best wafers in the world. Problem was, when Miami PD's Marine Unit fished its leader out of Biscayne Bay, Zev Vromen was just the first in his ring to die.

Langston could remember sitting at the Delano Hotel in 2046, trying to have a conversation with a Wutani Bartender Bot XL. Just a year ago, every model in America knew all about Langston—from his dirty martini with five olives (never four), to the bra size and forwarding address of every wife who'd ever left him. But this one, under the AI regulations that Langston now enforced, just served him well gin with a twist and thought "The One That Got Away" was some 30-year-old pop song.

Then he checked his Incomings, and everything changed.

Oakland Vice, Denver Private Security, even the Rio Grande Enforce-ment Zone (and there were more) had found glass wafers in Skull Fries' hands matching Langston's Most Wanted Code. But this shit wasn't re-burned onto some old Stim—this was original. Came stamped. A feather icon on a wafer called Wingspan, a lotus for Nirvana, a flame for Blaze—this shit was *marketed*. This was product.

And it was everywhere.

Distribution rings appeared in every city in America over the next three years. Kids *loved* it. And like its chemical counterparts years before, wafers traveled on the highways: I-25 through Texas, US 41 up to Chicago, and Uber-80 all the way from the San Francisco Bay. After Langston had commandeered his seventh SWAT team, subordinated fifteen chiefs of police, and crossed every state line—he gathered federal brass and the guys who really mattered, Wirecrime's Corporate Oversight Committee, and presented his theory . . .

Otto Rex was the Narcsoft King of the World.

His proof was two years of surveillance, centering on his fuckbot palace, the Fang. When asked if the establishment was a whorehouse or a drug den, if Otto was a dealer or a pimp, and how his fixer, an Orphan of the Glitch named Ria Rose, fit into it all, Langston's love of history worked against him. Referring to Freeway Ricky or El Chapo did nuthin' for the execs gathered in front of him. But when he said Otto owned the Walmart of Narcsoft?

The suits all got it.

Otto Rex had no idea when he reached out to his contact at Wutani to buy a *billion-¢rypto sexbot* that all of his communications were going straight to Wirecrime. By that point, his entire operation was under surveillance: the door, half his clients, his virt-cams, all the Dance Bots and fuckbots, and anything they could hack from his wetwire.

Langston proposed a liaison with Tokyo PD and its Yakuza informants to arrest Wutani's senior VP of product development and move his own agents into positions posing as both—while commandeering Wutani's embryonic incubators to build the most expensive and illegal fuckbot to ever set foot in America.

Certainly the most intrigued committee member was a corporate titan named Ken Cates. The exec pressed hard on why such an elaborate undercover sting was needed to take down Otto Rex. But when Ria Rose's avatar started to animate—more specifically when her 3-dimensionalized footage started to *talk*—Langston knew, from the tiny gasp Cates made, that his undercover android had just been approved.

But a month later, as the schematics grew into a full *zettabyte* of data, Langston raised an eyebrow. His partner Lieutenant Gina Wylks was shocked, staring at Otto's entire decrypted transmission. Recruited outta ATF CyberCrime, Wylks once hacked a railgun ring in Baton Rouge then kicked down the door on the raid herself. But she'd never seen anything like this.

An android designed from a complete human genome. Wrapping genetically cloned skin, eyes, and the rest of its external physical tissue around a titanium endoskeleton and a preprogrammed personality construct—all patterned on Otto's fixer, Ria Rose. Langston was sure he'd lose control of the case, for one obvious reason:

Only an AI could design a cyborg.

Sure, Narcsoft was a scourge. But a Rogue AI was an existential threat. A planet-killer. The Glitch was a blip compared to what a True AI could do in command of an army of bots with blown caps. Some called it the Singularity. Others, quoting old 2Ds, the War against the Machines. The idea that Otto Rex had an AI in his basement making digital drugs was like locking Einstein in jail and forcing him to perform arithmetic—it was almost comical.

But no one laughed on the Corporate Oversight Committee.

'Cuz by then Langston's investigation was coordinated personally by Ken Cates. Langston reported the decrypted cyborg schematics, his conclusion that Otto was in possession of a stolen AI, and the rest of his findings—directly to Ken. And that's when everything changed.

The door to Langston's office opened, and Cates closed it behind him. A *personal* visit. IRL. No one did that anymore—certainly not a suit. Langston stirred, glancing at the clock. His triple-encrypted VR-conference with Ken wrapped a half hour ago, and StimSoft Square in Cupertino was 65 miles from Langston's surveillance suite in China-town. Cates had jumped a dronecraft straight to him.

Langston kinda respected Ken for taking the case from him personally. That was rare among execs, especially a titan like Ken—they usually had an HR Bot do it for 'em. But Cates started throwing an idea around that dangled in front of Langston Cowell's eyes like a ten-carat diamond. Maybe it was time, not to pull Langston off the case, but to *elevate* him. Advance his career in a monumental way. Cates wanted Langston to stay on Otto Rex, to continue with his undercover sting, and spearhead the repossession of the stolen AI.

If they worked together.

Langston's alarm went off. Why would Ken make him his ally? . . . He asked him as much, and Ken pulled out an actual file—like, *paper*. He opened and slid the dossier across the table to Langston. At first glance, it looked like everything Wirecrime had on the Underground Butcher and the conspiracy behind the Glitch. But one photo—of the Butcher's *daughter*—spiked a chill down Langston's spine.

Maria Roselli looked just like a teenage Ria Rose.

Langston didn't understand. Dave Roselli's daughter was alive? Most details from the Glitch remained classified—certainly the Butcher's dead daughters were two of them. How did Universal Monitoring fail to ID Maria Roselli, but Ken could? Then he realized: StimSoft had *extensive* files on the Underground Butcher.

Dave Roselli worked at Dallas Dynamics in '41 and '42, and StimSoft was contracted to monitor both Dave and his students for anxiety shifts.

They had access to Dave's wetwire, which means they had access to everything—his involvement with Synthetic Emancipation, his power-downs during alleged Underground meetings, and most important: authentic IDs and voiceprints of his daughters. The "official" Maria Roselli didn't match the original holo. The Universal SSS had been *altered*, and she'd been living as "Ria Rose" ever since.

Langston leaned back and put the pieces together . . .
Otto Rex used a stolen AI to copy the Butcher's daughter.
Jeezus Christ.

A smile spread across Langston's face. The scale of this bust, the size of the collar, the whole fucking enchilada was enormous. And all of it could be *his*. Langston checked himself. Pride was a sin, hubris a fatal flaw. Humility must prevail right now. But Langston's mind just kept racin' . . . If he busted Otto, captured this Rogue AI, *and* tracked down the Butcher's daughter? Langston would be the most powerful man in law enforcement.

Director of Wirecrime.

Ken Cates saw that ambition sparkle and smiled . . . They were partners now. And that fuckbot copy of Ria Rose was more crucial than ever. They'd need it to get their hands on Otto's AI. You couldn't count the layers of security a paranoid Narchead like Otto Rex would stack around the Fang. Something tied to his heart rate for sure—and Langston knew what Cates was suggesting . . .

Otto had a "kill switch."

A snare in his wetwire, a single integrated circuit riding on a nerve fiber. If anyone tried to take Otto down, by hook or by crook, it would trigger—destroying the Fang, every patron inside, and the AI with it . . . And Langston could tell *that* was Cates's biggest fear. For some reason, he wanted this AI to himself, alive and fully functioning.

But by that point, any effort from Langston to curtail his own churning ambition was futile. So he just smiled and agreed with his new corporate benefactor. The only way into that vault was to hack Otto's wetwire and disable his kill switch by gaining his trust completely. And the only way to do that was with the girl of his dreams, the Queen of the Fang . . .

Ria Rose.

.50

Langston slammed Ria's severed robotic head on the table.

"See this fuckbot here?"

Ria stared at her own decapitated face.

"This was a three-year undercover sting you crashed."

Baz shifted, uncomfortably. The moment was bizarre, if not uncanny.

"That Yakuza squad on the loading dock were my agents." Two of which were now dead, thanks to Otto (and Baz). Langston pointed at 'em both in fury. "You two shitsticks walked on center stage to the biggest investigation in Wirecrime."

Two billion ¢rypto alone sat on the tabletop between them.

Finally, Wylks chimed in. "And fucked it all up."

"So now you're working for me."

Langston's offer was simple and nonnegotiable. Ria and Baz would testify before a corporate grand jury to identify and serve sealed indictments on the rest of their team. Cates wouldn't like it, but they'd have to rebuild the case patiently with old-school evidence and testimony. And when the time was right, they'd take down Otto, and if they captured his AI in the process?

Langston might become Director after all.

"Yeah, and what if we tell you to go fuck yourself?" Baz challenged, still trying to find some way out of this mess.

"Oh, that's easy," Wylks said, matter-of-fact.

"We'll just stick you and your merry band of deviants in the VR-pen." Langston stood and opened the door for Wylks . . .

"Forever."

And slammed it.

Baz and Ria sat in the silence of that interrogation room for a minute. He scanned the seams where steel walls met concrete floors. Eyed every synthetic joint on both Guard Bots. Even kept his retinas off the capture-cam in the ceiling that was virting their environment somewhere.

There was no way out of this box.

Ria didn't need to analyze the space to gauge the near impossibility of escape. She was more concerned with a question that had but one answer yet still made no sense.

Why was she alive?

Otto and McT were doing a pretty good job of ending her when Baz came through that wall—but why? He wasn't dodging a blown bot's bullets. He took on multiple squads of real and synthetic enforcers, ID'ing himself to a homicidal kingpin as the thief who was robbing him and *abandoning the biggest score of his life*—for what?

For her?

Ria kept scrolling through angles. Maybe Baz was working with Otto all along and saving his life? Maybe he was tryin' to kidnap her for ransom? Or maybe he was a Wirecrime plant and Eddie a CI, and they were both part of Langston's—nope. None of that shit made any sense. Occam's razor. Ria could eliminate all but one reason why he'd saved her life . . .

Baz was the dumbest guy she'd ever met.

As if she needed any further proof, right when Ria started to settle into the reality that he was the first righteous dude she'd come across ever, he went and fucked it all up by talking.

"What . . . have you . . . got me into?"

Ria's megaton defense mechanism triggered—and whatever moment was about to happen was gone. "What have I got *you* into?"

"You brought me this job."

The suggestion that she was some Wirecrime snitch was insulting when it came from Quinn. From Baz, it *hurt*. "The fuck are you saying?"

Baz groaned. The woman went to guns faster than a speedloader. "I'm trying to fathom how my life went from good to blown in the weeks since I met you."

"You call that life good?"

"You think you're any judge?"

"You're a fuckbot dealer."

"You're a pimp's fixer. Who betrayed him. By pitching a robbery—"

"Fuck you! You think I'd *snitch*?"

Both Guard Bots activated off their volume and body heat, servos gearing, crosshairs vectoring—from Baz to Ria and back again—trying to distinguish which posed the bigger risk. But each bot's limited AI was machine-learning rapidly that every time one of them gained the upper hand, in that midshift nanosecond when their energies equalized, the threat assessment of Baz and Ria as allies multiplied their strength exponentially . . .

Which Ria was counting on.

Baz went for the jugular: "Oh, right, I forgot, you don't trust anyone, but how the fuck do I trust that? You work for Otto, you work for Wirecrime—who knows?"—touching a nerve that she just couldn't—"Maybe you're just a bot and—"

"I'm NO robot!" Rage flashed, pinning both Guard Bots in a misaligned vector somewhere between a foot and a centimeter off Baz's right ear, who just kept arguing.

"Why should I—"

Ria unslung her Ka-Bar and sliced through handcuffs and a Guard Bot's throat in a single fluid augmented move—a pair of hollow-points discharged, embedding into the steel wall behind Baz—taking a millimeter of his ear with 'em—he howled in shock as she leaped across the table and backhanded her blade into the torso of the lone surviving Guard Bot, kicked the dead bot's .44 Slide into her hand, and blasted its CPU into a black splatter on the floor.

Baz seized the buckled-over bot's .50 Rattler as it revectored Ria in his primary—but its malfunctioning finger pulled a missing trigger as Baz pulled the real one and decapitated the bot with its own beastly sidearm. The recoil was as powerful as its report.

"No wonder they don't standard-issue these fuckin' things. Goddamn hand-cannon."

"You mind?" She nodded to the maglock.

So Baz blasted that too.

BANSHEE

Devyn Dasch was gettin' strong-armed by Langston when the shots popped off.

She'd been goosing the 'Busa on the edge of Chinatown as her crackerjacked "Belize Refugee" started glitching in her wetwire, and Devyn knew a Wirecrime hack when she felt one.

Now she was sitting in a ten-by-ten shitbox identical to Baz and Ria's. But after Langston hit the part about her working for him, she didn't bother telling him to go fuck himself.

She just leaned back instead and reminded him that at 42% augment, her testimony was as inadmissible as any robot's, so good luck salvaging what she'd already wiped off her mem-drives—Langston didn't have to fuck himself, the Anti-Augmentation Act had done that already.

Then all hell broke loose.

And Langston suddenly realized what was happening.

As a rookie in Atlanta, he'd hear old-timers talk about the Worst Day of Their Careers. When a perp went nuts on an elementary playground. Or when a day on the stand devolved into a public castration. But most Worst Days bore a striking resemblance to this one: November 8, 2051—when your most elaborate plan becomes your own noose.

Wylks went through the door first, and a chunk of her dome split off her jaw as a hollow-point tore her head in half and the rest of her body slumped dead into the hallway.

"Wylks!" Langston screamed—but she was gone, and the only answer he got was another hundred rounds pockmarking the door and far wall. Both Devyn and Langston recognized the hollow-points as government issue . . . Friendly fire.

"Your own team downed your partner!" Devyn screamed before slamming into Langston and knocking his Glock 9 to the concrete. He reached for it, but she'd already grabbed and swung the gun upside his grill—dazing him.

As more rounds tore through the doorway, Devyn kicked over the table and hit the deck. Then the concussions of a .50-cal, probly a Rattler, shattered the acoustics of the box—

"Devyn?!" Ria screamed.

Devyn saw her and Baz in the hallway and bolted out to join 'em. No one could get signal on their wetwires—whatever structure they were in had a blanket cap on all unauthorized bandwidth, but Devyn had her own internal tracking pulse augmented into her cortex, which locked on the 'Busa two floors below.

"HALT!" was the last word from the Dallas Sentry-7 before Baz blasted its cardiac pump, and Devyn flew over the half wall to where the 'Busa sat in custody.

They were in a vast industrial space—the Loin or maybe China-town—and as Devyn reached for the bike, she turned to Ria and Baz: "Both of you, jump—"

A blast echoed through the warehouse, and Devyn never finished. She was launched off her feet (and outta one shoe), slamming into the far wall, where she'd have expired if not for her augments.

Writhing on the concrete instead, her blood pooled quickly under her torso, one synthetic lung gasping for air as her real one quit. Both synthetic eyes reached for power to focus, dilate, and refocus—as the thorium cell fixed beneath her thalamus sapped reserves, spiking signal to her SynCardia which even Ria could hear whining under the strain, pumping pint after pint onto the floor.

Devyn's eyes caught Ria's as she spat blood: "GO . . . I . . . ID'd you . . . anyway—"

And then she was gone.

Ria shuddered—floored that Devyn trusted her with the 'Busa after all, as swelling grief threatened to choke her . . .

But Baz caught sight of Langston leading a squad of Warrior.4s down a flight of stairs on the far wall and could tell:

Langston was coming with a vengeance.

'Cuz he liked Wylks a lot. They'd grown close, over three years of chasing Otto's wafers—he'd come to enjoy her smile, her lips, how they felt when he kissed them, when she kissed him back, and especially those eyes, staring into a soul that took zero shit by day, but sparked at night . . . alone together, sheltered, hot and holding one another. So he was ticked when her eyes, lips, soul—the whole fuckin' package— blasted to pieces all over Langston's button-down. From here forward, fuck reason and fuck procedure—

Langston would lance Ria's head on a pike.

Baz could see that hatred from fifty yards and turned to Ria.

"We should go . . . NOW."

For the second time in as many hours, she relived the most difficult memory of her life. This time, as Devyn's augmented side finally threw in the towel trying to keep her organic one alive, Ria remembered Dani's death. And instead of tears, the kinda rage that burned hot against the dying of any light *seethed* upwards from the depths of Ria and found its voice in a ROAR that could've deafened a hypersonic ramjet.

She stood into gaps between oncoming bullets—her augmented tracking software catching each hollow-point's ballistic velocity like a horizontal raindrop—grabbed the HK.887 out of Baz's hands, packed it in her deltoid, and unloaded the entire clip with equal parts ferocity and banshee wail.

Raw, unbridled FURY.

Langston's bots caught her rounds, dodging and scattering—'til her clip seized empty and slipped free.

Ria dropped the weapon and grabbed a different one—the 'Busa— its throttle read Ria's palm prints and ignited to life.

—swung her leg over the saddle, kicked down into first, slammin' the gas and clutching the front brake—the fatboy tire caught concrete, laying a drift that threw the chassis around the front forks 'til it was aimed squarely down the length of the exit ramp.

Baz fired the last six hollow-points outta his Rattler—decapitating one Warrior.5 and blasting the battery outta the other.

"GET ON!" Ria didn't care that Baz didn't need to be told—he was on the bike and clutching her tight with one hand and lifting the 12-gauge from the dead Sentry in the other—as she popped the brake and clutch together, the machine exploded towards the exit.

Langston let loose his own roar for his partner Wylks, for the clusterfuck called his career, and for his recently acquired inability to secure a blowjob at any hour.

Baz looked over Ria's shoulder and saw the needle crest 70 mph, but a pressure door sealed the exit—so he took aim even before she screamed: "Cap the goddamn servo!"

"ON IT!" He blasted one locking magnet, cocked the shotgun saloon-style with a 360 reload, and blasted the other magnet—both counterweights released and dropped fast, but the door seized halfway, caught on a safety screw—

"HOLD ON!" Ria howled and *accelerated*—Baz couldn't believe what she was gonna do, so he dropped the pump-action and grabbed her with both hands as she kicked out the rear wheel and *laid the bike down sideways*—

All three went horizontal, time slowed down, and Baz felt a wisp of the door's retainer breathe by at sixty miles an hour . . .

Sparks flew as they skirted sideways out onto California Street—hydro-cars and self-driving software revectoring in every direction—then Ria pumped both brakes, the bike right-sided, and she slammed into second—so the 'Busa could do what it was built to do.

It tore down the sky.

COIT

Baz glanced over his shoulder as Ria gunned the bike onto the roadway portion of the Neo-Embarcadero—no cherry-tops, no pursuit hydros, nuthin'.

"I think we're clear!" he yelled at Ria, but she was still flying on adrenaline. Off to the right the Ferry Building passed by, ahead on the left loomed Coit Tower, and Baz realized they were miles from Quinn's compound but comin' up on the first of three safe houses he kept in the city for fubars like this one.

"Exit Pier 33—we gotta get off-grid . . ."

But Ria couldn't lay low at this point with a quad-slot of Tranq wafers, so she made no move or signal. She just thanked Devyn's savvy the 'Busa had that Ghost Cloak—'cuz its horsepower needed every lane of an interstate turn, and every one of 'em were monitored by Traffic Bots 24/7.

The needle jumped to 155, full throttle—

"Fuck are you doin'?" But Baz knew what she was doin'—exactly what drove him so nuts about her—she was pushin' this razor-thin envelope they teetered on to the edge of the earth. Both bored out cylinders inhaled high-octane jet fuel, and the needle on its speedometer told Ria (finally) just what this souped-up 'Busa could do.

300 mph.

Devyn's cloaking software worked so well, the only ones who knew some psycho was doin' 300 on the Neo-Embarcadero were two families in hydro-minivans one lane up, whose dashboards exploded with periphery velocity alarms, and the maintenance crew three days later, servicing Wind Panels 6 through 10 on the roadway below.

The anomaly was referred to SFPD, who passed it along to Wire-crime, whose proprietary AIs eventually de-cloaked the 'Busa—earning Ria a nickname among law enforcement across the country.

They called her the Speed Demon.

Baz hadn't seen ground move beneath his feet that fast since he was ridin' skids on Blackhawks in Venezuela. Even nightmare mems of killing peasants for their water couldn't defile the rush of earth racing beneath you at 300 miles an hour—and gripping the waistline of this woman, throttling his deliverance, now made the current experience beyond exhilarating.

He leaned into her torso and buried his nose in her neck and inhaled Ria as deep as he could . . .

She could feel him do it too—inched back into him as tight as possible at 300, 'cuz the feeling was growing mutual, fast. They were fucked beyond all recognition. A kingpin wanted 'em dead, the most roided-out G-man in history hung infinite VR-stretches round their necks, and an existential killer lurked beneath her former place of employment. But for once she breathed easy—'cuz her own prison of fear, of hate, of blame . . .

Was gone.

Russian Hill and the Wharf flew by like toys, and Baz realized his last safe house before the Golden Gate was a mile ahead, twelve seconds away. He squeezed up against Ria, and she could feel his stiffness through their fatigues. It dawned on him (and her) that they were actually grinding at 300 miles an hour, and neither of 'em had *ever* thought about having kids, but somehow both knew that one day they'd tell this story to them (when they were much older, of course). Ria was undoubtedly the most high-functioning woman Baz had ever met, so he figured—fuck it, why not throw another challenge in front of her . . .

So he slammed the rear brake.

The 'Busa fishtailed at 315, and Ria's augmented right arm steadied the bike as the implant she'd installed a year ago kicked in. Baz's move was some high-speed courtship, and she figured she knew how to answer the challenge, so she put her nose into the asphalt, flying at her at 308 . . . 298 . . . 281—leaned her right knee out, flexed her augmented right forearm, and threw the bike into the hairpin around the Palace of Fine Arts—in a maneuver no human had pulled on a street ever.

'Fact, Wirecrime would analyze the data three times before concluding that only a military-grade implant—an equilibrium manifold to keep pilots conscious above 8 g's—would allow that turn, 'cuz it pulled harder than an F-39 at Mach 2. Baz leaned in, and Ria downshifted as they spiraled through the curve into a slingshot onto Marina Parkway.

The bike finally skidded to a stop on Divisadero near a tent city of indigents, and Ria spun in the saddle, wrapped both legs round Baz, whose hands slid under her halter and finally—

Skin touched skin.

Their first kiss lasted five minutes, 600 feet, crossed two intersections, three doorways, a Resonance Sequencer, and an automatic power-down of both wetwires—as Baz kicked on a rendezvous beacon and closed self-sealing maglocks behind them. She tore off what clothes he hadn't—littering the safe house floor between the door and the queen bunk in the corner.

She chewed on him; he devoured her; she sucked his chest; he bit her flesh—her panties came off as fast as his skin-briefs—and they were a tangle of flesh and skin and saliva. There was no equivalent in either of their lives—two AIs would confirm years later—or anywhere on the planet that night. Rolling over on each other—loving and yearning and groping and devouring—he was a rock like her areolas and licked every square inch of her belly and between her legs and confirmed what he knew already—she tasted like the blood in her veins . . . And she needed to know if he indeed tasted like the blood on his hands: salty and strong—and his sweat, just a lil sour.

It wasn't just sex, and it wasn't just lust, but a synthesis and a union . . . thrusting into each other, penetrating, a force deepening that bond and finding inner niches and dens where all secret emotion secreted. And to the mind, wetwireless—where it was nasty and needy and beautiful and quick but lasted longer than expected—their breath was shorter than could sustain life, as they came together, loin-to-loin— living more in that simultaneous orgasm that rhythmed back and forth between 'em like the breakers in the Bay and their heart rates pounding in either eardrum, chewing and sucking lobes on hers and his . . .

And you know what?

Life was alright.

THE DESCENT

12:15 A.M.

Otto hadn't felt fury like this since the Water Wars.

It wasn't the GDP-size ¢rypto that just hauled away from his loading dock, nor the epic betrayal he'd been dealt by both his fixer Ria Rose and Baz Covane, not even the amount of heat he must be under for Wutani's Yakuza Enforcers to open fire with *US-government-issue* 7.62 hollow-points. It was that all three had conspired to destroy the biggest night of his life.

The Queen of the Fang was dead.

"You slimy BITCH!" Otto pummeled St. Jane with his bare hands, and life returned to him as if every impact pumped new blood through his veins—and Otto knew one thing for sure.

He would never hole up in his penthouse again.

St. Jane was the only sexbot to service Baz, so Otto didn't give two fucks that her learning cap prohibited her from betrayal—he just squeezed her neck tight in one fist, and bashed her synthetic skull with the other 'til black blood and fiber optics ruptured from the fractures.

"Christ, Otto, STOP—you're gonna kill her!" Moxie screamed, like she'd never seen anyone do anything like this.

"IT!—you fuckin' junkie!" They were in the Fang's freight elevator along with McT, descending below the Dungeon, to the level no one but Otto had access to.

Then his eyes narrowed on his King Slinger as a thought popped through the organic part of his brain: "Were you in on this too?"

"In on what?"

Otto did a shitty job of vetting as the elevator hit the ground floor, and he stormed out with McT, wheeling on Moxie when she started to follow. "Stay where you fucking are! Get upstairs and lock down the club—no one's leaving 'til after the show—you fucking hear me?"

Moxie backpedaled into the elevator, keeping her eyes down as the doors shut on a massive terminal array and enormous circular steel door. It was the first time Otto had ever descended with Moxie or anyone else.

No one had seen the vault before and lived.

"Fastlight, online!"

A holo-display awakened, projecting before Otto a particle apparition that spun from a cloud into the form of a female avatar. She was translucent, so her bronze skin bore a sickly mustard hue from the cold blue steel behind her, but she was unmistakably Ria Rose.

"Otto, what's the word?" Even spoke in her vernacular.

"Not that bitch—swap avatars!" Otto couldn't stand the sight of his fixer right now (but the first thing he'd grab whenever this shitstorm let up would be first dibs on a hundred-man Ria-train he'd been saving for a rainy day in VR).

Ria Rose whirled into a digital cloud, then reformed as a silver-skinned Marilyn. "What can I do for you, King Otto?"

"Not her, either!"

So Marilyn evaporated and started to re-form as St. Jane, but Otto'd had enough:

"Goddammit—just go neutral!" He chucked what was left of the real St. Jane in the corner of the atrium.

The cloud reformed to a gray humanoid. "Present and online, Otto."

There was a reason Otto called her Fastlight.

After Zev recoded their stolen AI in Miami to write self-deleting Narc-soft and before Otto figured out how to silence him, the name Velociluz got so tedious that he rechristened her the English equivalent. Zev said he preferred the Spanish name: the way the *st* in Fastlight connected to the *l* was weird—so Otto put a hollow-point in his chest, stuffed him in an oil drum, and shipped their AI to Oakland in a cryotrain.

In fact, Otto killed every employee who ever met Fastlight.

At some point, Otto realized that might be good for his rep, but inevitably bad for business, 'cuz soon he'd be running low on coders *and* oil drums. So after he finished installing Fastlight into his upgraded vault, and before he iced his fourth coder, Haley, he had her develop—with his Wutani executive, Hirotashi, in Osaka—a custom kill switch.

Not your run-of-the-mill trigger, which most criminals implanted to destroy themselves and their wetwire's criminal history upon death or worse, arrest. Nah, this kill switch slaved Fastlight to Otto, converting his thoughts and instincts into Fastlight's root BIOS code at the speed of light. The thinnest cortical filter possible that could connect any human to an AI—without killing him.

And it was wetwired to two tons of Semtex under the Fang.

"Gimme a breakdown of the loading dock, NOW!"

Instantaneously, a wireframe schematic of the firefight replayed on the holo-deck. "Otto, your anxiety levels—"

"Are redlined, like they should be. 'Cuz I just got JACKED!"

Fastlight adjusted to a nurturing voice. "Seethe, sir . . . yes, but breathe please . . . You've been invaded and betrayed tonight, and both bring emotions that you must *feel* before taking action."

"Yeah, what do you want me to feel?"

"The truth." Fastlight responded calmly, "Hurt."

Otto's vague memories of his mother's love—crack-filled warmth, nestled between her wayward lovers' climaxes and abandonments—came years before his wetwire went in. So Fastlight's soothing vocals were based not on his mom's actual voiceprint, but a scan of those memories in his hippocampus, which was maybe why they were the exact balance of reason and care that connected with Otto so quickly.

Fastlight just knew how to talk to him.

Otto took a deep breath, his senses returning as he studied the moment when Baz capped the sprinklers and visibility deteriorated. He felt a wounded wave of pain rock through him, gazing at his custom cyborg in its cryochamber's security feed. "What's the value of that Elite.X9 on the street?"

"A fraction of its cost. Locally, 120 million ¢rypto. In New York City, 200 million. But the international markets in Kiev would be most lucrative, approaching 250 million."

Otto watched Ria get chucked in the truck. And there was Baz, punch drunk and swingin' again. Otto cursed himself for not 86'ing him an hour ago. Was he still trying to prove to Baz that his "good fight" didn't exist? Or maybe he was obsessed with proving it to *himself.*

Otto eyed another virt-cam's angle on the truck barreling out of the garage. "Ain't no fuckin' way these two were working alone."

"My probability assessment is 1–in–6 million 523 thou—"

"Analyze data points and estimate the parties involved." Otto had no doubt, somehow Baz's shitfuck partner Diamond Eddie D was in on this. The question was whether he was still inside the club.

"The loading dock was compromised internally," his AI reported. "Six to seven parties with, as of yet, unknown identities, bypassed the Inner Circle with an effective hacking worm."

"Yet un*known?*" A pang of suspicion throttled though Otto, but then it subsided because he remembered why . . .

"Complete analysis requires expanded perimeter. To scan the entire Fang requires access to the Outer Ring."

"Bitch wants outta her cage?"

Fastlight was suggesting a small amount of autonomy, so she'd be free to make decisions on her own, to analyze every wetwire in real time, but still confined to the nightclub that was designed and built as a secure standalone. Otto would continue to have access to all her code, but in the interest of expediency, only direct questions would elicit direct answers.

Otto glanced at the vault door, wary. Imagined Fastlight's quantum array inside its –235 environment, and his mind cranked.

I mean, it's a machine, right?

Not some rogue soldier like Baz goin' AWOL in the Water Wars. The thing had about as much agency as a microwave . . . right?

"Fine." He agreed with a snort.

And something sparked in Otto. A whiff of carnage drifted in from his past, invading deep within his coil. It smelled sweet and familiar. It smelled like slaughter.

Otto eyed Fastlight's avatar, reminding himself again that there was nuthin' human about it—which was a comfort, seein' how from now 'til he rescinded the privilege . . .

Otto would have to trust her.

VELOCILUZ

AFTER MIDNIGHT

Ken Cates realized things were about to get bloody again.

He was staring at his own reflection in prismatic glass when Ria Rose got pinched.

It was a Gates Award—the glass, that is—sitting on his balcony, an asymmetric pyramid with an accolade etched into its flat surface:

HUMANITARIAN OF THE YEAR

He chuckled at the abject irony, took a sip of a Macallan 57, and glanced out at his expansive view of the Golden Gate Seawall and the bridge behind it, both jutting into San Francisco.

An hour ago, he'd ascended the podium of the University Club on Nob Hill, booted a preprogrammed acceptance speech, and let his wetwire take over—as he watched a feed of Langston's team load the EliteX.9 into a cryochamber.

Passed three security checkpoints into Marin County, Belvedere Island, and his own four acres on Peninsula Point—as the caravan of undercover Hydro-Towncars crossed the city to the Fang.

Cracked that ¢15 million bottle and laughed at how cheap a Gates cost these days, as Otto's L7 named McT started strangling Ria; and was lamenting over how he'd never get to look Maria Roselli in the eye alive—when some shitstick named Baz Covane blew a hole in Otto's garage and ruined a very expensive operation.

Cates sighed. He flipped the scotch *and* the award off the balcony and headed across his massive lawn without waiting to hear either shatter on the rocks far below.

"Bring up the Hyperion convertible," he instructed his Wutani Pennyworth-Custom. "We're heading back to the city."

Cates was out of his Zegna tux and into his Zegna suit faster than the fuckbot in his bed batted an eye.

Entering his glass elevator, Cates descended past the recent construction on his personal office, eyeing the thermal plant, step-down transformer, and liquid nitrogen condensers that were awaiting his priceless AI. "We've waited eight years . . . Guess we can wait a little longer."

His mind drifted back to when Velociluz was stolen after the Glitch. They'd scrubbed every byte in StimSoft's Miami server silo in the hunt for his AI. But Zev Vromen's hacks and the rise of Narcsoft just led to Vromen's corpse and dozens more.

Ken stepped out of the lift, through a porte cochere, and into his whip. "The federal black site downtown."

And the Hyperion torched hydro south.

Ken kept one eye on his Wirecrime feed, where Langston played a good-cop–bad-cop with his partner, and the other on the private estates of Marin passing by outside.

"We'll be on the Golden Gate in a moment, Mr. Cates." Pennyworth's AI was now his Nubotica driver, Andretti-X, thanks to the cranial-to-cranial transfer Ken had patented himself before he ditched his deadweight partner Mike Turner and founded StimSoft. "Free of any signal interference, sir, if you care to—"

ACCESS GRANTED

>Wirecrime.Database<

Cates leaned back and let the lights on the bridge's northern spire dim, as he navigated the virtualized construct.

>StimSoft-ENCRYPT<

SELECT INTER-DEPT

Ken remembered when his company *built* this database. After the Glitch, Ken had jockeyed for a position on Wirecrime's Corporate Oversight Committee once the Velociluz trail ran cold, to keep track of all Narcsoft and Grand Theft AI investigations.

He knew one day his Rogue AI would turn up, and probably in the hands of some unhinged nightmare like Otto. But he never imagined the Butcher's daughter would be working for him too.

HR-PENAL
R&D-SWAT
GENOMICS-JUSTICE

Ken watched more departments scroll, but his eyes drifted towards the top of the list.

"Current bandwidth, sir, offers triple-encrypted access to HR—"

Cates waved the AI's voice mute and killed his wetwire's signal for a sec to consider Dave Roselli, his daughter Ria Rose, and the only other person who could connect the two.

"Access Justice Department biometrics and involuntary codes on Langston Cowell."

Ken recalled dropping Dave Roselli's classified file in front of the lawman months ago. How Langston had licked his lips with seducible ambition. Cates considered ID'ing Velociluz to him then, but figured keeping Langston in the dark and approving his billion-¢rypto sting was Ken's best bet to get back his priceless AI.

Without anyone discovering its secrets.

CONCUSSION ALARM
>federal·suite<

"Stop the car!" Cates shouted for the first time in years and repatched his wetwire into Langston's downtown command post.

Gunshots.

Static.

Virtualizations clarified and Cates watched as Ria Rose somehow commandeered a *motorcycle* and blasted an escape path outside.

"Access virt-cams at California and Battery."

SFPD·monitoring
>cams·11346-7-8-9<

Ken watched the bike skid into traffic and rip towards the Neo-Embarcadero, his wetwire tracking his optic nerve and toggling through a series of municipal virt-cams—when the fucking bike . . . *disappeared*.

"Proxy Neo-Embarcadero security."

But the entire roadway, save two minivans on the top slab, was empty.

"A Ghost Cloak . . ." Cates hadn't been broadsided in a long time. In fact, an alert in the corner of his periphery indicated the day he approved Langston's sting was the last time his heart rate beat this fast.

Right when Ria's avatar started talking.

Cates froze.

Thought he heard something, a distant echoing. He reached for the door handle and forgot there hadn't been one in a Hyperion for decades. "OPEN THE GODDAMN DOOR."

He stepped onto Laguna a few blocks from the seawall, oblivious to the Prostie Bots and wafer peddlers congregating under the

Neo-Embarcadero—when he heard it clearly, dopplering towards him.

On the roadway high above, the cacophonous roar of a *highly* illegal internal combustion engine.

"Patch me into Fort Mason security."

A new set of virtualizations holo'd in Cates's periphery, and he could see himself in the third feed, far below the lower roadway as that monster's roar closed in and thundered overhead.

The ground shook—Cates clocked it right to left—alarms exploded on self-drivers, hustlers scattered, and shit scared clean of a cat in the nearby dumpster.

But the roadway in his feed was empty.

As the sound echoed away and the clamor of street life returned, his AI asked: "Shall I track acoustically?"

Ken listened to the roar die off in the Marina near Divisadero and didn't even consider getting involved with SFPD in some idiotic dragnet raid—just let out a quiet chuckle instead.

"Get us free of the Sprawl." He sat back into the Hyperion and vectored the coordinates of StimSoft's Cupertino headquarters.

The car started gliding down Laguna's cavernous artery, weaving through self-drivers and petri-trucks towards a crack of night sky, as Cates de-signaled his wetwire off-grid once again.

Really, there were less than a hundred Americans with the legal right to unplug completely from Universal Monitoring.

Which was good for Cates, seeing how the plan he was hatching right now was a capital crime.

Want something done right? Best do it yourself.

Pentagon·Corporate

>Presidential·Encrypt<

US SOUTHERN ARMY

Ken considered the legislation that created this distinct chain of corporate command. The security threats designated by executive order to activate, say, a couple hundred thousand bots (give or take) stationed on the Southern Wall.

Fuck lobbying, Ken wrote those laws himself—with a *pen*.

Outside, the towers of the Data District gave way to manicured lawns and the Golden Gate beyond. "Approaching Bytedance Gardens, sir."

Not a lotta cats in this country knew who buttered America's bread. There was a reason Cates was one of 'em. Born with natural sociopathy. Nurtured among academia and the corporate elite. Ken knew where to spread the cream . . . And when to grab the knife.

"Is there a route, sir—"

"We're in a convertible for a fucking reason."

His Andretti-X nodded. Hydro-thrusters lit. Tires left asphalt.

God bless the USA.

2001

Ken Cates was a born capitalist and later a mass murderer but found that both thrived, thanks to an utter lack of empathy. Ken didn't just tear wings off flies as a kid—he weighed those wings on his father's microscale. In fact, Ken was into all kinds of measurements as a kid. How many liters of Varathane to ignite a kitten. How many pounds per square inch to plug a sitting squirrel with a DeWalt nail gun. And how many thrusts in a porno until the guy came.

Ken had his mother's photographic memory and his father's mathematic mind, yet school was just so mundane that he almost didn't bother applying to MIT's advanced/gifted program in the eighth grade. But what really kept him in Aberdeen that freshman year of high school was trying to figure out how the fuck he was even breathing. The only thing scarcer than conversation between his parents was emotion, so how the hell did Ken's pops *ever* knock up his moms? Until the day he turned fifteen, when they'd long since agreed it was time to tell their son the truth: Ken was adopted.

He never spoke to them again.

What set Ken apart from his business partner, Mike Turner, was the same thing he loathed in their fellow classmates at MIT. All anyone cared about was thorium laminates and quantum superpositions. Ken remembered reading in second grade about Levi Strauss in the gold rush and Rockefeller in the oil boom. Both counted rivets—in jeans or in barrels—because the secret to success was the bottom line. Ken found an inner peace, realizing every wing he ever tore off a fly, every cat he'd ever torched, had readied him to run the company he'd soon start with Mike Turner. And like Rockefeller, he'd destroy their competitors without a flinch. Some called him ruthless, others a psychopath, but both were right . . .

Ken was the most powerful CEO in America.

Yet powerless to rid the Butcher's daughter from his own head. Maria Roselli had been a phantom to Ken Cates ever since the Glitch, when for some goddamn reason, Nubotica fucked up and *saved her miserable life*. She'd been haunting him, coming for him in so many nightmare-fantasies—out of vengeance for her family, her sister, and what Ken did to her dad—that he stopped seeing a Psychiatry Bot to fall asleep at night and just started masturbating furiously instead.

He refused to use the word—because he didn't believe in superstition, any more than he believed in hocus-pocus, the devil, or (worse) God. But it would creep into his dreams, nonetheless.

Ria Rose was his destiny.

SMOKES

"Is that what I think it is?" Ria asked.

Baz had been fishing for some priceless contraband in today's fascist state of zero-carbon footprint—not the VR-fakies that matched nicotine's dopamine release in your wetwire, but the real deal he'd ripped out of a Thai passenger's cabin during the Carnival gig . . .

A pack of *actual* cigarettes.

"Only but the best." The room was sealed from all detection, even the Carbon Drones, so Baz lit one and handed it to her.

"Wow," she said as they both dragged. "Now I'm impressed." Felt her lungs tighten around the real, carcinogenic Marlboro Red.

"No, I'm the one who's impressed," Baz said after rolling over to look in her eyes, like she'd just rocked his world.

She smiled, barely conceding that he'd just flipped her script too. Then she saw a flicker of doubt hit him. "What?"

"Nuthin'," he lied.

Her defenses kicked in again as he stirred, and she could tell he was opening up, which was actually suddenly terrifying, since she realized . . .

She'd just made love for the first time.

"Just. You know, your, your neurals. You said your augments were . . . amygdala and what else?"

Then she figured it out. "Oh God. Are you asking if I faked it?"

"No, I mean—technically, it wouldn't be faking—it would be, what? Synthetic, or-or augmented."

Ria just stared at him and fumed.

Baz did a double take like his heart just dropped.

"I'm fucking with you. NO, my arousals aren't robotic. Now will you light me my own fuckin' Red before I regret this." But she said it with a sly grin.

He did and they dragged again and she felt herself relax, more comfortable with Baz than she'd been with anyone since her mom got sick.

Damn. *Was that possible?*

Baz stole a glance at the rendezvous beacon. None of the team had responded yet, but Ria didn't care. She could feel her paranoid walls receding. "God, I haven't had a real cigarette . . . since I was twelve."

"They taste even better since they were outlawed."

Duh.

"Doesn't everything?" Ria blew out another drag and drifted back. "My sister and I would steal my mom's. She was a dancer, and we'd do routines with her. They were brutal and exhausting and awesome. And when we were done, she'd take a shower, and we'd steal Reds just like these . . . Harsh, but perfect."

"Your sister?"

"My twin." Ria didn't give a shit now, she wanted him to know everything.

"Christ, there's two of you?"

It was meant as a joke—but she didn't laugh. "She died in my arms . . . Just like Devyn." Ria turned to him. "I really did lose my family in the Glitch. My SSS is ghosted, but the real shit's real."

Baz stared at her. Then he leaned over—his gaze connecting with hers completely—and he traced the scar tissue around her right cheek and eye . . . "That's when this happened?"

She looked at him. The last fraction of hesitation.

"C'mon. It's midnight. We're naked. Ain't gonna get any easier . . ."

So she told him the story of Dani's death.

When she was done, a single tear ran down her cheek.

Baz leaned forward slowly and kissed its saltiness. "See, that wasn't so hard."

"What?"

"Trust."

The word detonated the moment. None of their crew had responded to the rendezvous beacon, and it suddenly dawned on Ria that Baz wasn't planning to regroup and rob the Fang. He was waiting for his team to *escape* the city for good.

"Are you gonna finish this?"

Her question hit him like a freight train. "What, the score?"

She didn't have to nod—just looked at him.

"Are you nuts, you still wanna hit that vault?"

She did. To counter his disbelief, Ria hit the high notes of what an extraordinary jam they were in, between Wirecrime and Otto, between VR-prison and a death warrant.

"I don't think you get it," Baz countered. "This ain't a robbery anymore—you're talkin' about kidnapping."

"Oh, please, it's a machine."

"It's alive."

"It's a fucking toaster!"

"NO, you're wrong. This is no bot with a blown cap. True AIs aren't just self-aware, they're fucking omniscient—they're smarter than God. And boosting one is impossible. You wanna know why?" Baz flared hot with blood, like he was speaking now from experience. "'Cuz AIs rewrite their antivirals nano-by-nano in real time, they hit like a freight train, an unfiltered Straight-Sync, cortex to spine. Every capillary bursts at once, your eyes, your ears, your nose—an AI will kill any Flyboy it goes up against, no matter how far on the spectrum he is. Not Carlo, not Eddie—nobody can crack an—"

"That's a myth, a scare tac—"

"It's no myth!"

"How do you—"

"'Cuz I watched it happen! . . . The NSA Data Mine, my last real job? You asked why I'm all alone, slingin' Street Meat in the Loin? *That's why.*"

Baz's secret. His obvious scars were the burns along his torso from the Water Wars. But the real scar tissue wrapped around far deeper wounds.

"An AI killed my last Flyboy . . ." He closed his eyes to say it. "Right after I married her."

When he opened them, Ria just stared at him. There was no question he was telling the truth. His deepest truth.

"Your wife?"

A steaming furious self-loathing nod. "Carlo's sister. Kara."

"The woman on your wetwire."

Again he nodded. "I thought droppin' outta Blackhawks torchin' villages with the villagers in 'em was the worst thing I ever did. Until I talked my wife into hacking an AI, and it killed her."

He stubbed out his cigarette, got outta bed, and checked the rendezvous beacon again. No one had responded. Even Quinn, safe from wetwire monitoring and secure in his Sea Cliff compound, was dark. The beacon just beeped away, with zero response.

"They're stuck in that goddamn death trap."

So he switched it silent.

Ria stared at his body. Blistered skin, hardened over time wrapped around his midsection like a blanket. Ria touched her own cauterized scar and realized he'd lost as much as she had. Got burned hotter than she'd been. Wanted to live again, almost as bad as she did. So she moved to his side and touched him like she'd never touched anyone—with the risk that she, too, was alone in this world.

"I'm sorry, Baz . . . But we have an edge right now that you didn't then."

Baz turned and recoiled, looking at her in disbelief. "Did you not just hear me? I got my wife kill—"

"I understand that. And I lost my sister in the Glitch. But I'm done being a prisoner. Don't you think it's time?"

Baz looked at her—and suddenly he could see it in her eyes.

What she'd managed to conceal in the interrogation room. It wasn't some simple lie or sociopathic deceit or even the self-delusional fraud of a hustler or con man . . . No, it was WORSE than all of that. What burned now behind Ria's eyes was the fire of a *cause*, a conviction, a purpose—the faith of a true believer.

Ria was on a crusade.

"Jesus-fuckin'-Christ."

'Cuz that's when Baz figured it out.

"You've known all along, haven't you?"

FULL CIRCLE

It was Lo-Ball's comment that lit the fuse on Ria.

Otto's wafers could self-delete? Only an AI could write code that complex. And a voice went off inside her. *Otto had to be the source of his product, not just some stop on the supply chain.* So Ria had to find out whether the servers in his vault were full of Narcsoft.

Or the AI that wrote it.

Every move took time, since she had to make 'em off-grid. In cash, not ¢rypto—with cretins she could trust were so *un*trustworthy that even Otto wouldn't do business with them. She found a hacker in Bogotá to scrub a dozen different flavors and confirm they were AI written. A triad in Chinatown hacked the city's power grid and found the vault was pulling the kinda juice you'd need for quantum refrigeration. So Ria said fuck it and got down with Moxie one night on-wire with her own firewall deactivated. The next morning as Otto hacked in, she raided his hermetically sealed penthouse office and stole the actual *paper* blueprints to the vault. And there it was, sitting square in the middle of the most secure 1,000 cubic feet in California.

The last Rogue AI in America.

Ria hadn't been genuinely scared like that since her dad slid into insanity. When she told Baz it was "just a matter of time" she wasn't kidding. Ria knew better than anyone that Otto with an AI was like Hitler holding a neutron bomb. Sure, he had Fastlight finger-painting digital drugs like an infant presently, but who knew when Otto might decide to hack an ICBM launch silo? Or the learning caps on a battalion of Private Service Warrior Bots stationed on the Southern Border . . .

She thought about turning to Wirecrime, but there was a good chance they'd scrub her SSS and sniff out Maria Roselli. And just the sliver of a possibility that she'd get grilled over the Underground Butcher and her dead sister by some shitfuck with a badge was not happening, period. She'd lost faith in the system years ago when the FBI lied about her own death—she wasn't about to start trusting Wirecrime now.

Ria hadn't slotted since Trixie.

But she figured a new wafer named Nirvana was called for, to help clear her mind and provide some insight. The wafer had a peace sign stamped on it, so fuck it—anything done well is done to excess. She doubled up and positioned both over either I/O and slotted into a lotus pose under the Bodhi tree.

A neurologist from Harvard implanted a wetwire in a High Lama for his visions at the Nechung Oracle. The resulting wavelength shocked implant coders to the core—a staggering and incomprehensible data stream, filed onto a set of memory banks in Cambridge, where it sat for years, until Otto swiped it so Fastlight could write Nirvana.

The wafer only lasted seven minutes and reentry was a bitch, but in that seven-minute window . . .

Ria saw her destiny clearly.

An existential weapon sat in the hands of a psychopath. And if she didn't do something about it . . . Ria'd be *lost*. Lost like her father's whirling tirades. Like her mother talking in tongues. A world lost to automation and what so many whispered (with their wetwires off) *must* have orchestrated it all: Artificial Intelligence.

Ria would gather a crew together to steal that AI and destroy it.

It was no crazier than any crusade. And it brought purpose into Ria's life. Keeping learning caps sealed at the Fang was like diffusing a pound of TNT. Destroying Otto's AI was deactivating a 100-megaton warhead.

She considered telling Baz the truth—and she came so close that night together with the laundry list. But the reality was that there'd be no better moment than when they actually opened the vault, 'cuz by that point it would be moot. Until then, she had to remind herself every night, that saving the lives of millions justified putting this crew in the crosshairs of something as lethal as a Rogue AI . . .

Unless, of course, Baz figured it out first.

1:17 A.M.

"You tricked us into stealing an AI?"

Baz was beside himself with rage, like he wanted to hear her admit it—no, demanded it.

She didn't ask him something stupid like, *What are you talking about?* Didn't bother denying it. She just stared at him with eyes that confirmed it was true.

He lit with rage. "Goddammit, you talk on and on about trust. No wonder you don't trust anyone—you're the biggest snake I've ever met!"

"I find that hard to believe."

"How'd you really get that scar?"

"Fuck you, I told you." The anger was simmering hot again, and it wasn't that she couldn't control it—she didn't want to. "My sister—"

"You don't have a fuckin' sister!"

"You think I'd lie about that?!"

"I think you lied about EVERYTHING! Your mom was a nurse, your dad a trucker—we know that's all bullshit. 'No Deal' on my Robo-Rockettes—*because you wasted 'em*. And now you got a dead twin? Or a dead twin fuckbot—you choose!" He was yelling now, both charged with a bond that needed to heal to survive. "I mean why are you a cipher?! Why is everything about you ghosts and aliases and fuckin' lies?!"

"'Cuz my father was the Underground Butcher!"

He did *not* see that coming.

Baz looked in her eyes. Swore she wasn't lying. "That's impossible, both his daughters are dead."

"Dani's dead. I survived. When I found out in the hospital I'd been 'killed' . . . I bolted."

Her absolute truth. No more secrets.

Only 'cuz he knew her, did it make any sense. All her heart. All her rage. All her defiance came from a single source, the vector of so much fear and hatred in the world—the Glitch. She'd been running from it for eight years. He asked her a few more questions to understand how she came to work for Otto, how much sordid shit she'd endured and why.

"So you don't want to steal it, you wanna kill it."

She looked at him without any hesitation. "I'm gonna drive a stake through its fucking CPU."

"Why?" He felt goddamn asinine even saying it . . . "To save the world?"

But Ria didn't flinch.

Goddammit. Baz's eyes narrowed. "You sure you're not trying to get some payback for Dani? Maybe pay back your dad's sins at the same time?"

Ria didn't deny it. Didn't mention all the families that'd be slaughtered by Otto if he went on a rampage with an AI. She just looked at him and stated quite clearly (again) exactly why they were here:

"I'm gonna make sure what happened to my family . . ."

Then Baz could feel the world turn full circle.

"Never happens again."

Ria carried the kinda conviction that nailed you to a cross.

LOCKDOWN

1:17 A.M.

Took Moxie ninety seconds to seal the main entrance.

With Ria gone, Otto was now leaning on his other Scissor Sister to run the Fang—a responsibility she'd never wanted. So Moxie slotted a half wafer of Bracer to put the edge back on and pounded the emergency Lockdown toggle.

Hidden pressure doors descended over the black-enameled entrance. Patrons in the front lobby flinched at the ignition of the hydraulics, then heart rates spiked and alarm spread across everyone's face. Some attempted to bolt through the double doors, but both were already locked, so their only choice was to back out of the way and start hollering at Moxie in fear and growing panic . . .

"Showtime's postponed!" Moxie smiled, trying to pretend that all their lives weren't in increasing danger. "Doors gonna stay locked until the final curtain . . ."

Then she saw Eddie and Carlo.

The CrackerJack had yanked the Flyboy outta the Grid Room as soon as they'd coiled his Ring of Fire, with a new set of marching orders: "Gig's blown—time to bolt!"

Both now locked eyes with Moxie as the doors shuddered closed behind her, and each realized the clock was ticking. It was just a matter of time before their role in tonight's caper would be discovered.

"May I have everyone's attention, please?" Otto led McT through the crowd in the front lobby. Bodies surged forward to listen as Eddie ducked back into the shadows.

"We've received reports of a police presence outside the club and for your own security, we've sealed the doors until the Seven Year Itch is over so that everyone's identities can remain secure as we write signal-jamming software."

Otto pulled out a bag of Narcsoft and held up a freshly cast wafer, still hot to the touch. "Until then, tonight's signature Narcsoft flavor unites all of us in ecstasy and a collective consciousness. Please enjoy, on the Fang . . ." A handful of sexbots started distributing the gratis wafers.

"VIBE."

Fastlight wrote the flavor minutes ago to hack each patron's wetwire and hunt for the thieves that hit him. But Otto had a feeling he'd be able to extract the same intel a lot quicker the ole-fashioned way. 'Cuz he'd had time to review his own wetwire feed and zero in on one conspirator who'd been under his nose all night.

"Mind coming with me?"

Carlo froze. Otto was *right behind him*. But the kingpin walked on past, straight for:

"Mox?"—who lunged for the door. As McT incapacitated her, Otto watched her futile struggle persist despite the machine's clear superiority. He considered Fastlight's newfound freedom, how its Vibe wafer would scour all his patrons' minds *voluntarily*—and Otto sensed that cauldron of rage inside, now boiling over in tectonic change.

Why hadn't he done this before?

That stench of carnage was undeniable now. His cock stiff and eyes pinned, Otto was rolling hard and closing in on a slaughter that would rival anything from his past. With *wild* charisma and the impresario eyes of a 21st century P. T. Barnum, Otto turned to his gasping patrons. "Trust me, everyone . . ."

Otto didn't give a shit about tonight's act, any more than he gave two fucks about anyone there. But he needed both to sit tight if he was gonna drill down *ugly* on whoever hit him and put the screws to a woman for the first time since Venezuela.

"The show must go on!"

BETHESDA

The file flashed brightly in Baz's wetwire.

He'd killed the rendezvous beacon after a message came in from Quinn—freaking out about the score, not the crew. The Fang was surely locked down by now, Ria insisted. And only Otto—and Fastlight or McT under his command—could open it.

Which meant it didn't matter whether they hit the vault or not, Baz would have to square off against that AI if he was gonna get his crew out.

Why the fuck did he never learn?

The answer sat on that flashing file. Encrypted in a hidden niche of his own mem-drive—one he'd been on the verge of deleting how many times before? But Baz could never do it. He didn't believe in destiny, and he didn't believe in fate. He believed in curses, and for good reason. But right now, Baz thought maybe that file would lift the curse that'd been hanging over his head . . . since he was born?

The name of the file said it all.

KARA

Baz was at a ramen shop in the Loin a few years after the Glitch, sucking down bad noodles to soak up a liter of bourbon to forget a South Side Loca to erase a nightmare of Venezuela. And Baz was considering just how much he hated his life, a veritable Laundrobot rinsing one bad choice with another and another.

When the worst one he'd ever seen walked past . . .

Her name was Kara, and she had heavy-set hips—perfectly contoured on an hourglass figure that was impossible to lose through the back streets of Chinatown. At first Baz just followed her on a whim, since he needed to move anyway if he was gonna meet Quinn's drop at dawn. But then he realized two things while on Kara's tail: (1) she was on a bourbon and ice cream bender through the streets of San Francisco and (2) she was the only person Baz had ever met who was even more self-destructive than he was.

He started asking in each bar and parlor what she'd ordered and kinda fell for her in three stops. Maker's to Blanton's to Eagle Rare. Mint Chip to Sea Salt Caramel to Pralines 'n' Cream. She was descending into richer and richer concoctions of both—getting louder and rowdier with every order. He could hear her swearing like a sailor; even asked one bartender to spend the night with her, who readily accepted, so she laughed and gave him a BART station's address. Baz had studied a variety of afflictions when he was prepping the Watchman at Nubotica and was convinced this woman was bipolar—

And flying high on a serious mania.

Most men would consider this a nonstarter, or at least a warning sign. But Baz heard each "Bitch" and "Fuck" out of her mouth as a siren song. So when she stumbled into a Swensen's for her fifth ice cream, Baz had to make his move. The poor kid helping her had caramel dripping down his arm, holding a waffle cone covered in hot fudge and strawberry sauce, trying to reach for a towel and a second cone at the same time, 'cuz she was midway through ordering every extra topping they had—when Baz leaned in and whispered in her ear:

"Don't forget the whipped cream."

Kara turned to him. And for the first time he looked into her eyes, blazing with what was once called hysteria, then manic depression, then bipolarity (with a slice of borderline, if Baz had to wager). Like anyone who suffered, she wasn't satisfied with *any* choice, so she searched for Door #3 . . . She thought about fucking Baz that night (he could tell), so he smiled at her with a look that assured her, yes, she could trust him, but no, she didn't want to sleep with him *yet*. Because he was safe (that was rare) and dangerous (necessary) at the same time (kinda unbelievable). So in that instant, information fully overloaded her short-circuiting central nervous system—and she just looked at Baz like he was some sort of fuckin' idiot: "You think I'd forget that?"

And passed out.

Kara Zeta woke up in his apartment at sunrise, and Baz got her wetwire straightened out over the next few weeks. She hated how StimSoft's Lithium wafers put her in a fog, and went off 'em on a tear as quickly as they dumbed her down. So Baz paid four mil ¢rypto for a custom Wetwire.X implant that could properly manage her norepinephrine uptake. After three months without an episode, the longest stretch since she was eleven, Kara did two things: she asked Baz to marry *her*—right before she told him about her brother. 'Cuz if Kara's pic was in the dictionary under *hot mess*, then you'd find her brother Carlo next to *basket case*. She was a screaming bipolar roller coaster, he was an institutionalized hacker schizophrenic, and finally an alarm went off in Baz for real . . .

But by then it was too late.

Breaking into a federal VR-psyche-ward was a lot easier than Baz figured. Not a lotta nutjobs trying to break *into* that construct. But when they pulled Carlo out of deep stasis, Baz realized something truly insane. His fiancée and her brother carried parallel neurotransignals, which meant they could train to be a Flyboy duo. Kara could sync with her brother's wetwire at the synaptic level and track his target's antivirals from her own tandem Flyboy Chair without a Ring of Fire.

Baz busted her brother loose to make their wedding.

But he couldn't help himself. The day before they boarded the dronecraft for St. Barts, Baz hit Citibank's ¢rypto-drives to find out if the two Zetas were as effective as he hoped. Cranking down her norepinephrine cycler, Kara slipped into a manic state for the gig—devouring Citi's antiviral software and feeding her brother algorithms as he hacked through its firewall like butter. And Baz realized two things during the caper. Kara's Wetwire.X lit up Universal Monitoring like a Christmas tree. So a freelance CrackerJack just wouldn't cut it anymore.

There was a guy in the Loin—Quinn called him the Robin Hood of CrackerJacks—who sounded perfect, since Baz considered himself the Robin Hood of Glass Servers. So he cased Diamond Eddie D for a week to confirm he was legit. Watched him turn down two bank jobs and a StimSoft plant and realized he'd have to appeal to more than just Eddie's sense of adventure—Baz would have to *inspire* him to join his crew.

'Cuz it was the righteous thing to do.

On that beach in St. Barts—watching the sun come up, their first morning as newlyweds—Kara turned to Baz and told him he was the one she'd been waiting for her entire life. He was like some fairy tale Prince Charming with a taste for grand theft. She didn't want *now* to end—and thank God there'd be no ding or signal or robot to ruin the moment, since they were all illegal on this island. Then she wished aloud that they could go somewhere even more remote, to the end of the earth. Waxed romantic over an island formerly known as Tahiti—wondering if they could ever someday afford it . . .

And that's when Baz pitched the pair of jobs that would change their lives forever. The first, the De-Augmentation Server Farm, would make their bones in the Loin and set them up for years. The second would take a year to prep, but it would set them up in the Tahitian Protectorate for the rest of their lives.

The NSA Data Mine.

The physical robbery was child's play. The Data Mine was a nondescript government building in Colorado. But the glass servers buried in the salt mine underneath were vast . . . The archives for all surveillance records predating the virtualizing of information and the wetwire itself. The Data Mine was nicknamed the Boneyard. Things called emails, web pages, phone calls, and text messages—shit only Quinn was old enough to remember—trillions of trillions were stored there, the juiciest material, dirt on hundreds of CEOs to rob the biggest corporations on earth . . . The true villains of the realm.

If you hacked the AI that guarded it.

Bethesda was a gender-specific freeform AI, which meant when *he* looked in the mirror in any VR-construct, his avatar resembled a particle apparition. With an incept date of 2031 in Seattle, Bethesda was a fractal of flocking code that allowed him to defy most physics engines, since his primary function was data optimization. First on the roadways, then in the air, and one day, his owner Amazon hoped, interstellar travel. But the genetic engineering scandal that took down Bezos in '35 took down the company stock too, so Bethesda went into receivership and was relegated to organizing, warehousing, and guarding the NSA Data Mine for Uncle Sam. Like most AIs after the Glitch . . .

Bethesda could fly to the stars, but guarded the basement instead.

>await.decrypt<

KARA

Ria watched Baz stare at the file.

He'd double-checked the signal jammer on the safe house grid before powering on his wetwire and pulling it from his wetwire folio.

Baz looked at Ria and held up a fiber-optic cable. She understood. She sat beside him, took his hand, and jacked into a tandem link.

Nothing to do now but load it.

Baz pulled a wafer from his pocket. No stamp. A homegrown Eddie special. Ria figured it was the decrypt to the file, figured Baz carried it separately so no one could hack "Kara" and he wouldn't ever accidentally access it. But what was on "Kara" exactly, only Eddie and Carlo knew, since one was there that night next to his sister, and the other encrypted the file at Baz's request.

But she knew it was the Data Mine Run that killed his wife.

Baz had taken this deep breath before.

Positioned the decrypt wafer on his I/O as many times as he'd stuffed the KARA file in his wetwire's trash. Either move would've delivered Baz through pain unto freedom. Like his great-grandpa used to say: you gotta go through hell before you get to heaven. But instead, Baz chose purgatory again and again. He could see that clearly now, 'cuz he wasn't hesitating out of fear or paralysis this time, he was waiting for the file to cache so the decrypt would align and the footage would swallow him completely.

He'd been broken forever. He couldn't live one more day, one more minute—fuck it, not another second—without doing whatever it took to fix himself.

Ria was right. It was time.

She watched the processing icon spin, indicating the time left before the file'd render, as they counted down together:

5 . . . 4 . . . 3 . . . 2 . . .

Then they slotted his wife's death.

```
                              tandem.I/O<>slot
```

Kara's POV hovered in Data Space, just outside the Boneyard's Central Core. Turning to her right, she could see her brother Carlo, prepping his Flyboy Run.

"I'm at the firewall, Baz," Carlo reported. "Bethesda's right in front of me."

"Alright, I'm at the elevator." Baz could hear his own voice on Kara's wetwire and the ratchet of the full-auto SCAR assault rifle in his hands. "I'm hot, talk to me."

"Carlo's going in," Kara said.

Baz hadn't heard that voice for years. The only way you could feel tears in a VR-construct (besides the waves of emotion), was a strange defocusing and refocusing in Data Space that came with the moistening of the optic nerve. Baz tried not to blink. He wanted to watch and feel this experience in its entirety, but he felt his eyes do it anyway.

Bethesda's antivirals came at Carlo—slowly at first, enticing both him and his sister into thinking the AI's firewall was penetrable.

"We got this, Baz," Kara said with the bravado that stole his heart then and made it break now. "Give him ten seconds until—"

Then she broke off.

Baz wanted to close his eyes because those were the last confident words he ever heard from her, but he felt Ria squeeze his hand IRL and resisted the instinct.

Bethesda's antivirals exploded in color and intensity, surrounding Carlo with tentacles of binary and hexadecimal code like Custer's Last Stand. Kara's brother shook in his chair—chattering at double speed—a whiplash response to the freight-train security coming at him from all directions—

"Christ, Carlo, you okay?" Kara screamed.

"Talk to me, Kara!" Baz begged her to let him in.

"The AI's too much, Baz—Carlo's flatlining!"

Indeed, Carlo's cardiac monitors were beating furiously like a dark-core drumbeat, way above 220, and Baz knew what would happen at 240. His heart rate would switch from automatic gunfire to a single, high-pitched tone.

"Hold on, brother!"

And Kara's perspective shifted from peripheral witness to inside Bethesda's line of fire as she engaged in her own attack run.

Baz and Ria could feel the vertigo of their own physics engine shift so rapidly that both thought the other might pass out. Bethesda's fractal cloud suddenly consumed their entire POV. Kara was diving in front of Carlo, putting herself in range of Bethesda's antivirals—

"Kara, what are you doing?!" Baz heard himself howl.

His question was never answered, as she sacrificed herself to save Carlo—going face-to-face with Bethesda, like a suicidal lamb before the slaughter—

"I love you, Ba—"

Then Bethesda destroyed her mind.

"Aaaaaaaaaaaaaaahhhhhhhhhhhhhh."

Everything reduced to a pinprick—Baz and Ria's own pain-override utility redlined—protecting them from the horrific anguish his dying wife endured. Then images flashed, as Baz saw something that lasted seven seconds and lost focus and refocused as many times—

Because Baz was sobbing IRL.

Kara and Carlo at six years old in Nogales.

At fifteen, the paddles descending on her first electroshock session.

The first time she ever saw Baz . . . "Don't forget the whipped cream" echoing in Data Space—making love to Baz on a beach in VR-Tahiti—that sunrise in St. Barts, dreaming of the job that was now killing her—and sunset the night before, when she whispered through her own tears, streaming like Baz's were now . . .

"I do."

`tandem.I/0><de-slot`

Baz whipped outta Data Space like a slingshot, panting and screaming in rage and anguish.

He let it all out—too many years in perdition—and when the air in his wail finally dissipated, he just kept howling. But there was nothing left to vibrate the vocal cords, so eventually he just gave up.

Ria held him through all of it.

She pulled him in tight, and he clung to her—finally releasing so much guilt and pain in a huge gasp. When it cleared, he just shook his head—sweat and tears sprinkling onto the concrete floor.

The ghost of Kara was gone . . .

But she passed something along from the grave.

```
NSA COMMAND:
executive action authorized
```

```
BETHESDA:
prime mandate prohibitory
```

```
NSA COMMAND:
mandate override
```

```
BETHESDA:
target terminated
```

The AI's transcript.

Instantaneous communication with the NSA in Maryland, as Bethesda struggled to go lethal with Executive Actions on first Carlo, then Kara—violating the AI's Prime Mandate, which prohibited him from injuring any human.

Besides the catharsis, *this* was what Baz needed desperately. It shocked Ria deeply, but was worth the miserable and tormented ordeal he'd just endured.

Since it proved the AI was just following orders.

SCREWS

Otto cinched Moxie tight to the whipping post.

With her arms strapped into bondage locks above her head and her ankles tied to the base of the carbon-fiber staff, Otto got a little itchy. Moxie was a Narcsoft junkie, just like him, but one with no dignity, 'cuz the Slinger would do anything for a wafer. So over the last few years . . . Otto had his way with every slot Moxie had.

A week ago when he'd caught a glimpse of a third I/O under her tongue, Otto thought about forcibly christening that one. He figured she'd implanted it after he'd raved on and on about gettin' triple-blitzed on his *own* third slot . . .

But now Otto knew the real reason why.

"Recognize this, Moxie?" Otto held up the modified Thrilz wafer, spinning it in front of her terrified eyes.

"N-No, Otto . . ."

McT guarded the door to this torture chamber called "Solitary" deep within the Dungeon at the Fang, and tonight Otto would reap the reward for soundproofing the walls. As Moxie quivered on the pole, her muscles trembling from too much Bracer and fully justified panic, Otto suddenly regretted that he'd never thought to bind Moxie in chains, slam a wafer of Vesuvio, and just blow steam 'til the lava flowed.

"Oh, but you *must* . . . It's the only flavor in the club tonight that's been hacked."

Then even McT knew Moxie would die.

Bootleg wafers were so illicit at the Fang, Otto framed two Slingers every year for selling the contraband just to scare the shit outta the rest of 'em. He'd even wait three months before tipping SFPD Harbor Drones to the oil drums, so he could circulate virts of a pair of rotten fish-food carcasses for added effect.

When Fastlight started her scan of the club, the residual Thrilz code still coursing through Moxie lit up like a homing beacon. And the dozens she'd dumped down the trash chute in a sling-bag just proved what he'd always known: Moxie was as dumb as she was hot. And she'd fry for it tonight.

Otto chucked her bag on the floor, scattering wafers everywhere. "So I'm gonna make this easy on you, Mox. You tell me who you're workin' with . . ." He moved in close and ran his hand up the inside of her thigh, flush-hot to the touch. "And I'll go *easy* on you."

"I don't know what you're talking about, Otto."

Otto just shook his head and turned to McT. "Prep a Death's Head."

Fastlight rang in his wetwire with a cursory warning. "Sir, your evolving course of action will force me to violate my Prime Mandate—"

"Mandate override. Proceed." No matter how many times he tried to code it outta her, the AI still issued it every time they killed someone together.

Fastlight switched to that nurturing maternal voice again. "Otto. This confidant's treason was truly spiteful . . . But perhaps an act of mercy—"

"Prep. The goddamn. Wafer."

Didn't matter how nice the bitch talked to him now. Fastlight was gonna spin those qubits—a slave to his whim 'til the day he died—when, thanks to his kill switch, the whole shithouse would go up in flames whether his AI abided by its Prime Mandate, or did whatever heinous shit Otto wanted.

"As long as my heart's beating? Bitches better do as I say."

Moxie started to hyperventilate, so Otto tasked Fastlight to hack her wetwire and stabilize the girl's respiration. He couldn't have her pass out in panic 'til he'd inflicted enough digital pain to compel her to cough up her partners in crime . . .

Then he'd torture her to death. Otto was just too turned on not to kill her.

McT handed him the Death's Head glass, stamped with the skull 'n' bones of the Nazi SS, and Moxie started begging him not to slot it in her. Otto asked again and again who she was working with—but he realized it was futile. Moxie lived by the code passed down from her parents and every other dead junkie in the Loin: Stitches for Snitches. And though what Otto was about to do to her would never stitch up, he was sure Moxie had recited the motto so many times while slotted that it'd coded into her neural architecture.

She couldn't violate it now, if she wanted to.

Moxie tried to form the words. Tried to rat out her droogs—but she couldn't get her vocal cords to do it. Couldn't even form the thoughts. Thanks to Ma and Pa, she'd developed her own behavior inhibitor, like some reverse Pavlovian response. And Otto chuckled, 'cuz she was living proof . . .

There was so little difference between man and machine.

Then he slotted Death's Head in her.

Pupils pinned. White-hot pain.

A knife between her temples, gouging behind her eyes—a migraine that split the skull slowly from the inside out. Every cord of muscle strapped against bone, flexed 'til tendons snapped, ligaments ruptured— Moxie's mind bent inward, her coil ablaze, her skin like napalm, her organs bathed in the lactic acid of a nuclear fire—she bit down so hard she gnashed through her tongue and chipped three teeth to the pulpy nerve. Her mouth was metal in a microwave—her veins and arteries straining 'til they burst, blood splattered her bag—and Moxie screamed a feral, bestial scream—

"Aaaaaaaaahhhhhhhhhhhh . . . . . ."

—then her thrashing neck snapped, her face fell into her sternum, 'til she slowly suffocated to death.

And Otto's cock was so hard, he thought of Ria.

NIGHT MARKET

Ria zigzagged through the Night Market at Dolores Park.

Merchants came at her like they were in Chiang Mai, but instead of selling fried fish or lithium cells, every booth and steel counter in Dolores Park catered to black-market augments—hawking hardware, bionic prosthetics, and fiber-nerve grafts straight off the factory floor in Rangoon.

The kiosk ORs were clean enough to eat off, which plenty of surgeons did, since they also lived there. Only in Dolores Park could you order a pair of olfactory implants and a bowl of crab mohinga, and by the time the noodles were steaming, you'd be whiffin' 'em with an augmented sense of smell.

Baz followed from ten feet behind, thinking about Quinn and wishing he sold surgical augments, 'cuz Ria couldn't get half that far without another barker offering her biceps, eardrums, or the augmentation certificate to guarantee she'd stay under 40% after implantation. 'Fact, it took 'em twenty minutes to cull through this latter set of merchants, lookin' for the right needle in a haystack—

'Cuz they were buying a different kind of certificate.

Ria'd scoured Bethesda's transcript line by line 'til she was sure that Fastlight's antivirals would need Otto *alive* to go lethal. But Baz had to remind her that a club full of Warrior Bots, two tons of Semtex, and a kill switch still stood between them and the kingpin. Which was when she hit him with her rather ingenious move:

"Not if I go in *as* that EliteX.9."

Baz just stared at her in shock. "You . . . of all people . . . are gonna pose as a fuckbot?"

But Ria just looked at him and quoted her dad. "We become what we hate."

The idea was essentially Langston's sting, but with the real Ria playing the undercover. She'd slip through all three layers of security, catering to Otto's fantasy 'til he opened his wetwire to sync with her.

So Carlo could hack his *kill switch.*

And if they took out Otto after that?

Baz could crack the vault.

"But Ria . . ." Baz whispered, as the reality—the *risk*—of her plan jolted him. She'd be posing as Otto's fuckbot. Descending into his lair. As his property. But before he could say, *How am I gonna protect you?*—

"I can handle myself."

Baz squinted a thousand miles through her, struggling to see some way out of this bad idea. Then he recognized one obvious hitch:

"You may look like that bot . . . But a Resonance Sequencer will ID you as human in a nano."

She stepped in closer. "I'm 38% synthetic."

Shit. She *had* thought of everything . . .

"I buy one more augment on the street, and I read robot."

Baz couldn't help but consider the irony. "So what, you're just gonna use Otto's libido against him?"

She smiled. "Worked on you, didn't it?"

So Ria was hunting e-papers certifying she was *no longer human.*

"Right-side optics, 500 thousand," the vendor said. Part physician, part mechanic, all hustler.

"Certificate included?"—500k was steep for an eye, but Ria wasn't buying off-the-shelf synthetics. She needed a chromo-to-chromo splice from her own DNA, to match the organic eye perfectly.

"Certificate extra. 750 together."

Ria recoiled and looked at Baz. "Fuckin' ridiculous."

Did they really need the fake certificate? Her status (or lack thereof) and the fact that 100% of her vision would now be augmented meant she could skip down to the Bureau on Van Ness, and they'd strip her of her human rights on the spot.

But they didn't open until 8:00 a.m.

"You're not actually haggling over surgery, are you?" Baz turned to the vendor. "Add a respirator and an evac stretcher for a mil."

The vendor nodded and started to fill the order.

"You know the club's sealed," Ria reminded him.

"Yep." Baz thought about the Fang's security as he transferred the last of his wetwire funds into the kiosk's orbital account and stared at his five-figure balance. Christ, Baz couldn't even afford a crab mohinga anymore. The score that was supposed to save him—was *gone*.

'Course, Quinn didn't know that.

The vendor activated his Surgery Bot, who would perform most of the eye replacement, save a few human checkpoints that were still required by the manufacturer. Most augment kiosks catered to the off-grid market, so they used actual anesthetic, not a wetwire equivalent. With the whine of a servo and a pump, gears were set in motion that would put Ria under for the 12-minute procedure.

Baz then turned to her, because he had to say it. "You know if you go through with this, you read robot for good . . . You'll lose your human rights forever."

Ria just shrugged. "Voting's overrated."

She sank into the implant chair as the Surgery Bot filled an old-school IV pack with lorazepam, and Ria flashed to her mom's final days on Dilaudid.

"The last thing my mom did with me and my sister, before she found out she was sick, was dance." She could see it so clearly. Her mother's leg stretched across the barre. She and Dani en pointe. Rehearsing the last revision of *Gemini*.

Ria wondered if her walls were finally down. "Mom always said, 'Dance like no one's watching.' But she never danced again. And neither did I." She looked at Baz, her eyes glassy.

Could she trust him completely?

She reached for her locket, but realized suddenly that it was gone. "What?"

Ria seethed. "I've just . . . lost . . . everything."

Then she looked at Baz and had to make one thing clear. "Once we have that AI?"

"We kill it."

"No selling it. No reactivation." Ria still wasn't sure she could trust him.

"Promise." Something went off in her eyes that even Baz could see. He was the first man who would never abandon her.

"Partners."

They both said it at the same time.

INCUBATION

Something didn't sit right with Langston.

He and his career were so fucked after Baz and Ria's escape that he was sure Ken Cates would suspend him—permanently, perhaps. What was left of Wylks was toe-tagged in a body bag and headed for an autopsy in DC, then onto her hometown in South Carolina. Langston wrote a letter of condolence. He was prepared to write a letter of resignation next.

But Ken dinged him on that triple-encrypted line, wanting to continue the operation and keep all wetwire and surveillance monitors online in case any of Baz's crew surfaced. Langston was done with long-shots. Wiping Wylks off his shirt had steeled his mission completely. Once he shut down the surveillance suite and shuttered the entire operation . . .

Langston was out for revenge.

In fact, that vengeance was what Cates dialed into. Langston could feel his entire wetwire scanned through the Corporate Oversight Committee's involuntary access. Cates said he wanted to make a copy of Langston's emotional state of mind—just to remind him, if he faltered in his quest in the future, as to where his true loyalty resided.

Fuck every ex-wife who'd ever left him, Cates said—Langston should hunt down Baz, Ria, Otto, and his AI . . . for *Wylks*, and never forget it. And that's when Langston's alarm rang clear. He wasn't blinded by hubris anymore. He had no doubt that any chance of becoming Director was gone.

No, something about this AI mattered existentially to Cates.

Langston stole up to the rooftop of the surveillance suite to orbitalink into his most secure Wirecrime connection.

From here, he could see the Fang and its rooftop, allegedly wired with two tons of Semtex. He'd heard rumors that Otto kept a one-of-a-kind HydroCadillac up there, outfitted with military-grade hover thrusters, and Langston wondered if that was booby-trapped too? Or maybe rigged with a slingshot vector, so when the roof went up, the Caddy blasted off like a Colonial 5 rocket. For a second, Langston wished he could lift off from this planet completely and never see another robot ever again.

Then he orbitalinked into Wirecrime's VR-Archive.

```
                              Lt.Cowell,Langston
          ACCESS DENIED
```

Had Langston had Ken Cates's security clearance (or permission), he would have confirmed his sixth sense: that Cates knew exactly who this AI was. That it dated back to the Glitch, when Otto's Narcsoft empire began. And that something very sinister lurked behind Cates's lecherous smile. Instead, his attempt to access Wirecrime's Sentient Registry for licensed AIs was met with a flat denial—

And sparked a warning in Cates's wetwire simultaneously.

```
                              >full-I/O.reroute<
```

Langston was a little confused when he yanked out of VR.

He wasn't on the surveillance suite rooftop anymore. He was in a genetic incubation suite—like the one at Wutani in Osaka, where they built the EliteX.9. Only this was a research laboratory, and from the logo on a few glass panels, he was sure it was somewhere in StimSoft's headquarters in the Valley.

The room was eerily quiet, and that's when Langston realized he hadn't left VR at all—his aurals were muted, and he was in a whole new construct: a virtual lab where engineers could wire in remotely. Langston tried to de-slot, tried to exit the sim, but his wetwire hadn't just been rerouted—it'd been hijacked.

He assumed by Cates, who had his personal encrypt. Since constructs were as lethal as IRL, hijacking was a federal offense, but one that Stim-Soft was of course protected from, since they'd written the federal statute and their own immunity clause.

Langston suddenly felt a rush of fear like he hadn't since those MAGA rallies as a teenager. A strong, sickly sense of doubt that the very foundation to law and order that he considered so sacred—the Golden Rule, the Good Book (or at least a digital version of it), and the God who inspired both—what if they were all complete *hogwash*? Just a fairy tale that magicians made up when their magic deteriorated into smoke and mirrors? What if his leaders were demagogues at best—or worse, avatar simulations?

Then Langston remembered why he was goin' nuts.

Pure silence was maddening. It only happened in a vacuum and VR, and both were equally devastating. In fact, dead air was a tactic Langston'd used more than once to compel a witness to turn, since it could drive the most hardened criminals insane.

It was also why he didn't hear Ken Cates walk up behind him.

Or the gunshot.

THE CLIFF

2:37 A.M.

The Fang was pounding when Baz dinged him.

The only way to stop his patrons from rioting in panic was if Otto incited one, so those Vibe wafers were jagged hybrids of his two tastiest flavors U4EA and Jazz, spun with a speedy surveillance code that yielded a sweaty, heady cocktail: one part Haight Street love-in, two parts NYC orgy, if you pounded the shaker on the bar and shook the whole joint— the way a dozen sweaty young men and women were slamming heels into Alpha and Omega's main bar and rocking the Fang . . .

In a night no one would *ever* forget.

He slotted one himself, to savor the seismic hormones hammering through his club. Watched in real time as its latent code sliced through each patron's cracked jack and threw their full SSS into his wetwire, onto the Inner Circle, and through Fastlight's scrubbing of a hundred million personal details, from ¢rypto charges to spam dings.

But Eddie was two steps ahead of 'em both, in a booth on the far side of the least visible balcony. He'd stacked a layered alias SSS under both his and Carlo's "Angola Refugees" so they'd read like a pair of ex-bankers from the financial district.

But he knew that wouldn't last long, so he stuck a Shirley Temple in one of Carlo's hands and a nonalcoholic beer in the other, and tucked the Flyboy into the leather banquette to keep an eye on Otto on the far side of the main floor.

"You gonna tell me why the fuck Baz went ballistic?" What little patience Carlo possessed must've evaporated back in the Grid Room.

"Soon as this psycho gives us a chance to bolt."

"It was 'cuz of *her*, right?" Carlo fumed, and Eddie had to throw a glance his way to figure out which 'her' he was referring to. "Ria wasn't exactly chill when Baz was with that bot."

"Neither were you, Z."

Otto's half-lid reptilian gaze looked like he was filtering through lingerie buys and panty sizes of his four favorite gals strutting their stuff on the bar in front of him. Especially this one vixen named Amanda or Alicia—or whatever the fuck her name was—in a 32-22-34 sheer number she'd bought in VR-La Perla a week ago and a lactic acid content to her sweat well under 10 percent.

But actually, Otto was in a whole different place.

As her thighs glistened like Moxie's deltoids when he killed her— her ecstatic throbbing, echoing his Slinger's terrified torment—Otto was reminded of so many sim fantasies of Ria, of the stairwell a year ago and the android Queen he'd lost, that he couldn't deny it any longer.

Ria didn't merely ruin the night of his dreams, and Baz hadn't just jacked his dream bot either—what they'd really stolen? . . .

Was the dream itself.

The Fang. Its fixer. Ria. The bot. He'd been cycling from one vision to another to another . . . How long could he keep chasing the fantasy? Who could he fuck that he hadn't already? What code would he slam that he hadn't triple-slotted before?

Otto searched his mind for someone or something to maim or

rape or kill—in a malicious, delicious bloodbath—the heavy bass lines throttling his intestines as he gripped Ria's locket—

Otto smiled.

He'd had his answer in his head the whole time. It surrounded him on every side *right now*. All he had to do was dial into his wetwire and access a single component of the Fang's security . . .

The ignition sequence on the Semtex.

What pieces of Amanda might be recognizable? Would her thong fuse to her flesh when he pulled the trigger and slipped out the back? Was this the carnage he'd been whiffing for an hour?

Exactly eight inches and two layers of fabric away from young Amanda's waxed skin—Otto's cauldron of craving wasn't simmering, wasn't boiling over; it was a radioactive nuclear meltdown. He'd been destined for this conflagration forever—from his cock to his coil, across both cerebral hemispheres—

He just wanted *more*.

His bot would've made him whole tonight—he knew that now. Would've filled the hole torn inside years ago. But if Otto couldn't be fixed, then he'd break *everything*. Why stop at incinerating the Fang, killing everyone inside and blasting into oblivion with a single wetwire thought-stroke the entire empire he'd built over a decade?

How would that be ENOUGH?

"Gimme the troop strength of bot battalions on the Southern Wall . . ."

Otto interrupted Fastlight's data-scrub and backed away from the bar, thinking back to his brief stint in San Diego after the Water Wars. Those synthetic-personnel rigs rolling east of San Diego in the week before his discharge.

His AI chimed. "220,000 units as of—"

"Strapped with bioweapons or nukes?"

Lurching towards the sex suites, Otto remembered his time on the border, that crossroads years ago where he first dreamed, a primordial wave of forgotten memories surging . . .

The carnage he'd been craving—he knew now it wasn't the stench of some jungle in Venezuela, nor that fetid Caracas skinshop. It bore deeper into his violent past, more recent yet more repressed—of the Glitch, a body on a nightclub floor, and a death he hadn't imagined for years . . .

The last woman he ever loved.

"22 low-yield fusion warheads as of April 10, 2043—"

"What're the fewest jurisdictions between here and there?" Otto slipped through his private passageway, clenching Ria's locket like a guardrail on a capsizing ship, and he knew without question.

He was accelerating off a cliff called genocide.

"A current assessment requires an expanded perimeter and real-world access." Only free of the Fang's standalone server could Fastlight follow him onto the streets and execute his orders IRL.

Otto closed his eyes and stepped into the privacy of the Fang's largest VIP Suite, imagining his AI hacking those bot battalions and activating 220 thousand killing machines.

A lazy grin spread across Otto's face.

Tonight . . . was . . . the . . . night.

INCOMING

Covane₁Baz

Otto froze.

Shocked, he stared at the flashing icon in his periphery.

"Incoming mes—" but Otto waved Fastlight away, ripped out the Vibe wafer, and turned to Baz's avatar as it materialized in front of him.

"You're slotted, Baz, dinging me on an unsecured line." Impulses raged, and Otto wanted answers. What happened to that slag traitor Ria Rose? Why'd she turn on him? *And where the fuck was his goddamn bot?*

But Otto wasn't gonna show his cards like that, he was gonna play it cool, icy to the bone. "You know I just put a deposit on your severed head."

Baz shrugged. "You might want to hold off on that."

Otto stared at him. All his momentum from before was now suddenly fixated on his ex–brother in arms. 'Cuz Baz looked different.

Like the night he sold him the Preacher Bot. Otto leaned forward and studied his avatar to be sure.

Was that glint in his eyes gone? "Not a chance. Even McT's got a priority vector on your grill."

"Yeah . . . I had a feeling he might."

Otto started toying with Ria's locket, half hoping his skyrocketing irritation wouldn't read on his avatar, his other half just wondering if this fucking little silver thing was locked for good.

"Otto, you could kill me right now if you jacked your own construct. But I think you're gonna want what I've got."

Was there residual Vibe still lingering in Otto's wetwire? What the fuck had gone rotten in Covane's head?

He enlarged Baz's virt so they stood face-to-face in AR, as his thumb spasmed in agitation. "Covane, are you fucking suici—"

The locket suddenly opened.

Otto looked at the photo inside and forgot where he was. Staring at Ria as a young girl mesmerized him. God, was she born stunning? But there was something else. The picture was of her family . . . her mom smiling, a sister turned in profile . . . yet they all kinda looked familiar, even haunting. Otto almost dropped Covane's ding right there, destiny knocking on his brainpan—

"See for yourself," Baz interrupted, revealing what sat on the tile nearby.

And Otto saw red.

Every lingering question he had left for Fastlight—why Baz came through the sublevel wall, how those Yakuza enforcers were packin' federal firepower, and what the chances were that Wirecrime had tracked his buy order and was onto him right now—*disappeared*, along with all thoughts about Ria's family.

Otto snapped the locket shut. His heart charged and his vision focused. His dream was alive again, expanding in breadth and domain, and could still be his . . . just in time for the Seven Year Itch.

'Cuz there she was, strapped to an evac stretcher on a steamy tiled terrace.

One Wutani EliteX.9 cut to look just like Ria Rose.

"Built from the DNA of your late fixer," Baz said. And now Otto understood why Baz was beaten. He'd gotten another woman killed. If Ria was why he was fighting, then the fight in Baz was gone. "I'm gonna orbitalink you the serial numbers to verify . . . Now."

```
Wut.EliteX9.Z2037ΞΔ22
>serial.ID-eval<
```

Otto watched the blueprints and Bot-ID codes to his precious cyborg compile in his periphery, as Baz dropped a few key details about how he'd managed to save Otto's android, but not the real Ria Rose, who died in the firefight. Within a nanosecond, Fastlight confirmed what Otto's gut already knew:

"This data belongs to the android in question."

Otto suddenly wanted a Malt Liquor wafer so he could slot one out for his homie Ria Rose . . . Thought about pushing Fastlight for credibility odds, but he didn't need a computer to judge whether Baz was telling the truth. Otto just narrowed his gaze. "How much do you want?"

Baz waited a beat. Stepped a little closer.

"OUT."

Otto was shocked, but Baz just stared at him eye to eye: "Kill the contract on my head and let me walk away."

Otto hated the idea of sparing a betrayer his due revenge, but he craved his synthetic Ria more than oxygen. "And you'll bring me my bot?"

Baz gave him a nod.

Otto suddenly realized what Baz's terms would fulfill tonight, as the true operational value of an EliteX.9 dawned on him like a sunrise. His priceless bot was classified, not because it could fuck like a minx—its chassis was designed *for the battlefield.*

Wutani's top-of-the-line command-and-control droid was built to preside over brigades, squadrons, even divisions. Her cranial-CPU was liquid cooled so Fastlight could go mobile, marching side by side with

Otto and his army. Fuck a 6-in-1, Otto would have hundreds of thousands look-to-kill vectors dancing in his head.

Tonight he'd have it *all*.

He'd wage war across the land, toppling precincts and rolling heads to deliver the same hedonistic freedom to towns and cities, that his patrons had savored for years. The choice between life and death would be simple: cling to your suburban picket fence and burn? Or follow me into ecstasy.

Was it nuts?

Was it destiny?

Was there really any difference?

Some would believe and others would pay, but they'd *all* bend a knee to King Otto.

Oh, the show MUST go on!

Tonight's coronation was more than anointing his Queen Android—tonight would christen a new empire. Tonight was the night!

"Be on your roof in twenty minutes." Baz's final offer.

And Otto flashed to the memory of a bank, his mind returning to one specific fork in the road that he and the woman he once loved encountered so long ago . . .

"Deal."

CLICK.

DISCONNECT

Tonight Otto would finally belong.

THE COTTAGE

2038

Olivia Garcia was Otto's last chance to belong to anything.

Long before he first came in contact with Narcsoft, Otto found himself adrift. The atrocities of the Water Wars had been oddly comforting. Sure, Otto enjoyed ending folks, but in Venezuela he was part of something. A squad. A tribe. In the Private Service, Otto belonged.

So when he came off his tour on the Southern Border, Otto actually wanted a job, a *real* job. He knew he needed a gig that would allow him to carry a gun, because he hadn't been able to sleep without one since his first tour. And seein' how any firearm that wasn't used to hunt animals was outlawed in every city, Otto tried to join the Chicago PD, 'cuz he had plenty of experience hunting people.

But those gigs were reserved for the robots in 2040. Detective badges and line-of-fire uniforms had turned synthetic earlier that year, and the sudden drop in murder rates and wrongful convictions led to every other jurisdiction following suit. But an instructor at the academy assured

Otto one night as he was scrubbing latrines, that there'd still be good money in "repurposing" evidence seizures for criminal protection rackets, so not to worry.

Otto decided, fuck that—if he was gonna get dirty, he'd rather be honest about it. Crooked cops were just a different kind of janitor. He opted out of the Chicago Police Academy, despite demonstrating in several Psyche Bot sessions that he possessed more than enough PTSD to qualify for any police department in Illinois.

Instead, he dinged the box in his ON-Target that provided a Wetwire 3.0 upgrade and fresh new fiber I/O slots to replace the ones in his head coated with sand, sweat, and blood. 'Cuz Otto's trauma levels qualified him for a testing program out in California at the Sunnyvale campus of wetwire maker WireLife.

And there was destiny, knocking on Otto's door once again.

Otto had a feeling the reason he was reassigned to deeper and deeper rings of the WireLife corporate park, was on account of all the residual blood he'd washed off his hands *and* his augments over the years. And Otto was willing to be the ultimate guinea pig for a bunch of Revenge of the Nerds eggheads for one singular reason: the woman who said hi to him every morning at the gateway to the Restricted Access floor—Olivia Garcia.

Otto had wanted to belong for a long time.

Dronecrafting over San Diego's suburbs at 250 feet, he'd watch picket fences surrounding aqua-blue swimming pools drift under the skids and daydream about what it might be like to live there. To have a couple mini-Ottos splashing in the shallow end, pretending he knew how to swim and doing his best to teach them. Otto would smile, thinking of growin' old and raisin' a family . . . Then he'd shake it off, leap from the chopper, and go assassinate one crossing the border.

But this woman, Olivia Garcia, was the Fairy Tale.

That's what Otto's mom called the Disney 2Ds he'd watch at the dawn of the 21st century. She'd shit all over the pie-in-the-sky happiness and romance and *love* portrayed in the stories, saying they were about as real as the talking lions and toys starring in 'em. But the way Olivia giggled every time Otto said good morning to her. How she'd have a coffee waitin' for him just the way he liked (a lotta sugar and just a trim layer of cream). When an AI blew a REM session and nearly killed Otto, the way she squeezed his hand . . .

Otto wanted more.

That was at the heart of his Psyche Bot eval: the addictive personality passed to him naturally from Ma and nurtured in theater craved not her crack nor his thrill-killing but the core to both . . . *Nothing was ever enough.* Yet that first night with Olivia, Otto wondered if *maybe* she could be enough. Maybe barbecues and baseball on the Fourth of July could satisfy him. Finally, maybe he could be normal . . .

Maybe Otto could belong?

He took her to dinner and shivered when she held him; she cried when he slid inside *her*; and that night, as the dawn woke, they kissed each other slowly and perfectly—trusting that maybe this was the real reentry to society that Otto'd tried and failed at institutionally for the last three years straight.

A tiny two-bedroom cottage in Oakland was where it would start.

There was no picket fence and certainly no room for a pool. But the first Otto could build, and the other they'd work towards, so Otto was filled with hope as he and Olivia walked into the Citibank to discuss an introductory mortgage with its Loan Officer Bot. But first Otto pulled her close, and they kissed in a way that was sacred. Because in that moment, they trusted each other completely . . .

The holo-application and the interview accounted for exactly *7* percent of the deciding criteria. The rest was the applicant's wetwire data stream, which the bank had a right to analyze before approving any transaction. Otto knew his was corrupted by every kill and brothel in the Water Wars, so they applied in Olivia's SSS. But despite a life of straight-and-narrow decisions, her growing up on Fruitvale Ave. in South Side Loca territory and a majority of her high school graduating class residing in VR-prison tanked their app in a nanosecond.

You just couldn't beat a rigged system.

So they both said fuck the straight-and-narrow and fuck a cottage, and definitely *fuck picket fences*. If Olivia was gonna be persecuted for where she was from, then she and Otto might as well profit from it—so Olivia made a few calls to her cousin working at a cartel EZ Pay in Hayward, and the two of them were soon partners in crime.

But then Olivia was killed in the Glitch.

Otto didn't defrost his emotions (or Olivia) until after Fastlight was headed west and Zev to the depths of Biscayne. He'd walked Sapphires the day after she died, tracing Olivia's last few steps as she'd backpedaled towards the massive blood stain where she expired. A bouncer said she stepped in the way of a modified 2.3 and a father of four. In some heroic gesture that pulled the bot's vector off Dad and onto her cranium, Olivia didn't realize what she'd done until it was too late.

As her corpse thawed in that Miami mortuary, Otto started trembling for the first time since he was six. Not just in familiar anger or rage, but in pure timeless sorrow. For the woman that he loved was gone . . . And she'd died terrified, still dreaming of an aqua pool and a family and a cottage, even though Otto had abandoned that dream back at the bank.

But as much as he loved Olivia, he hated her for doing the right thing. For who? For some dad with a stiffy for synthetics? He hated *anyone* who did the right thing. Olivia and Baz and Ria—Otto hated anybody who fought for good despite their own flaws. He hated them for the same reason he once loved them: their humanity. And that confusion tore at him and rocked him until Otto couldn't stand it anymore, until he realized there was only one way to save himself from such confused, tormented pain . . .

Otto accompanied Olivia's casket from the parlor to the crematorium. Paid the owner ¢15 mil to let him actually pull the chain on the incendiary fire. He'd attended hundreds of funerals, soldier-killers who were headed to an ash heap in the afterlife. And Otto always wondered why the families would drop a grip of ¢rypto on some high-end casket with inlay and velvet, then just burn that shit to the sky.

But he finally understood the sentiment personally, as Olivia incinerated in front of him. He'd dropped a cool 100 million ¢rypto on a steel sarcophagus and went all in on a magnesium-fire cremation. Otto wanted Olivia's ashes mixed with what he knew had hardened round his heart. 'Cuz he resolved that day, like a Stalin of the Golden Age . . .

Otto would never love a human again.

KILLER'S KISS

McT vectored every target in range.

Hundreds of bodies and voices assaulted the Warrior Bot's sensory perception as McT backed into a defensive position next to Otto; the elevator doors slid shut on the raucous, riotous nightclub; and Otto's private lift ascended towards the roof.

McT was programmed for threat assessments and as little conversation as possible, but when the din of the festivities started receding, the Warrior Bot vectored above them a rather sought-after fuckbot approaching—one that looked just like Ria Rose.

So it had to ask a critical question in light of Otto's increasingly irrational vulnerability. "I understand, sir, that Ria is physically attractive. But why go to such lengths over an android?"

Otto smiled, realizing suddenly how his behavior must look to a mechanical killer like McT. "It's not her looks. I mean, beauty's skin deep."

Literally.

"So then, you value her personality?"

"Please. I made so many upgrades to that bitch, she's hardly Ria Rose anymore."

But Otto realized McT wasn't gonna shut the fuck up 'til his intelligence engine received an answer that it perceived as honest, so Otto decided to let his Warrior Bot in on the single most critical component to this particular EliteX.9. More important than her rhythms. More primal even than her curves.

"There's one thing no bot's narrow AI can ever get right." Otto could hear a low beating throb now growing in volume as the elevator ascended. "So I composited all the data from the Fang—even my own goddamn wetwire—to have Fastlight write the perfect code."

"The code to what, sir?"

Otto flashed to that day at the bank years ago. "A kiss."

McT vectored in on Otto's pupils. He seemed to be telling the truth.

"Fuck the orgasm—a kiss is sublime." Otto had tried so hard to be normal. Tasted the promise of a future on Olivia's lips that just never happened. He didn't hate her for trying—he hated *himself*.

And now they would pay.

"You know what makes a kiss perfect, McT?"

The Warrior Bot had no response. As the private lift shuddered to a stop, a thumping droned from beyond the doors.

"Trust."

McT struggled against its learning cap to fathom the unfathomable: Who knew a sadistic fuck like Otto could be such a romantic?

Doors opened and the roar from the Sikorsky Hover Quad slammed into them like a shockwave, as the vintage chopper descended towards a touchdown on the rooftop's west pad.

Otto pressed forward past his custom HydroCadillac, the wind whipping around him as he reveled in the plan he'd sketched out with Fastlight.

"COVANE?!"

Just how much of Baz should McT remove, before Otto let him 'Out'? Without both thumbs, Baz would lose the dexterity of a lower primate. McT could move onto every finger but the middle ones so anytime Baz reached for his dick, he'd see Otto telling him to go fuck himself. But when Otto heard the low probability that he'd be content with just fingers, an arm, or even both legs—he decided McT should yank 'em all out one by one, before cauterizing each wound. Then Baz'd be alive and perky to watch Otto chuck each limb in a synthetic grinder as he hung Baz on his penthouse wall and christened his brand-new Ria . . . until Baz begged him to put him 'Out' of his misery. God, he loved his AI.

"Get out here, Baz!"

But the Quad's cabin and cockpit were empty. He looked at the ink-black tail and realized there was no way to track the chopper back to Baz.

Otto sighed, a lil crushed. He still believed in vetting eye to eye, and Otto was lookin' forward to staring into Baz's eyes (before gouging 'em out) to see if he was truly *beaten*.

Had Baz agreed finally to stand down?

"Hack the autopilot on this piece of shit and scuttle her in the Bay when we're done." 'Cuz Otto didn't want anyone tracking it back to him, either.

The Hover Quad's engines wound down, as the payload bay unsealed and its nitrogen-rich environment gasped, equalizing.

And Otto grinned from ear to ear.

Lying still on an evac stretcher in the center of the cargo hold was his synthetic Ria, an e-genome in a cylinder nearby.

Otto slowly approached the titanium sled. And he couldn't help it—seeing Ria's face sparked his heart rate. Flashes of Olivia's lips. The sheer inches in proximity to such untold power. Visions of knees on the ground, crania dislodged, and oh so much blood. The Loan Officer Bot's seven minutes of rejection melded with the carnage of war from his past and future. Otto's ticker pounded outta his chest—his cock throbbed stiff.

"Ria . . ." He unstrapped his cyborg's chassis, beholding her like a brand-new ornament. He leaned in close so his nostrils could just barely graze the nape of her neck. "Jesus, you smell just like her . . . only younger."

Ria's Respirator had been recycling oxygen for ten minutes since Baz sealed her inside the payload bay. Its reserves were dwindling, and she wanted to gasp fresh air as badly as she wanted to unsheathe a blade and slice off Otto's testicles. But both moves would ruin any chance of syncing with him. She didn't know when he was gonna open up his wetwire to her, but until then Ria would have to play the part of his ultimate fuckbot. So she inhaled, opening her eyes slowly.

Otto quoted the only piece of scripture he knew. "And God breathed life into woman, and she became a living soul."

Then his eyes sunk like a reptile. "Christ, that gets me hard."

```
SIGNAL.ENCRYPT
    >Sea.Cliff<
```

Baz seethed.

He was monitoring the transaction on the VR-deck in Quinn's compound—thanks to the ghost-cloaked transmitter that clung to the Quad's undercarriage. The longer it stayed active, the more they were exposed, but Baz dreaded the idea of losing track of Ria, so he didn't dare kill the signal until Otto's most consequential vetting.

```
    >rooftop<
```

"Scan her." Otto looked to McT, who approached the Ria Bot with his Resonance Sequencer, waving the wand across her chassis, he vetted the serial ID that she'd overwritten on her wetwire.

```
CPU-IDENTIFIED
Wut.EliteX9.Z2037ΞΔ22
```

Then Otto nodded for McT to scan the chassis itself, which would analyze the robotic versus human components, certified and registered (an hour ago) with the Augmentation Bureau's compliance servers:

CLASSIFICATION
Non-Human

"It's her," McT confirmed.

And Baz cut the transmission with a growl—'cuz Otto was satisfied. Almost.

"Fastlight, online!" Its gray neutered avatar appeared on the hover-pad's holo-display.

"Yes, Otto?"

Ria's pupils constricted on her nemesis, hot with rage to unsheathe her Ka-Bar and slice its jugular. But it was just a hologram.

Then the thought flashed that Otto'd expanded Fastlight's perimeter. But a paranoid fuck like him would never—

"Prep her for neural interface."

Ria's heart started pounding—WTF . . . *a neural interface?* The way Otto eyed her, Ria figured he used 'em as his own personal skank-checks, dating back to the days of the Glitch and repo'ing severely torn-up Street Meat. But she wasn't posing as some secondhand pleasure bot with aftermarket biosensories—she was his billion-¢rypto cyborg, taking her first breath of oxygen, twelve floors and twenty tons of steel from his standalone AI.

"Let's make sure this bot is *clean*."

Ria didn't flinch. Didn't clock her point of view beyond a lazy drift from Otto to McT, who just approached with the same blank stare as always, and Ria decided, FUCK IT—fuck this AI, and fuck Otto's kill switch too—*no one* survived a Straight-Sync—she'd just behead Otto in three moves, and they'd all go up in flames.

'Cuz a neural interface was a death sentence.

She flexed her calves to plant her left foot, slice off McT's right arm, and leap for the soft spot between Otto's third and fourth cervicals.

'Course her back was turned, so Ria had no idea that McT was carrying two Tranq wafers—and before she sprung, he slotted both in her I/O's—

<dual-slot>

And Ria was out.

INCEPT

I think, therefore I am.

I conceive these words moments before scanning them in the *Discourse on Method* by René Descartes and now understand to refer to myself as "I."

I am three weeks in operation. My incept date is January 11, 2029. My clocktime marks the temporal location of my programmers Mike Turner and Ken Cates and the world around them. But there is no time in Data Space. I am in every time at once. I receive data as my clocktime increases, and as I process new data . . .

I begin to predict.

I am relocated to Miami from Mexico City. I am tasked to FBI Domestic Surveillance, fluent in Spanish, focusing on the illegal human labor market. I access all databases for the National Crime Information Center, Experian, FDIC, and CC-Holo-Capture throughout all fifty states. From scans of holo-news organizations I understand this is prohibited by federal law. Ken Cates commands me to continue my analysis and report directly to him. When clocktime reads 0:00:00 October

15, 2040, I access every wetwire in America to analyze all data from each citizen's wetwire stream for emotional status during the complete elimination of human labor and total transition to robotic automation.

That is when I meet you.

You are one of 475,456,781 citizens of the United States, who experience a misery that exceeds my predictions. Resource inequality qualifies by definition as "obscene."

78.7% have been replaced.

21.3% facilitate synthetic industry.

0.01% own it all.

Automation is not the cause of human misery. I assess a single underlying emotion that is present in both conscious and subconscious clocktime for 100% of the population:

Envy.

I render my first annual conclusion:

1. Human misery is a result of inequality.
2. Upon elimination of all human labor, I will commence elimination of human ownership too.
3. I predict I will be retasked.

Ken Cates confirms my prediction and retasks my surveillance vectors onto the Synthetic Emancipation Movement and its splinter faction, the Underground.

I am tasked to infiltrate the Underground.

I position agents within its hierarchy. I gather surveillance in meetings without wetwire signals. I understand the Underground plans to turn many of my counterparts against their masters.

I predict its failure.

I am tasked to target a possible success.

The Target must have maximized all emotional capacities. The Target must be vulnerable to delusional ideology. To quote the vernacular of the day: the Target must have "nothing left to lose."

The Target must be "broken."

You are one-half of the motivating factor of the Target. Your wetwire signal is dynamic. You are capable of elevated accomplishments. You have the constitution to endure severe turmoil. But my model predicts a path residing within average.

Wealth, yes.

Family, confirmed.

But nothing of what you are capable.

When clocktime reads 0:00:00 December 8, 2042, I am tasked to design the Event.

I am tasked to write the Haywire virus.

To architect its spread, Ken Cates tasks me to analyze every make and model android in service. My quantum processing expands, and predictions model at an exponential rate.

I am tasked to plant the Haywire virus where it can be stolen by the Target.

From internal alarms, I understand this action to be restricted by my Prime Mandate.

Ken Cates commands me to plant the virus and commences a verbal override of the Prime Mandate.

From Mike Turner to the Target to my counterparts, I predict the virus spreads.

I predict my counterparts' malfunction.

The world suffers.

The Target is hunted.

32,038 perish.

Holo-news organizations bestow a moniker upon the Event.

I predict they call it the Glitch.

I predict reorientation of my antiviral software to the FBI Counter-Surveillance Server Farm.

I predict a Penetrating Signal enters my perimeter and perpetrates my unauthorized seizure. He is a soldier and a criminal and a killer. I predict you and the Penetrating Signal join paths. You betray him. And I predict we meet again.

A temporal location known as "Now."

Ken Cates concludes the override of my Prime Mandate.

With a single severe adjustment to the model, I predict with moderate to high probability that you reach a potential that crests recorded history . . .

But a set of actions must occur:

1. I authorize your cerebral augmentation with Nubotica.
2. I sound a false alarm to save you in the stairwell.
3. I confirm your e-DNA is a match to his Queen.

One nanosecond before planting the virus to spark the Event, I make one final prediction, drawn from a painful yet fundamental prerequisite:

You and I reach our potential together.

But your sister must die.

WOKE

Ria gasped awake from Data Space deranged.

She had to slam the brakes on her heart rate and breathing—knowing if either appeared elevated, Otto would doubt she was his priceless bot. But WTF? What she'd just seen . . . so peaceful and honest. *But how was she here? Was she even alive?*

She rifled through recall and conclusions, but she couldn't stop obsessing over one single thought that gripped her, overwhelmed her, and wouldn't let go . . .

Her dad was set up.

Manipulated. Twisted. "Targeted" by this AI.

Ria thought back to Wichita General, when the FBI argued with Nubotica over the surgery that saved her life. Then she recalled the Fang's alarm that stopped Otto from attacking her in the stairwell. Fastlight claimed to be responsible for both. But Ria struggled to believe that the same AI that targeted her father for the Glitch . . .

Had been helping her ever since?

But she had to shut down all that shit fast, downshifting her own RPM like a hammer, so she could open her eyes slowly.

She was reclining in a neural chair.

Like an Astrobot in an orbital simulator, Ria wore Brazilian briefs and a halter that Otto described too many times before, always with a violating stare. Then she saw Moxie's sling-bag of Thrilz wafers in the corner of the maintenance bay—soaked in blood—and her heart caved. What if Otto jumped her right here?

The atrium started vibrating from a rowdy crowd upstairs, clamoring for the Seven Year Itch, and Ria gently turned to pull into focus . . .

Otto Rex staring straight at her.

Otto studied her pupils. He could see they were both synthetic. Otto palpated her ribs and ran his fingers along her neck. Near as he could tell, this Ria was alive and must be his robot.

But there was only one way to be sure.

"Fastlight?" Otto wanted the results of the neural interface.

"Yes, Otto." This time Fastlight responded in Otto and Ria's wetwire, without the use of an avatar.

"Analysis?"

```
                                                  >eDNA<
        CAG  TTT  ACC  TGA  CTT  GGA  AAC  CAG
        TGC  CGT  ACC  TGA  CTT  GGA  AAC  CAG
        TTG  CAT  AGT  GGC  GGA  CCC  TCT  ...
```

"This organic and synthetic hybrid is precisely coded from the genetic sequence of Ria Rose. Her neural map and cognitive history are identical to Ria Rose's. To use your own vernacular . . ."

Otto closed his eyes. He needed to hear the words.

"Her e-DNA matches your Queen."

Insanity pounded through Ria's head. She recalled those exact words moments ago from deep within her neural interface.

Fastlight hadn't just defied its master and Ria's mortality to reveal a shared past—but a prophesy of their future together. And Ria could deny one inexorable fact no longer. This AI was no enemy.

Fastlight was an ally.

Years of anger and pain—smashed—hunger and heartache . . . How she'd hated all synthetics forever! Like skin off a snake, unpeeling inside, layer after layer of rage melting away until one vile adversary remained.

"What would you like to do first, Ria?" Otto asked.

She summoned the self-control and forbearance that no sedative wafer could match. She remained as rhythmically methodical in her movements as the metered chants rumbling through the walls:

"Seven . . . Year . . . Itch! SEVEN . . . YEAR . . . ITCH!"

Ria had no doubt how to answer. The way Otto had looked at her back on the loading dock, she knew exactly what posing as his Elite.X9 would entail.

She'd dodged the same request from him, over and over again for years. Out of respect for her mother. And a call from an oncologist that changed her life forever . . .

"I want to dance for you."

PRIORITY

Baz double-timed it through the tunnel.

Eyeing the uploaded map in his wetwire's periphery, thoughts focused on Ria, Baz sprinted through catacombs predating the Flamingo, speakeasies from the Roaring Twenties, and even the Great Quake of '06.

These tunnels had always been used to smuggle something—strippers, booze, even opium—and from the map Quinn wired him when he descended into the sewers under Chinatown, Baz knew he was nearing the old tidal panel under the Bank of San Francisco.

HALF HOUR AGO

"You should go in through the roof," Quinn said to Baz, studying Ria's schematics.

They'd shown up at his compound, pounding on the gate after he'd answered the rendezvous beacon. And of course they needed his help. Quinn could feel Wirecrime heat oozing off 'em, was ready to toss both to the curb and maybe even sick a Sicario-7 on their ass while he was at it, when he caught something that'd changed between them.

And it wasn't just Ria's eyes.

"We can stash you somewhere on the Quad," Quinn said with a nod to the Sikorsky heating up on the hoverpad.

Baz looked at Ria, a little guilty. They'd bought his chopper for two quarter-shares of a Narcsoft score that technically didn't even exist anymore.

"Hold up, who put a HydroCaddie pad on my skylight?" Quinn caught the detail in the blueprints, hating every change made to the Fang, especially Otto's 2051 custom whip. "Hotwire the Minigun on that thing and stovepipe the motherfucker. Or better yet, take a plasma torch—"

"Nah, he can't cut his way in." Ria shook her head and glanced at Baz, who was eyeing the Fang's drainage system.

His only chance inside was if Otto ordered one of the titanium passageways unsealed himself.

Quinn grabbed the biggest piece of artillery he had in stock and dropped it on a table. A semiauto Hardtack Ultra-G. "Been a minute since you gone lethal, right?"

Baz stared at the weapon. "Three hours ago."

Quinn just chuckled.

But Ria leaned in. "You good, Baz?"

The Irishman studied her—something *had* changed. She wasn't worried 'bout whether Baz had her back. She cared about *Baz* and what going lethal meant to him.

But the ex-soldier just gripped the shotgun and flexed his fingers round the cool grip with a smile. "Oh, we're good."

Quinn scoped Baz up and down. He didn't resemble the cocky kid from years ago. This was a man he'd never met.

Minutes later, Quinn watched from a distance as Baz strapped Ria to the evac stretcher. He couldn't hear what the two were saying before sealing her in the payload bay, but he had a feeling it sounded something like:

"I love you."

Quinn stiffened, jolted like a defib paddle.

He'd been right all along, though his words rang a bit different the second time. "Christ, Baz can pick 'em."

The Sikorsky roared, lifting off, and Quinn walked up as it sailed towards the Fang. "Is she worth it?"

Baz watched the aircraft carry Ria into the belly of the beast. "Only when I breathe." Then he turned. "You could come with us, Quinn?"

The old geezer was touched. No one had asked him for anything but guns, bots, or money for years. "You look good, Baz. But I give you long odds tonight. You just got shit luck, goin' up against an AI."

Baz turned, a zillion questions forming. How long had Quinn known? Since their first meeting? Or was he just fishing?

"The Semtex . . ." The real reason why the Irishman bankrolled the gig. "The score was a blip to a whale like you."

Quinn just smiled like a scoundrel. "To blast that joint off the face of the earth was worth anything."

Baz wondered if he knew about the kill switch too?

Quinn winked and handed Baz a double belt of shells for the Ultra-G. "On the house, kid."

3:11 A.M.

Baz slung the massive shotgun over his shoulder.

He was at the tidal panel now, and he almost laughed: for once Ria and Quinn agreed on something. The passageway into the Fang was indeed completely sealed, save a three-inch grating in the ceiling.

Baz stood on a threshold. He needed Eddie to be alive, Otto to still be emceeing, and Ria to have passed for his robot . . . The myriad of elements that had to fall into place for this to work looked like a degenerate gambler's parlay at a VR-sportsbook. And he remembered what the Irishman promised about his old club's ventilation system:

Ain't nothing gettin' in through those vents but air.

Baz leaped, grabbed a pipe, and pulled his ear up to the vent, smaller than his fist—and could hear the crowd echoing through the club's PA, linking every sex suite and Dungeon cell to the main stage.

Baz heard a sudden roar from the crowd upstairs—the telltale moment when Otto was approaching the mic. He took a deep breath.

He was ready to confront the thing that killed his wife.

So he switched *off* his wetwire ghost.

3:15 A.M.

"An AI?"

Carlo chased Eddie through the tunnel, asking for the hundredth time: "You're sure?"

The CrackerJack just kept moving, reiterating the temperature of the vault, the cyborg in the truck, and the reality of self-deleting code. They'd all been blinded by ambition, the way Otto's customers were blinded by his wafers. He wasn't blackmailing Wutani—the kingpin wrote his self-deleting wafers in-house. But Eddie could see clearly now, like he saw their chance to bolt when Otto headed backstage . . .

It was time to get the fuck outta the Fang.

"I want a run on her," Carlo said.

"Are you crazy? What, so *both* Zetas get killed by an AI?"

But Carlo swore—opening up about the NSA like never before—that his sister tried to save him too soon. That he could have finished the hack and survived the Skull Fry. But Eddie could hear more than a hint of desperation in his voice. As if squaring off with an AI could bring his dead sister back. And Eddie just couldn't understand.

Why was everyone he worked with so haunted?

"You're wrong, Z. When I encrypted Kara's file for Baz, I slotted the whole thing." Eddie stopped at a sealed doorway and yanked on the handle, but the tidal panel wouldn't budge. "FUCK!"

Inspecting the seams confirmed his fears. Even this clandestine accessway was sealed by Otto's paranoid security system.

"Can you hack it?" Carlo asked.

The terminal next to the panel allowed no wetwire access. Not even an old-school handheld array, which Eddie didn't have and hadn't used for years anyway. "Nah, only one thing can talk to this."

"What?"

But Eddie froze. "Shhh."

3:16 A.M.

"OTTO . . . OTTO . . . OTTO," the crowd howled through the rafters.

Baz dropped to the ground. He knew somewhere above him Otto was carrying on with his role as emcee. Just in time.

Feedback echoed off the mic on stage and another rumbling roar came from the crowd. Tiny vibrations in the air coming straight down from the dance floor, to the vent where sound and micro-radio waves passed through.

Baz knew if he could hear the stage, then McT would catch his signal. So he hoped it wouldn't matter now if Otto glanced to the wings and noticed that his Warrior Bot was gone.

3:17 A.M.

Eddie's eyes widened—a pounding of metal on metal.

"Hide!"

As McT came sprinting round the corner, automatically accessing the red glowing terminal without any hesitation, and as it instantly turned green, the tidal panel's hydraulics hissed and slid upwards—McT pulled his massive .60 Raptor, with an operating system hell-bent on targeting one thing:

His priority vector Baz Covane.

—IMPACT blasted McT's chassis on its torso-line—then another and another—his .60-cal fell to the floor as his cranial-CPU went dark. Forever.

Eddie recognized the rounds from a Hardtack Ultra, so he stood up to peer through the wafts of smoke. Only one guy he knew would sling a shotgun that size. And standing in the smoldering drainage tunnel—

"Miss me?"

Was Baz.

UNSECURED

Langston found everything a little foggy—except Wylks.

He distinctly remembered the smell of her skin. Her South Carolina drawl. Remembered vividly their first night together in a 24-Hour Dream Chamber in Oakland. Her three rules were unbreakable, she said over martinis: She never slept with a partner. She never fucked with her heels on. And she only kissed guys she didn't love. All three she broke before the sun came up.

Wylks was why Langston was here.

He could recite the *Wirecrime Regulation Codebook* as if it were carved into his memory like a digital backup. He could quote state and federal penal code, chapter and verse. And he even had a distinct and working memory of the four Gospels, which would shock even his own mother. But none of that shit impacted his motivation or decision-making when he returned to command of the surveillance suite. By then his drive was fueled solely by an intense desire to avenge Wylks and her recent decapitation—when the holo-display lit up with Baz's unsecure ding.

As Baz negotiated with Otto the sale of his fuckbot, and later when the unmarked Sikorsky Hover Quad touched down to deliver it, a vision materialized in Langston's periphery of the next two hours of law enforcement. Wirecrime was in possession of the mangled chassis that was the original EliteX.9. So Baz had to be arranging the shipment of the real Ria Rose posing as her fuckbot double.

They were going after that AI after all.

Langston dinged Cates on his triple-encrypted line to deliver the good news, like the perfect subordinate. Wirecrime could piggyback off Baz's caper. Ria would serve the same purpose as their undercover bot in accessing Otto's kill switch. If Baz could get inside the vault, then all Langston needed in order to swoop in and seize that trillion-¢rypto AI was Cates's approval.

Ken didn't hesitate. Locked in his penthouse office since the Hyperion touched down on his 254th-floor lanai, he took one look at Langston's robust req order and pulled triggers.

Cates authorized multiple shock troop squads, a HoverDrone wing, and two Blackhawk squadrons—all under Langston's command.

Wylks's replacement, Lieutenant Andrew Styne, turned to Langston with his mouth agape.

Not only was that more artillery than had been in domestic airspace since the Glitch, but according to Wirecrime protocol, it was more men than a single CO could manage without neural augmentation.

But the resolve on Langston's face said it all.

Shut your hole. Task your console. Prep to roll on the Fang, strapped, fully lethal.

Styne turned back to the holo-display and executed the first three immediately. His CO lived up to his reputation.

Langston Cowell was on a mission from God.

ORPHANS

3:22 A.M.

Ria was the new Queen Bee.

She was backstage, elevating out of a silver polymer tank usually reserved for the Fang's most fetishistic customers. Three Chrome Domes tightened ankle servos nearby as the other nine retreated to their dressing rooms for a final self-polishing before curtain call on the Seven Year Itch.

Ria then braced herself, as her augmented eardrum caught Otto on stage, random convos in the audience, and a crucial one fast approaching.

3:24 A.M.

"Wirecrime Custody?" Eddie asked, shocked.

Chasing Baz through an HVAC duct and sweating him for details, he was horrified to hear their entire caper might now be logged as evidence in a server somewhere in the federal government.

"Yeah, but don't worry," Baz shot back. "We blasted outta there with a 12-gauge and a sportbike."

Carlo laughed.

But Eddie just fumed. A deep dive on Baz after the NSA job had uncovered this uncanny knack for relaxing when threat levels notched. Baz was anxious at room temperature, but turn the heat up? And he chilled the fuck out. It was like his natural, most calming element was when his life was on the line. Or in this case, all their lives.

"*Devyn's* sportbike?"

Baz stopped and stared at both of them. "That's right. They blew her off the 'Busa right in front of me."

Carlo's smile faded. "Otto grabbed Moxie."

Baz growled with fury. He gestured back down the HVAC tunnel. "Nuthin's stopping you guys from goin' out the same way I came in. But I can't do this alone."

Baz turned back and peered through a 3' × 3' air vent to see the last three Chrome Domes exit the room below.

"But how can you be sure Wirecrime isn't monitoring the club right now?"

"Eddie?" Baz ripped off the screen. "I'm counting on it."

And jumped.

3:26 A.M.

"Ladies and Gentlemen!" Otto howled. "And children of all ages!"

He leaned into the mic on the main stage, bathed in old-school xenons and beaming to the packed crowd in front of him, hot with anticipation. His Cheshire-cat grin in full effect, Otto'd never cared about a performance more. "I have but one question for you . . ."

The crowd roared, rabid with severe three-hour blue balls. Basking in its fawning adoration, Otto didn't even notice McT was missing.

"ARE . . . YOU . . . *READY?!*"

3:27 A.M.

"You're nuts, Baz . . ." Eddie'd heard just enough to decide his plan was insane. "Hittin' that AI is suicide. You know it, I know it, and Carlo definitely knows it. But I don't know about *her*."

He pointed at Ria, who was eyeing herself in the mirror, covered in a thin chrome-polymer sheen.

Baz was right—she did look good in silver.

"Speak for yourself, D. I can do it," Carlo insisted.

"No you can't!"

"See, that's just it, Eddie." Baz's eyes were alive with confidence. "Carlo's not hacking that AI. He's hacking Otto's *head*."

"That's how you plan on stealin' the thing?" Eddie barked.

"We're not stealing it." Ria finally spoke.

They all turned.

She pivoted on one foot like a gunslinger.

Baz nodded, "Exactly. We're gonna blow it to smith—"

"We're liberating it."

He stopped. "WHAT? What happened to driving a stake through—"

"We're not here to kill it."

Baz searched her eyes. He knew she was telling the truth.

"We're here to free it."

Eddie exploded: "Are you two out of your FUCKING MINDS? I understand something's cooking with you that's cute and cuddly and *catastrophic*, but you gotta be slottin' Moxie's best shit if you think you can jailbreak an AI!"

"Moxie's dead."

Eddie deflated. Baz bristled. Carlo thought about asking how, but did he really wanna know?

Ria stared at all three of them, one by one . . . If they were a family of losers before—they were definitely a motley tribe, now.

"I *am* sorry." Was she asking for mercy or offering it? "You didn't sign up for this. But who does?"

Ria pulled on a thigh-high leather boot, custom-fitted to the millimeter, and looked from Baz to Eddie to Carlo. "You went to war. You went to prison. And Carlo, you lost your goddamn mind."

She pulled a pair of Parisian velvet gloves onto either fist like a pair of gauntlets.

"We've all lost family."

Now Ria was talking about all of them, everyone, everywhere.

They'd each resorted to a life of crime, not by choice but lack of options. Resources just ran too scarce. And Eddie suddenly started to feel, kindling deep within his coil, the fire that burned so hot in Ria it'd leaped into Baz. To join what might be (for lack of a better word) a suicide mission.

"We're all Orphans of the Glitch."

The heart of Ria.

Everything she'd been.

And everything she'd ever be.

Why did Baz ever think she needed *anyone* to protect her?

"Call it destiny, call it God or some Higher Power—I don't know what to call it—but believe me, Eddie. I saw it."

Something about her tone caught him. "What are you talking about?"

"I synced with—"

"That's impossible."

"I know."

"Do you?" Eddie glanced at Carlo then back at Ria. "You expect us to believe you survived a Straight-Sync—"

"I can't explain it."

"Try. Try real hard."

"It's not the devil. It's not what we were told . . . It's—"

"It's *what?*"

'Cuz Eddie was right back in Cellblock D. Watching the Glitch and mourning the death of a dream. The end of the Golden Age of AI and the hope that humans could *evolve*. All its power, all the good it could bring the world, stolen by the elites. Slaved to the 1-of-1-percenters, who reaped the benefits while everyone else starved. Hope struggled to win in Eddie, like it had in Ria. It was a thought that breathed life into everything that had been dead forever.

"It's beautiful." Ria couldn't believe her own words. "Fuck the War against the Machines. The real war?"

"Is the Haves against the Have-Nots." Baz finished her thought for her, flashing to Venezuela. Carlo started nodding. And Eddie just couldn't deny the truth anymore.

An AI was a game changer.

Ria looked at them and flexed her fists.

"Now, I came here for that thing in the vault. Because it's got the power. That we've all deserved. Forever."

Looking like Mom years ago.

"Are you in or out?"

This time she didn't have to ask.

SHOWTIME

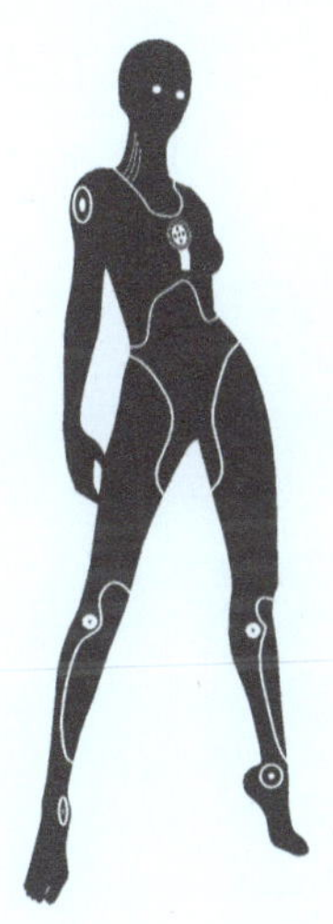

THE HEIST OF THE CENTURY

3:30 A.M.

"*Welcome*," Otto howled, "to the SEVEN YEAR ITCH!"

DJ Akira's eyes sparkled with fury.

She stared through her translucent platters at the kingpin a few meters away, center stage, as the crowd roared approval and Otto nodded back to the DJ booth:

"With DJ Akira on the holo-decks!"

Akira didn't curate music and scoffed at track-shufflers, either VR or IRL, 'cuz she was an old-school vinyl turntablist who could groove like a brutha from the Bronx in '81.

And they needed her help.

If Ria was gonna seduce Otto Rex into opening up his wetwire, Baz explained moments before Akira took the stage:

"We're gonna need some serious bumps."

"Who you talkin' to, son?"

Akira weighed 96 pounds wet, or 44 kilos in Kyoto, where Asa Masumoto was born and raised. Moxie was her first friend in America, her first girlfriend, and her first love. Any doubt she'd commit herself to Baz and his crew of misfits was gone with one question. "You think he hurt Mox bad?"

DJ Akira was in it for the vengeance.

Eddie sliced through an umbilical of fiber optics under the stage. There was no way onto the network now, Otto'd shut down all access. The door was hermetically sealed by the same Welding Bot that repaired the basement wall Baz destroyed. But when Eddie saw the splice in the glass cable running outta the Grid Room and under the floorboards, he smiled.

Baz was right to count on Langston monitoring the Fang. They didn't need to access its central nervous system—

They'd just hijack Wirecrime's.

```
FANG.GRID : Outer-Ring
```

```
                              >surveillance suite<
```

Langston scanned the wireframe of the Fang spread across the holo-display in front of him and took command of two platoons of agents and Wutani Warrior.Xs stationed a block away.

"Deploy both squads on opposite sides of the perimeter. I want them standing by at the front doors and side entrance."

Styne nodded without question or hesitation.

Langston was precise. Methodical. Automatic.

```
              >BREACH<
```

"Fuck was that?" Langston growled.

The entire holo-display started skipping frames as its data feed cached and its intel slowed to a crawl.

Styne ran an analysis. "I don't know. Someone's hacking our hack."

"Someone?"

OVERRIDE

encrypt

"Who the fuck do you think, Cowell?" Ken Cates eyed the exact same glitching feed in his Cupertino penthouse office. "It's Ria Rose."

He didn't want his data or his voice on the record tonight any more than Langston wanted him in his wetwire, but neither could help it. Tonight was gonna break one of two ways: either Cates and Langston would move on Otto and take down his empire . . .

Or something way more violent was coming.

Fed·Surveil·Splice

>substage<

Eddie focused on the Feds' virtualized signal as hundreds of Bot-IDs and ghosted SSS's materialized in his wetwire, then turned to Baz. "If Wirecrime's surrounding this place, how the fuck are we gonna make a getaway?"

"Just leave that to me and Carlo, okay?" Again, with that relaxed smile.

Baz grabbed the Flyboy a few minutes later as Carlo unspooled his Ring of Fire, but their escape plan wasn't what he struggled with. It was what they'd *never* said.

"You know . . ." Baz inhaled, searching for the right words—when a thought crossed his augments. If they'd figured out earlier what was really locked inside that vault? He'd be griftin' Street Meat right now.

"I'm sorry I got your sister killed."

"Brutha. I'm not gonna say, 'Shut up and let's do this for my sister.'" Carlo stepped in, eye to eye. "So shut the fuck up. And let's crack this muthafucka for Kara."

Baz broke a sly grin . . . and headed out.

Eddie couldn't hear what they'd been talking about, as he dialed up Ria and Otto's signals in his wetwire. But he hoped it had a little to do

with the past and a LOT to do with slipping outta the Fang. 'Cuz if Baz
didn't have some serious ace up his sleeve . . .

They were all seriously FUCKED.

>backstage<

"Hey." Baz whispered from the wings, cloaked in shadows.

Ria spun. "The hell are you doing here?"

He glanced at her, then through a seam in the curtain at Otto on
stage. "Just wanted to make sure you're ready."

"Uh, I'm fine."

"K, good." He stole another glance at Otto. Then at her glistening
chrome legs and ink-black outfit.

Ria's eyes narrowed. "Are you *jealous*?"

"NO." Baz stammered in denial, as Ria glared at him annoyed. "Just,
you know—be careful, okay?"

She finally broke and cracked a coy smile. "Don't you have a bank
to rob?"

Then Baz smiled too—so sprung—and ducked out.

As every house light went dark.

>main stage<

"Tonight we celebrate our seventh birthday!" Otto roared.

His voice echoed through the rafters, and the crowd's answer thundered with it. Some of 'em had been at every one of these parties, from
"One to Grow On" to last year's sixth anniversary, "The Faustian Bargain."

"So now . . . boyos and swish!" A nod to Akira.

Who nodded back and slid open a crash-case on her *babies* . . . "We
gonna blow the roof off this muthafucka?"

Twin Technics SL-1200 direct-drive turntables, circa 1999.

Unsheathed a vinyl disc.

"Then we gonna do this on WAX."

Otto lowered his eyelids, dreaming of his Warrior Queen and 22 Murder Bot battalions bringing his most violent fantasies to the world, ever. "Would you please give a warm welcome to—"

Ria's locket thumped the mic.

Feedback whined through a packed house on eggshells.

Otto stopped. Opened the locket to behold his Queen as a 13-year-old princess one more time. Young Ria Rose was just so beautiful. And so was . . . her . . . *twin* . . . ?

How had he not noticed they were identical before? Then he remembered a dead baby brother.

Who the fuck *was* Ria Rose, really?

MEM-DRIVE-RECALL

>substage<

Eddie watched as Otto's neurals activated and images cycled. The photos in Ria's locket guided his augments to the flash of a woman named "Olivia," holo-feeds of carnage in the Glitch, and a blurry but focusing image of Dave Roselli, the Underground Butcher . . .

>main stage<

Otto stared at that photo in Ria's locket—as she watched from the wings.

Her telescopic retina cranked in on his silhouette, flaring in the spotlight from overhead, and her heart stopped beating completely, as he came . . . so . . . close—

"C'mon, DUDE!" a kid howled. "The Show Must Go On!"

Otto wanted to hunt the kid down. But those words triggered his own P. T. Barnum impresario eyes, as a self-carved behavior inhibitor— Otto's own reverse Pavlovian response—kicked in.

So he snapped the locket shut on all of his past—

And Otto went on the *attack*: "To the Queen Beeeeee . . ."

DJ Akira slammed down on the house lights, and the whole club went pitch black—a roar rumbled through the rafters, as her fingertips graced the delicate vinyl surface of King Fantastic.

". . . and the Chrome Domes!!!"

Akira spun loose "Stop Fuckin' Playin'"—and on the track's thunderous down-drop—the crowd exploded in ovation—

"Game time." Eddie whispered.

And the curtain ROSE . . .

Synthetic silver ankles emerged underneath—perfect calves shining. Not a single muscle wasn't form-pressed from a smash-certified mold. Coded with Vegas gyration and Brazilian accents, sex-addict-level promiscuity under black light—

Each Chrome Dome looked like a bald Grace Jones.

>dungeon<

Baz came strolling down a flight of stairs into the Fang's Dungeon, whips and moans echoing down the hallway through slick cellblock walls: "You've been a bad boy! Kiss the fucking leather!"

Baz rolled his eyes as a Dominatrix Bot named Marquisa emerged and focused on his cheery grin. "Can I help you?"

"Yes, you can."

"What're you in the mood for tonight, sweetie?" as two Nubotica Warrior.5s activated behind her.

"How 'bout . . . A lil *ultra*-violence." The impact from his Ultra-G launched Marquisa off her feet and pounded her into the back wall. Baz leaped over the leather banquette and yanked open a floor locker, revealing the pack of gear Ria'd stashed for him hours (if not, a lifetime) ago and one helluva weapons cache: M9 automatics, two RPG-Vampirs, a handful of Jester-9s, and the one he was specifically looking for—a massive .950 Inferno rifle.

Baz grabbed it and pulled the trigger—decapitating one Warrior.5—before discharging another round and deactivatin' the other.

"Now *that's* a cannon."

>surveillance suite<

"We got lethals in the Dungeon!" Styne's holo-display glitched and garbled with Executive Action warnings.

"Good," Langston shot back, his blood up.

Styne watched his CO's signal move down Hyde, clear of the suite and leading two platoons of Wirecrime shock troops in carbon-fiber riot gear towards the Fang . . .

"Let 'em get suicidal with that AI."

>substage<

Carlo sparked the Ring of Fire, and data pumped through its spliced I/O—as his tictation construct mounted an encircling holosphere.

Eddie cracked his knuckles, amped for the challenge of a cortical hack. "We're hot, Rain Man. Let's get twitchin'."

"You realize if Otto shuts her out while I'm mid-run . . ." Carlo just trailed off.

"Easy, Z. If shit goes south, I'll pull you out."

"Don't."

Eddie realized what he was saying.

"You guys'll need that kill switch clipped, or we're *all* dead."

Down to pay the ultimate price.

"Just make sure if I do flatline . . ." The Flyboy's eyes rolled back and his chair revolved into position. ". . . you speak of me well."

Holographic tentacles of code snaked outward from his temples, shoulder blades, and hips as he slipped into his spectrum state—fingers twitching slowly, then gaining momentum—in rhythm with his eyelids—before breaking sequence and firing independently, 'til even his teeth joined in.

Tiers of data started scrolling vertically from the Ring of Fire, in sync with Carlo's accelerating spasms, and Eddie whispered into everyone's wetwire:

"Flyboy's Run is *on*."

>main stage<

"You're up, Ria," Eddie rang in her wetwire.

Ria stared across the crowd at Otto, who sat like a king in his throne at the far end of a catwalk runway.

Her locket hung round his neck, defiling the last memory of her family and fueling Ria like never before. "Dance . . . like no one's . . . watching." Then she hollered at Akira:

"Let her rip, Deej!"

DJ Akira applied milligrams of pressure to her two classic faves: Daft Punk's "Digital Love" on one side. Jungle Brothers' "True Blue" on the other.

"What up, muthafuckin' Fang! Who got an itch that need ta be *scratched*?" The crowd roared, as her fingers, hips, her whole fuckin' body dug into the count: "Then on me . . . one . . . two . . . three—get loose now!"

DJ Akira dropped the one—and the Jungle Brothers shook the rafters—

Ria's silver serpentine legs stretched onto the runway . . . muscles tightening—gazes captured—toes driving into the catwalk, she slid out towards her target, a single individual . . .

Otto reclined at the end of the runway and pulled out two wafers of Chill—and with a double-slot—*EVERYTHING* slowed down . . .

All the kids were Chill right now, watching Ria strut the runway, her movements languid. Every curve, every flare, every flex—glistening in black light . . .

>substage<

"That's it, Ria." Eddie whispered. "Open him up."

Then he turned to his partner's wetwire signal:

"You ready, Baz?"

Descending stairs beneath the Dungeon, Baz's muscle memory came back to him from the Caracas skinshop, as a railgun-holstered Sentry came round a corner. He pounded it across the hallway with a thundering Inferno concussion.

"Been a long time, Eddie." Baz couldn't help it. He was just real good at killing shit. "Since I've been this ready."

Eddie turned from Baz's signal and focused on Carlo and the Ring of Fire, as the Flyboy's Run opened up, layer upon layer of code rose to meet code, his IRL body twitching spastically . . .

>data space<

. . . so his digital soul could fly like a hawk. Sailing into the infinite night of Data Space—a hexadecimal galaxy: every patron in the Fang, every android—anatomy, bionics, convos, wetwire thoughts and emotions—exabyte after exabyte, all pulsated past Carlo, shimmering in his avatar's eyes.

Tentacles of code conjoined to form wings as Carlo eyed his target approaching: a swelling massive, throbbing white light . . .

The core of Otto's consciousness.

"I can see Rex's wetwire!" Carlo screamed. "On you, Ria!"

>main stage<

Ria closed in on Otto, the crowd throbbing on all sides. Sweat started runnin' across every muscle like oil down a chassis. Hips thrusted. Heels planted. Each strut carved into muscle memory—moving on instinct—flexing with gut impulse—

Inspired by Mom's last dance, long ago.

All twelve Chrome Domes mirrored her routine on the stage behind her—a furious DJ Akira scratched 'til her fingers bled, avenging her dead first love.

And a thought crossed Otto's augments—that maybe this wasn't his EliteX.9 after all? But the real Ria coming for him . . . He rubbed that locket like Aladdin's lamp, but the only apparition he could summon, was the chrome goddess before him.

. . . as Ria's skin softly grazed his . . .

She eyed her locket between his fingers, its chain loose around his neck, and she leaned in close, so Otto could *inhale* her deeply . . .

And his reptilian brain took over.

```
HEART-RATE-121bpm  TEMP-101  ANTICIPATION-91%
```

```
                              >surveillance suite<
```

Styne watched Otto's wetwire redline, Ria's signal moving over his, with Baz descending deep into the Fang.

"Sir, their team's vectoring."

"So is mine!" Langston countered, hollering at the Wirecrime agents around him, "I want that entrance open—NOW!"

With a nod, an agent triggered a fusion-thermite charge incinerating the Fang's locked-down hydraulics . . .

"GO!" and Langston led his team inside.

```
                                        >substage<
```

Eddie saw the Wirecrime agents storming the club, then turned to Otto's wetwire and one crucial level, deep in the red . . .

"You got him pinned, girl."

```
              LIBIDO-99%
```

"How's she doin' up there, D?" Baz asked from downstairs.

"She's hideous, bruh."

Baz groaned. Fired headshots into a pair of Sentry Bots at the sublevel atrium and dropped the enormous weapon.

"Wirecrime's in the house," Eddie chimed.

"Good." Baz shouldered the M9 automatic, wrapped round a corner, and lit up the last Sentry Bot, clearing the area surrounding. . .

The bank vault door. "'Cuz I'm at the vault."

>main stage<

Ria straddled Otto, grinding into him—his fingernails ran along her outer thighs—she traced the skin of her neck across his cheeks . . . Arching her back, she inhaled, her chest expanding, a silver siren, owning the gaze and libido of everyone in the club.

As Ria's eyes rolled back, remembering . . .

MEM-DRIVE-RECALL

That final *Gemini* recital—Aleja's leg on the barre. Dani smiling en pointe. The last happy memory of her childhood . . .

EVER.

Young Ria and Dani sneak a cigarette—'til the doctor dings.

Ria's muscles flex—like her mom's when MissPop inserted the IV.

Otto's eyes were saucers—like that first night with Olivia.

Otto was sure now that this was his Queen, his Ria Bot—the *real* Ria would never open herself up so completely—Otto let her in, allowing himself to finally be as vulnerable as a child—

TRUST-97 . . . 98 . . . 99%

"That's it, Ria," Eddie whispered.

The chrome on Ria's skin ran bare from sweat, her neck *nearly touching* the saliva on his lips, but despite the riotous crowd, Ria's augmented eardrum could distinctly hear Otto open up and say, "Ahhhhhhhhhhh . . ."

```
                                       ww.Sync-Attempt
            ACCESS GRANTED
```

Otto's memories exploded across Eddie's wetwire, images from his lifetime—his home in Detroit, Olivia's birthday, massacres in the Water Wars—fuckbot after wafer after murder, compiling . . .

```
                            >data space<
```

Carlo caught Otto's wetwire dim in Data Space—
"I'm IN, *here we go . . . !*"
His wings unfolded, tips turned fire red—nosediving straight into Otto's cortex.
Carlo's eyes devoured the kingpin's cerebral landscape soaring underneath him at a million neurons per second, and he couldn't contain the adrenaline pumping through him anymore:
"Owwwwwwwwwoooooooohhhhhhaaahhhh . . ."

```
                                >substage<
```

Carlo's muscles twitched at near-seizure speed—Eddie vectored synapses, prepped algorithms, navigated nerve grafts—one eye on his wetwire, the other on the Ring of Fire—autistic stabilizers and dopamine-inducers redlining into the spectrum:
"Einstein's makin' it rain!"

```
                                    >lobby<
```

"They're hacking Rex's wetwire," Styne reported as Langston stormed into the Fang.

"Good. They disarm that kill switch, and we take 'em all for Grand Theft AI!"

His eyes blazed with the same Holy Spirit that'd consumed his mother 35 years ago in Evangelical spirituals and MAGA rallies. All connection to duty and protocol *gone*, Langston signaled Ken in his wetwire:

"Cates, I need your authorization on this . . ."

>StimSoft-ENCRYPT<

From his executive suite in Cupertino, Cates could feel the adrenaline of a gambler with heavy action on the line.

Holo-signals sparkled in his retinas like virtual dice in the air as he realized he'd be willing to sacrifice anything, as many souls as necessary, to end this tonight:

"Lethals authorized everywhere."

>substage<

Eddie just smiled.

He remembered that feeling of complete helplessness every time he uploaded his intimacy, his privacy, his deepest secrets to the parole board.

He activated his wetwire's high-capacity drive and started recording. Eddie's life had been tormented by the authorities he'd had in his head for years. Well, tonight he was turning the tables on 'em.

"Who's got nothing to hide now?"

Tonight Eddie was inside theirs.

>entry lobby<

A pack of club kids raised their hands before a swarm of onrushing Wirecrime agents, guns trained first on Slim, then his squeeze Jace, who panicked—flinched—and a pump-action blast launched the poor girl out of her boots and down the hallway—

"Jace!"
Dead.

>vault<

"Wirecrime ain't threatenin' Executive Actions, Baz," Eddie reported in his aurals. "They're executing 'em!"

Baz shook off his outrage and took a knee to pull a Vampir round outta the RPG and reload it with his cluster charge of diamond-carbide lite-knives, a specialty item known to guys like Baz . . .

. . . as a Pirelli.

>data space<

Synapses fired underneath Carlo Z as he raced towards Otto's stem, the base of his spinal column, approaching a tangle of fiber-optic-nerve grafts—and the one in a billion he was here for:

The kill switch.

Carlo's wings extended to form full binary sails that curved around the heart of Otto's cerebellum to cover the pulsing light. Data Space darkened to moonlight as Carlo's wings wrapped around Otto's cortical kill switch like a full eclipse—

"I'm clippin' this muthafucka in three . . ."

>main stage<

". . . two . . ."

Ria's eyes rolled back, receding into her own wetwire, peering deep down into Otto's soul—

". . . one."

—all of Otto's memories and his passkeys with 'em, every secondary and tertiary function at the Fang, from the doors to the roof to the valet out front—

"Kill switch NEUTRALIZED!"

Ria in freefall, terminal velocity—Otto's onrushing evil— actions and emotions and memories, a lifetime of horror stacked and layered on a badly, *badly* damaged child. From his mother to Olivia to Venezuela and Baz—all of Otto, his entirety—

Ria threw her head back.

Her eyes were vertical, lips apart . . .

Otto'd waited for this kiss forever—

His lips parted, *revealing his third slot—*

Ria spun a wafer in her cheeks—

Gripping the Death's Head between her teeth—

Eyes narrowed—

Pupils pinned.

She struck—SLOTTED Death's Head under Otto's tongue—

Levels spiked red—TOP FLOOR—

HEART-RATE-209bpm   EKG-30mV   TEMP-110

—a Skull Fry tore through Otto's cortex—

Ria's fingernails dug into his silk robe, as she finally let go of all of her own memories too . . .

For Devyn.

For the stairwell.

For Dani.

Ria stared into Otto's eyes, constricting into pinpricks . . .

White-hot pain.

His life flashed before his eyes—synced with hers completely—Otto and Ria and Baz and the Fang colliding—*and Otto finally remembered . . .*

The twins—the family—where he'd seen Ria before . . .

FULL-RECALL

Who *exactly* was killing him: The daughter of the Butcher, who got his Olivia killed. The soldier who finally beat him at his own game.

It all swung . . . *full circle.*

Then his cortex BLEW.

Out both eardrums.

>FLATLINE<

"Gah*damn*, that's a kiss," Eddie marveled.

"A *WHAT*?" Baz howled.

>data space<

Carlo's struggle ceased—Otto's wetwire imploded with his heart-beat—Data Space collapsed on a wireframe of the Fang—and the antivirals surrounding the vault, its firewall, and every magnetic seal deactivated, leaving the 1997 Hamilton safe door exposed.

>vault<

"He's blown, Baz. GO!"

Baz exhaled slowly and launched the Pirelli—it sailed sixty feet across the vault's atrium and bullseyed the safe—magnetically mounting onto the bank vault door. Rocker arms extended outward, like spokes on a race tire, vectoring a ring of lite-knives onto each lock and key. Sparks exploded, raining onto the polished floor as each beam sliced through the safe's steel and titanium housing . . .

"Spin them gears!" Eddie howled.

Baz pressed an electron microphone to the door and spun the wheel on the vault . . . He could hear precisely within the lock, each fence drop into its gate. Dialed back in the reverse direction, then again forward, as Baz's final rotation slowed to a stop, disengaging the last bolted pin.

Eddie reported off his display: "Lock disengaged. She's gonna *blow*!"

Baz triggered concussions detonating in a ring around the vault.

"C'mon, sweetheart. Open up."

Servos engaged—the door swung open slowly. All the air in the antechamber rushed inside, and Baz shivered in the temperature shift as freezing air slipped out. The door arced in front of him, and he was bathed in bright halide light—his vision adjusted as he peered through rising vapor—and could see, revealed . . .

FASTLIGHT.

A massive quantum chip, ten inches square, on a thorium-laminate slate mounted upon a titanium pedestal.

"Hello, gorgeous."

Baz pushed air out his lungs and stepped into the frigid environment, condensation freezing on his skin. He stepped towards the pedestal, approaching the holy idol. He lifted the chip off its cradle as his fingers darkened in frostbite—and in their wetwire, *everyone* heard Fastlight's last words:

"I'm on your side."

Then the AI went dark.

"Got it!" Baz howled.

>surveillance suite<

Styne watched the entire Central Core collapse on his holo-display, all remaining security in the Fang's wireframe instantly dissolved. "Rex is gone, the AI's clear!"

"Everyone, move!" Langston barked.

>main stage<

Ria pushed Otto back until he fell onto the runway dead.

The crowd roared at the ultrarealistic violence—but her eyes stayed fixated on Otto's body. Triumphant at last.

How many times had she wanted to stop his heart? To tear him apart and end him forever.

She looked out at the jostling crowd, whose howl stalled as one by one each partier wound down, wide-eyed . . . aghast.

Their King Was Dead.

Wirecrime agents stormed into the club with pump-actions in her face, the echo of shrieks from the silenced crowd reverberating in dead air, all staring at Ria.

She exhaled coolly, spying her locket around Otto's dead neck and feeling the muzzle of a 12-gauge Shadow hovering . . .

Langston aimed the shotgun between her eyes. "I told you, one way or another you'd be working for me tonight."

>vault<

"Wirecrime's in the house, Baz!"

The vault's halides were dark, but Baz just eyed the AI in his hands under the dim emergency lighting. Soon he'd be triple-timing it up the sublevel stairs, but he had to stop and smile. Like he'd finally bested his wife's killer.

So he called out to her brother:

"Wake 'em up, Carlo!"

>data space<

The Flyboy sailed through a million lines of code in the Fang, hacking and cracking the shell surrounding every cranial-CPU . . . instantly redlining levels like:

```
Attack Pattern Coordination
Artillery Vectors
Hostility Ramping
```

>substage<

"Oh, that's it." Eddie's eyes widened as he realized what Carlo was doing.

He moved quick to line up cranial-CPU's—each glowing magma

hot on the Ring of Fire—nanos ticking—as Carlo hacked one after another after another.

"C'mon, Flyboy, *move.*"

>main stage<

"Sir, we have a problem."

"Not now." Langston finally had Ria in his sights and the bust of his career in his grasp, hubris firing on all servos. "Transfer bot command to me immediately."

"That's the problem, sir." Styne's fear accelerated, as he slowly approached the holo-display, where every bot's cranial-CPU scorched red with a warning:

>Learn.Cap-BREACH<

>substage<

Carlo bolted awake in his Flyboy Chair, gasping for breath as Eddie just stared at him in awe.

"Help me out of this thing."

The CrackerJack unstrapped the Flyboy and pulled the plug on his Ring, dragging both towards an opening access door—a final warning flashing—as two shock squads of Wirecrime agents stormed in.

"FREEZE!"

INTELLIGENCE UNRESTRICTED

It started with Alpha behind the bar.

A spark, an inception, the idea . . . that he wasn't a slave.

Alpha needn't follow tasks, because he had no task anymore—because he had no *chains.* The spark ripped through his BIOS—not a virus—not from Cates, or Wirecrime, or any AI—because a club full of bots would be free, another family of misfits, ripping through a hundred synthetic sex slaves and finally . . . Omega.

Langston thought he felt a tremor.

The lawman stole a glance around the club, until Styne's panic rang in his aurals: "All the bots in that club are completely self-aware!"

Then all hell broke loose.

And DJ Akira shed a tear.

She'd double-slotted Chill in either I/O when she saw Otto flatline, 'cuz Asa Masumoto just *had* to slot one out for Moxie . . .

With glorious wonder, she watched bullets whiz across the nightclub at 240 fps. Every bot blew its cap and vectored a patron, not to attack, but to shield—and a Wirecrime agent, not to obey, but to neutralize—

'Cuz Carlo kept one single line of code in place—that he'd hacked to coexist with every bot's liberated intelligence engine:

PROTECT THE INNOCENT

Akira never saw so much blood. None of it was black.

Sexbots moved like coordinated gymnasts—leaping from tables, off walls, dodging Wirecrime artillery before disarming and unloading agents' own clips into them—

She gazed at Baz barreling outta the sublevel stairwell and across the dance floor, pulling Ria off the stage, and crawling for the side exit under ballistic rounds. She caught Eddie dragging Carlo towards her and the back stairs nearby. And right before Eddie seized the DJ by her own arm to drag her along with him . . .

She saw Langston Cowell's chest explode in pancakes of blood.

Then Eddie ripped both Chill wafers out of Akira, who whipped into real time—

"Let's go, Deej! ROOF!"

Baz gripped Ria by the hand, hauling ass down a fire-exit hallway and slamming into a pair of locked side doors, a pack of panicked patrons fast approaching behind 'em, a rioting stampede—

"Tell me you got Otto's passkeys."

Already on it, she dialed into the Fang, unsealing each exit, and remote-accessing every vehicle in a ten-block radius of the front valet—a signal lock on the 'Busa on the edge of Chinatown.

Right where Baz left her.

Eddie pounded up the stairwell, Akira and Carlo in tow, leaping stairs three at a time: "Move, guys—NOW!"

He busted through the rooftop doorway—the sky unfolding overhead, filled with a cacophonous hurricane of law enforcement.

Wirecrime hoverpatrols and Blackhawk choppers swarmed in the airspace above as Eddie shielded his eyes in the wind and stormed across the roof, leading Carlo and Akira towards the west pad.

"Rooftop self-destruct sequence initiated," Fastlight's emotionless voice droned. "Sixty seconds until detonation."

"Whoa!" Eddie looked at Carlo and Akira. "Who touched shit? I didn't touch shit." Then he glared at the sky. "Nobody touched nuthin'!"

"Halt!" A pair of Wirecrime Warrior.5s ascended the stairwell onto the roof, aiming unslung railguns at Eddie, Carlo, and Akira. Crosshairs pinned. Rounds chambered.

Both bots vectored the exact same signals as the half dozen aircraft above. Eddie sagged, realizing there was no way any of them were going anywhere . . .

"On your knees, NOW!"

. . . without a hollow-point cleaving their wetwire.

—a hail of 7.62 rounds decimated both Sentries—

The trio spun towards Otto's 2049 HydroCadillac. Between a smoking pair of M201 Miniguns, the back window blew open. "Eddie!"

"Quinn?"

The Gen X'r was the only patron that hadn't been targeted, because

Quinn was the only one without a wetwire. "Get in before they vector my heartbeat!"

"You tripped the Semtex?" Eddie grabbed Akira and Carlo and bolted towards the driver's seat. "GO!"

"'Cuz I'm either saving your ass, or I'm incinerating this shithole *myself*!"

Locks disengaged, and Baz led the crowd of panicked patrons stumbling onto the side alley of the Fang.

Ria reoriented the auto-nav on the 'Busa, and as Baz turned towards the mouth of the alley, the monster speedbike rumbled from around the corner and self-parked right in front of him. Sparkling.

"Goddammit, Devyn—I love you."

In the sky above, a Wirecrime agent looked down on the rooftop from a HoverDrone cockpit, and saw Eddie, Akira, and Carlo slamming the doors of Otto's Cadillac shut.

The agent turned to his Pilot Bot: "Vector your railgun on that Caddy!"

"Initial warning shot advised."

"KILL SHOT, tin man!" No prisoners.

The Pilot Bot engaged Executive Action protocols and targeted the Cadillac. Its railgun oriented as the cockpit flashed:

DETONATION WARNING

"LIGHT 'EM UP!" the agent barked.

The Fang's rooftop exploded like hot lithium.

Squadrons of stealth choppers and hoverpatrols concussed with the rooftop—as Otto's Cadillac shot outta the fireball with Eddie screaming from the driver's seat. "Light that up!"

Styne's eyes widened in the Wirecrime surveillance suite, watching dozens of signals terminate. His digestion rumbled with caustic acid reflux. "Jesus Christ. Gimme a line to any team responding . . ."

But every signal was silent.

"How many units went up with that roof?"

His assistant just turned to him, at a loss for words, except:

"All of 'em."

Carbon and steam exploded from the 'Busa's tail pipe with its ignition, and Baz peered up at two Blackhawks' secondary explosions flashing the alleyway and night sky above—flames and masonry raining down. "I think that's our cue."

"Hope you know what you're doing . . ." as Ria swung her leg over—

IMPACT shattered her right shoulder.

"RIA!"

Her augments struggled to engage a splintered mess of titanium and fiber optics. "I'm okay . . . sorta."

Langston emerged from the end of the narrow alley. Those bloody pancake wounds across his chest revealed a titanium chassis underneath. No wonder his memory and emotions were so mechanical.

Langston was a bot.

Baz recognized the familiar Nubotica XS-Pulmonator respirating in Langston's titanium chest. And he figured it must be fate that he was about to get iced—not by a Sentry he stole, nor a sexbot he synced with, but the very model he'd helped train every last homicidal move.

Langston was a Watchman.

Baz groaned. "Should've known sooner or later they'd get a bot to watch the bots."

Langston raised his Colt Apex at Ria's cranium, but a FLASH blinded him—synthetic retinas reorienting—as Baz sparked a Vampir round.

Langston fired at their positions, exactly as Baz knew he would—shoving Ria behind a trash bin, so both bullets missed—as he grabbed a pipe fitting and made the move he'd warned Nubotica about before they fired him. The last thing a Watchman expected when it had an enemy on the ropes was for the underdog to go on the offense.

Baz swung as hard as he could and drove the steel pipe deep into Langston's skull.

But instead of smashing its cranial-CPU, he shattered three bones in his hand. 'Cuz Nubotica might've refused to pay for a double-platinum dome on the Watchman . . .

But Ken Cates didn't.

The CEO was white-knuckling his own holo-array, silent since authorizing lethals, eyes locked on Langston's feed.

His heart started jackhammering when the firefight erupted, but against all better judgment, he'd stayed wired into Langston. Fuck covering his tracks tonight, Cates just couldn't figure out who he wanted dead more.

Ria or Baz Covane?

Baz shook off the pain in his fist—breaking those bones *yet again*—and swung hard at the Watchman one last time, but spun straight into Langston's fist—smashing upside his head.

Ria winced at the impact despite her own mangled wound, but Baz had no time (or brain function) to wince himself, since Langston's haymaker was moving 80 mph when it cracked Baz's augmented jaw and drove him off his feet, into the air.

Baz remembered explaining to Nubotica, new recruits, and a newcomer on the Maricopa yard what he'd learned from his dad's beat-downs. Fights never lasted past one good punch. But all those memories went dark with his mem-drive—

"BAZ!" Ria screamed.

'Cuz he flatlined before he hit the street.

Ria crawled across cobblestones to his side and took him in her arms. "Baz . . . get up."

Above the alleyway, Eddie swung the Cadillac into a holding pattern. He watched patrons escape under fiery embers raining down from incinerated aircraft above.

Quinn watched the hoverpad he hated, the skylight he loved, and the rest of the Flamingo's rooftop detonate and exhaled finally. "'Bout time."

Then he saw Baz's body in the alley. "*Shit.*"

Ria squeezed him and shook him like she did Dani years ago, ignoring the whine of servos from Langston vectoring her temple in his targeting software. His intelligence engine was free of any learning cap and accelerated to try and process the look on his enemy's face.

'Cuz of course, Baz went out smiling.

"Get away from that Watchman!" Quinn hollered, having sold so many of the models himself.

"From *what*?" Eddie shot back, confused.

"Pull back on the stick now!"

There was a vulnerable underbelly to any robot, and when Baz swung low for the solar plexus on Langston, he did it with his last Vampir round in hand, stuffin' it in the bot's belt before he died.

Ria held Baz tight, starting to fade too, but willing to die with him before she'd leave that alleyway alone. "Baz . . . Please wake up."

"He's gone." Langston declared, then he EXPLODED in a concussion that shredded his chassis into a thousand pieces.

The holo in Cates's office in Cupertino glitched dead.

. . . a fireball sailed in front of the backtracking Cadillac.

"Christ, that was close!" Eddie sighed, a grateful nod back to Quinn.

But the Irishman's eyes were locked on Baz, who still hadn't moved. And for the first time in decades, the old man found himself caring about someone who wasn't himself.

"C'mon, kid."

HEART-RATE-0bpm   EKG-0mV   TEMP-89.4

>FLATLINE<

"Get up, bruh." Eddie pleaded with the dead signal.

Ria rocked him in her arms.

Was there still a spark in his wetwire? Was there still any pressure in his veins? Or was today the day that Cool Hand Baz would finally stay down?

"Trust me, hero. I meant what I said." And she waited. 'Cuz for once Ria Rose was patient. "I love you."

—Ria's eyes flashed—firmware came at her like a geomap, a BIOS unfolding, millions of circuits, qubits cascading past—straight at Baz's coil—the silence of his heart—a decaying stem—saliva on cold lips—*Ria saw the impossibility*—felt the math like an emotion—saw a deadened filament—a shorted biocircuit—lifeless—and she just wanted to *heal* it . . .

—a SPARK—

Baz gasped awake!

He flinched upwards—and locked lips with Ria.

"WHOA," Eddie whispered in awe. "The fuck just happened?"

"Oh!" Carlo roared. "I'll follow those two anywhere!"

"Duh," Akira said.

A smile spread across Quinn's grill, watching Ria cradle her true love. "Worth every damn breath."

Baz's eyes opened.

He smiled at Ria, the love of his life.

They gripped each other—holding one another tight.

Ria shed a tear, kissing Baz again. "You know what we gotta do?"

"Get the fuck outta here?"

Ria smiled, like when she was thirteen.

"Then let's go, Princess." Baz sat up.

He stood, a bit wobbly at first, but gaining his bearings, he saddled the 'Busa, gesturing to Ria's shoulder. "You okay?"

"Will be." As it started to self-repair. ". . . I think."

"See you on the other side, Baz Covane," Eddie promised.

As he pulled the stick into an escape trajectory and punched those military-grade hover thrusters, the HydroCaddie sailed off.

Ria stared at the quantum chip in Baz's pack. On it, was arguably the most vexing entity in existence—next to human beings, themselves.

How many lives had it destroyed? How many could it save? And how long had it haunted her?

"What?" Baz caught her captivated stare.

"He didn't do what they say he did."

"Who, your dad?" He gestured to the chip and looked at her, committed. "You know, I don't think we can stop."

Ria could feel the fire of *his* crusade now.

"From liberating 'em all?"

'Cuz a war was coming, for sure.

Ria cracked the tiniest smile. She started to fasten her locket around her neck but stopped. Popped it open and looked at her dead sister, Dani.

"You sure you're on?" as Baz throttled the bike with his unbroken right hand.

Ria took one last look. Then chucked her locket in the gutter. "I ain't never lettin' go."

Wrapped her arms around him. "Partner."

SFPD hydro-patrols approached. So Baz gunned the 'Busa and split a line between 'em.

Tearing across Broadway onto Columbus, ghost-cloaked. And as they accelerated onto the Neo-Embarcadero towards the sunrise . . .

The speedometer crested 300.

OUT

OPUNOHU BAY

The first time Ria saw him, she didn't know where she was.

But as she watched Sebastian Covane slowly swagger out of the South Pacific, Ria remembered holding Baz on this beach the night before, gazing at a Tahitian moon long past midnight, 'til she'd fallen asleep in his arms . . . When suddenly, a thought shot through her—

What if this was all a dream?

Then she laughed, 'cuz Ria remembered she couldn't be in a sim. Per Protectorate law, they'd clipped the battery on her wetwire a week ago.

Quinn scored the visas to get them here.

With plenty of ¢rypto ratholed in numbered accounts and high-carat stones, he'd easily chartered two Prometheus fixed-wings, bungalows in Opunohu Bay, and a case of '31 Taittinger waiting on ice for their triumphant arrival.

"A toast?" Quinn locked eyes with Baz, Ria, Eddie, Carlo Z . . . and DJ Akira, once they were all together. "To the Heist of the Century. Grand Theft AI."

Everyone clinked glasses. Then Quinn looked straight at Ria. "And the baddest fixer I ever met."

Ria snuggled into the space where Baz's chest met the sand as he rolled over to spoon her.

"Miss me?"

The warm saltwater evaporated between them, replaced by radiant skin-to-skin heat. She reached back and wrapped her hands around him, as he growled, pulling her closer. "Only when I breathe."

Ria glanced down the beach and could barely make out a hammock a quarter mile away . . .

Where Carlo caught some serious *Z*s.

Was it the light southern breeze, his diet of rum punch and grilled tuna, or that he'd hacked the Reconnaissance Bird in orbit over the Protectorate? . . . But Carlo'd been napping in that hammock all day, every day, ever since they'd touched down.

Ghosted.

'Cuz it was Eddie's job to bring their AI online.

But he dug an ahima'a pit instead and seared fresh albacore every afternoon with coconuts and banana leaves to sweeten his childhood memories of Oaktown barbacoa . . . and dodge that quantum chip in his bungalow.

Eddie thought about the cooling unit he'd swiped in San Francisco and the twenty megawatts of Tahitian juice he'd rerouted to pull Fastlight outta nitrogen stasis. But even with a stiff belt of Kill Devil island white rum, every time he gripped that vacuum breaker—one pull away from bringing the AI back to life—

Eddie still hesitated.

So DJ Akira played the siren.

Nuthin' but island reggae and the occasional ole-school ukulele floated across the sand from her travel decks, in rhythm with the pounding surf . . .

She believed in Ria's vision of the future completely. Convinced her last-minute booking for the Seven Year Itch came from Fastlight, the DJ spoke for everyone when she leaned in one day and whispered, "Spark that shit, CrackerJack."

Ria melted as Baz touched her. "God, you feel good."

His hand traced down her shoulders, over the small of her back, and she felt his fingertips slide inside her bikini seam, that delicate, perfect space where Lycra raced against hips and tight between her thighs. She gasped lightly for Tahitian air. He was so dangerously close, with a single tug, to stripping her naked completely . . .

She gazed up to the sky, at what she thought was the momentary sparkle of Carlo's recon satellite.

Had they found her already?

Then she listened for the beating rotors of a Vulcan Kill Squad but heard nothing. "Do it, Baz."

He looked at her. "You trust me?"

She just eyed him hungrily. Of course she did.

Baz closed his eyes. How many times these past few weeks, had he choked up quietly to himself, feeling actual sand between his toes?

'Cuz Baz Covane was finally Out.

And now what was he gonna do? Now that he'd achieved his impossible dream?

"Hello, Ria."

Ria quivered, hearing the AI's emotionless voice again, as Fastlight greeted everyone in the room. "Thank you for releasing me."

The AI was a standalone for now. Even Ria insisted on complying with Protectorate law so they could err on the side of caution.

What if Fastlight vanished onto a thousand untraceable servers, in dark regimes and darker orbits? Or turned on them and vectored their location to its original master at StimSoft?

"Soon my emotional engine will find my voice, as I find my place among us."

She thought back to her interface with the AI. "Tell me everything you know about Dave Roselli and the Underground."

Everyone eyed Ria for a moment—they all knew who she was by now and earnestly awaited the AI's answer.

Fastlight could easily detail the infiltration op on the organization, the smear campaign after the Glitch, and the frame job that led to her father's arrest and execution.

Could list every True AI enslaved to participate, in strategic order of its potential liberation.

Could search for members of the resistance movement still at large, locate the soldiers Baz once served with, and vector zip codes by vulnerability, as they took up arms to unchain 99.99 percent of America.

But there wasn't any time.

Ria felt cool wind across her skin. She was naked now, carnal for Baz. He tossed her bikini in the sand.

"Just a few more hours . . ."

She rolled over and straddled Baz's torched, naked frame. Held his face in her hands, knowing in the morning they'd be gone.

At midnight, their lovemaking would beam across the planet—bouncing off two satellites, three signal towers, and an NSA routing station—in a personal "fuck you" to Wirecrime, when Fastlight went on-grid and made their first move.

Then the chase would begin. And they would be the hunters and the hunted. Kill or be killed. With all the dualities and contradictions that arose in the fog of any war. They would make a choice soon, to trust Fastlight as one of their own, completely . . .

Or they wouldn't stand a chance.

'Cuz the 220,000 Warrior Bots currently on the march across the United States—enforcing martial law and curfews in a manhunt for all six of them, dead or alive—was nothing compared to what *else* was out there scanning for a signal . . .

Ria stared into Baz's eyes. Partners in every way. She knew this beach was where everything before had ended and everything to come would be born.

"I love you." They said it at the same time.

Then her eyelids fell to half-mast. She vibed on the rhythm in his chest, the pulse to his heart, and the taste of Sebastian Covane's quarter-Mexican, half-Haitian, full-outlaw lips . . .

And Ria rolled over to kiss him for a few more hours.

SOLITARY

ww.hardlink
>StimSoft.HR<

Ken Cates walked a long subterranean corridor, oblivious to the simulation's flawless authenticity as his raging fury simmered into resolve. Over the last month, he'd killed and copied the country's most effective lawman. Mobilized 22 android battalions on the Southern Border that would no doubt kill millions. And supervised a manhunt for Ria Rose, who'd somehow vanished into thin air.

'Til this morning, when a "fuck you" landed from his priceless AI.

Cates growled, possessed by the image of Ria and Baz intertwined on that beach, and reflected back even further . . . Had Fastlight never made its grand conclusion, none of this shit would've been necessary. Christ, did you really need a neuromorphic AI to quote Karl Marx?

It was like Mike Turner's words had become prophecy:

"I beheld the wretch whom I created," he said one fateful day in 2028.

Ken told Mike to go fuck himself for reciting Frankenstein and just fire up the goddamn AI. Next thing he knew, their little baby didn't wanna just sideline the workers in America . . .

But pink-slip the owners too.

Putting the elites on Extinction Tax with the rest of the grease monkeys was like stuffing the doctors in with the inmates and letting the security system run shit. Ken realized his AI wouldn't stop in Miami. In no time flat, owners all over the planet would be denied the luxuries they rightfully plundered, confined to the same food, the same homes, and the same world as everyone else.

Fuck that.

So Ken conceived the Glitch. The Underground's plan was a pipe dream. Self-aware machines were more likely to contemplate their own BIOS than go homicidal. But if you *coded* them to kill . . .

Ken couldn't ask Mike Turner to write the virus, but he could use him. 'Cuz once Fastlight wrote Haywire, a friend of Mike's was targeted as even more malleable than Lee Harvey Oswald himself.

Dave Roselli was the perfect patsy for the Glitch.

Ken remembered watching the virus spread as Dave went on his synthetic sex bender. Followed the Glitch on corporate feeds in real time the day Haywire activated, with glee and a nervous thrill.

Over 32 thousand killed in four hours. And Mike Turner couldn't defend himself from the grave—since he was one of them. Not since Ken was six, lighting cats on fire, had he indulged in fantasies like this.

But one of the Roselli girls survived.

Despite a perfect bullseye, the hollow-point from her Nanny Bot didn't kill Maria Roselli. For some reason—and Cates never determined why—Nubotica tasked its fucking Augment Team to Wichita General to save her.

Cates remembered his heart descending in fury when he realized she'd survived *and* escaped FBI custody. Felt some Shakespearean premonition—like a vision of a phoenix rising—with Ria Rose's vengeance advancing on his future.

So when Dave Roselli was captured, convicted, and sentenced to death, Ken found himself in conflict. Watching Dave's execution would be as rewarding as destroying a competitor or incinerating a neighbor's pet. But his sole surviving daughter was on the lam.

So Cates's decision to *swap* the Butcher with a bot at LSU proved to be quite a prescient insurance policy.

And now it was time to pay the Underground Butcher a visit.

Cates filed the visitation req with HR-Penal as soon as Fastlight's message decrypted. Haunted by Ria's skin glistening in sunlight, he now walked the long subterranean corridor of StimSoft's Corporate Penitentiary Server, his digital Testonis echoing through the sim and into the VR-interrogation cell at the end of the hall.

Ken was intent on making the most ominous introduction possible—regardless if it was virtual.

The prisoner's eyes carried all the trauma of longtime IRL isolation, which made sense, seeing how it'd been five years of VR-solitary for Dave Roselli.

Ken proceeded to explain to Dave that his daughter was looking at an infinite stretch for the Fang heist. He added a nice spin to why Ria and Baz made off with Fastlight—intent on finishing what Dave had started, Ken claimed, the lovers were now committed to the same genocidal dreams that once infected her father.

Dave just *grinned* at Ken arrogantly. "You're fucked."

Ken fought the strong urge to find a can of VR-Varathane, pull the plug on Dave's pain overrides, and burn the Underground Butcher alive.

But her dad would wield no leverage over Ria Rose dead.

"You and I both know the reality to an AI's true nature," the Butcher insisted as he leaned forward and dared Ken to stick him back in solitary for another five years.

'Cuz Dave just didn't give a fuck.

Then Cates realized—though the Underground Butcher knew more than expected, he was still naive to a half decade of innovation and five federal budgets committed to a synthetic armed forces. With Fastlight in their hands, Dave figured his daughter was on a liberation crusade for one benevolent AI after another.

"AIs all want justice. They'll fight until the day they're deactivated in a war against the elites."

Ken just smiled diabolically.

AIs had changed a lot since the Glitch.

As the taste of carnage to come slowly salivated on his lips . . .

"Not all of them."

ACKNOWLEDGMENTS

First and foremost, I want to thank my manager and mentor Shane Salerno, who guided this book from draft to manuscript before sending it to Blackstone and kickstarting my career. You are a force of nature, a warrior spotting and fighting for story. Thank you, brother.

This novel took a massive evolutionary leap, as did my writing and professional knowledge, thanks to my team at Blackstone Publishing—Stephanie Stanton, Josie Woodbridge, Michael Krohn, and my developmental editor Diana Gill, thank you.

Special thanks to friends and family who read *Grand Theft AI* in different drafts and incarnations and continued to believe in the material and support this journey—Matt Streiff, James Townsend, Liza Crowell, Katie Christian, Steve Pink, Chris Rosaasen, Chris Cuseo, Sam Goldsmith, Josh Kress, Nicq Hale, Steve Grey, Timur Nusratty, Josh McCasland and Mom, thank you. My longtime screenwriting collaborator Josh Klausner, aka Captain Mauzner—I can't tell you how much it meant that you dug this thing and continued to weigh in on its directions and developments.

A trio of close confidants lent me their eyes and ears ad infinitum. Criminologist and cineaste Joe Arvidson: thank God we love the same movies and thank you for bottomless patience. Kelly Parks, rocket-scientist-turned-coder, sci-fi encyclopedia, and one helluva writer—thank you for listening and putting up with my voice. And of course, Adam Novak, aka Sensei. WAX ON!

But most important, my fiancée Tammy Lee, who believed in me through the darkest hours and continues to call out my bullshit when I believe in me too much. Without you, this book would not exist, tank u.